Ann Lingard was brought up in Cornwall and after graduating in Zoology and gaining a PhD in Parasitology held a Research Fellowship at New Hall, Cambridge, before moving to Scotland, where she taught at Glasgow University for fifteen years. In 1989 she gave up research and teaching in order to write fiction, and a year later moved to Oxfordshire. She is married with two daughters.

Alongside her fiction writing, Ann Lingard has broadcast regularly on radio and contributes both short stories and non-fiction articles to a wide range of magazines and journals. Her interests include sculling, hill-walking and amateur dramatics. Her second novel, THE FIDDLER'S LEG, will also be published by Headline.

Figure in a Landscape

Ann Lingard

First published in 1996
by HEADLINE BOOK PUBLISHING

First published in paperback in 1996
by HEADLINE BOOK PUBLISHING

A HEADLINE REVIEW paperback

10 9 8 7 6 5 4 3 2 1

All characters in this publication are fictitious and any resemblance to real persons, living or dead, is purely coincidental.

ISBN 0 7472 5296 3

Printed and bound in Great Britain by
Cox & Wyman Ltd, Reading, Berks

HEADLINE BOOK PUBLISHING
A division of Hodder Headline PLC
338 Euston Road
London NW1 3BH

For John

One

As midmorning approaches, the sun burns away the last remaining wisps of mist that lie in strands around the feet of the mountains. The two peaks and the narrow, toothed ridge that joins them have been free for some time, and now the details of the crags and scree and steep, grassy slopes are plainly seen in the bright, clear light.

A figure is plodding relentlessly up the western skyline. In a hollow, next to a boulder, the figure stops and stretches, and is seen to be a woman, dressed in jeans and short-sleeved shirt. She brushes back her short, greying hair, holding it up at the back to let the air cool her scalp. She wipes the sweat from her top lip with the back of her forearm and, smiling, closes her eyes and tilts her face towards the sun. She unbuttons her damp shirt and spreads it on the rock to dry; sweat glistens between her breasts as she lifts her arms to the sun and welcomes its heat. Her body is lean and fit, but her breasts, though small, sag a little, and there are deep creases around the eyes and mouth in her tanned and weather-beaten face.

Fifteen hundred feet below and to the west the sea is calm and blue; dark reefs break its surface near the shore and support cormorants with spread wings. Further out, several small islands lie huddled in the sea, inhabited only by sheep, birds and rodents. At the foot of the hill where the woman lies is a flat plateau, an ancient beach raised twenty feet above the shore, and now colonised by short turf, plaintain, yellow cinquefoil and lousewort. The plateau has been gnawed away to form a rocky bay and, squatting in a hollow above the northern shore, protected from the gales, yet facing south, is a low stone cottage with a roof of rusting corrugated iron. A low stone wall surrounds its garden, and a single rowan tree grows by the front door. There is no road to the cottage, but a trail, such as sheep or deer might make, leads down from the moor, following the burn. At the top of the moor, this trail joins a stony track, suitable for a Land Rover, that winds across the island to the village on the far side. Several miles further east, across the water, the white houses of the nearest fishing port shine in the morning sun.

The woman has been lying down, but now she stands up and scans the mountain with her binoculars. There are deer, thirty or forty of them, in the bowl-like corrie between the peaks. They have scraped and trampled dark gashes in the peat. Several of them have calves with them and other calves are lying quietly, half-hidden among the rocks. The woman turns to stare down at her cottage and, as she looks, a large, dusty-brown fox trots briskly down the trail and stops, sniffing, at the cottage gate. He scentmarks the rowan tree and walks restlessly around the garden, looking up at the windows. The woman, incongruous in her half-naked state, whistles and waves her arms, even though the fox is too far away to hear her.

At this moment a fishing boat putters around the northern part of the bay, the throbbing of its engine echoing off the cliffs. Crab-pots and orange buoys are heaped on its deck. A red-haired man dressed in oilskin dungarees steers the boat towards a floating buoy. An older man, short and swarthy, stares through binoculars at the mountainside. He speaks to the skipper and laughs, handing him the binoculars. The skipper braces the wheel against his knee so that his hands are free and, after a few seconds he, too, laughs, then turns and spits overboard over his left shoulder, muttering and shaking his head.

Small waves spread out in a vee to mark the boat's passage from the further bay where, on the raised beach, stands a mausoleum, an airy thing of polished pillars. A kestrel hovers nearby, then plunges towards the ground.

Two

The lowing (or was it bleating?) at first made me uneasy. In the thin darkness of those nights when May drifts into June, there were unseen herds of cows (or were they flocks of sheep?) moaning in the corries and beneath the skyline. Heard, but unseen, for by dawn they had disappeared: yet there were no cattle on the island, and the sheep were several miles towards the east.

In the village, I asked the shepherd (I was still speaking to people in those days, seeking basic information). It was the hinds, he said, when they were calving; the normally silent red deer hinds, groaning with their birth-pangs and welcoming their newborn.

Each year the forgotten nocturnal sound takes me by surprise, and then I remember that the females, too, have voices, to cry out their love but not, like the stags, their anger. They are silent again now, and the calves, still camouflage-spotted, are strong and leggy. They have seen me, of course, and the calves have become part of their background, melting into the hollows of yellow grass and speckled gneiss, waiting for me to pass by. Down in the cool, shadowy bowl of the corrie, the hinds stand and watch me, their long necks reaching up so that their ears, huge furry funnels, can trap the slightest tremor of sound in the air. I stand and watch them, listening to the rustle of my rapid heartbeat in my ears, and squirming as a trickle of sweat runs down beneath my breasts.

Somewhere in the distance, unseen, a boat putters, but the ears below remain trained in my direction, sensitive trumpets, so unlike the small hard triangles on stuffed trophies, dead heads.

Belinda also shrank in death. When I went to wash my clothes I found her lying in the bracken by the burn; her big ears were still, and I knew she was dead. Although I didn't want to look closely at the hind, I knew it must be Belinda because no other deer would come down to the croft in early summer. She had been my friend, preferring her own or my company to that of the herd; in the winter she hung around the croft and I fed her whatever scraps I could spare, an apple core or carrot tops or peelings from potatoes. If I walked on the moor or in the hills, she would eventually appear, grazing calmly, avoiding my eyes but keeping pace. I talked to her, even though she didn't listen, and I thought that she, too, was outcast, banished and untouchable. So, when my sleep was disturbed by the lowing of a hind, I hadn't associated the sound with her, as she now lay, motionless, in the bracken. Later in the morning, when flies buzzed around her head, I knew I should bid farewell to my friend and I saw then that she had not, after all, been untouched, for a small dead calf hung from her body, still within its now-dull, pink membrane. And so much blood – dark congealed crusts. When she wandered gracefully alone, had some young stag, safe from the watchful eyes of the dominant male, leapt upon her, hoofs flailing against her flanks, and impregnated her resisting body? Or had she succumbed to a brief moment of mutual passion, unknowing or uncaring of the consequence? I hated her for allowing it to happen. I hated her for dying. I hated her because she had been an undemanding companion and had now left me; but most of all I hated her because, finally, she had demanded too much, she had forced herself, by her death, into my life. She had made me feel responsible for her by dying on my doorstep, and that was unjust because I could not have saved her. I could not have helped her calve. And if the young one had survived without her, what then? There's no cow here to provide thin milk. I'm not a lactating female, like Romulus's she-wolf. I can no longer produce milk to order: Tom took all I had.

Figure in a Landscape

I had to move her, of course. The smell became too strong, and I couldn't get near the burn. Even now, years later, I can remember my sick anger at the trick she played upon me – and at the waste. God sees every sparrow fall, does He? Well? How does that help? What sort of comfort is that to the sparrow, as the pellet from the catapult penetrates its breast? Oh, but sweet Mary, Mother of our Lord, protect me from His anger at my blaspheming thoughts, and help me to banish mine. Instead, let me admire the blue milkwort flowers, blue like your picture-book robe. And remind me to rejoice at the blue of the sea, that sparkles with laughter. Come, Harriet! Rejoice, and love the beauty of the day! Climb higher, and throw yourself from the mountain-top to possess this view!

The heat of the sun and of the climb soaks my shirt with sweat. My hands smell of warm rock and lichen, a delicate sweet smell, a smell caught on pullovers that reminds one of summer days. And here, in this hollow, I can catch my breath and open, like a flower, to the sun. There, sun! Look at me! I'm a sunflower, turning my face to follow you. See, I lift my pale breasts towards your gaze, and embrace you with my brown arms!

That must have been a week ago. Something Robbie Ferguson said yesterday has fixed it in my mind. How careful I have to be, even here, where I thought I'd escaped . . . Yesterday began simply enough. I rose early, as usual (how can one not, when the sky awakes at four?) and pampered myself, heating water for washing, and cooking a luxurious breakfast – the last of the ground coffee, the last two eggs, scrambled, with rancid butter, and oatcakes because there was no bread. I packed what I needed and walked over to the village. From the pass, the track is downhill and, with an empty pack on my back, it takes me about two-and-a-half hours. Coming back, laden, I'm slower.

The tops of the hills were hidden in cloud and the air was still and humid beyond the pass. The midges were out in their thousands and, although it was so warm, my sleeves and the neck of my shirt were tightly buttoned. There's an unpleasant story about midges that should strike terror into the hearts of adulterers (well, perhaps not their hearts). At about the turn of the century, a ghillie on one of these islands (he was, of course, dark and strong, with gleaming black eyes, adept at hiding his thoughts yet burning with tumultuous passion) had an affair with the laird's wife. The laird came to hear of this (no doubt some kind neighbour of the ghillie's was responsible) and the man was left tied to a tree overnight, in punishment. The punishment was not just the tethering, but that he was stripped naked, as a feeding-ground for the midges. It's said that shame and midge-bites killed him, for he died a few days later. No antihistamines for hypersensitivities in those days, but perhaps they would have been denied him, in any case, placed tantalisingly just out of reach. And what became of the lady?

The tide was out when I reached the village. Two children were playing on the slippery green rocks by the river outfall; the midges were obviously bothering them, too, for they occasionally flailed their arms and grumbled, but that didn't stop their game. They had found a large metal tray with raised edges, rusting and barnacled, and had set it horizontally, propped carefully with stones. It had been filled with water, and the smaller boy searched the beach for weed-covered pebbles, which he arranged in this aquarium. The elder boy was lifting stones and guddling in pools, collecting animals into a yellow plastic bucket.

'Look! Watch them pee!' he shouted.

He held out a stone on to which several reddish-brown sea-anemones had fixed themselves. He slithered over the rocks towards his brother, then pinched one of the round red lumps between his thumb and forefinger, so that a jet of water squirted into the younger boy's face.

'Eeeyah! Stop it! Let me have a go!'

'No! Get your own. They're mine!'

The elder boy squeezed all the other anemones, taunting his brother, then threw the stone away, so that it cracked against a rock. I shuddered as I thought of the pulped red bodies, crushed and split. But I couldn't interfere. The boys, crouching and slipping among the rocks, both searched for more anemones. A dank smell of seaweed, with faint overtones of sewerage, drifted up from the shore. A man was walking on the path that ran along the top of the shore from the distant quay; there were two yachts anchored in the bay and I assumed he had come from one of them. I turned to go into the shop, to avoid a chance meeting.

There was a high-pitched shriek from the younger boy.

'He bit me!' He was bent double, hugging his hand into his armpit. 'That crab bit me!'

A small green shore crab, no bigger than a few centimetres across, lay on its back on a rock, its legs waving pathetically as it tried to right itself. The elder brother, now protective, seized the crab at the back of its shell and held it up.

'Fuckin' little bugger! Let's fix it!' And he ripped off one of the crab's front legs.

'Don't! That's cruel!'

The man's voice snapped out across the shore. He sounded shocked, disgusted.

'Why not? It bit my kid brother.'

The boy, only nine or ten years old, was unrepentant, even insolent.

'It was defending itself.' The man's authority was weak. He noticed that I had stopped to listen and looked at me as though to include me in the discussion, but I opened the door and slipped into the shop.

The village shop, the island's shop, was no more than a flat-roofed extension at one side of the MacGregors' house; its windows were small and the interior was gloomy. A bell jangled when the door opened, but John MacGregor must have been watching from a window because he was already on his way through from the house.

'Morning, Miss Falmer.'

He leant forward over the high counter that crossed the width of the small room. Behind him, the shelves, stocked with packets of cereal, tinned food, jam and coffee, were inaccessible to the few customers. Trays arranged with tubes of Polo mints, sherbet Refreshers and other sweets were tilted in display at each end of the counter. A locked, glass-fronted case of cigars and cigarettes hung on one wall, and a collection of miscellaneous fishing-tackle, shrimping-nets with pink plastic handles, cards of gaudy fishing-flies, plastic bubble-floats and wooden frames wound with strong brown line, was jumbled in the corner by the door.

'Good morning, Mr MacGregor.'

Our dealings are always polite, coolly friendly yet uninquiring at a personal level.

'A bit sticky out, today – midges'll be bad, no doubt.'

'Terrible. Clouds of them by the burn,' I agreed. 'Is there any mail?'

'Aye, a few bits and bobs – a couple of letters and a parcel.'

The big man limped slowly back into the house and I searched my pockets for my list. He came back with the mail, and inspected each item carefully as he put it down on the counter.

'Mail order parcel from Smethwick's. The new catalogue should be coming soon, Mary's waiting on it, too. It'll be a heavy thing to carry across, will I put it in a carrier bag and leave it with the Calor, next time I'm over? One letter – Ms H. Falmer . . . Mzz indeed, like bees buzzing. And one from the bank, by the look of it . . .'

I smiled and nodded non-committally and thanked him, and diverted further questions by asking for some provisions. There was a store room off at one side where goods were stacked in cartons and in the freezer. No customer was allowed to see inside the store room, so the hidden treasures could only be guessed at, but MacGregor brought me out a frozen loaf of bread, some butter and cheese, a tin of ham and two wizened grapefruit. I wrote him a cheque for these and for the goods on the previous list (I rarely used cash, it meant a trip to the bank on the mainland) and I left my new list with him for the next boat.

'I don't think you've got any mackerel hooks, have you?' I pointed to the list. 'I think I asked you once before.'

(I had lost most of my hooks last year, when the line snagged around a rock; I had been too close inshore, but didn't want to have to admit it.)

'No, we'll have to order them.'

As he peered at the mess in the corner, the door opened and Robbie Ferguson came in.

'Ah, talk of the devil,' MacGregor said.

Ferguson and I looked at each other briefly, surprised, then he came over and leant an elbow on the counter.

'Which one?' he asked, ignoring me and smirking at MacGregor.

The older man looked at him for a moment, unsmiling, one eyebrow raised.

'We were talking about mackerel – and so of course it was of you that I was thinking. The mackerel are running now, aren't they? Miss Falmer needs a packet of hooks. Maybe you could let her have some of yours, Robbie, and save her waiting for the order.'

Ferguson turned his head slightly and looked at my face, then his stare shifted to my chest. After three or four seconds' pause, long enough for me to become unpleasantly certain, without daring to look, that my shirt must have come unbuttoned, he looked back at my face again, and nodded, coolly.

'Aye. I could.'

It was spoken with qualification, as though his generosity might be dependent on some other action, on my part.

'No, no . . .' I shook my head. 'There's no rush, I'll wait. Don't bother, please.'

'You can spare a dozen or so, can't you, Robbie?'

'No, really, it's all right, I don't mind waiting.'

I wanted nothing to do with this smirking Robbie, to whom I had scarcely spoken since the witch episode a few years ago. And then I suddenly remembered: last week, climbing Sgurr Mor, half-naked in the sunshine on the hill. It was not possible the Fergusons could have seen me from their boat! But I had been waving at Finnghail, far below, shouting and uncaring. Perhaps Robbie even thought I had been waving at *him*; nothing else would explain this change in attitude. My face became warm at the memory and I had to clear my throat to speak.

'Thank you, Mr MacGregor. Please just order them for me. I'll see you in ten days or so.'

I quickly pushed the package and the letters into my rucksack, so that the address of the top envelope smudged against the damp wrapper of the frozen loaf. But as I bent to lift the pack on to my back I saw the stranger, the unwilling protector of crabs, pass the window. He was about my age, but with darker hair, and wearing a flecked woollen pullover. A bell rang in the house and we could hear Mrs MacGregor walking briskly along the passage to open the front door.

'A priest. From one of the other islands.'

MacGregor nodded his head towards the window, assuming, rightly, that we would want to know. (My prohibition on asking questions doesn't mean I'm never curious.)

'He came on the boat this morning.'

'What do we need a priest for?' Robbie scowled. 'He's wasting his time here.'

'Ach, he'll be here on holiday,' MacGregor shrugged dismissively. 'Oh, goodbye, Miss Falmer. I'll get this stuff ordered for you.'

I nodded my thanks as I shut the door behind me. The priest had gone into the house, and I walked away up the track as fast as I could. There was too much to think about, and I felt threatened by the morning's human contacts: small boys, learning cruelty at an early age, then Robbie Ferguson's smirk, and now a priest! Were there other Catholics on the island? I doubted it; it was a Presbyterian stronghold, if it was anything at all, and Ferguson's attitude was probably typical. One or two of the nearby islands were predominantly Catholic, and the priest had apparently come from there. It was disturbing, but I was almost sure I recognised him, even though his facial type was not uncommon – round, clean-shaven, a strong nose and heavy eyebrows, a pleasant, smooth face. But where could I have met him? I walked up the track, oblivious of the insects and the weight on my back, and puzzled.

Then I remembered, and with the memory came the certainty that the priest was here on this island to see me, a shepherd come to check the sheep. It must have been two, even three, years ago; I had been spending a few days on the mainland and, knowing that the local priest would be at the church that morning, had gone there to make my confession. The church was a small stone building, tucked away in a street halfway up the hill behind the harbour. I had been there on a Sunday or a Holy Day only a few times (circumstances force me to worship alone), and the congregation on these occasions was small, perhaps thirty or forty people. As I entered, that weekday morning, I heard two men talking quietly and seriously and, as my eyes adapted to the dim light, I saw the priests standing by the altar steps. One was the local priest, Father Simpson. Because he was clearly busy, I knelt in a pew near the back of the church, trying to calm myself and compartmentalise my guilt into tidy packages for absolution. Soon, Father Simpson glided down the nave towards me (why do priests seem to glide like mechanical toys? Is it because they are propelled by faith, or merely because their legs are hidden?) and asked, cautiously, softly, if I wished him to hear my confession. As I followed him to the confessional, he called the other priest over and introduced us.

'Miss Falmer,' (Father Simpson knew all his parishioners by name.) 'This is Father Peters, who is visiting us for a few days. He's almost a neighbour of yours, from the next island.'

We exchanged a few words, I no longer remember what, something about the weather or boat travel, perhaps, and I continued on towards the confessional and my catalogue of pride and lack of charity.

And now this crab-man, this priestly visitor, reminded me strongly of Father Simpson's guest. When I reached the cottage, I searched through the pages of my diaries (they are not proper diaries, but soft-backed exercise books in which I occasionally write down events, such as when I planted the peas, when the first swift arrived, or if I have seen an eagle; Belinda is there and a visit to the bank manager, and there are detailed records of Connan's arrival and recovery, and of Finnghail's development). At last I found it: February, two years previously. Of course, now I remembered; I had been trapped on the mainland. I wouldn't have met Father Peters if the weather had been calmer.

> 'Feb. 21st. Boat not running because of bad weather, had to stay on 2 extra days. Mrs S' son was due home, so had to move to 'Sea View' instead; evening meal not as good, and costs more. Went to St Thomas's, for confession. Father S. introduced me to one of the island priests, Father Peters; quiet man, distant. Bought more galvanised nails, polythene sheeting for windows, new glass for lamp.'

Even that brief comment in the diary made me certain it was the same man. And now I was certain too, that he had come here to find me; an island priest, come to talk to a woman trapped in her insularity! (That's interesting, I have twice spoken of myself as being 'trapped' – am I trapped on an island or was I trapped on the mainland? I think the answer is that I am trapped, but willingly so, within my own self-imposed isolation. This insularity encloses me wherever I am. I can imagine it as a kind of egg-shell around me; I can bend and stretch out to touch its warm protection, it is a shell yet it enfolds me. It excites me, and it is a dangerous luxury. I *am* an island, and I can laugh out across the seas. But that is to consider only my secular existence. There is also God, thank God.)

So Father Peters had come to see me. I needed to prepare myself for him. I was calm, filled with a certain warmth and tenderness towards this man who had thought I was worth seeking out. I imagined him, tall and straight, black cassock and biretta, his Bible clasped to his chest. He would walk along the track with measured tread, the air would be still around him. (There must not be wind because, if he were to bend forward, clasping his hat and with his robes streaming out behind him, I found that he became, instead, a witch.) Would it not be better if he were dressed in white and gold, glittering with purity? And then he would become a Christian soldier, with tanned face and piercing eyes; he would leap off his richly-caparisoned charger and lay his gauntleted hand on my imploring head. (But would he also pick me up and throw me over the saddle, claiming me for God – and for himself?) He had not been so strong by the village shore, but here, in the face of duty and the empty sea, he would be strengthened once more. I was elated with the love of God, and I knew that, by His authority, stern words and wisdom and healing would spill out from the hands and mouth of this far-seeing priest.

I stood in the open doorway, staring along the track. It was cooler on this side of the island; a light wind blew off the sea and stirred the still-green clusters of rowan berries. It was early afternoon, and the sea-birds dozed on the rocks. He will come this afternoon, I thought. He will have had lunch at the village. No, he will take Mrs MacGregor's cheese sandwiches and a foil-wrapped chocolate Swiss roll; he will stop and sit on the stone bridge for lunch and throw pebbles in the water. He will be here in two hours, otherwise he'll not get back in time for his evening meal. But of course not; he'll expect that I will feed him. Then he'll walk back in the long evening light and watch the deer.

Then the reality of the expected visit hit me. Suddenly I couldn't breathe properly, and a pulse started beating hard in my temple. I began to rush around inside the cottage, panicking, tidying away clothes, packets of food and dirty plates. I cleared the table that stood in the centre of my living room and lined up the prayerbook and the Bible, Tom's Bible, neatly at one side. I straightened the books and papers, and wished that I had a cloth to hang over the worst of the fish-boxes that supported the planking shelves. Where would Father Peters sit? In the big old armchair by the fireplace, or on the single wooden chair by the table? And then where would I sit? To sit at his feet adoringly would be to over-act.

But, looking around at this room, the room in which I sat and cooked and ate, at the scuffed wooden floor, the peatsmoke stains on the chimney breast and the kitchen cupboard that wouldn't shut, I realised that, worn and untidy as it had become, this was, nevertheless, my home, my fortress. And I would be stifled if I met him here. It would not work. We must, instead, meet on the moor. I would watch for him.

I watched for three hours but there was no sign. I tried to work in my garden, but I felt ill with anxiety. I couldn't eat, and walked on the shore until it was dark.

Next morning I awoke with confidence. I had been stupid to think he would come yesterday; he had arrived only that morning and it was to be expected that he would need to find his way around and to absorb the atmosphere. Today, though, if he left the village at nine, he could be here by one o'clock – he looked fit, but of course he would have to walk more slowly after he had changed into his cassock. I knew he'd leave the village wearing his normal clothes, his pullover and, perhaps, breeches; he wouldn't want to stir up gossip in the village, and his priest's clothes would be in his rucksack. He would probably change in the copse, or even closer. I had it all worked out. I was no longer afraid. I prepared myself carefully and I went to sit on the moor and wait.

Consequently, late in the morning, a figure appeared at the pass. I could see through my binoculars that he was not in black. He strode purposefully along the track, then detoured amongst the lumpy hillocks of moraine. I laughed to myself, pleased that I had anticipated this ruse. I waited for him to reappear, tall and dark and majestic. So it shocked me when he came into view again, only minutes later, dressed as he was before. I stood up and cried out, quietly so that he wouldn't hear.

'No! Stop! You must change there! There's nowhere else.'

But the man continued marching towards me. This was completely wrong! I was unprepared. And suddenly I was frightened to meet him; I crouched down and watched as he stopped and pulled out a map. He turned his body and the map to face the sea, then, instead of taking the path to my cottage, he began to cross the rough ground towards my hiding place, placing his feet with the confidence of a seasoned hillwalker. I was sure he couldn't see me, but now he was between me and the croft. I would have to move ahead of him to Camus Dubh and hide there, to watch what he would do. I thought he must be wanting to reach the crest of the moor behind the cottage, perhaps to look down and pray before he met me. I could skirt around on the shore out of sight, and meet him as he came down by the croft to Camus Beag. I was shaking with anxiety. We were required to meet, but this was not going according to the plan, and I was no longer certain of the rules.

I leapt down the slope, hidden by the low hill. The polished stone pillars of the mausoleum shone in the sun, the grassy plateau was smooth and bare. I imagined the priest reaching the top of the moor and turning to admire the view in all directions. He would be framed by the sky and he would look down into Camus Dubh, Black Bay, Death Bay. Yes, that was a fitting backdrop, after all; I should have thought of that. He would see me, and the glistening mausoleum. He would lift a hand, fingers gently curved in the sign of peace, then come slowly down the hill, and I would kneel, waiting.

But of course reality wasn't like that at all. I ran, jumping over boulders and squelching on the bright green moss that marked a sluggish spring. I ran towards a small rockfall at the side of the valley, and I slithered through the ragged hole that was the entrance to the crypt.

Even as I peered out, panting, to see what happened, my priest strode on to the skyline. He didn't even pause to look down towards my croft, but came straight down into Death Bay and walked towards the mausoleum. There he climbed over the rusty chain-link fencing, stepped on to the plinth, and stood motionless between the tombs. I don't like to do that too often; I always feel that I'm in the way, interrupting the continuous comment and conversation that flows between those three bodies as they lie there, inside their marble boxes, watching the sea. The priest stroked the smooth marble of a tomb, then walked out on to the grass at the far side. He was quite still, his back towards me, and I imagined that he prayed for the souls of the long-dead corpses. Then his knees bent briefly, so that he was momentarily bow-legged, and he turned round, zipping up the fly of his breeches. Comfortable again, he sat down on the step, facing the sea, and pulled his lunchbox and thermos out of his very small ruck-sack.

As for me, I watched and I waited, while he slowly ate his lunch and yawned and stretched and stood up to read the inscriptions on the tombs. God had deserted me for the day, and I was empty. My knees were dented from pressing against the gravel and pebbles that littered the entrance hole, and I longed to be out in the blustery wind instead of breathing the unstirred air of the crypt. But I was trapped; the crypt was dug into the hillside and, though the entrance was well-hidden, the ground on every side was smooth and open.

So, as the priest lay there, a priest on holiday, I lay, too, and watched him, and wondered what he thought about, this strong and celibate priest, a priest apparently unaware of my existence and upon whom I had expended so much energy and love. And I woke from the confused imagery of my thoughts to see him looking at the hillside, staring at the rocks where I was hidden. He picked up his pack and started to walk towards me. He must have known the crypt was there, and although he might well fall down if I rose up from the tomb, I could not stay there to be found.

I pulled myself through the hole and, muddy and scratched as I was, smiled and nodded in his direction, as though we were two old acquaintances in a shopping arcade.

'Lovely day today!'

I smiled again briefly, raising my hand, and limped stiffly but very rapidly away across the hillside.

In less than a minute, I was out of his sight. I wish now that I could have seen his face. No doubt he crossed himself.

I can put Tom's Bible away now. It has sat here on the table for the past two days, but Father Peters didn't look at it. Tucked inside is a felt-penned drawing of a balloon-shaped, brown animal lying on its back, with its stick legs in the air, upon a yellow circle. It is the 'fatted calf' laid out on a table for the returning son.

Tom was born to us within a year of marriage. It was too soon (I had forgotten to take my Pill) and 'hordes of children' echoed in my ears. ('Do you realise, Graham, what it will mean to be married to a Catholic? Candles and beads and graven images! Gilded trappings, Graham! A matriarchal society – do you want to be the father of endless hordes of children, ground down by their wailings and smells, spending hours at the office to escape from home? And they'll all be Catholics, too – Harriet will see to that. It's her role in life, didn't you know?') Graham's mother's voice was so quietly evil: but she was wrong about my role, about the hordes. I brought Tom up as a Catholic; he was baptised, he went to a Catholic school and made his First Communion, and Graham tolerated it, I thought, although, due to his absence on business, I was accompanied by my mother at both ceremonies. Graham and I hoped to have more children, and I rejected further contraception, but no other was conceived. So I began to feel guilty, the fault must be mine. Perhaps my mother-in-law had been right, I'd been unable to be a true Catholic, allowing life and death to take its ordained course. Tom's extra chromosome, his disability, and this sterility were a punishment upon me, Divine retribution. It was a terrifying thought. One was observed.

I started to go to Mass several times each week, using a smaller church that was closer to our home. I went early, so as not to disturb the breakfast routine. But I worried about Tom – the sins of the mother should not continue to be visited upon the son –

and I began to take him with me. Tom woke early anyway, and, perhaps surprisingly, he rarely grumbled about the early morning outings. I loved Graham, I didn't want this to be a cause of conflict between us.

But on Ash Wednesday, Tom sat down to supper with a grey smudge on his forehead. Graham asked him what he had been doing, to get his face so dirty.

Tom laughed, Daddy was so silly!

'It's a cross! It's Ash Wednesday. We had pancakes yesterday!'

There are occasionally moments when you realise that something has just happened that will permanently alter your future life. I'm not talking about major events like deaths or weddings, but sudden insights, intimations that everything is not as you had supposed.

'Go and wash it off!'

'But I have to wear it until bedtime! Father Joe said so!'

'Wash your face, Thomas. Now.'

It was said quietly, authoritatively, and with no further room for argument. They both surprised me, Graham and Tom. Our son did as he was told, and his father and I sat in silence until he returned.

Three

Peace ... sweet sleep ... and pleasing ease. Streams ... green leaves ... and distant seas ... bees are buzzing; dozing, dreaming, my eyes are closing ... sun-steeped, serene. Lazy breathing, chest barely moving, air trickling in and out, arms heavy in the sunlight. A grasshopper rattles near my ear, its sound stirs the air like flickering heatwaves. I open an eye and watch a lustrous green beetle, metallic in the sun, crawl slowly across the golden lichen, an Egyptian amulet, rich and warm and gleaming. Ripples slap soporifically against the black and silver shore, where quartzite sparkles in the ebony peat. Dry grasses, dead brown stalks of asphodel, *tempus fugit*, slowly; scent of thyme and beds of amaranth and moly. I am lowly, God is Holy, my mind turns slowly. This peace is mine; peace, deep pleasing peace and teasing ease. A Garden of Ease, reached from the mausoleum at Death Bay! A heavenly, living, life-endowing secret.

I can remember when I first came here. I was searching for the lochan that is shown on the map. I was quite unprepared for this hidden wonder. I had followed the burn up from Death Bay, treading the beaten track (made by deer, or my croft's previous owners?) through the grass and bracken, and ducking through the alders and pale thin birches. Gradually, the stream-bed narrowed and the valley sides steepened until, suddenly, I was at the bottom of a gorge. There was no way through, the walls were sheer and dank and glistening; ferns and liverworts clung to dripping ledges and the air was cool and moist. The river spilled out of the gorge in waterfalls and deep, clear pools, that would have been inviting were they not so cold and sunless. I backtracked until I found the traces of the path that I had missed, and I scrambled and sweated amongst boulders and loose gravel until I had reached the top. Then I knelt at the edge and looked down; a bird's nest was propped, improbably, against a stunted birch on a ledge beneath me, and round, polished stones shone bluish-white in the water thirty feet below. There was no bird-song, and the river was silent and purposeful, trapped in its narrow channel. Thick, luxuriant bushes of blaeberry grew by the path, their berries swollen and waxy in the damp air. I followed the gorge for half a mile, and then the upper valley opened out and the river was running free and noisy. I walked on dry grass and heather, dotted with patches of silky bog-cotton. The salty wind would howl across here in winter, funnelled in from the sea, and the rowans and willows were scrubby and hunched. I could see that, in the distance, the land rose steeply, its southerly face in stern profile; this must be the area of crags marked on the map, that sheltered the lochan that I sought. I worked my way towards it, leaping from tussock to tussock to avoid the soggy sphagnum and, as I got closer, I began to appreciate the understatement of the map. The crags formed a dark, vertical cliff, eighty to a hundred feet at its highest point. From each side of the cliff-face, the land curved and sloped gently down, so that the whole massif was shaped like a horseshoe.

I climbed to the top of a rocky hummock to get a better view, and saw the lochan, protected by the curved feet of the cliff. I whooped at it, shouted 'HALLO!' shrilly, to hear the echo bounce back from that perfect sounding-board, but was at once ashamed as a pair of mallard scampered across the surface of the water, wings outspread and necks stretched in panic, and took to the air.

When I first saw this lonely dark lochan, where waterlilies, rocked on the ripples, opened their pale, chaste centres to the sky, and where tiny toadlets crawled wetly on the shore, I almost cried. Its empty beauty overwhelmed me; I wanted to disintegrate into a thousand pieces and be scattered on the breeze, so that I would be absorbed and re-integrated into this pure wilderness. Even when a gale screams down the valley and whips spray from the dark wavelets, I feel at peace here, in this place. I shelter here on the south shore, amongst the hummocks, slabs and outcrops, lulled by thyme, where time floats free. I have knelt here many times and prayed (at first self-consciously, contrition out-faced by majesty, damp knees in an alien landscape); it is my cathedral, where I lift up my eyes to the natural vaulting of the hills, and I give thanks and ask forgiveness. And I know He sees and hears me, and offers me another chance, because why else would I be permitted to continue to feel the considerable spiritual impact, the healing peace, of this place?

Who was the Harriet of fifteen, or even ten, years ago? It doesn't seem possible that she and I have inhabited the same body. If we had all been here then, Graham, Tom and I, here on the island, the outcome would have been so different. Knowing what I know now. If *this* Harriet had been the wife and mother, not that other, that confused, rejected Harriet. . . . *This* Harriet, who has learned to accept her punishment (punishment upon punishment), and who lies here now, replete with repentance and weak with worship.

We could have brought picnics up here, and become lazy and drunken with the sweet peace that falleth, like manna, as the gentle rain from heaven. Grasshoppers and heather honey, in a human desert that throbs with life and God's love. A natural paradise for you, my little Tom.

'Mummy?'

We would have managed, my love. Sweet Holy Mary, with her mother's touch, would have helped me to help you, and your father could not have failed, in this perfect place, to have succumbed to the purity of her charms.

'Mummy! Mum-mee, Mum-mee, Mum-mee!'

'Hush, Tom! What is it? Why are you pulling at my arm?'

'Mum! Come and make a den. In that cave.'

'Where? Oh, in that hollow beneath the cliff. Yes – soon, when we've had a rest. Let's just lie here for now, and plan what you'd need. It could be a perfect den. . . .'

'Get a box for a table. And cook sausages on a fire!'

'Sausages? We could cook some fish!'

'Fish? From there?'

'No, not from the lochan. But I caught some sea fish yesterday, so you can have one.'

'No, sausages. I want David to help me with the den. We'll sleep there.'

'But David doesn't live here, love.'

'Phone up and ask him to come over and play.'

'But we haven't got a 'phone. And he'd have to wait three days for the boat.'

'There'll be boys at school . . .'

'Oh. The school's on the mainland, Tom, the children go by boat then stay there, it's a boarding school. But I think, Tommy, we'd have to teach you ourselves, here – you'd have lessons with Daddy and me. It would be fun, wouldn't it?'

'We could watch TV, about lions!'

'We haven't got television, Tom – there's no electricity.'

There's no road, no transport, and no hot water. And there's a hole in my bucket, dear Tommy, dear Tommy . . . An implausible Paradise, Tom, for a young, demanding boy, and an impossible Paradise for three interdependent adults. But a perfect haven for a single, self-reliant soul!

'You're so fidgety, Tom. I know, you want to build your den. But talking of dens reminds me of something else. What do you think it is? Foxes! You wouldn't need to watch animals on television, there are plenty of wild ones here. Let me tell you about Finnghail, my fox. You would have liked him as a friend, my Tom-whose-time-has-stood-still, seven-year Tom. Finn would have been very happy to have shared your den and your food.'

'A fox! I didn't know you had a fox! A real one, not pretend?'

'A real one. Here, come and curl up next to me and keep an eye on the water-lilies. I've never seen a frog sitting on a lily-pad, have you? Keep watching, and tell me as soon as you see one! Now – Finnghail. I found him not far from here, you know – at the bottom of that deep, dark gorge that the river runs through. He must have fallen down from the path along the top. He was just a little cub, and he was nearly dead when I found him.'

'Poor little fox.'

'Yes. He'd broken his leg. It was just luck that I saw him. I was already on the top path and I leant over, as usual, to look down at the river and saw a little black bundle lying on a rock. It had a tail, and I could see it was a fox, but I thought it was dead. Then suddenly, it gave a little twitch, just like this—'

'Ouch!'

'—and I saw it was alive! It was very difficult getting to him, I had to wade through the river in places, and scramble over slippery boulders. I got wet right up to my knees, boots and all! But I managed to reach him, and he was so limp that I rolled him up in my pullover and put him in my rucksack and took him home.'

'Was he heavy?'

'No. He was about the size of a big cat, and very skinny-looking because his fur was wet. I'd never looked after anything like a fox before and I wasn't sure what to do, but I rubbed him dry and put him by the fire with a hot-water bottle next to him – he looked very sweet. And I managed to get some warm sweet milky tea into him. He was very weak, which was lucky because it must have hurt when I strapped his leg.'

'How?'

'I hadn't the faintest idea what to do, Tom – only what I'd read about in books when I was young – "Secret Seven" or whatever! But I bandaged it on to a bit of wood as a splint, to stop him moving it. He hated it, of course – but it seemed to work! It wasn't very easy getting him to eat at first – little bits and pieces, bread and egg, eventually tinned meat, all odds and ends.'

'I wish I could have helped.'

'Yes, you'd have got on well together. You could have played with him.'

'Like a dog?'

'Yes, almost, although he was a bit wild, and had a very sharp nip! He chewed everything in the cottage! But he used to follow me everywhere once he was able to hobble around again. He lived at the cottage for about a year, then he started to go away, for longer and longer periods. I tried to encourage him to go, and didn't feed him very often. He was – *is* – a wild animal. And then, when he was about two years old, he left altogether.'

'Then I'm glad he wasn't my friend, I don't like it when people leave.'

'He still visits me sometimes. And I've seen him once with a vixen, a female. Perhaps they've got cubs by now.'

'Finn's mummy left him.'

'Perhaps she couldn't reach him after he fell down. And her other cubs were hungry, what could she do, poor thing? Oh, Tommy, she cried and cried, but he was taken away from her and out of reach. . . .'

'There's a frog! Look! A frog!'

'Chase it, Tom, quickly. Who will it turn into when it's kissed?'

Chase away the darkling monsters, embrace the pale beauty of the lily. Curl safely into the foetal position, fold and unfold like a lotus, let the radiant peace enter your soul, and call on His Holy name. Forget, forget; forget the dark power of human misery. . . .

Four

An orange wart on the clifftop, a lurid barnacle! Marching in and claiming this as his living quarters. Study area, indeed! Well, he won't be able to stay there in the summer, there'll be no water. Unless he learns to drink seawater like one of his precious seals. *His* seals! I suppose he thinks he'll have exclusive rights to them now. 'The Jos Allen Seal Colony. Keep Away.' Jos – what sort of a name is Jos, anyway?

I feel ill. I can't eat, my stomach *hurts* I'm so angry. And how does he think he's going to watch them from there? He needn't think he's going to borrow my boat, either – I saw him looking at it. He can get his own ruddy boat. Go and camp out there on the ruddy rocks with your precious ruddy seals. Let the tide come in! Camp underwater! Drown, for all I care!

Oh, please, please, go away. Please, Jos Allen, don't stay here, please go away, leave us alone. O dear Lord, sweet Jesus, help me. Help us all. Keep the peace, please, keep him out. Sweet and blessed Virgin, intercede; you're a Mother, you know the seals won't want to be spied on. They're God's seals, not his. Oh, I beg you. 'Hail Mary, full of Grace . . .' Hear how I beseech you, a hundred, two hundred times if necessary. Oh go away, Jos Allen, go away, oh please go . . .

I must have cried myself to sleep. My cheeks and eyelids are crusty with tears. And the tent is still there. He hasn't gone. The flaps are open, his hand is reaching out towards the saucepan on the stove. He's eating. I shall never eat again, there's a terrible dull sickness inside me.

This man, this Jos Allen, came to my cottage yesterday. He came to me on purpose, to deliver a letter. John MacGregor had asked him to deliver a letter. He came to introduce himself, he said. Arrogance! As if I should want to know. I suppose he just came to pry, to find out about me. But perhaps I'm the one who is arrogant, to think this. I don't know what to think.

I was in my bedroom, cutting my hair. That's very difficult, another of those tasks that I haven't quite managed to master. It's very confusing in the mirror, trying to make sure that all the hair is being cut to the same length. I have to do it very slowly so that I can work out how to angle the scissors. I once tried cutting it without the mirror, by feel, but my fingers tended to get in the way of the scissor blades. This time I was sitting on my bed, a towel around my shoulders to trap the cut hair, and concentrating on my little rectangle of reflection, so I didn't see him arrive. There was no warning: there's no gate to squeak and the front door was open, and he must have been stepping very softly.

'Hallo! Anyone in?'

I was frozen, as in a film, my two pairs of eyes linked in mutual shock. His voice boomed through the cottage, echoing down the years of solitude.

'Hallo there!'

Undoubtedly the voice was real.

'Wait!'

I threw the towel on to the floor; I remember pushing my fingers through my half-cut hair, to fluff up the wet strands (and the memory of this action surprises me, it appears I do have some remnants of vanity left). My hands and legs were shaking.

I couldn't see him clearly; his huge backpack shut out the light from the front door, so that the living room was dark and his figure black and featureless. He was right next to me, hugely blocking escape. I remember I was holding the frame of the bedroom door.

'What do you want?'

He stepped quickly backwards, possibly realising how large he loomed. The light returned, and I saw that he was in his mid-twenties, brown-haired, bearded. I do remember his eyes; they are deep-set and dark. Is it his eyes that are arrogant? He looked surprised when he saw me, and I remember how his eyes kept watching me, assessing.

'I'm sorry if I frightened you.'

His voice was surprisingly quiet, as though he had consciously modulated it in appeasement.

'I was passing, and John MacGregor at the shop asked me to deliver this letter to you.' He held it out. 'He wasn't sure if it was for you or not.'

'Oh. Oh, thank you.'

I took the envelope, but didn't look at it. It was irrelevant. I wanted him to leave. But he was insistent, forcing me by his words to examine the letter.

'It's addressed to Mrs G. Falmer, you see.'

It was, too. But that was completely impossible. I looked at him, sternly, determined that he should not see the effect of this second shock. My jaws were stiff with the effort to stop my teeth chattering. I forced myself to shrug and smile, shaking my head in puzzlement.

'How odd. It should be addressed to Harriet Falmer if it's for me. A strange mistake. Well, I'll look at it, and if it's not mine I'll take it back next time I'm in the village and get it returned to sender. Thanks for delivering it.'

I shrugged again, dismissively. Pieces of cut hair slipped down inside my shirt and prickled; I wriggled my shoulders slightly.

'It was no trouble on my part. As I said, I was just passing this way, anyhow. I'm Jos Allen, by the way.'

He stuck out his hand, and there was some confusion as I tried to shake it with my left hand, because I was still holding the letter in my right. He smiled, briefly, giving a small, amused snort.

'I'm going to be a neighbour of yours, of sorts. I'm hoping to camp a bit up the coast, beyond Camus Dubh, to look at the seal group that lives along there.'

'Why? What's wrong with them? They looked all right last time I saw them.' (He couldn't be intending to *stay*?)

'Well, nothing's wrong with them, I hope.' He looked surprised again. 'I'm a zoologist. I've been employed to look at the behavioural ecology of the seal group for the next three years. With Peter Metcalfe – you probably met him when he was over? Short – grey beard . . .? No? We want to see what affects the size of the seal population, what they eat, and so on.'

'Why?' I suddenly felt trapped; his bulk still blotted out the sea. 'Please, let me get outside! I need to see . . .' (The sea, to see the sea, to see the sea.) I pushed towards him, still talking. '*Why* must you watch them? It's nothing to do with you, is it, what they do? You're intruding, a voyeur. How will your knowing what they do help them in the future? You just want to use them so that you can write an article in some dreary journal.'

He was backing away now, out into the brightness. I followed him, to stand on the doorstep, to turn the stranger from my door. The daylight reduced him. I was pleased that I had pushed, physically and verbally. He looked less certain of himself, and his eyes were hidden from me as he looked down at the ground. I no longer felt intimidated, and beyond his shoulders a small choppy swell bobbed and nodded in encouragement.

'I hadn't actually thought about it from the seals' point of view.' His smile was guarded, and his eyes no longer tried to force contact with mine but seemed to have gone blank.

'I won't disturb the seals, though, Miss Falmer. Or you. And the study will help them, or the common seal population in general, in the end. I hope.' He looked up at me again. 'Perhaps you've noticed yourself that there have been fewer seals around in the past few years? We want to work out why this is happening, you see. If we can understand the reasons, perhaps we can do something to reverse the trend.'

He walked over towards the wall and turned to face me, leaning back and hitching up his pack so that the wall took its weight and he could be free to concentrate on rationalising his work. It was the introductory sequence of a talk, a lecture to a lay audience. I thought hysterically, briefly, that I could turn back into the cottage and shut the door, but he might carry on talking, regardless, and never leave. He must, though, have sensed my desire to flee, and he raised his voice.

'Distemper, of course, wiped out a lot of seals, especially the common seals. With the increase in fish-farming, though, there are probably many more being shot at than we know about. Perhaps there's been a decrease in their preferred food, perhaps the waters are being over-fished? I wondered if you'd have some ideas, yourself? You must get a fair picture of what goes on around here – ecologically speaking.'

Not in any other sense, his tone implied. He was watching me again. The bottoms of his shorts cut into the tanned muscular flesh of his thighs as he braced himself against the wall. A strange, mocking tension came from him, and I realised that I had been mistaken to think that I had gained superiority. He persisted, despite my silence.

'I was wondering, Miss Falmer, if you knew when the colony had moved down this way? We're fairly sure that this is the group that used to be up at the north tip of the island, that Jamieson worked on in the fifties, and it looks as though the shift in territory has been fairly recent. It should be very interesting to compare our data with his. If you could give me any snippets of information, I'd be very grateful . . . Harriet.' He raised an eyebrow as he spoke my name. 'Local knowledge is often extremely valuable, you know, especially where it's long-term.'

My neck and back itched intolerably, and I winced and squirmed angrily. Why couldn't he stop going on about the blasted seals and leave me alone?

'No, I don't know anything about them. I'm sorry, I can't help. I hardly even know where they live.'

'Did you notice any pups last summer? It could just be that

they're not breeding very successfully here, for some reason.'

'I didn't notice. I'm not interested. For all I know they're probably not even there any more.'

I hoped to God that they had left for good!

'Ah well. Thanks anyway. I guess I'd better be off then, and find somewhere to set up camp. Can you recommend a good site near the seal colony? Ideally, flat and smooth, with freshwater, hot sun, sandy beaches, and a great view. Topless, if possible!' He grinned.

'You're on the wrong island!'

'Oh, I don't know. That bit just there in front of your cottage, where the burn comes down, looks good. Your beach isn't sandy, but it would do. A bit far to the study area – but nice neighbours!'

He was still grinning as he pushed himself away from the wall, grunting as his shoulders took the weight of the pack.

'I could drop in and fix things for you, in return for tea and home-baked scones. Nice meeting you, Ms Falmer . . .'

He nodded, and waved a hand, and turned sideways to squeeze out through the garden gate.

I stood in the doorway and stared at the shore. A wave, larger than the others, broke with a soft roar and hiss, and I started counting the bands of swell that followed it. One . . . two . . . three . . . The seventh wave was, as I expected, large, and I was comforted by the natural order of things and continued counting groups of seven for several minutes. By the time I had finished, Jos Allen had disappeared.

I went round to the back of the cottage, to be certain he was not, through some cruel joke, pitching his tent within sight of the croft. My washing line had broken with the weight of so many wet clothes, and they lay, besmirched and hidden, among the yellowing pea-vines.

The letter, however, remained: 'Mrs G. Falmer'.

I went back into the cottage, into my bedroom, and shut the door. The room was dark and cool, smelling faintly, familiarly, of damp walls and fusty carpet. The aged staleness used to bother me at first; by then, I had forgotten the smell of cheap rented bedsits, and had become accustomed to accommodation with a carefully regulated internal environment, whether it was the renovated Victorian flat that I shared with my husband and son, or my mother's modern house: vacuum-cleaners to remove trampled earth, washing-machines and spin-driers to pummel and suck at dirt and damp, central-heating, extractor fans, and large windows that opened easily. But these walls were thick, and the white emulsion with which I had covered the internal walls was flaked and discoloured by rising damp. The windows were small and protective against the gales, their wooden frames alternately swollen and shrunk by rain and sun, and the mice above the plasterboarded ceiling were part of the history of the place. At first, I had tried to disguise the smell with the perfumed smoke of joss sticks; I bought them from a small Asian shop on a visit to the city. I remembered how I surprised the polite and ancient shopkeeper by purchasing all the packets (eighteen? twenty?) that remained on his shelf. Two packets contained incense-scented sticks, inappropriate, I felt, for my bedroom (would I be struck down by a suddenly-materialising censer as I undressed for bed?). The heavy scent of religion also brought back memories of early morning Mass (and Tom, heavy with sleep, beside me on the pew, his feet unable to reach the ground), and I wondered whether I should burn the incense at my Sunday morning prayers. But the idea provoked images of absurd drama: an isolated cottage, fog-shrouded, is seen against the muffled hissing of waves breaking on the shingle; inside the cottage, a lonely, kneeling woman, muttering prayers and plucking at her rosary, emerges briefly through the drifting fog of incense-laden smoke.

Instead, I luxuriated in the exotic scents of sandalwood and patchouli. I drifted out of the cottage and strode back in, alternating between sensual images of richly-embroidered floor cushions, silk scarves and golden filigree, and the practicalities of digging potatoes and repainting the windows. After ten days or so of perfumed indoor air, the unreality of the indoor dreams contrasted so incongruously with the reality of the natural environment that I allowed the odours of organic life to dominate once more. Somewhere in a box above the ceiling, if the mice haven't eaten them, there is still a large pile of joss-sticks.

A faint scent of dried bog myrtle came from the sheets as I lay down on the bed. I propped myself upright against the pillow and examined the now crumpled envelope carefully. My name and address were typed, and I could make out enough of the postmark to see that it came from Edinburgh. The only people who knew where Mrs G. Falmer, wife of Graham and mother of Tom, lived, were my bank manager and my solicitor, both of whom were based in the capital, but they both had strict instructions never to address me as such, and never to reveal where I lived, to anyone. If my husband needed to communicate with me (I hadn't heard from him for many years) he wrote to my solicitor, who forwarded the letter inside a newly-addressed envelope. With a bank account, a chequebook, access to a mail order firm, and a solicitor, I had all I needed as Harriet Falmer, Ms Harriet Falmer, if need be even 'Miss'. I cannot, will not, deny my marriage, I am not Harriet Longmore, I will never be Harriet Longmore again. But living here, on my own, it is not safe to be identified as the wife of someone; my husband might be found and informed. It's safer to pretend (without specific statement) that I am an ageing spinster. Better that they imagine my shrivelled, middle-aged body and merely speculate on whether I've 'had it' or 'need it', rather than know that I, widowed or married, 'know what it's all about' and must therefore be desperate for a man to thrust himself between my legs. Was it the married title that accounted for Jos Allen's arrogant eyes – that he hoped to deliver himself rather than this letter, into the clever hands of an older and experienced woman? My clever hands don't need joss sticks!

I could just throw this letter away, unopened. That would be simplest, to forget that it ever existed. It can only bring me disquiet, and hours of worrying, and the need to reply. I don't want to be disturbed any more, the seal-watcher is enough disturbance. But there is something inside the envelope, I can feel it, a thickness;

boxes within boxes, perhaps leading to something tiny in the centre, too small to cause anxiety. Think of it in those terms, and opening the envelope becomes easy. There! Tear it apart so that Mrs Falmer is fragmented. But there remains another folded envelope, another 'Mrs G. Falmer', redirected from our flat, in blue ink, to my husband's present address. A memorial tablet, remembrance of times past, postmarked two weeks ago. My solicitor – but no, a substitute, an incompetent subordinate who cannot read instructions as to my form of address . . . 'Mr Falmer has requested that the enclosed letter be forwarded to you.' Nothing else; my husband requests nothing else. There is no danger, then, in this outer box, apart from dangerous incompetence. And now, the inner box; what ancient archive is chasing out-of-date addresses? I haven't the courage to open this, after all, it is a time-bomb and will explode into dust; but it's been opened already and resealed. Has Graham checked the contents and left danger lurking in their place? It is a *cheque*! A cheque for fifty pounds. And a letter from yet another solicitor, explaining away the miracle as a cheque from the estate of a deceased aunt, my father's sister, long unseen, almost unknown. She came to my wedding day. Fifty pounds will be her widow's mite. Dear, kind lady; I'm glad you didn't know. I thank you, and I shall celebrate your name. I'll send your cheque to the bank, and tomorrow – tomorrow I'll go to the village and buy some more whisky and a cake, a frozen cake. I'll have a party, and we – I, the seals, and your memory, will celebrate.

(The letter, of course, was not for me, Mr MacGregor. I'm returning it to the sender, you can feel the envelope inside. Some other Falmer, they must have picked out the wrong address, we were next to each other on the list, I suppose. One cannot trust anyone to do their jobs properly these days, can one?)

Five

The seal-watcher has been on the island for less than two weeks; not even two weeks since he first blundered on to my croft and claimed the seals as his own.

Saturday

Dear Miss Falmer,

For the past ten days I have been aware of you watching me. You have tried (unsuccessfully) to scare away the seal colony. I am very sorry that my presence here disturbs you to the extent that you would like me to leave.

I am sure it would help if we could discuss this. There is no sense in us both upsetting each other like this, and we must surely be able to come to some arrangement. This study is my *job*, and will also be my life for the next three years. I can't just abandon it because you don't want me here! Please, Miss Falmer, can we meet? I don't want to disturb you at your cottage.

Yours sincerely,

Jos Allen

The letter was written on a sheet of lined file-paper, torn from an A4 pad. The writing was neat and careful, and I imagined the boy attempting two or three drafts before he got it to his satisfaction. It possibly took him several hours; the first draft was probably angry and accusatory, but as time passed and he thought about what he needed to accomplish, he modified his tone. And then, having written the letter, he put it in an empty half-bottle of whisky, salvaged from the shore, and came silently to my cottage (at night? early this morning?) and left it by my back door.

I sat down to read, resting the letter on the kitchen table because I was shaking so much. As soon as I had seen the bottle by the door, I'd realised, at last, that I had not been playing a one-sided game, but that Jos Allen, although he had apparently ignored my presence (apart from responding to my deliberate provocation at the Pied Piper's party), had been very much involved. I don't think, until that moment, I'd seriously considered any alternative outcome to my campaign other than that he would just quietly give up, pack his bag and steal away into the night. I had chosen to interpret his pretended ignorance as passive endurance that at last would crack. Yet I'd met the man (he was not, despite the letter, a boy); it had seemed then that he was confident, analytical, capable of physical and verbal domination. But for all that, it had only now occurred to me, when he had cast his message upon my shore, that my behaviour could have goaded him into anger and physically threatening behaviour. I was very vulnerable; and I would have earned no sympathy. The letter suggested I had escaped physical threats, if nothing else.

When I'd finished reading it, I rested my head on my arms on the table and sobbed. For the second time in ten days, Jos Allen had caused me to cry, and this time it was with relief at the ending of a time of tension, and with remorse and pity. The tall, tanned, bearded invader of my imagination shrank back to a lonely young man anxiously looking over his shoulder. Poor boy! I had spied on him relentlessly. When he sat still for hours, his binoculars trained on the rocks and sea, so did I. Sometimes my binoculars were trained on him, but usually it was sufficient to know where he was. If he walked along the cliff or shore searching for the objects of his study, so did I. I sat and watched him prepare his food, I watched him as he set off along the track to the village, I watched him as he returned, re-provisioned. Every day I watched him, but I was always careful to remain in the distance so that there was no possibility of verbal contact, and, used as I was to watching animals and birds, I was able to remain hidden. Of course, I occasionally showed myself, briefly, so that he knew I was watching – standing up to stretch, or to remove my red pullover. Twice, I had motored past the headland in the boat, far out, ostensibly fishing, but I had stopped briefly and had stood and stared towards his tent. Jos-watching: my mind was full of nothing else, it had become an obsession. My waking hours had become focused on harassing the seal-watcher, and I believe now that I no longer knew the purpose of the vigil. I had neglected my daily routine and the hundred tasks about the croft of repair and preparation for autumn. I scarcely ate, my stomach was contracted with hate so that food made me sick.

The bottle-letter, although it solved nothing, brought me back to life. I became frightened at my madness, at how quickly it had taken me over. My guts churned and groaned in emptiness, and I made strong, sweet tea because solid food was, as yet, too much. And all the time I thought of the young man, not much more than a boy, (not much older than Tom), whose precarious hold on this island, alone, unbefriended, protected by no more than a fragile nylon shell, I had eroded. Like the black acidity of a peat bog, I had crept and spread, and worn him down. How I had wounded him; O Lord, forgive me, forgive me, forgive me. And protect the seal-watcher. I walked and ran to Jos's campsite, over the moor, past the pillars of the dead, along the paths where dry heather stalks tore at my ankles and dark mud smeared my legs. I reached the headland and looked down – and his tent had gone. He had gently laid his stone at my back door, and he had gone.

'Jos! COME BACK! Jos!'

I stared inland, hoping to see him on the track, but the landscape was empty.

'Jos! Jos!'

I called and shouted. There was nothing left; no further note of explanation (his acknowledgement of my behaviour was explanation enough), nothing except a rectangle of yellowed grass and a ring of blackened stones. I climbed down and sat on the grass where his tent door had been and I looked out to sea. I lay down where Jos must have lain, suddenly wanting to imagine what it was like to eat and sleep and live in a tent full-time. I had driven the boy away. A great weariness swamped me, and I rolled on to my side, hunched in my sleeping bag against the cold, peering out of the open flap. Two seals lay on the rocks, slapped by the cold grey spray. They didn't mind being watched, they probably didn't even know.

'You could have stayed,' I said. 'It would have been all right. You could have stayed.'

'Actually, my head's usually at the other end. But I'm camped in a hollow round the corner.'

I felt very silly. The ground was wet, too. I wiped the tears from my face and stood up, without the help of his outstretched hand. He had managed not to smile.

'I thought you'd gone.'

'Obviously! This site got too windy. Thanks for coming.'

He inclined his head slightly; his face was gaunt and serious.

'Thank you for your letter.'

'Hmm.'

Silence hung heavily, broken by gulls' screams.

'We need to—'

'Perhaps we should—'

We spoke together but I let him continue, it was his play now.

'We need to discuss this business, Miss Falmer. Shall we sit on the rocks over there?'

'This business.' It sounded cold and legal. What did he intend to do to me? The rocks were damp and close together, so that the hems of our waterproof jackets touched. We made a strange picture: a thin, middle-aged woman with wild grey hair and tear-stained face, her muddy-kneed jeans almost touching the knees of the slim, dark-bearded young man next to her. Despite the man's youth, there are deep grooves each side of his mouth, and the skin around his eyes is pouched and tired. Both people have the weather-beaten appearance of outdoor people, and yet the faces of both are tense and pale with weariness. Together, they are apart, and each stares at the far horizon. What are they talking about?

I had to take the initiative, or I would be lost.

'I came to say that I promise to leave you alone. I won't bother you ever again. We can each keep out of the other's way. Please stay. And I hope your project goes well.' Amen. Lord, forgive me. Lord, take care of him.

'Can you not even say you are *sorry*? Why did you do it to me?' He thumped his wrists down on to his thighs, and his face twisted with his anguish. 'Do you know what it was like, thinking you were there watching me all the time? I couldn't even have a *crap* in peace. I don't understand why you did it. Why?'

The cool, let's-discuss-this-in-front-of-our-solicitors approach had gone, and Jos Allen was no more than an overwrought boy who could no longer suppress his misery, who might even weep if he lost control still further.

'I just wanted you to go! I thought I could make you go away and leave me in peace,' I whispered.

'You scared me, Miss Falmer. I didn't know what you were going to do to me. You were always there. You were *crazy,* with the seals.'

'I know, I know. I just didn't want you here.' I was crying again, silly, weak woman.

'But I won't be in your way. We need hardly see each other, I won't bother you. I told you that.'

'I see that now. But think back to when you came to my house. You scared *me*. You were so sure of your own right, you gave the impression that you were checking up on me – and my boat – and you were just going to come and use us when you wanted.' I was indignant and bitter at the memory.

'Use you?'

He looked startled at the word. Then suddenly his face went

quite round with delight, and he bent back his head and shouted with laughter. The barely-suppressed tears poured down his cheeks. I didn't understand him, but his laughter blew away the clouds.

'Oh, Miss Falmer! Harriet! We are such fools! What misunderstandings. We've made each other sick, all for nothing. I could hardly eat all week.'

'Me neither.' I began to smile. 'But I don't understand what you misunderstood. Or why you think your behaviour was so funny.'

'It wasn't. I know I was rude. Jokes about topless views and things. You were so prickly and unwelcoming, I just got pissed off and wanted to make you snap out of it.'

'So you're not always like that, then? Arrogant? Full of yourself?'

'Very rarely, actually. I hope. Really.'

I met his eyes properly, for the first time, and I believed him.

'Come round to my new campsite and I'll make a brew. I could use a cup of tea even if you couldn't. I'm practically out of biscuits, though.'

I was being invited out to tea! What a strange, exhausting day. I smiled wryly, and followed him through the sodden bracken. At the top of the path, Jos stopped and turned to look at the seals; there were now three on the rocks.

'I can recognise several of them individually now. Did you really think you'd lead them away? And what would you have done with them if you'd succeeded?'

'I don't know.' Although I had always had a secret dream.

'If you *had* succeeded, I would have been even more scared of you, terrified, in fact, do you know that? I would have thought very seriously about abandoning the whole project.'

'Why?'

'It would have been too much like magic. Someone told me you were a witch.'

So they had been talking about me, discussing me.

'You said you'd leave me alone, and that you wouldn't interfere. Gossiping and prying is interfering. I wish I had succeeded in taking the seals, then nobody would ever dare come here again!'

'Hell, no. I haven't been gossiping. I thought we were reaching an understanding. You're so bloody prickly! All I knew about you before I came here was that a recluse called Harriet Falmer lived near my study site. MacGregor asked me to bring a letter, I suppose he thought it might be important, or maybe he was just stirring things up out of boredom. Hell knows it did that all right. I asked MacGregor if he knew if you had a boat and would you be likely to lend it to me. He said, "Yes. And No." Okay?'

'He was right about that. But what about the witch? That was Robbie Ferguson, wasn't it?'

Images of long black skirts and crooked, pointing fingers and, sweet Mary, my naked breasts in the sunshine, were in my mind.

'What did he say?'

'Nothing. He came into the shop when I was there, a few days ago. He knew who I was, apparently—'

'Everybody knows everybody's business.'

'—and he asked me if I'd seen the witch yet. That's all. MacGregor told him to shut up, or mind his manners, or some such thing.'

I stayed silent, and Jos must have realised that I would give no further explanation.

'Come on, then, let's get the primus going.'

The tent was pitched in a dip that provided shelter from the westerlies which, by now, were daily sweeping up the coast with dreary regularity. I noticed that the burn was not easily accessible, and commented on the fact.

'Yes, you don't have to tell me! I'm still looking for a good spot for when I come back in October.'

'Are you going away soon, then?' (It was already mid-September.)

'In a couple of days. Aren't you glad? The job doesn't start officially until October the first. I just came over for a quick look round. To work out what I'll need to get, and to do. The nature of the problem, so to speak.'

He raised an eyebrow and gave me a sardonic look.

'I see.'

'Don't look so worried. I'm not going to come knocking on your door asking for a cup of sugar. I'll keep away. I won't gossip.'

His tone was patient, as though he was speaking to a child rather than a woman who was probably old enough to be his mother. But his smile was kind, and I thought how lucky I had been that the outcome of all this stupidity had not been more damaging; Jos Allen had a maturity and perceptiveness that one would not expect from someone in his early twenties. He was still speaking, though.

'Could you tell me a good place for firewood? Unless it's too rare and precious to give away the secret. Drying clothes is always a problem. Mine got soaked, by the way, trying to get your message in a bottle. It came back on the next tide. Pied Piper, indeed! Pity you didn't leave me some booze in the bottle – though I would have expected it to have been poisoned.'

'Huh. There's not usually much driftwood, but it's your best hope because you'll have to carry it and the copse is too far away. Anyway, that's mine! You're always limited by what you can carry, though. There's a rocky promontory on the north side of the next bay, you'll have seen it, and that usually traps quite a bit. All yours – it's too far for me.'

'Great. A fire's good company, too, keeps the bears away. You know, you look quite normal in jeans, even wet jeans. Not like a witch at all. You did look pretty weird when I first met you. I think that scared me, too.'

I stared at him, puzzled. What had I been wearing?

'Oh. Yes! The long black skirt.'

'Yeah. With holes in it. But it was your shirt that was, shall we say, interesting. One long sleeve and one short?'

I tried to imagine how I must have looked, and I couldn't help smiling.

'Ah yes. All my other clothes were wet. The clothes were supposed to be drying, but the washing line had broken. I blamed you for that, too, it just completed the misery of it all. Oh – and I was cutting my hair when you arrived. Of course! I had to stop and lots of the cut pieces kept getting down inside my clothes. Yet another reason for being angry.'

'Yes! And you kept squirming. That explains it all. You were really scary, Harriet.'

Oh, it was good to laugh, even though I slopped the remains of my tea on to my jeans. Jos chatted gently about this and that, and I listened to him talking about his ideas for the seal project, and I liked to watch the way his face changed with his conversation, how the grooves came and went, and how his left eyebrow rose with his enthusiasm. We seemed to have survived. As I finally walked away along the path, I turned and called back that I had, by the way, given seven or eight of the seal cows individual names, but I wouldn't tell him what they were until the end of his study, when he would presumably recognise all the individuals, too. Actually, I could scarcely tell one seal from another, but I did enjoy seeing his expression change. He'd survive!

Six

When I was young, seven or eight years old, I wanted to hurt a bird. I went around with my pocket full of tiny stones, carefully chosen so that each was the size of a pea, and I lay in wait for blackbirds, thrushes and even robins. At first I hid behind the *lonicera* hedges, or crept in amongst the ornamental shrubs, and waited for the unsuspecting birds to come close, but the blackbirds always found me out and set up such a loud berating clatter that all the birds flew away. As a result, I was forced to build a hide. I built it at the edge of the lawn, near to the shrubbery, out of a mixture of flattened cardboard boxes and sticks and an old green curtain that I'd found by someone's dustbin. I borrowed the garden shears and cut leafy shoots and twigs from the herbaceous plants and trees, and I stuck the vegetation into holes that I had poked in the curtain. The construction bristled with camouflage, most of which became pale and limp overnight, but I was convinced that birds were too stupid to see the difference between the hide and a real bush.

At first, my father had been rather upset about the untimely pruning of his herbaceous border, but when I explained to him that the 'den' was actually a hide, for watching birds, he was proud of my initiative and became very enthusiastic. He borrowed a book of bird identification from a friend and searched through his desk until he found an old notebook, from which he tore the used pages. Even better, he gave me a smart new pen, one with a click-down button for pushing out the roll-tip. I was to make a record, he said, of the birds that I saw, and what they were doing. Since this was at the time of year when the garden was loud with the squeaks of baby birds, insistently begging for food from their over-worked parents, he thought I would be kept busy. I put my bird-watching kit in a polythene bag in the hide and laid a cushion on the ground on top of a plastic carrier bag (to stop it getting damp – I was very practical, even in those days).

There were several small holes in the curtain through which I was to spy on my feathered friends, but the problem was how to hit them. I decided that I would have to wait until a bird was in a suitable position, then reach out of the back of the hide and take aim. I rushed home after school, to practise. The pea-sized pebbles were hidden in a wrapping of paper hankies inside a plastic carton, on the lid of which was written: 'Private. Do NOT open.' I placed a fledgling-sized stone several yards from the hide and practised leaning out and throwing pebbles at it. The target had the advantage that it did not move and, surprisingly, my aim quickly improved and I soon had quite a high success rate. I collected the scattered pebbles and returned them to the carton.

The following Saturday, I announced that I was going to spend the day bird-watching, and I persuaded my mother to make up a bottle of orange squash, and a small bag of 'provisions', containing crisps and biscuits and an apple, enough it seemed for several days. My parents were amused by my enthusiasm and happy that I had devised a 'worthwhile' scheme to occupy myself. As part of the game, they agreed that they would keep away from the shrubbery and lawn, so as not to disturb the wildlife.

I took out the notebook and the treasured pen and, using my mother's watch, kept a record of avian activities. Counting the minutes and seconds was rather tricky:

> Blue tit on tree, pecking leafs, 15 secs.
> Starling running around, 2 min 5 secs.

Ring ouzel with big worm on grass 42 secs.

(I had to copy the spelling of that one. I identified it myself from the pictures; it was very exciting to see one in our garden. I didn't know about blackbirds with albino streaks, in those days.)

The book, like a brown paper alibi around a dirty story, was filling up. At long last, the opportunity for which I had been waiting arrived. A young thrush huddled underneath the lilac bush, gaping plaintively at its harassed parent. The adult left to seek more food, and the fledgling fluffed up its tiny wings and hunched down against the ground like a small, brown stone. This time I didn't make a record of what happened. I selected a pebble, then leant out and flung it at the bird. The target was a sitting duck, and my aim was perfect. The bird reared up, then fell on its side. For a few seconds, I couldn't actually believe what I had seen; it seemed impossible that I could have hit it. And now it would be mine: I would nurse it and it would depend on me and become my friend! I crawled out of my hiding place to where the young thrush lay, and carefully picked up its tiny featherweight body, cradling it in my hand and loving its warm softness. But its head lolled back on its broken neck and a spot of blood oozed from its fractured skull. There was a sudden pain above my eyes and I felt cold and sick. I pushed the little body far back underneath the bush, hiding it under scraped earth and torn-up grass, and I went up to my bedroom and emptied the waiting shoebox of its soft handkerchiefs and crumpled paper. When I brought in the bird book and the damp cushion a few days later, my parents made no comment. Had they discovered what I had done? I expect so; I discovered later, for myself, that very little escapes the eyes and understanding of a parent. I only hope they understood the motive.

Years later, I tried to explain the motive to Jos when we discussed what had happened at my party with the seals. He had come to the croft on a grey cold day in late autumn. This time he hadn't come secretly, he had taken care that I should hear him coming;

he stamped his feet loudly as he approached (quite a feat considering the size of his load), and stood outside the gate and called.

'Harriet. Halloo. Harriet, are you there?'

He looked away from the cottage, pretending that I might be on the shore or in the back garden. I knew at once who it was, of course. I hadn't seen him since he returned to the mainland a month ago, and I was a little apprehensive about his attitude and mood. I had been wondering what he would have reported about me to his research supervisor. How had the supervisor instructed him to 'deal with me'? But as soon as I heard him calling, I slipped on my boots and hurried round from the back door.

'Hallo.' His smile was slightly anxious, as though he was uncertain of his welcome. 'No letters! But I've brought you a present. Picked fresh from the fruit shop window yesterday.'

He held out the object that he had been hiding against his chest, arms extended and hands cupped underneath it like an offering. It was a pineapple, greenish-orange and rolled up in its spikes. I took it from him and I couldn't think how to reply.

'I think it's ripe, I tested them all to find one that was all right.'

I squeezed the sides and felt it yield a little.

'It's perfect. In fact, it needs eating right now, I'm sure it'll be over-ripe in an hour or two. You must come in and help me eat it.'

Jos's anxious smile grew broader and more secure. I suddenly wanted to hug this nice young man who had brought me a peace offering. Of course, I did no such thing, but I dismissed his protests that the pineapple was for me alone and, hurriedly, before I could lose my nerve, I led him round to the back and showed him where he could leave his pack. He no longer seemed to fill all the space and block out the light, as he had on his first visit; he was not much taller than I. He took off his boots and I sat him in the big armchair, wishing I had not let the fire die out. I lit the gas ring and filled the kettle from the tap, to make us tea. The silence was awkward, and I tried to fill it with the noise of preparation, rattling the plates and raking through my small store of cutlery for a sharp knife.

'Shall we wait 'til the tea's made, or shall we start on the pineapple now?'

'Oh . . . uh, let's have some pineapple . . . if that's all right? Shall I cut it for you?'

'No. I can manage, it's fine.'

I sliced off the crown, and juice dripped out on to the kitchen table. I was becoming nervous again, and hacked untidily at the skin, then placed two dripping slices on a plate and handed it to him. The orange flesh was crisp and scented.

'A minute more and it would have melted away.'

Jos smiled and sniffed. 'Mmm. It smells good. Thanks.'

'No, thank *you* for bringing it.'

Juice ran down Jos's chin and dripped from my fingers, and we sucked and slurped and then laughed at the noises we were making. The kettle boiled and I made tea, and the awkwardness that had prickled the air disappeared.

'It was really kind of you to bring the fruit. You seem destined to arrive bearing strange gifts! At least this one was welcome!'

Jos looked puzzled for a moment, then realised what I meant.

'Oh, the letter, you mean. The first time I came here. *Was* it for you?'

I certainly didn't want to discuss that. Why had I reminded him, poking at an old sore?

'It was just a mistake. It doesn't matter. I dealt with it. How was the boat trip?'

'Rough. Awful. I suppose one has to get used to that, living on an island, though.'

'I don't think it's something you ever get used to – you're either the sort of person that feels sick or you're not. John MacGregor never goes on the mainland at all, if he can help it, he hates to be out on the sea. He says he can't see the point of it – the sea, that is!'

'It seems strange to live on an island if you hate the sea, it's so, well, dominating, isn't it? I wouldn't like the feeling of being trapped. Does the boat get cancelled very often?'

'No. The south-westerlies are all right – for the boat! A bit noisy here, though, but I get used to it.'

I pointed to the ceiling, above which the familiar creaking of the corrugated iron could be heard. The polythene sheeting, with which I had lined the front windows for extra insulation, billowed gently in and out with the draught.

'It'll be a bit wild at my campsite,' Jos said. 'I thought I might use the bothy up the coast as my base, instead. I had a look at it last time and it looks pretty waterproof – more comfortable than a tent, anyway. There's even a fireplace. Luxury!'

He grinned, his teeth showing between his beard and moustache. He was sprawled comfortably in the armchair, his feet in their thick woollen socks propped against the cold hearth.

'That's good.' I nodded approvingly. 'I'd wondered how you were going to cope with camping at this time of year.'

I'd been worrying, in fact, but not entirely on his account. The winds could get very strong in the winter months, and I didn't want him to think that my cottage would be available as a safe haven. I wanted nothing to do with soaked sleeping-bags and sodden notebooks. (Oh, come on, Harriet! He's just brought you a *pineapple*, for goodness' sake. In his rucksack. It must have weighed a ton!)

'Yeah! I'd been wondering, too!' Jos was laughing. 'I've brought an extra tent – it's down at the village. But that crossing – and your roof – have convinced me that the bothy's a better bet. I'm quite looking forward to it, actually. And the walk to the haul-out rocks will keep me fit.'

'Did you sort out your plans with your supervisor? How long do you have to be here for?'

This was the question I'd been waiting to ask; I had almost come to accept that Jos Allen was going to be around, on and off, for three years or so, and that we would both do our best to avoid each other, but I still prayed regularly that his visits would be short and infrequent.

'Well, that's one of the reasons, apart from the pineapple, that I came to see you.'

He looked out of the window, although the polythene distorted the view, and picked at a spot of tar on his jeans. His obvious displacement activities made me nervous.

'I thought you'd like to know my plans, so that we can keep out of each other's way – or whatever. Basically, I'm going to have to be here from about the end of March to October, although perhaps not all the time. The rest of the time I'll be back in the department, reading up, and working up data, stats, stuff like that. When I'm here, I'm going to have to try to identify the members of the colony, try and work out their interactions, see how often they haul out, and when, and so on.'

'Mmm. Sounds ambitious. But you'll be here, let's see, three . . . six or even seven months of the year, roughly.'

Bad enough, but at least he seemed to be counting on keeping out of the way; and his territory would necessarily be very limited.

'Something like that. On and off. It's hard to say at the moment. I've got to work out the feasibility of some of the things. Like collecting shit – faeces, excuse me – for analysis of what they eat, for example.'

'Ugh!'

Jos grinned at my disgusted expression. 'Nasty job. Perhaps I can train them to come and crap in a toilet. I don't know how I'm going to collect it, though.'

He was serious again, and was clearly puzzling over the matter.

'I always assumed – not that I've ever considered it at all before! – that seals just did it at sea, as they swam. You don't see toilet rocks – not like badgers. And foxes are usually quite particular, too. You've probably seen the piles of white droppings on top of tufts of grass?'

'Yeah. There's one that visited my campsite once or twice last time. Quite bold, though I never saw him. He left his stink around as well as his droppings.'

I laughed. 'I expect that was my fox, Finn. He wouldn't be

frightened of you, and he's always been nosy. Make sure your food's secure next time you camp. If you see him, you'll know it's Finn by his limp. His left back leg was broken when he was a cub.'

'*Your* fox? Does he live with you? I can't smell him!' Jos looked around the dark little living room.

'No, he's gone back to the wild again. But I found him with his leg broken and I looked after him.'

I told Jos about how I cared for Finn, and then about Connan of the evil yellow eyes, whom I had found on the beach. smeared with oil, after a storm. Connan had been a brief and unwilling visitor, lacking dependence or affection. He had fought against restraint, and he had pecked and screamed, his voice echoing around the cottage, but he had been forced to accept food from me during his short recuperation. He still returned occasionally to look for scraps and, once, to shelter in the lee of the outhouse from a sudden blizzard. Jos was interested and asked questions, and I made more tea as I answered and we talked, and we became more comfortable with each other.

'Why don't you get a dog? It must get a bit lonely here, a bit eerie on your own?' he eventually asked.

'I thought of it once or twice, but dogs are so unnatural in a place like this. It would intrude. A dog would frighten away the natural inhabitants. Actually,' I looked at him briefly, interested in his reaction, 'I've always liked the idea of having an otter as a companion – or even a seal.'

Jos sat upright, frowning; his beard seemed to curl with irritation.

'A seal! How can you say that, after what you did? It's a wonder there are any left.'

He was really cross, yet I had been unable to resist the temptation.

'Oh, please, don't get angry all over again. We went through all that last time. Anyway, they're all there again. I've looked.'

He was surprised, ready to question me, but I stopped him.

'No. Listen a moment. I've thought a lot about what I did, and

I think that it was partly because I was hoping that I'd get close enough to make contact with them. Befriend them in some way, show you that I knew them better than you did.'

'But you were doing the exact opposite!' Puzzled, he shrugged and shook his head. 'It's obvious you could never befriend them —' scornfully '—*that* way!'

'I want to try to explain. When I was little I always wanted a bird as a friend . . .'

But even as I began to tell him about the garden hide, I knew I was making a mistake, because I could never tell him about the stones, so he would never see the connection. I could never tell him how, amongst the pilchards and the cake, I had placed three carefully-selected stones, each the size of a potato. That evening, a terrible madness had caught up with me, driven by whisky and the desperate struggling against the imagined rape of my islandness . . . As I walked to the village, the morning after receiving my dead aunt's money, I planned my evening's outing. At that stage I thought merely (*merely*?) in terms of creating a disturbance. I buzzed with irritation but I could still think rationally. I would take the boat to the seal rocks, and we would have music, and eating and drinking. We would have a party. There would be sufficient disturbance to attract Jos Allen's attention, and to cause the seals to stir themselves and slip down into the water and out of sight. And the seal-watcher would recognise the fragility of his plans and would be forced to reconsider for, with my boat, I was omnipotent.

My business at the shop had been quick and polite. I left my letter to the solicitor on the counter while I made my purchases. It contained 'Mrs Falmer's' empty envelope and a note of complaint, and was thick between John MacGregor's fingers as he felt it, in a friendly way, and shook his head at my story of secretarial incompetence. Four tins of pilchards, whisky and the only frozen cake that he had, thick discs of pale plastic sandwiched together with jam and something that looked like shaving cream, made up my load.

It had amused me to imagine the seals lying like fat ladies, uncorseted, gently gossiping, upon their rocky sofas.

'Oh my dear, not fresh salmon *again*,' one sighs, dismissively gesturing with her flipper. 'One gets so tired of it.'

'What I could do with right now, love, is a nice boil-in-the-bag kipper,' yearns another. 'And caviar's so *tricky* to eat. But I've heard that sturgeon are enormous. Even bigger than you, dear – beautiful!'

So I bought them tinned pilchards. There was a potential problem in that seals might not be very partial to tomato sauce, but on the shore at home I opened the tins and carefully washed the chunky little bodies at the edge of the sea, coating the shingle with an orange slick. I cut the thawed cake in slices and put it in a box, and I propped a glass inside the bailer, near the stern of the boat. I don't want to talk about the stones, they were easy to prepare. Because I would be returning against the tide, I put the outboard engine on the transom and checked the fuel. The boat was ready, and all that remained was for the hostess to dress for dinner. In my wardrobe hung a heavy woollen skirt, thick, and glowing red. It had a few moth holes, but not enough to cool its insulation, and its colour and the whisky warmed my body to party temperature. But it would be cold on the water (a marine party is a party with a difference) so I pulled on thick pullovers and covered my head and shoulders with a shawl. My dead aunt would appreciate the shawl; it was old and frayed and its swirling green and red Paisley teardrops were faded with age, but it had been given to my mother by my aunt's brother, my father, and I hoped she would enjoy the connection. I picked up the bottle, and lit the hurricane lamp and left it on the shore as a beacon for the homeward journey, then I hitched my skirt around my waist and pushed the boat out. I don't often drink; I know too well it's the curse of lonely people, it dehumanises and destroys perception. But I wanted to enjoy my party and I wanted to get drunk; not completely and dangerously drunk, but drunk enough to sing and dance and celebrate.

I motored at first, to save time, but as I rounded the point of

Camus Dubh – the Black Bay, Death Bay – I cut the motor and took out the oars. Rowing was warming and exciting; the waves were small, my rhythm fast. The bow butted into the waves, tossing spray on board. Pull tight, reach out; legs splay, lips pout; breathe in, breathe out; talk and laugh, sing and shout; stomach in, knees out; twist your body, shake it all about. I stopped to drink more whisky, I ate a piece of cake; the rhythm of my rowing made my body sing and shake. One, two, three, four, here's the rock and there's the shore. In, out, in, out; see, Jos Allen, what it's all about!

Seals lay plumped on the rocks like old sacks. Two or three turned their heads to watch, but they were as yet undisturbed by my presence. I shipped the oars then slopped the brown liquid into my glass and stood and toasted my guests. What had I prepared to say to them? I couldn't remember, so I shouted 'Cheers!' and 'Welcome to the Pied Piper's party!', then, from my pocket, I took my wooden penny whistle. I'm no musician; I can barely read music and my fingers are stiff, but I have mastered several of the easier folk tunes. As the boat rocked in the swell, I stood and played 'Speed, bonny boat' . . . but the rhythm was not mine, it was too slow, so I switched to a jig, instead. A seal slithered heavily towards the water. I threw two pilchards in its direction, but they sank quietly beneath the waves.

'Hey! Seals! Come and join the party!'

I sat down again, and rowed closer, singing and shouting. I threw more pilchards, I stood and waved my shawl about my head.

'Yoohoo, Jos Allen! Come and join us!'

Seals now plopped heavily into the sea from all sides of the haul-out rocks. Several smooth dark heads were raised above the waves, regarding me reproachfully. I played my whistle again, badly, loudly, and threw more food, fish and cake. I waved my shawl and swayed and danced on the spot, bracing my legs against the seat.

And I laughed and cheered as I saw a figure running and jumping along the clifftop; he was swinging his arm, gesturing me away. I hoped very much that he would jump up and down and wave both arms, like an angry figure in a cartoon. I checked that no seals remained upon the rocks, and I waved again at the seal watcher. Then I took a piece of paper and a pencil from my pocket and wrote: 'Mr Jos Allen is cordially invited to the Pied Piper's Party.' A drop of whisky remained, so I lifted it to my mouth and drank, waving the empty half-bottle with a flourish. The folded invitation was pushed down into the bottle, the lid was screwed on tightly, and then I yanked the outboard motor and sped as close towards the shore as I dared. Jos was watching through his binoculars as I hurled the bottle-message into the sea. He was still watching when I circled the rocks like a marine sheepdog, and when I reduced the speed to a gentle putter and raised my penny whistle to my lips.

Few seals had cared to stay and listen, but one rose nearby and snorted in surprise. How I longed for her to follow me. I wanted to caress her smooth kind head, and look into those deep eyes that held aeons of understanding. Nothing remained to give her but stone potatoes and a lump of cake, but I knelt, nevertheless, and stretched my hand towards her and entreated her to be my friend. She pinched her nostrils together in disapproval, and sank beneath the waves, so I dropped the stones overboard and turned the bow towards the south. My head and throat ached, the rocks and sea were empty behind me, and I sang quietly, 'Speed, bonny boat, like a bird on the wing . . .', as I motored homewards and tried not to cry.

Jos had sat quietly as I told him about the hide and the dead thrush. Even as I was talking, I couldn't understand why I had thought it necessary to tell him about this childishness, but I seemed to be unable to stop. He'd be shocked at my cruelty and perhaps, after all, he would make the logical jump to the seals and think that I had indeed stoned them. But he didn't speak when I reached the end of the story and, after several minutes, the silence made me uneasy, and I peered round at him from where I stood by the sink, endlessly washing my mug in cold water. He was staring down at the cold ashes in the hearth, so that his eyelids almost covered his eyes and he might have been asleep.

'I did something like that to my dog,' he muttered, eventually. 'My dog seemed to like my mother more than me. I realised later, of course, that he was a greedy dog, and she gave him his meals – you don't bite the hand that feeds you, and so on. I wanted him to like me most, to be devoted to me and no one else. It was an accident, really. I was painting wood preservative on to a fence for my dad – nasty stuff, he'd made me wear rubber gloves and everything – and I flicked the brush because there was a spider's web stuck to it. Then I looked round and saw the dog was there, and the stuff had flicked into his eye. He had his head down and was rubbing his paw over his eye, you know the way they do. So I flicked more preservative at his face, deliberately. It was in both eyes and he was really whining and rubbing.'

Jos looked up at me and his face was tragic in his self-disgust.

'So I bent down and cuddled him, and then I carried him into the kitchen and bathed his eyes and held his paw. I explained to my mum and dad that he'd got something in his eyes, it might have been the preservative, and they fussed over him. But I held his paw and hugged him and stayed with him, and I gave him his food when he felt like eating again. I did everything I could to look after him and to show him that *I* was the one who loved him and would care for him. But of course he knew that I'd flicked the stuff, and he never trusted me again. He was sort of *polite*, if you know what I mean?'

I nodded, because he expected it, but I couldn't think what to say. Why was he telling me this? Could it possibly be true? Or had he just invented the story for some purpose of his own? And yet it was hard to imagine what the purpose would be; was it really possible that he, too, could have shared the same perverted motive?

'Were his eyes all right?' I asked, wanting to see where the story was leading.

'No, not really. One of them became really cloudy, the cornea was damaged. It was a bit like a cataract, so he couldn't see out of that eye. And he sort of blundered around after that, he didn't have a proper sense of distance any more. I'd damaged him, and he just kept near my mother all the time. She guessed it was my fault, but not, I'm sure, that I'd done it on purpose. When you talked about hurting the birds, Harriet, I just couldn't believe you at first. It was exactly the same thing, wasn't it? I didn't think it was possible that anyone else could have done that sort of thing, for the same reason. I'd managed to forget it . . .'

'So you're saying we're as bad as each other, are you? Did your dog's cataract cure you of the misguided idea that animals feel gratitude, and that gratitude induces dependency? Perhaps you became a zoologist in order to understand better?'

'I don't know, I've probably never thought about dependency since then, and even if I had, it wouldn't have been in those terms, would it? As for my career, if that's what it is, that just happened anyway. It's an interesting idea. I guess I've been cured of interference, though. I don't want to interfere with the seals. I want to worship them from afar, not have them worship me!' He grinned, briefly. '*Did* you throw stones at them, Harriet? Is that the point of your story in relation to the seals?'

'Of course not! You seem to forget, Jos, that I'm about twenty or so years older than you are. You've still got to learn to sort out the barriers and interactions between pain and pity and love and dependency. The Lord knows there is enough human and animal pain around to create pity and dependency without confusing the situation by the use of sadistic cruelty!'

He was such a child! And the memory of the stones burned at the back of my mind, as I tried to blot out my guilt with anger.

Jos stood up, a hand raised, pleading.

'I'm sorry, that was tactless. And now I've spoilt our talk. I don't think I've talked to anyone like that before.'

He was genuinely contrite and, yet again, I knew I had over-reacted. We had been reaching some sort of mutual understanding on this topic, but perhaps neither of us had dared explore it further. Twists of pineapple skin lay damply on the table, and the room was becoming dark and cold.

'Well, you've never eaten a pineapple in the house of a wild old woman before, either.'

'No, it's bound to be an unusual experience. Hell! It's late, nearly six o'clock. I've still got to walk to the bothy – it's a good hour from here.'

'I'm glad you came here, though. It was good of you to tell me your plans. Have you got a candle for the bothy?'

'Yes, of course! You're so practical, Harriet. I could become dependent on you.'

'And you're a cheeky young man. If you're not independent you shouldn't be here. I'm a recluse, and you're a hermit. And don't you forget it! I don't want to see you again.'

We both laughed, as he heaved his pack up from the ground, but he knew that I was nearly serious.

Seven

For three days the rain had been driving in across the sea. Dark squalls flattened the wave-tops and slammed against the front wall of the cottage, and then rushed on, to leave angled lines of water pouring relentlessly out of the low grey sky. Water crept insidiously into every cavity. It poured down the corrugated runnels of the roof and seeped under the front door. The cottage seemed to have tucked in its shoulders and hunched down in a hopeless attempt to escape the damp and noise. Inside, the living room was warm and dim and steamy. Its warmth came from the peat fire that burned dully on the hearth, and the humid air came from outside and from the walls and from my damp pullover that sagged over a rope stretched between two hooks in the ceiling. The grey midday sky shone only dimly through the small windows, the noise of wind and rain on the metal roof numbed my brain, and the shortest day was but two days off.

Whatever theologians and historians may say, the date of Christmas must have been fixed by influential northerners, who recognised that the human spirit is at its lowest at this time of year. Trapped inside the house and oneself, by long hours of darkness and stormy days, one can sink into despond and idleness; the devil makes work for idle hands, and minds, and so on. So the feast of Christmas was opportunely placed four days later, to lighten our darkness (we beseech Thee, O Lord), and to stimulate anticipation (the thrill of anticipation, the heated imagination, all so much better than the real event!) and preparation. Light and festivity in the midwinter gloom! It has been gloomy enough these past few days. The dark days, rain and wind, wind and rain. Can people really be sunbathing on the beach in Australia? The wild gales and storms are exhilarating, they're loud and extrovert, spray hurling into the sky and crusting the windows, wild white sea and the bursting, thundering burn. There is a thrilling frightfulness in the power that arouses and stirs. But not this, this dreary rain; this is merely perpetual noise and wetness. I'm restless and, unusually, bored. And apprehensive about Christmas.

When I first came here I worried how I'd cope with the winter and a solitary Christmas. I suppose I was pulled by two opposing forces: on the one hand, I desperately wanted to be alone, and on the other, I was frightened at the prospect of enforced solitude, especially at that so particularly family festival. But I soon found that there were ways and means for coping. I'd known that I would no longer be able to rely on books for company (the nearest proper bookshop is seventy miles and a boat trip away, and books are heavy to carry) so I chose my few books with care, like the pampered castaway on 'Desert Island Discs'. And yes, I have the Bible and a complete Shakespeare and the Shorter English Dictionary. I also brought my French and German dictionaries, small relics of my working past, but they're more or less redundant. There's a poetry anthology, and there are now two shelves of novels. I read them and re-read them, I browse through the reference books, and I try to learn epic poems and passages from Shakespeare. 'Rolled to starboard, rolled to larboard, while the surge was seething free . . .' declaimed from a rock on the shore, and 'How fearful and dizzy 'tis to cast one's eyes so low . . .' from Sgurr Mor! And, of course, 'Eye of frog and leg of newt' while stirring the sauce, the witch's brew. Wonderful words, rolling off the tongue like clichés! The theatrical world doesn't know what a talent it has lost! I'm not interested in time-filling cottage crafts, woodcarving, embroidery, or painting pebbles, and I never learnt to knit anything more than small crooked blankets for my cuddly toys. But there are always indoor tasks to occupy the daytime, they expand to fill the time available, and I go to bed early in winter to economise on candles, paraffin and peat.

In preparation for each Christmas I buy myself two novels, this year one fat paperback and one thin, one chosen for bulk and the other for content. I've wrapped them up in Christmas paper, and look forward to opening them and starting to read on Christmas Day. I have also, as usual at Christmas, bought myself more batteries for the radio, a very special treat indeed. Music, talk and laughter! Instant entertainment and undemanding companionship, that can be instantly banished as required. My first winter here was the worst, and I bought many batteries, but at the end of the second summer my mind was already occupied with Schemes, and I enjoyed planning future work around the croft. I haven't been afraid of the solitude for many years now, and I've almost forgotten that this isn't the normal human state of existence. So, why am I now so restless? I surprised myself this morning with the thought that, if Jos Allen had been at the bothy, I might even have asked him over for a Christmas drink. Not for the day, or even to share my dinner, but for a drink, an indication of Peace and Goodwill. I think it would have been all right. I suppose he will be with his family. If he has a family. I don't know. I have not, of course, asked. I've respected his privacy as he has respected mine. Yes, we seem to have reached a good agreement, really. I suppose he will be back in March. I think that's what he said. March.

I wonder what seals think about in this weather? I went to look at them a few days ago, in the wind and the rain, because I felt desperate for air and exercise. I just thought I'd see what they were up to. Not much, really. I don't suppose they're terribly impressed by Christmas. Do animals appreciate the Glory of God? And the birth of His Son? The seals obviously don't appreciate Christmas as a family time either, no Christmas flipper-socks for their pups! Certainly no warmth and festivity at the haul-out rocks, just rain.

Not like the MacGregors' house. Light shone out of their windows into the afternoon, and the smell of mince pies followed John into the shop. I could hear the television, silly cartoon voices, and the giggles of his grandchildren who had come to visit. I bought my frozen chicken and my pudding, some vegetables, tinned cream and other treats and necessities, and I suddenly longed to stay there in that brightly-lit comfort, instead of battling back across the pass. John MacGregor handed me my mail ('Three cards by the look of it. That's a nice thing, now.') and a paper bag patterned with holly leaves and berries. Inside was a large bar of fruit and nut chocolate!

'Just a little treat for you for Christmas, then, Harriet, from Mary and me.'

My second present in three months!

'Thank you! That's really kind of you! I've almost forgotten what chocolate tastes like!'

'We were wondering what you'd like – I'm fond of a bit of chocolate, myself, almost an addict, you might say. And you're not in danger of getting fat, now, are you!' He shook his head, then changed the subject. 'What about that chicken, now? Do you need more onions? Or do you want to try some of this packet stuffing? It's quite good.'

I reminded him that I didn't have an oven and would have to cut up the chicken, in any case, and he continued chatting as he added up the prices and I wrote him a cheque.

'Can you manage all that, now? It's a pity that young lad – what's he called? – Allen, isn't still staying over your way, or he could have carried something across for you.'

An assumption has been made. It doesn't take much, does it? It has been automatically assumed that Jos Allen would be willing to help me and that I would be happy for him to do so, to be dependent upon his help. After all these years that I have lived here! I build an obvious fortress, one that seems to be acknowledged and respected as more-or-less impregnable, and they assume that the accidental geographical proximity of one young lad will instantly breach the wall. What on earth do they imagine? They'll be labelling him as the witch's familiar, the sorceress' apprentice. Poor boy! Suddenly the shop's heat and cheer and electrical lighting were no longer so seductive.

'I'll manage, don't worry. And I'm really looking forward to the chocolate. Please thank your wife, too, and wish her merry Christmas from me.'

'Happy Christmas, Harriet! Take care, now.'

'Happy Christmas. And thanks again.'

The Christmas cards were nothing special. I had, in any case, guessed who they were from, because I had three cards every year – my solicitor, the bank and Father Simpson. More interesting was the quarterly newsletter tucked inside the priest's card. There was the usual parish news, notification of coffee mornings, Senior Citizens' outings, and so on, all of which were irrelevant to me, but Father Simpson's 'personal' photocopied letter contained a shock.

> 'As most of you will already be aware, I have decided to retire at the end of January. Father Peters, whom many of you have met during his recent visits to the parish, has been appointed as my successor. As you know, he has had great experience of the particular needs and difficulties associated with pastoral care within our scattered West Coast community, and I am very pleased . . .'

Father Peters stands there, a black and white column; his arms are bent and raised at his sides, and his hands are pale, his fingers loosely pointing towards the simple roof. His legs are hidden by the lines of the pew. He is like a motionless glove puppet, waiting to be squeezed into activity.

He hasn't seen me enter, and I duck down, bent double, between the pews, and kneel there, quite still. Then I pop up, stiffly vertical, and raise my hand and smile.

'Lovely day today, isn't it?'

Father Peters' head jerks back and his fingers are rigidly splayed in shock. At that same moment, the grey light is split by a sharp white flash so that we are both caught, as by a stroboscopic light, in the act of grotesque jerks. Thunder crashes like the Wrath of God.

Alternatively, I await my turn, eyes piously downcast. The dark hair curling out from the edges of my head-scarf masks the edges of my face. The priest, dispassionate and absorbed, suddenly pauses in front of me, so that I raise my head anxiously. Our eyes meet, and the priest's face sharpens briefly. His lips scarcely move, but his whispered words burn inside my head, so that my scalp prickles with heat beneath my wig.

'Miss Falmer, I presume?'

The sacrament of reconciliation has the texture of stale bread within my parched mouth.

I can't face him without shame, yet I must. Each time I go to church, he will be there. He deserted me, was unaware of my need – and I humiliated him. Our relationship could never again be impartial; each time – at the confessional, at Mass – there would always be the unspoken *awareness*, and the dread that either of us should let slip an acknowledgement of what had happened. Each time I enter the church, I will feel that he is standing in the shadows, watching. It would be impossible to use him as my intercessor and divine-empowered arbiter, in such a situation.

How can I escape? Yet I once longed for him to come here to my house, I wanted to feed him and be warmed by his presence!

Father Peters and the physical entity of St Thomas's are indivisibly linked: to stay away from one is to be exiled from the other. What am I going to do? A Christmas conundrum for a solitary Catholic.

Could I fulfil (dare I even think this?) – would it be accepted that I could fulfil – the requirements of the church, in total isolation? I could go to Mass at Easter – go to the city, to a different church. Take an 'Easter Break'! I could do that!

I wish the Lord couldn't hear me while I try to think this through. Perhaps I could cover my head with aluminium foil to hide my thoughts, and, conclusion reached, present Him with the answer and ask His blessing.

Completely alone: can I do it? And yet, it's but a step along my present path. Even by coming to this island, I've been forced to reconsider the practicalities of the faith, to adapt to the limitations and the possibilities of an island in a winter sea. I know, even now, that the Lord sees and hears everything, wherever I am. My thoughts are not secret. (Even the contraceptive in my blood scintillated visibly with sin. And *how* I have paid!)

Will I ever be forgiven? Will my lonely attempts at faithfulness be accepted? Separated from my husband and my dead son, have I not earned absolution by my suffering? I am tied for ever, I am not allowed to forget, it's part of my mental and physical being – scar tissue, stretch marks, the remembered heat of hands, the dialogues and shared dislikes. (And has *she* also suffered, for the way she cast me out? She knows what it is to be a wife and mother.) Surely the Lord hears my prayers! O Blessed Virgin, look upon my son, and love him for his simple innocence. Help me in my loss.

I sin in my thoughts – for I have nothing else. Should I therefore chastise myself, wear a hairy thermal vest and bind my taut nipples with wet bandages? Should I douche my body in the cold sea, or snow-melt? I have acknowledged my lewd and lustful imagery, and I have confessed (in words of classic formulae, conveying no hint of passion or reality) to the patient ears of Father Simpson. I have confessed my mischievous hatred of Jos Allen – and I shall never hurt him again. But I have not confessed to Father Simpson about my meeting with his successor; I confessed that to my God direct, and sought forgiveness. If I have, alone, implored Him once, I could do so again. O Lord, give me guidance! There's no minister here to interpret Your command – but give me guidance.

The knowledge that I'm always Seen, and that there is a running account of credit and debit, should be conducive of good conduct.

Guilt, too, is a powerful guide. And an unexpected concomitant of insularity is that soul-searching is unavoidable!

It is not such a big step, practically. Yet to sever myself, even from those few brief contacts with priest and Church, is to throw myself across a vast spiritual chasm. Have I the courage? Will I be burnt at the stake twice, once as a heretic and once as a witch? I'm so afraid. (Yet so relieved. There's a curious peace in this detachment. It must be the right solution, the answer to the conundrum, towards which I think I've been working for many months.) Perhaps Father Peters was sent here to help, for he has forced me to accept the solitude.

I have the time and the need to examine and appreciate everything around me, from the grains of mica sand and sea-smoothed pebbles, to the yellow breast of the wagtail dashing across the burn and the jewelled red cups of lichen in the grass. We are all overseen; God perceives our difficulties. The lilies of the field don't toil to get to church on time.

'Am I now free, then, Harriet?'

'Graham! No! Why were you listening? What brought you here?'

'Christmas, Harriet. We tend to lurk in each other's thoughts at Christmas, don't we? Thinking of families and thinking of Tom. Things could have been very different, Harriet, if you had opened yourself to your "greater freedom and understanding" earlier.'

'No! You're deliberately misunderstanding me, I'm not talking about freedom from beliefs. I'm talking about the freedom of faith and understanding that results from freedom from the imposition of physical constraints.'

'What are the physical constraints, Harriet? A wedding ring? Contraception? Where does faith fit in with or without these, in your new-found freedom? Your new ethical code has to explain the place of your husband and son, doesn't it?'

'You're just tying me in knots with words! You're confusing me. And contraception was chemical, not physical, so stop trying to re-write my life with pseudo-clever word-play. I was eternally damned if I did, and I would have been damned by your mother if I didn't. She would have enjoyed that, wouldn't she, pointing a finger at the trail of children? But she never had the chance, I'd been damned enough already. Tom was the first and last of our line.'

'My poor love, poor Harriet. So confused and so full of self-recrimination. *I* didn't damn you, Harriet.'

'But who are *you*? Not God! Not your mother! The son of the mother, though, and the father of the son. Even now, all these years later, there's still no fire or logic in your arguments. What happened to all that passion you used to have, why didn't it spill out into words, as well? You didn't damn me, of course not, Graham – you are my husband – but you failed to save me.'

'Harriet, if you bring out the old arguments about matriarchal dominance, I shall leave. You never understood.'

'Nor did you, all those well-worn statements about Catholicism and the family, and the cult of the Virgin!'

'Yes, and all your well-worn arguments in pre-Tom contraceptive days, Mary as a sop to women's consciousness, women oppressed by relentless child-bearing, and so on. How could I forget all those tedious, repetitive, boring arguments?'

'Tedious, repetitive, boring arguments about a mother's rights. My own rights. And where your mother's stopped! Who was Mary's mother-in-law? Does anybody ever pay any attention to what she did?'

'Harriet! Are you comparing yourself with Mary, now? Has your reasoning, or lack of it, reached such lengths? Her problems bore no relationship to yours, anyway. And in any case Joseph was irrelevant in that particular procreative event, so his mother probably lay low and tried to live down the scandal!'

'Don't joke, Graham. I was thinking of you and your mother. And I wanted to think about Tom.'

'Harriet, my dearest one-time wife, I wish I could have helped. I did love you, Harriet.'

'Graham, I want to think about Tom. Just Tom.'

The other night I awoke during a dream, trying to think about him clearly. It was a confusing dream, in which Tom had come here with Jos. Not *here* to the cottage, but to the island. it was difficult to see them, they were in the distance on the skyline, and I think I woke because I wanted to see Tom more clearly. But he and Jos kept changing and merging with each other. They were laughing: Jos – his beard was sharp and stabbed at the sea as he tipped his head back and laughed – touched Tom's shoulder and pointed at something down below. There were two ravens, twisting and tumbling in the air currents by the cliff, and I could sense that the birds were happy as they swerved and spun and cronked. But the boys were looking at the shore, where a large black bird, a shag, perhaps, lay dead on the shingle. Its wide black wings trailed beside it, almost as though they were flapping in the wind. Jos started to go down towards it (I remembered later that he collects birds' skulls; he boils them up, or soaks them in bleach to make them clean and white) and I was scared for Tom, although he was Jos's age. Tom was looking towards me, waving his arm.

'Can I go down, Mum?' he was shouting.

I tried so hard to zoom in on his face that I woke, but I think he was beardless, happy, his face was round and his eyes were slits with laughter. But I suppose his appearance was only an older version of when I last saw him, smooth and round and still babyish. A happy, loving child, who trusted everyone to help him; in the playground, the children looked after him and cuddled him and wanted him to join their games. It's strange that Tom was with Jos. I wonder whether he was helping Jos or whether Jos was helping him? I had the impression that Tom was also a zoologist, perhaps because he had binoculars around his neck! But I can't imagine him as a zoologist. Once he brought me two halves of a worm; he couldn't understand that he had cut an animal, a complete entity, in half, and he laughed as the pieces wriggled, pleased that he'd made two animals. It was hard to explain what he had done and to spoil his enjoyment, but I worried secretly that he might imagine that he could make two cats from one, four goldfish from two, and so on (with a kitchen knife?). I remember his soft little hands, hardening into a steely grip that wouldn't let go of mine, as he cried with disappointment.

Those little short-fingered hands, so trusting even at the end, reaching out towards me. And Graham's mother reached out for her son, so that when Tom was gone there was nothing left to bind us, and I was banished to a childless Hell. My own mother led me away, chained to her by a rosary; and the door, loudly protesting the glory of the presbyterian Lord and the irrelevance of the Mother, swung to behind me.

They allowed me back later, briefly, to collect clothes and personal treasures, and Tom's pretty Catholic Bible, that had been a present from my mother, was tactfully tucked inside my case. Are not all Christian Bibles the same? The words are the same, but it seems the pictures differ. But a Bible given at Christmas should not be an inflammatory object, that sparks cold fury and chills the atmosphere. And, that Christmas, Graham once again failed to warm us with supportive love and heat, and instead tried to melt the ice, the quiet and deadly storm of his mother's hailstones, with Christmas chit-chat and the noises of toy cars. Tom was saved from sinking beneath the floes by the distraction of hot mince pies – and drawings of feasts and fatted calves. For which, only a few months later, he would not return.

But he returns to me in my dreams and conversation. You and Jos could be friends, Tom. If you lived here, Jos could visit us for Christmas, and we could conquer the noise of this wind and rain with talk and laughter and companionship.

I'll put the kettle on the fire again and turn on the radio, and eat chocolate in the company of loud music.

Eight

January 25th

A cold, clear day. To the top of Sgurr Mor – glorious views, snow on far hills, islands within touching-distance. Two white ptarmigan on S. slopes. Came back via raised beach – saw otter on shore.

Failed to see puffin-burrow and fell flat. Unable to move, great pain; thought I'd broken my ankle, terrified and got into a panic. Eventually crawled/hobbled to burn, soaked foot for 10 min. – numb with cold, but reduced swelling and pain. Took 2 hrs to get home; medicinal whisky very welcome. *Not a good experience!*

IF I HAVE AN ACCIDENT OR IF I'M ILL – NO ONE WILL KNOW (or care?)

Intimations of mortality – at last! (Until now, have I thought that I was invulnerable? Answer: I didn't think!)
Pain; fear; and *interesting conclusions*, written down here for future ref. (NB. further ponderings still required, when sober.)

QUESTION: what to do if I'm wounded/ill (*Is* this the question? I'm not sure.)

Given:

minor 1st Aid kit ** check expiry dates and renew**
no phone/radio
no neighbours (cf. trusty collie/fox fetching help)
no transport (cf. trusty steed carrying half-dead rider to doctor's door) (*What* doctor?!)

Types of accident/illness:
Concluded: can probably manage with heavy dose painkillers (aspirin not enough – *get something stronger*) if arms/ribs broken – not needed for walking.
broken neck/skull – presumably†, therefore not too much problem.
broken leg/lower spine – no hope, apart from hoping for unconsciousness and 'blissful release' (overdose if poss.)
internal injuries/heart, gut disease etc. – probably no hope anyway.

Now I know what *not* to get, in the manner of accidents and so on!

But this rationalisation induced irrational and abject terror, temp. mental collapse, and further resort to medicinal whisky.

Later: WHY WAS I TERRIFIED?
Analysed this at length, and reduced the fear to 2 components:
(i) fear of pain. It hurts!
(ii) fear of alone-ness, dying on my own.
And thus proceeded to examine these concepts.

(i) Pain.
Experienced real pain today; have experienced pain at Tom's birth. But there must be worse pain: I don't know how I'll react – must maintain balance between will to survive and to

help myself, and acceptance that damage too great, no help forthcoming, and death inevitable – 'fatalism'. In latter case, acceptance *should* lead to loss of fear. In former case, concentrate on using pain *positively,* removing negative effect of fear.

Thus: fear of pain *unnecessary* (so simple, on paper!)

(Another thought: it's *more* terrifying to know that rescue possible, but hospital is many difficult hours away – neither Pegasus nor Lone Ranger's 'Silver' available.) (Hospital itself terrifies?)

Conclusion? Because absence of help/rescue is certain, acceptance of likely death must be absolute (but beware fatalism – do everything poss. to survive, but don't be frightened). Pain is to be considered only as a step along the road to death. Thus, fear of pain is irrelevant – the *fear* need exist no longer. (Hope I never have to test this.)

(ii) Fear of alone-ness.

Why fear loneliness in death when I don't fear it (indeed, welcome it) in life?

Atavistic fear, from my earlier life in composite social and familial structure? – 'they won't know where I am?', 'they'll worry', 'who will look after them?' Such questions no longer applicable.

(The future of the croft is unimportant to me, dead.)

Fear that no one will hear my famous last words?!

Fear that no one will have understood my *raison d'être*? – mere vanity.

Conclusion? If I don't fear pain, I should also welcome the

alone-ness. *There is no cause to be afraid.*
EUPHORIA, THE ASCENDANCY OVER FEAR.
Remember that feeling always, it will give you COURAGE.

(Fear of the state beyond death: a different question entirely. To die unshriven and alone – as have many others.)

Nine

What was that?

A scream! A crash!

I sit up, my ears straining, trying to remember the noise that woke me, to put it in the context of the house. Nothing: except the roar of the sea and the slamming gusts of wind.

There are screeches from overhead, and I recognise the cries of corrugated iron, crying out at the brute force of the gale. Outside, something, the metal bucket perhaps, crashes against the wall. The bedroom door rattles, and the polythene sheeting at the window snaps in and out like an uncleated sail. Branches of the rowan tree tap and scrape the roof and window.

I huddle back down again into the warmth of the bed and pull the cover tight against my body like swaddling clothes, burying my head and ears so that only my nose and forehead are exposed. But I imagine that the cottage shudders and that the bed itself is shaken by the wind. Half-heard noises are more menacing than those fully heard and understood, so I uncover my head and lie tense and listening.

Each lump of wind approaches the house like a train, sweeping up the beach with a whistling roar, and the noise of the surf fills the bedroom. I feel for my watch and for the matchbox – two o'clock, that lonely and dead hour of a winter night, when both dusk and dawn are far away. I'm made uneasy by the noise of the sea, it's so loud and close. And then I remember that it will be high tide within an hour and, with the wind this strength and in this direction, the sea will be piling high up the shore. The boat! It's the boat that is making me uneasy. Suddenly I am convinced that the boat is in danger and must be dragged even higher up the beach on to the grass. I need the boat. How can I coexist with the sea without a boat? Now, suddenly certain of the boat's imminent death, I drag on my clothes in a panic of haste. The torch beam is too feeble, so I snatch the hurricane lamp from its hook by the back door; even inside the cottage, its flame gutters in the draught. When I open the back door, it seems as though the air is sucked from my lungs and from the room, into a vacuum created by the wind as it races over the roof and up the slope.

The world is made of the noise of rushing air – air that hisses through holes in the drystone wall, buffets the rolling bucket against the house, clatters the roof and howls over the moor. As I turn the corner, the air hits me, spinning me, breathless, against the corner of the cottage. The lamp slams against the stone and the glass shatters. I clutch at the house until the gust lessens, then take the broken lamp back to the outhouse. There is a spare glass, but the lamp would be useless in this wind. Once my eyes have become accustomed to the dark, I'm surprised how clearly I can make out shapes and outlines; it is as though the furious gale has so whipped the earth that everything gives off a pale glow of energy. And now I see that the sea itself is fiery white in the darkness; the white wave-tops are fighting the dark clouds and the shore, and the air above them is white-hot with power. But I'm weakened by the noise and savagery, and I cling on to the gatepost.

It's fifty yards to the shore, and the rocks and air are wet with spray. I'm confused by the nearness of the sea and I can almost hear the boat calling out its fear. Bent double, hanging on to boulders and vegetation, I push myself down towards the shore. The small bay is a cauldron of black and white water, and I stumble over driftwood and other shapeless jetsam where there should be only salty close-cropped turf. I'm already soaked, and salt stings my eyes so that I cannot see. I cannot see my boat! I strain at the darkness, protecting my face between cupped hands. It's there, at the edge of the water, a dark, bucking shape. Its bow is still aground but the sea is sucking at it, twisting it, pushing it from side to side. As the boat swings sideways, waves smash against it.

I hobble across the shingle, terrified at being so close to this grasping monster, that threatens to reach out and twist and suck at me. I reach the bow, and grab and pull, but the boat is heavy with water and the shingle rolls beneath my feet.

'Come *on*!' I cry. 'Help me, boat. Come on, try!'

It pushes its bow into my hand, trying to oblige, but the sea sucks it back again and grips my ankles. I'm not frightened any more, I'm with my boat.

'We'll win, together.'

We must. I strain and tug, and scream and curse in my desperation. But the greedy water spills over the stern and caresses the planking. With a roar, the seventh wave – or the seventh son of its seventh son – flings towards the shore. I see it coming in the darkness and try to move, but my boots are full of leaden water. I hold on to my boat, but the wave knocks me face down and tramples me into the pebbles. The world is made of the noise of rushing water – and the air is squeezed from my lungs.

Terror gave me strength (I looked back, weeks later, and remembered this self-preserving force of fear). I hump and crawl from the grasping arms, and abandon my boat to the sea. I sit high up on the grass, shivering and crying, and I watch, even in the furious darkness, as my boat is swamped and pounded. Something flips from a wave-top, and is grabbed and spun by the air to land at the edge of the sea; it somersaults up the shingle, bowled over and over until it's trapped in a hollow near my feet. The bailer, the red plastic bailer – flung mockingly at my feet.

'I HATE YOU!' I scream. 'I hate you,' and I fling stone after stone at the laughing monster. The wind and spray batter me in the darkness and I stagger home, to the warmth and safety of the cottage. I strip off my soaked, stiff clothes, but the fire is dead, the updraught has sucked the life from it, and my teeth begin to chatter with cold and misery. I light the gas ring and find more clothes, because there is no point in going to bed. I wrap myself in the cover from the bed and huddle in the armchair with hot tea.

Far from appeasing the storm, the sacrificial boat has given it greater strength. The curtains are rippling fiercely, the doors are rattling and the roof screams more loudly. I'm too frightened to go to bed. I wish I could drown the noise with music, but there's nothing – apart from the penny whistle! I almost laugh, and then wonder where Jos's seals are. Lucky he's not on the island. Imagine a tent in this! Though the bothy wouldn't be so bad, it's protected by that hill. Hope nobody's at sea. 'Hear us, when we cry to Thee for those in peril on the sea.' I've heard that hymn on the radio, it made me want to weep. I could imagine the wives and sisters of the fishermen standing on a clifftop, shawls over their heads, staring white-faced out to sea, and praying for their men out in the herring boats. One would start to sing, and then their thin, uneven voices would join together in the prayer, praying that the Lord will bring the boats home, with their men. Oh, my boat, my poor boat. It hadn't hurt you, sea; why have you taken it? The tide should be on the turn now. Are the pieces of my boat being dragged out to sea? Should've pulled it up on to the grass. Wish I'd weighted the roof with rocks, too, or turfs. Where is it they do that? Rocks tied on to wires, stretched over the ridge. Listen to that damn bucket! So much noise!

I don't recognise the noises any more, everything is joining in a raucous cacophony. Dear God! What's that? Clanging and banging down the roof? Please, God, keep me safe. From the chimney? I don't want to sit here, what if something falls down the chimney? Just stand here by the sink. Please, please keep me safe. It was nothing much, just a bit of rubble, loose piece of coping stone. The wind is *punching* the house. The chimney is whining. I've not heard that sound before.

'NO! No, stop! Help! Don't, please. Oh, I beg your forgiveness.

I'm sorry, forgive me, I'm sorry. No! . . .'

I don't know how long I've been sitting here. The sky is lightening. I brought the cover with me. How strange. The bedroom is safe. I'm safe in this corner. How did I shut the door? Perhaps there's nothing there any more; nothing left. Were the mice blown out, too? I pushed a chair against the door! As if that would have helped. Is all now forgiven? Have I atoned sufficiently, do You think? Is this my Purgatory? O Lord, I'm sorry, forgive my sins. What else can I say? You listened as I turned the arguments to suit myself. You just bided Your time, didn't You? Waiting to see if I'd 'See the Light' again. Solitary Catholic indeed! Not afraid of a solitary death! But my time just ran out. 'The Lord Thy God is a jealous God.' Punishment time again. Oh yes. You've taught me another lesson.

A house built of sticks, blown away on the wind. O Lord, I'm scared. What have You left me? I'm even scared to go out through that door; there may be nothing there, nothingness, this room hanging on the edge of an abyss that reaches down to Hell.

How did I end up crouched in this corner? I cannot remember. I can scarcely move my legs and my fingers are locked tight around the bed-cover. The whining warned me. You warned me with the whining, and I moved. You didn't want me dead, not yet. I remember the chimney, the crash and screech, and the room full of dust and noise and the wind. The storm had entered the house and was fighting to get out, battering and sucking at the doors and window. And the window blew in and the back door blew out, and the darkness was full of the wrath of God. And I still can't remember how I got here.

The rain is slashing against the bedroom window. It came with the dawn and will dampen the gale's passion. Soon I will get up from this corner and look out of the window. I need to see. I need to think what to do. Soon, I'll open the door.

Can this be the house whose body I have inhabited, whose shell has protected me for so long? See, here is the bloody wound His hand did make. Chimney stones on a smashed armchair. Rain splattering through the window and the ceiling. There are the clouds rushing overhead – look through the ceiling, look up from the sodden hearth. The fire shall burn no more. Reach up and touch the clouds, feel the rain on your face. And weep. Dust and ashes. Damp destruction. Torn curtains, wet books. Was this once a *room*? Listen to the scream of twisted iron and the banging of the broken door. Rusted iron, its corrugations buckled over the garden wall. A sheet of iron embedded, like a hatchet, in the soil. Sodden plasterboard sticking to the moor, and torn cardboard in the grass. The broken shards of half a habitation.

But look! The outhouse is intact. A dry toilet seat from which to survey the wreckage, the only dry seat in town. Dry boots and oilskins, spare waterproofing, all spared. The Calor Gas cylinder dented but intact. Selectively sparing, sparingly selective. I could make myself a hot drink and go to bed and close my eyes, because this is merely a nightmare, that has galloped in on a selectively guilty conscience. But I need to look further, I need to see the full extent of this *atonement*.

Here on the moor, the ground squelches and everywhere small streams find new pathways to the sea, trickling over the grass and amongst the heather stalks. The pressure of the rain against my back is lessening, but the wind buffets me upwards, pushing me towards the ridge. It forces me to keep my back towards the broken cottage, and to see the sea.

Ah, the sea! Line after line of boiling whiteness, stretching to the horizon; dark grey clouds meeting dark grey sea, air and water shifting and intermingling. Waves are tumbling in towards the coast, they promise to overwhelm the island. But the rocks are immovable, punching holes in the white water. Spray explodes over the cliffs, lumps of white froth are being blown upwards, rolling and darting over the grass. Gulls slice and wheel through the thick air, but the mind-numbing roar of the water drowns their screams. Such excitement, wild frenzy; the ground trembles with the power. And now I see the gannets! Powerful and purposeful, cruising the air low over the seething water, teasing the leaping spray. The wholeness of it all frightens me; they are all laughing and teasing each other, earth and sea and living things, showing their strengths, each showing the others it is stronger. But all are dependent on each other and playfully interlocked in aggression. Here is such power – and *ecstasy.* Wild, joyous, ecstatic unity. Oh, why do you exclude me? I want to be part of you, I want that joy!

I could be one with you, sea, but you have stolen my only strength, the means whereby I could have lain with you.

A barricade of kelp, knee-high, bars the entrance to the beach. The sea has gathered the pebbles and pushed them into a high bank, leaving the beach clean with hard-packed sand. The boat is nearly buried, a lidless coffin. It lies skewed across the shore, filled with a cargo of small pebbles and weed. Around the sunken bow is a deep pool whose outflow trickles gently and continuously down the shore. The boat's upper outline is intact; but perhaps there is no hull, merely large holes through which the sand has risen? I will have to work fast to dig it out before the sea returns. I hurry back to the cottage, ignoring its ragged upper outline, and hunt for the spade and the dented bucket.

Hurrying to rescue my boat I don't know whether I should first empty it of sand or dig a pit around it, and I try to do both, jumping from one task to the other. I have, at most, three hours! But now I'm shaking with hunger – I haven't eaten or drunk since I woke, or came out of my trance, or whatever it was that held me – so I go back to the cottage once more and rake around in the cupboard for oats, and make porridge and tea. Everything is covered in soot and mortar, but, by concentrating on the food, I'm able to blank out my surroundings. Later, later! The boat's survival is dominating, its importance somehow connected with the gannets and the spray, but there is not time to search out the reason.

Strengthened, I begin to dig. The rain has stopped, and I throw off my waterproof jacket, and then my pullover. I dig a pit around the boat, clearing the sand from its sides, loosening its grip with bucketfuls of water that are grabbed from silted pools. I start at the stern, scooping a wide, long channel so that the sea will help me lift the boat – if the boat is intact. My arms and back ache as I lift up spadefuls of silt and throw them out over the gunwhales.

The waves are crashing on the shore and the wind is driving them in quickly, so that I can have barely a half-hour more. I still can't see the hull; I sluice the inner surfaces with water, feeling for cracks. I dig, and scoop, and then my spade hits stone, large pebbles like those now high up on the shore. So, there is a hole; the pebbles have pushed through and I have reached the underlying shore. I pull at the pebbles, fumbling in the murky water to find the jagged edges of the hole. But I find boards, smooth boards. The first foam-edged waves are already licking at the back of the trough and I scoop and shovel in a frenzy to clear the boat's insides. It is whole! Quickly I widen the pit beneath the bow and slope its edge towards the upper shore, in the hope that, as the water fills the pit, I will be able to pull my boat from its unwelcome berth. O God, please make it float. Please don't let the sea swamp it again.

Silty brown water pours over the lip of the trough, and suddenly the water is trickling, then swirling, around my feet. Even here, at the very edge, the breakers scarcely lose their power, and I'm certain that the boat will be overwhelmed; it is so heavy, sodden. I scramble up the pebble bank to fetch wood, and push planks underneath the hull, hoping to free it from the sucking sand. There is still a rope fixed to the bow, and I strain to pull the boat free as the water crashes into the pit. The top of a wave slops over the stern, but I daren't relax the tension. My legs and arms are weak with the strain, but I continue to worry at the boat until it begins to move. Then I push at the stern, and pull at the bow, and scoop out water. And gradually, the boat begins to lift; I can pull it a few inches up the ramp. Sometimes it slips back again and the puddled sand gives way beneath my feet. But we gradually advance, and the waves help, pushing at the stern and nudging it upwards until my boat rises up out of the pit and rests on the sloping shore.

It is whole! Scratched and scarred, with its wood rubbed rough and splintery: but it is intact!

Yet still the waves come thundering in, one after another after another; and we are still vulnerable. So now I dig and scrape a passage through the pebble bank. I make another slope and fetch wood and plastic to make a slipway; and, finally, we reach the turf. I want to rest but the boat is still unclean: dirty water is still pooled against the ribs, evidence of our battle.

Then I remembered the plastic bailer.

The world suddenly shimmered around me like an unfocused kaleidoscope. The grey light burned my eyes, so that the dead brown heads of thrift flowers, the ochre bladders of wet kelp, and the mottled surfaces of pebbles, all sparkled and blurred. The pounding, tumbling sea filled the horizon and its noise and light swelled up to Heaven. For I saw that the bailer had been a tease, a hidden challenge whose prize was a promise of things to come. The certainty brought a shocked breathlessness and a hot pounding in my head.

A strange laughter began to swell inside me. I ran back to the outhouse to find the square red bailer, then I scooped it down inside the boat and flung the water at the waves. The laughter burst out of me in a tired smile, and I held the bailer, that powerful symbol of unity, aloft in salutation to the sea.

Ten

The clouds form a solid, flat-bottomed mass that stretches across the low sky, and yet moves swiftly over the island. The mountains are hidden and their feet are black. The sea is grey and white, the land is shades of grey, everything in the landscape merges in tones of black and white. A dark Land Rover appears over the pass and lurches towards the west. From the driver's window an arm appears and points towards the copse, where trees lie flat and shattered.

Antlers are silhouetted blackly against the sky, as a stag turns his head to watch the vehicle, and the rumps of hinds flash whitely in surprise.

The Land Rover stops abruptly, and a man jumps down and walks forward. He bends one knee and reaches down with his other foot into a gully that crosses the road. The gully is deep, and rough with boulders that have been swept there by the water which rushes off the hill. The man gestures, and two more men, one with a stick, climb down to join him. They cross the gully on foot and continue to the west. White ribbons of water are draped down every hillside, and the burn has burst its banks and swirls darkly down beside the track. An uprooted rowan in the water snags twigs and grass, and forms a leaky dam.

The men walk down the narrow path in single file, the older one with the stick going carefully on the slick surface. The leader stops suddenly at a corner. He turns and shouts to the second man, who hurries to catch up, and they both stand and stare.

Below them, by the sea, is a cottage. Its smooth squat lines are disrupted by a jagged black hole and there is only a stump where once there was a chimney. The cottage winks with one black eye. The men hurry now, slipping and twisting on the path. They reach the flat ground by the croft, and shout and call, but the place is empty. Bare rafters and bent, torn corrugated iron are exposed starkly at one end. A window is roughly boarded.

One man walks round to the back. Debris has been stacked neatly in the garden, and tattered sheets of roofing materials have been salvaged and piled against a wall. Black bonfire ash is warm, and sends up white wisps of smoke when stirred. The back door has been nailed shut, so the men return to the front, and knock. One opens the door, and they disappear from the landscape, one by one.

But now they reappear, talking, gesturing. They shut the door and move about in the garden, nervously. One man stands looking towards the shore, and points at the boat.

The three figures make shifting patterns, dark against the grey land and sea. As they stare and talk, another figure appears on the ridge of moorland behind the cottage, and walks slowly down towards them. This figure is startlingly bright, dressed in oilskins, and she shines with yellow light as she descends the hill. The men draw together, then the older man with the stick moves towards her. They meet by the cottage garden. The man waves his stick at the cottage, obviously questioning her. He nods his head in the direction of the track and seems to be agitated, perhaps imploring.

But the women is quite calm and still. Her yellow brightness provides breathtaking contrast to the grey. She shakes her head. She shrugs slightly and touches, briefly, the man's arm. She continues shaking her head, and she smiles, gently, but the strange light of that smile is like an aura about her. She turns away, and climbs back across the moor.

The men stare after her. They are still. Eventually, their group re-forms and they walk close together, greyly, back up the path towards their Land Rover.

Eleven

'Harriet? Harriet!'

I was sitting on the mausoleum steps, resting in the pale March sunlight, and the granite pillar was cold against my back. I'd been expecting him, though not quite so soon. and I was suddenly nervous, half-tempted to stay hidden by the sarcophagi. But that would be stupid! I stood up and walked around the corner of the mausoleum, where he would be able to see me.

He waved, and came bounding down over the grass and heather at a knee-cracking speed. I could see that there was an anger about him, the sort of anger that derives from fear turned to relief.

'Hallo, Jos.'

I hadn't seen him since November, and he was paler than I remembered, his face a little slack from living in the city.

'Harriet! Are you all right? I was so worried – the cottage! I just came by there. I heard about the storm, it was on the news, even. What happened? What are you doing?'

I smiled, touched by his anxiety. He'd brought me another present, his concern.

'So many questions! I'm fine. Are *you* all right? You look tired. I didn't expect you to be back for two or three weeks. It must have been a bumpy crossing! Anyway, come and sit down, and tell me about everything.'

I indicated the step, a hostess graciously offering her guest a comfortable chair.

'You're so calm! How can you be so calm? Are you popping Valium or something, Harriet?'

Jos seemed unable to stop staring at me; he kept opening his mouth to speak, then shaking his head.

'Look!' I tried to distract him. 'See – there! There's Matilda!' The sleek black head of a seal turned and stared in our direction. 'Wave to her! Now the news will get round that you're back.'

'How do you know that's Matilda? You can't possibly recognise her – can you? Hell, my binocs are in my pack!'

'Oh, Jos!' I couldn't help laughing at him. He was so cross and worried and, now, indignant that I might have usurped his authority with the seals. 'Jos, you're so funny! And it's good to see you again.'

He had jumped up on to the top step to get a better view, but now he looked down at me. His legs seemed to stretch upwards like dark pillars; from where I sat he was a stilt-legged man from a circus. A small gust of wind blew hair across my eyes, distorting the picture, and, quite unselfconsciously, he reached down from his great height and brushed it away, apparently so that he could see me more clearly. I was too surprised to flinch and he seemed oblivious and continued to stare at me.

'After what MacGregor said I came hurrying over to see what had happened to you. And here you are, sunning yourself in a graveyard, and laughing your head off over daft jokes about seals. As though nothing had happened. I don't know, Harriet.'

'All right, so what *has* happened? What did John MacGregor tell you, then, that sent you to me in a panic? And where's your pack, anyway?'

'My pack's at the cottage. The cottage, for Christ's sake. Harriet! What a mess! And MacGregor said that you didn't seem to be living there any more. That you just sent them all away again, said you could manage on your own, thanks. Poor man. He's really upset and worried. Do you know, he's even given me one of those awful frozen cake-things for you. Said he remembered you liked them!'

'What frozen cake-things? Oh no! – not that yellow sponge and cream! Oh, he is good. But you keep the cake, Jos, I'm not in a position to entertain yet. Matilda likes that cake, by the way.'

He nearly fell for it again, but I quickly changed the subject.

'Are you going to stay at the bothy?'

'I was thinking of it, for a bit, anyway. Why! Oh – *you're* there, are you? Oh. I see.'

'No. I'm not staying there. You're welcome to it. Perhaps you'll invite me over to eat MacGregor's cake. "MacGregor's cake." It has a symbolic ring about it, hasn't it? I'm sorry he's upset, though. I know he meant well. And I didn't "send them all away again" in that tone of voice, Jos! But I did explain that I was all right – I am all right – and I can manage. I'm fine, truly. You can tell him that next time you see him – or I'll tell him, I need to go over for some more food. And then everyone can just forget about me and leave me alone again!'

'Okay, if that's the way you want it. I don't know what the bloody Hell you're playing at, Harriet. I'll be off, then, and get my pack.'

'Jos! Don't. Thank you for worrying about me. But you really don't need to. I'm getting things organised again.'

He had turned away, and he stood between the tombs, his hands stretched out at each side to stroke their smooth surfaces.

'They've weathered a few storms, too,' I said, reaching out to pat the nearest slab. 'The tombs, I mean.'

Jos was staring at the hillside further up the valley. Unfortunately, the sledge, with its piled load, was clearly visible. His voice was very thin, as though his throat was strangled.

'What are your things doing there? MacGregor said your mattress had gone.' He swung round to face me. 'You're not sleeping *there*, are you?'

I shrugged, and nodded.

'You can't. You're mad. Oh my God, Harriet, what has happened to you?'

I thought that he was going to run away from me, for a terrible moment, there was such fear and disgust in his expression. Then, worse, he began talking to me quietly, in a reasonable voice, as though he were soothing a dangerously unpredictable lunatic.

'Harriet, I don't really think the crypt is all that comfortable, is it? It must be a bit dark and cold. You like to see the view, Harriet, don't you? You like to be outside. Look, I have an idea. Why don't you stay at the bothy? I can go and fetch my tent from the shop. And I can look at the cottage with you, if you like, and help you sort out what to do. It must have been a bit of a shock, I can see that . . . The bothy's really very comfortable. Wouldn't that be a nice idea?'

'No, Jos. I like it here. The view is – wonderful. It's like lying in the door of your tent and looking out. I'm not mad, I know exactly what I'm doing—'

'Harriet, please. You need a few days—'

'No, don't interrupt, please. Once I've sorted everything out, you can come and see. You'll be very impressed.'

'But it's underground! Damp! Poky! *People* don't live in holes.'

'I'm not "people". It's what I want. It's meant.'

'Meant to be what?'

I'd used the word in the sense 'pre-ordained', part of the intricate pattern of interrelationship, but I knew that he could not possibly understand that, so I merely muttered something about how the crypt was meant to be a refuge.

Jos was frowning down at his feet, clearly trying to think of new persuasive arguments.

'Look! I'm doing what I want, I'm not hurting anybody, just leave me alone. Please!'

'Oh, not that again.'

'Yes. That again. I allow you to come and talk to me a few times, and look what happens. This is exactly why I don't like getting involved with anyone, Jos – as soon as anyone knows the smallest thing about anyone else, they want to start pushing in, offering help, advice, whatever. I know you mean well, but I don't want this, I want to be left alone. John MacGregor means well, too, but the others don't, they just want to pry and poke fun, and . . . and . . .'

A vivid image of Robbie Ferguson came to mind, and I lost track of what I was saying.

'Very condemnatory. We all mean well. Like upper middle-class ladies, charity shops and meals-on-wheels. Just a bunch of interfering busybodies, eh? Great!'

'No, that's a simplistic view. And I didn't include you in that, anyway. Oh – it's too complicated, and you know it. And, Jos – please don't stand between the tombs like that, it interferes with . . . oh, damn! Let's just walk over to the cottage so you can collect your bags.'

The sun had gone, hidden by a layer of thin low cloud, and a light drizzle was drifting in from the sea as we left the mausoleum. I wouldn't let Jos come with me when I went across to push the sledge into the shelter of the crypt. Perhaps I would show him some other time, perhaps not; as yet, it was too private a venture, and I didn't feel that the rationale was deeply embedded and inherent in my living. I would need time to accommodate, mentally and physically – and to be accommodated.

I was panting by the time I caught up with him; he had set off at a fast pace and his face was pink with the effort. Tiny droplets of moisture clung to his hair and beard. He was sulking, and obviously disturbed. I couldn't blame him, and I suppose I was both pleased and annoyed about his concern. I'm a grown woman, after all, and it is not his business to dictate or dissuade, but I couldn't tolerate the thought of this young man stamping crossly about the island. It was important that we returned to the state of peaceful, unintrusive co-existence that we had begun to find last year.

'Wait, Jos! Let me catch up.'

Grudgingly, he waited.

'Did you have a good time back at the department? I imagine it's rather a contrast from this.'

'It was okay.'

'What about the seals? Have you planned out a schedule of what you're going to do?'

'What about the seals? You haven't even told me if they're all right, after the storm.'

'Oh.' I was taken aback. 'I don't know. I suppose so. But I've been rather busy this past week.'

'That's why I came back early. Everyone was saying how severe the storm had been, and I didn't know what would happen to the colony. Perhaps some of them were hurt, and I wanted to be here to find out. It's probably too late now, anyway – but I couldn't get a boat any earlier. The ferries have all been cancelled until today.'

'Today! You mean you've only just arrived? How on earth did you get across here so quickly?'

'MacGregor brought me over in the Land Rover – as far as he could, anyway. The road's out. Didn't you know?'

'No. I'd almost forgotten that the mainland, let alone the rest of the island, existed.'

Although dwindling food stores were beginning to remind me about the shop. And, although I had watched the sea, watched and watched the sea, I hadn't thought to visit the seals.

'But I'm sure the seals will have been all right. After all, we just saw Matilda, didn't we? Or was it Roberta, or Susan, or even Jim?'

'Huh!'

As we reached the ridge behind the cottage, a curlew hooked up into the air, and its cry bubbled and swept across the moor. My skin grew cold and my spine tingled with love as the wild sound touched the corners of the wilderness. Jos had stopped, too.

'That,' he gestured at the sound, 'is what makes all this essential. When I hear that, I want to lie down in the heather and bury myself.'

He didn't elaborate, and I was afraid that I might not have understood what he was trying to say. Then he pointed down at the half-wreck of the cottage.

'That intrudes, Harriet. It's not right, you know.'

'No.' I answered him slowly. 'It's no longer part of the landscape, is it? It's not even in harmony. But I think it will find its place soon. It will merge.'

'They'll never let you stay there, you know, in the crypt. It's not yours. You'll get thrown out – cleared.'

'I share it with a sheep already. They don't need the clearance.'

'What?'

'Nothing, just an obscure joke. Who is to know, though? And who should care, that a solitary woman lives in an empty cave on the far coast of a far-distant and almost desert island! No one need know, Jos. Please don't tell anyone. You must promise me. Please! You have no right to tell anyone.'

I gripped his arm, and his pullover was damp with mist. He sighed, and chewed his lip.

'You're pretty odd, Harriet. But you're right in that I have no business interfering. And I've no right to come here and mess things up for you. Ah well, I'll away to the bothy. What about MacGregor's cake?'

'The Pied Piper's cake! Oh – just eat it yourself, or feed it to the gulls. The seals didn't like it, actually. And thanks!'

'It's okay. Or, at least, it's not okay – but take care, anyway.'

Damn! I thought I'd convinced myself of the rightness of what I'm doing. It *is* right; but the bastions of confidence are not yet strong enough. Build up the bastions, fortify the battlements! One person can so easily demolish them, with a blast from a trumpet.

Jos has gone striding off to his seals. He's not going to let this go, is he? He's going to keep on worrying away at the problem of Harriet the cave-woman. He probably thinks that I'll get tired of the troglodytic existence and recognise the foolishness of my ways. But he's wrong. I'm sure he'll understand, in time – as long as he doesn't talk to anyone else about it. If only he had never come here: just one person, one person with a trumpet, intruding like a big brass band!

But I'm so selfish. I intrude upon him, too; he sees the cottage's ugliness and my unexplained and erratic behaviour as disrupting the natural order. It nags at him, disturbs him. He cares about this place too, Harriet, you have to acknowledge that: I thought you had acknowledged that, indirectly, last time he was here. Have you forgotten so soon? *Laissez-faire* needs mutual tranquillity. He'll be better placed to understand when he starts camping again. Closer to the grass-roots! Yes – and the heather. That was interesting. I think it could be the same phenomenon, but incipient, still undiscovered.

But perhaps Jos never will be able to fully understand; he'll never make that single great leap, because he can never (even though he may understand the curlew's call) be the recipient of the same signs and clues. The meaning of the crypt had been shown to me after the storm.

After my battle with the sea for the life and body of my boat (and I understand, now, belatedly, that it had been a spiritual as well as a physical battle) I had slept deeply. The terror of the night and the morning's exertions had exhausted me, so that I was too tired to worry about my home, but I also felt curiously relaxed. When I woke, it was late afternoon; the rain had stopped and there was now only a strong wind rather than a storm. The cottage sounded completely different, different bangs and rattles and squeaks, outside noises had crept inside, and the echoes of the sea bounced back from every corner of the shell.

I cleared the dust and soot from around the gas rings, and hammered old boards and driftwood across the window. I couldn't even begin to think about the roof: it was too late in the day and I was frightened to climb on to the roof in that wind. I went for a walk instead, crossing the burn (with difficulty) at the head of Death Bay and following the path above the gorge, up towards the lochan.

Water was spilling out of the gorge in a thick brown stream, thundering down the rocks, piling up against branches and torn clumps of turf that had been rolled into tangled heaps. Nothing would have survived in that turmoil, and I was thankful that Finnghail had not fallen on such a day as this. The rock walls trembled with the force of the water, and the path was slick with mud, so I climbed cautiously. In the upper valley I found deer, their coats dark with water, browsing in the lee of the hill. The wind skimmed over the top of the island and caught the waterfall that normally fell, straight as a white ribbon, down the distant cliff, and threw it upwards, disarrayed, in a flurry of white spray. The ground squelched water as I walked; strands of yellowed grass had been pushed into tiny dams between the tussocks, and black fluid oozed from peat hags. There had been an onslaught, but it had been accepted philosophically, and everything around me was silently gathering inner strength for recovery. I sat on a rock, and watched and waited, reaching out quietly to the edges of my own strength, pulling it together and consolidating it.

The herd of deer moved steadily across the slope, now browsing, now raising heads to check for predators. A movement at the bottom of a nearby rock caught my eye and, as I looked, a pointed brown face, whiskers twitching, peered out of a hole. The vole came out slowly, hesitantly, then trundled rapidly along a straight, compacted surface run, and disappeared into another hole. I've always liked voles, I like their sturdy little bodies and their kindly faces, so I sat still, hoping it would return. After a few minutes, it poked its head out to check that all was clear, and then it disappeared, to re-emerge tail first, busily kicking with its back legs to clear its burrow of debris. Unperturbed by my presence, it pottered around, sniffing, poking, scratching for insects, until it finally wandered back into its home. I felt the vole's inner strength, its ability to carry on normally with its life despite the temporary adversities of storm and flood. It made me unaccountably and quietly happy, and I left the valley, and wandered back to my damaged home, along my own compacted surface run.

As I walked, I thought about the vole's burrow and its several doors. I thought about puffin burrows, and then how Finn's mate might, even now, be curled in a burrow with their cubs. Burrows were so ingenious, warm, buffered against the external world and yet very much an integral part of that world. I tried to imagine how it would have felt, to have been a fox or a vole during the storm, and my imaginings were tranquil, replete with the sensation of contentment. So, when I reached Death Bay and saw, in the darkening valley, the pile of stones that marked the entrance to the crypt, I assumed that there had always been the presupposition that I would move into the crypt. It was as though I had been expecting this solution to the problem of the cottage, ever since that startling, soul-swamping ecstasy of the morning.

I returned to the cottage, and sat on the bed. There was no ecstasy now, just a quiet certainty. I didn't need to argue with myself about the decision, or to look for reasons for or against, because the proofs lined themselves up logically, presented themselves to me one by one. There was a clear pattern: the partial destruction of my cottage ('partial' was the crucial step because, if it had been completely destroyed and my belongings scattered into the hills and the Atlantic, I would certainly have rushed into the wrong decision, perhaps even have gone to live in the village; instead, I was given time in which to become receptive to the right solution); the partial damage to the boat was another sign – salvage of the boat had been permitted, and of one, cracked, oar. And then the vole-hole! What a beautifully subtle signpost, the more pointed because my walk had taken me past Death Bay. Perhaps . . . perhaps even Father Peters' visit to the mausoleum could now be put in context, for he had forcibly, if unintentionally (ah, but had he not been Intended to guide these events? Herein lies a Mobius strip of cause and intended effect!) shown me the four-dimensional value of the crypt?

But here my guilt re-surfaced, my very Catholic guilt. Only a few hours previously I'd been convinced that the chimney had been smitten by my vengeful God, as a punishment. Had He also, through terror, shown me the way forward? Did both atonement and enlightenment, or rather, fulfilment, derive from living a simple life? Was this to be my punishment and my *reward*? The wind moaned in the fractured loft as I finished my supper of tinned tuna, crackers and a shrivelled orange. My body and mind ached with the struggle, but I was comforted by the certainty that, although I might not yet understand the complexities of the argument, the answer at least had been revealed. The thought of the safe intimacy of the crypt enveloped me in warmth, and as I undressed for bed, I tried to imagine myself as a female, Catholic equivalent of the sadhu. So terribly impractical in this climate, a loin cloth; and who would fill my begging-bowl . . .? And why?

Twelve

I want to describe the crypt, as I found it on the second morning after the storm. First, the entrance: this is hidden, a little way up on the slope of the hill. It is hidden by a group of rocks and dead vegetation, grasses, nettlestalks, brambles. The entrance hole is small and rough, formed by rotten wood. A person can walk in, bent double; there is no need to crawl.

Inside the hole is a pile of earth, stones and soft, fragmented wood. The wood comes from the remains of a rotten door, one of a pair. The other door is covered by earth and turf outside, and so is visible only from the inside. It is stained with rot and damp. Its top curves, and the tops of both doors together would have formed a convex curve, to match the roof. The pile of earth by the entrance is damp and slippery, but further back the floor is dry and dusty, hard-packed earth.

A person can stand up inside the crypt. The roof is arched, cut into the bedrock and lined with mortar. Fine dust has sifted through the cracks. It is caught in cobwebs and lies in small piles on the floor.

The side walls are lined with hand-cut stones, the gaps between them neatly mortared. A few stones are streaked with green algae.

Further back inside the crypt is windblown debris – dry grass, crisp brown seaweed and thistledown. There are also animal bones, the scapula and disjointed vertebrae of a deer calf. Also on the floor, near the back left corner, are two polished chunks of slate, spaced approximately four feet apart. Each slab is almost three feet long and two inches thick, and projects upwards by a foot.

The back wall is completely covered by a mosaic of half-inch, coloured tiles, depicting a dragon with scaly wings and with flames coming from his mouth, facing a long-nosed sheep. The background of the picture is pale blue, the dragon is green and gold and red, and the sheep is white and gold. There are some bare patches in the pattern where the tiny squares have fallen off; they are lying in the dust on the floor.

The crypt measures approximately nine feet wide by fifteen feet deep. Because the entrance is overgrown, daylight doesn't penetrate more than a few feet into the crypt; it would not be possible to see the mosaic or the roof without a lamp.

There is a smell of unstirred air and damp earth. There is also a smell of animal. And there is the continuous sound of the sea, and of the wind hissing through the rocks.

Here, then, is buried treasure! My burrow contains buried treasure and the wild music of the sea. Such unbelievable riches, concealed beneath the ground! How is it that I was so ignorant of this truth, had not found this trove? All these years! Even the size of the crypt surprises me, there is such spaciousness buried there. I have a suspicion that, only now, at the appointed time, have the scales been lifted from my eyes.

I came here once, many years ago, with my torch, but the entrance was smaller then, so that I had to crawl. The smell of dead meat frightened me, so that I didn't explore but merely shone the beam around the walls and perhaps mistook the dragon's gleam, half-seen, for glistening streams of algae. And when, years later, I lay dreaming of sleeping priests with exquisite hands, only my lower body lay within the tomb. The rest of me crouched in cryptic colouration amongst the entrance rocks. 'All the better to see you with', *mon père*.

It is almost intact, built to survive for aeons, like the pharaohs' tombs. But when the tomb was emptied, and the metaphorical rock was rolled across the entrance, earth was piled against the doors. Did they forget the effects of time and tide, when they thus imprisoned the dragon with the sheep? How rain and wind turned hard-packed earth into honeycomb? Aeonic fractions pass, and water filters through the soil, insect larvae burrow through the wood, a rock sinks deeper in its slippery bed, fungi ramify and digest – and the land slips, the wood rots, a hole appears for wind and spray to play with. The dragon roars at the storm, and there is a new entrance, and a pile of rocks to provide footholds for nettle roots and brambles. And, much later, a storm, assisted by a vole, creates an entrance foothold for a hermit!

I brushed my sleeve over the dragon's dusty face. His golden neck-scales flashed and sparkled in the lamp-light, and his tongue flickered and warmed the air. The sheep blinked a haughty yellow eye, and deigned to remind me that her heraldic horny brother ramped erect upon the mausoleum's shield, lord of all the lords and land surveyed. But I stroked her nose and told her, gently, that she was out of date and that neither sheep nor goats had inherited this earth, but that air and water and all living things had risen up, as one, against the ovine intruder, and that the natural balance had been restored.

I want to describe how I imagine the crypt to have been. I don't know why Sir Laurence Hunter wanted to be buried over here, but he must have ordered the crypt to be built in readiness for his death. Men from the village and from the scattered crofts, and perhaps imported stonemasons, came trekking over here on foot. They must have carried their food, and tools, their spades, pickaxes, axes, saws and hammers. I hope they built the crypt in the summer when the days were long and warm; I like to think of them lighting a fire at dusk to boil their water and to provide companionship, but they must frequently have been tired and hungry, and persecuted by the clegs and midges. Was there a safety-conscious foreman, who took care that the walls and roof were properly shored, or was the digging a haphazard affair? Skilled men cut those stones and lined the walls, but there would have been a need for coarse labour, to fetch and carry stones. They must have brought the stone by sea, because it isn't local; or was the track wide and sound, suitable for carts and small, sturdy ponies?

When the walls were finished, children came to see their fathers and to help. They cleared the floor of rocks and chipped stone. They carried sand in buckets from the beaches, and mixed it with earth, and stamped and rolled it flat. Several children stayed behind to watch the joiner shaping and planing the timbers of the doors, and they fingered and played with the heavy iron latch and bolt.

Then came the polished slate, shipped over from the mainland, the pedestals sitting snugly in their beds of straw. But it was the coffin table that caused the biggest transport problems. It was thick and shiny, solid yet brittle, easily chipped or cracked. And what expense! How the workmen marvelled at the cost! As the cart lurched and bumped across the island, the foreman carried the table's future, and his own, on a bed of prayer; until, finally, Sir Laurence's coffin table was prepared, in the rear left corner of the cavern.

I like to imagine that the visionary mosaic was a surprise to the dead man and his family. Sir Laurence and his wife have just returned home to their large, beautifully-proportioned house in the most fashionable part of Victorian Edinburgh. Lady Mary felt most unwell on the boat trip back from the island; she hated sea travel but she had felt it necessary to accompany her husband on this tour of their island estate, because she particularly wanted to see the family vault, of which dear Laurie was so proud. Personally, she would much rather be laid to rest here in Edinburgh, among her own family and friends, but Laurie had this peculiar idea that he must lie on his own land, in sight of the sea, and he would, of course, want his beloved Mary next to him when her time came. Well, he was not to be dissuaded – you know how he is when he has set his mind on something that concerns the family's future – and, anyway, she supposed she would be past caring when her own time came. But, after yesterday's boat trip, she did rather wish that she would be the first to die, so that she would never have to accompany his coffin on the trip!

Dear Laurie! He did so inspire respect, and a willingness, in others, to serve; the men had made such good progress with the vault, and were obviously delighted that he would be making use of their handiwork. Yet, it was such a gloomy place and, really, so terribly – well, simple. She would have preferred something rather grander.

Lady Mary quietly confided something of her worries to her daughter-in-law that evening, as they all sat in the drawing room after dinner, and she – dear creature! – suddenly startled them all by saying,

'Tapestries! What about tapestries?'

Of course, it took a moment or two of explanation before everyone realised what the sweet girl was talking about, but then Alfred completely flattened all their enthusiasm and merriment by just drawling, 'Moth and rust – earthly corruption, darling. Tapestries are so ephemeral.'

Alfred was such a strange, *aesthetic* young man; her ladyship always found it so hard to believe that he could possibly be Laurie's nephew. He always seemed to be lying around in odd poses, and sometimes his face held a curious glazed look, his eyes became quite blank and dark. But he was said to be quite unconscionably artistic, so much so that the muse quite overwhelmed him on occasion.

Then Lady Mary had a brainwave (or whatever was the Victorian equivalent for a flash of inspiration).

'Do you remember when St Margaret's was being repainted, and all those extraordinary wall-paintings – frescoes, weren't they? – were uncovered? Religious scenes, that were painted straight on to the plaster on the walls. We could find an artist to do that, my dear!'

She was so thrilled with her idea.

'But that would mean plastering all the walls. You saw for

yourself, Mary, the fine stone that they were lined with. I had it specially imported. It would be completely wasted!'

'And paint and plaster flake with age, Aunt Mary. But I have an inspiration. When Oscar and I were travelling through Italy last summer we spent some not inconsiderable time examining many exquisite mosaic designs. It's quite extraordinary what fine detail can be achieved with the aid of tiny squares of coloured pottery. Perhaps you would permit the back wall to be plastered, Uncle, and then embossed with a mosaic design? It would reflect the light of candles most satisfyingly . . . an effect guaranteed to lift the soul towards perfection. I would venture to suggest that such a scheme would present a most unusual and impressive prospect.'

Alfred's idea rather gripped the collective imagination, and the family spent a pleasant hour or two discussing how such a scheme could be accomplished. A few months later, Alfred, who had wide acquaintance within the society of painters and sculptors, brought to the house the young artist, Douglas, and subsequently a semi-religious design incorporating a kneeling angel and a sheep, symbol of the family's new-found wealth, was evolved. Sir Laurence, who had promised his widowed sister-in-law that he would 'keep an eye on Alfred', suggested that the two young men should remove themselves to Florence, to find both ceramic tiles and expertise. It was suggested that, if Douglas had any sense, he should ensure that he became the new Scottish expert and exponent of mosaic design and construction, under Sir Laurence's patronage.

Three months in Italy satiated the aesthetic sensibilities of the two companions, and Venice in particular proved exquisitely delightful. As they lay, dressed in loose-fitting silken robes, languidly limp with lack of desire for the voluptuous erstwhile maidens who wobbled around them, and surrounded by aromatic swirls of vaporised poppy-juice, Douglas had the sensation that he was flying, gliding amongst gilt-edged clouds. Images of angels and centaurs confused themselves in his mind, and he tried to explain these pictures to Alfred, so that a cleverly artistic conversation wove itself dreamily through the smoke. Fairies, and dragons, and Puck, emerged briefly, and cloven hooves, until the complex integration of the angel and the sheep presented itself to their joint memories. The juxtaposition of images of wealth and religion was incongruous and absurd, and Alfred, who wanted to return to the theme of fantastic flight, suggested that the angel could be easily converted to a dragon.

'They both have wings. A dragon rampant!'

'Ah, flaming passion! What progeny!'

Douglas tried to produce a sardonically aesthetic smile and was mildly startled to hear someone on his couch produce a cackle of dirty laughter. But Alfred was envisioning the flames, and tried not to think of Hell-fire but to concentrate on food.

'Barbecued lamb!' he managed to whisper, thereby jumping almost a century.

They returned to Edinburgh with several hundredweights of assorted richly-coloured tiles, and considerable knowledge of Italy's delights and skills, including, in Douglas's case, a practical knowledge of mosaic construction.

Douglas, sulky at being abandoned in a cold cave on a grey and inhospitable island, consoled himself with large volumes of the local 'water-of-life', and was considerably inspired to create a vibrant and colourful dragon in place of an angel-of-mercy. He didn't tell Alfred (who would have disapproved, because he always took care never to drop his bread on the floor, irrespective of which side was buttered) and he certainly didn't tell his sponsor. He was banking on the likelihood that Sir Laurence would be dead the next time that he visited his estate and crypt.

Lady Mary was in Edinburgh, prostrate with grief and the fear of *mal-de-mer*, when her dear Laurie made his final journey to his place of rest. Only his son, with the local agent, the ghillie, and a gaggle of local peasants accompanied the heavy coffin across the island. The new laird was depressed at the wildness of the scenery and the crypt's unstately simplicity and, when the gorgeous dragon flickered hotly at him like the eternal fire, his knees became weak with shock and shame. The attendants assumed he was weak with grief and the thought of his wealth and new responsibilities (they, after all, had known about the dragon for years and assumed it was merely another of Sir Laurence's charming eccentricities). But the new laird vowed privately, there and then, to build a more fitting monument to his family's life. When the mourners left the crypt with its lonely coffin, and closed and locked the doors, the sea was blue and sparkling, and the small islands shimmered across the water. Sir Laurence's son saw what his father had seen. He looked down at the bay and he had his own vision, of pillars of shining marble and sun-gilded tombs caressed by zephyrs of balmy air. When the mausoleum was completed, his father would be moved to that, more fitting, resting-place, and finally the three of them, himself with his dear parents, would be united once more. He conveniently forgot about his wife (there would only be space for three, and she was becoming so obsessive with her tapestry-work that they could hardly be said to enjoy the marital status any longer), and returned home to order (cheaper) polished granite and to set in motion, once more, the cycle of transport and construction.

Nobody else in the family ever discovered the angel's transformation, and Douglas never had a chance to broadcast his secret because he became the first, and probably last, person in this region to die from sea-sickness. Sir Laurence's earthly remains were discreetly transferred to their new home two days before Lady Mary's cortège arrived, so that there should be no unpleasantness to greet the mourning family, and it was ordered that the crypt be closed and its doors buried so that it need never be entered again.

And now I want to describe the crypt as it is today, twelve days after the storm.

Today, Jos is coming. I've told them at the shop that I'm all right. I did my best to arrive there looking fit and healthy, and I tried to be cheerful and full of enthusiasm for life. Now I need Jos to come here, so that he can confirm, if he's asked, that I'm sane and happy and need no help. After that, everyone will leave me alone again, and we'll all return to the *status quo ante*.

I've worked very hard to rationalise my requirements and re-develop the crypt as my new home. I think it's going to work well, but I need to convince Jos, perhaps also as a way of convincing myself. I'm very nervous about this visit; I didn't even invite him to the cottage, let alone the crypt!

Do I look all right? It's been dirty, hot work, but I've washed and I've trimmed my long and windswept hair. The woollen skirt smelt a little of mothballs, but I hung it outside to air. Dark green and navy tartan, matched with a thick navy pullover over a white shirt, and thick blue walking-socks, the darned heels hidden within my boots. Quite correct and dapper, I think, nothing eccentric, just a sensibly-dressed middle-aged lady. I can't remember when I last dressed like this!

Here he comes! Perhaps he is nervous, too. He thinks I'm very unpredictable. Walk slowly to meet him, and bring him down to the entrance.

'Hallo! And welcome to my new abode. "Home, sweet home", and all that!'

'I should have brought you one of those doormats as a house-warming present, one of those that say "Welcome". I brought you this instead. Close your eyes and hold out your hand.'

'Will it wriggle?'

'No.' Jos laughed, and put something smooth and cool into my palm. 'You can look now.'

I looked. It was a pale milky-blue agate, sea-washed until it was smooth, and patterned with concentric squares, the lines reaching deep into its interior. I held it to the light to see its cloudy transparency.

'It's a beauty. Thank you. From the beach?'

'Yes. I found it on the beach by the bothy. It was actually in the water and I had quite a job to get it out before the waves got me!'

'I can put it on my mantelpiece.' I smiled at his surprised expression. 'I was only joking. Come and see, anyway.'

I led him down the narrow path, little more than a deer track, towards the entrance to my home.

'You look smart,' he said, behind me. 'I like you in those clothes, they suit you. But very – proper, somehow.'

'Did you think I was improper?'

'No. Oh, you know what I mean!'

'Yes.' I did, and laughed. 'Anyway, here we are.'

We had reached the rockpile that had hidden the entrance. I had cut back the vegetation and, where possible, had piled smaller rocks upon those that were firmly rooted to make a low wall. Below this, protected from the wind and next to the entrance hole, was a circle of stones, my fireplace, at present guarding a soft pile of grey ash. I had also tidied the edges of the entrance, removing rough wood and loose pebbles.

'I'll go in first. It's rather dark, so go carefully, and stand inside the doorway until your eyes get used to it. And mind your head!'

I had not yet decided what to do about a door, but, as a temporary measure, had nailed a spare blanket over the hole; now, the blanket was tied back to one side, so that as much light as possible could enter. I gathered my skirt in one hand and stooped through the hole. Jos's body blocked out the light, just as it had done at his first appearance at my other home, and then he was through and standing beside me, closing his eyes so that they would accommodate quickly.

I had placed lit candles and the hurricane lamp at various points but, purposely, had left the end wall as dark as possible. I was very pleased with my efforts at home-making! I no longer thought that the crypt smelt musty but it was possible I had ceased to notice. I was also very conscious that I *had* to like what I saw, and that it was not necessary for Jos to see it in the same way. I waited while he opened his eyes and stared round; there was a long silence, and a wave of disappointment clenched my stomach as I watched him thinking what he should say.

'I'd no idea it was so big!'

'No, nor had I. And look at the doorway behind you.'

'How on earth did you get all this over here?'

He pointed at the gas burner and the Calor gas cylinder, set up next to the entrance hole. I tried not to remember the terrible sweating struggle I'd had in order to bring them here. It had taken me most of one day and twice I'd nearly given up, but desperation had been my goad. Now that I had reconnected the system, I was worried about the lack of ventilation in the crypt, and had resolved to cook outside on the fire, when possible.

'I brought them over on the sledge. I think I'm going to have to get another sledge, or try to make one – it's badly cracked after all this work. Do you like my sofa-bed?'

I was proud of that! I had initially intended to make a separate wooden platform, to raise the mattress off the floor, but, after tripping and bruising my shins several times on the slate pedestals, I realised that the stones were – of course! – ideally spaced as supports for my bed. Who had removed the coffin-table? Presumably some last-minute grave-robbers, before the empty tomb was sealed; but the slate would have been chill and hard, and now I had planks and salvaged plasterboard as my mattress-base. Bed-making had been one of my earliest tasks, because I wanted to move into my burrow as soon as I possibly could. The mattress had come across on the sledge, too, rolled and roped and covered with polythene. If the road had not been washed away, and the Land Rover forced to stop, John MacGregor and the others would probably have arrived in time to see that energy-sapping struggle. But now the bed looked bright and cheerful, covered with the faded Indian bedspread from the cottage.

Jos nodded slightly as he looked around, but his cheeks had fallen into the sad grooves of thought. He stood still and looked around him at the single wooden chair, at the box of plates and pans and cutlery, even at the small plank-and-crate bookcase.

'It's amazing what you've done, Harriet. And I can't imagine how you brought everything over. I think you must have persuaded someone from the village to come and help, after all!'

'No! You know I wouldn't!'

'Magic, then! But it's so dark and damp. And it does smell a bit odd.'

'I'd hoped the smell was going. It will soon be spring, the weather's improving every week, and I'll be able to let lots of fresh air in. And herbs – bog myrtle. And rushes on the floor – if I can find any. Dry grass, anyway. Don't forget, it hasn't been lived in for nearly a hundred years, it's been closed up.'

'*Lived* in?'

'I didn't mean that. "Occupied", then. But look! Let me turn up the lamp now so that you can see properly. I've been saving this as a surprise for you.'

I went over to the lamp by the door and turned up the flame, then walked past the bed and held the flame against the back wall. I tried to see the expression on Jos's face, but the shadows were too deep and I could only see the white glitter of his eyes.

'Christ! That is incredible! Let me look. Did you know about this before?'

'No. That's what so strange.'

I watched him touching the small knobbly tiles, fingering the dragon's wings, the sheep's dark nostrils.

'And how could I not live here, now that I've discovered them?'

I gave him the lamp, and went to my cooking area to light the gas. The steady roar of the flame merged with the continual, fluctuating hiss and mutter of the outside world. Jos was looking round again, holding the lamp to the ceiling and the walls.

'Is it safe? I wouldn't feel too happy about the thought of the whole hillside above me.'

'It's cut back into solid rock, that's just a stone facing. And it's been here a hundred years, give or take a few, so there's no reason why it shouldn't last for another twenty or thirty, or so.'

'You're not going to live here for ever, Harriet? This is only temporary, isn't it, until you get the cottage sorted out?'

He was really horrified. And I was horrified, too, at the scale of my intentions; until that moment, when I had spoken those words, 'twenty or thirty', I had not thought beyond tomorrow. For years, I have been accustomed to living from day to day, my most advanced planning concerned with ferry timetables or schedules for planting vegetables, and I have never had the need to think about my future (here on earth). My assumption was that I would live in my cottage until I died; and now my assumption would seem to be that I would live here in the crypt until that time (and presumably beyond, for it was indeed a tomb). It was difficult to imagine, and I was not sure that I was mentally prepared for the image. But, at this moment, my future plans could only be my own private concern and Jos, after all, was a mere transient.

'The main point is that the crypt is completely safe, and that I'm happy. You can see how comfortable it is.' I tried to sound persuasive. 'Sit down – yes, sit on the bed – and I'll brew the tea.'

Seeing him sitting on the bed while I made cups of tea brought back very ancient memories of student life, and I laughed.

'You see, this isn't much different from a student bedsit – a basement room, in a power-cut! Dark, a bit damp, very small but with room for a bed, a chair and a kettle. You must have lived in places like that, or had friends who did?'

'Were you a student? It's odd, I can't imagine you doing—'

'Normal things, you were going to say? Yes, I was a student – BA in modern languages. Same place as you, but rather before your time!'

'I saw the French and German dictionaries in the cottage, and I did wonder why you had them. What did you do before you came here, then?'

'Various things.' I slammed down my mental shutter, before scenes of family life intruded. 'Now, I've forgotten – do you take sugar? It may be slightly damp.'

'No, thanks.'

He stood up from the low bed and took his mug, then, because there was nowhere else, he put it on the floor by the bed.

'I did wonder whether to bring the table across, but it will take up so much space. Low-level living is simpler!'

'Very Japanese. Quite the thing these days, you know.'

'No, I didn't know. But then, as you might imagine, I'm completely out of touch with what goes on anywhere but here.'

'Mmm. Strange, really.'

'Not really. It doesn't help to know who's fighting whom, who is the Home Secretary, or what are the latest fashions in literature or cocktail wear. That knowledge doesn't contribute to the quality of my life. I'm too busy doing things like repairing the boat, finding firewood, watching flowers and birds!' I shrugged. 'You know how it is. Talking of watching, how are the seals?'

'Great. They're getting time-consuming, too. There's one female with a badly torn flipper, it looks quite raw. I wonder how many get damaged in storms, if anyone's ever looked at that. It must have been quite some storm.'

'I've never known one like it, Jos, and nor, presumably, has the cottage. I should go down to the cottage, because I need to try to block off the remaining bit of attic somehow, to stop the rain driving in and wrecking that ceiling, too. It's still my storage room, my clothes are in there.'

'So you're still using the cottage? You haven't abandoned it entirely?'

'While it's still there . . . But of course I'm not going to abandon the earth. It's coming up to a busy time for vegetables!'

'Do you want me to help with the roof? I will – if you think you need a hand. Just to be there to hold the ladder, if that's what you want.'

'That's kind. Thank you. I might take you up on that. Oh – and keep your eyes open for an oar, or something that might do as an oar, would you, on your walks? I've only recovered one so far. It's cracked, but I think I can bind it.'

Jos was amazed that the boat was safe and, because I couldn't think of a reason why he shouldn't know, I told him the story of my battle. I didn't explain my strange feeling of kinship with the sea, or of my new certainty that the sea was a living, spiritual entity, but I did tell him the joke about the red bailer. He wouldn't know why it was so significant, but that didn't matter.

The heat from the gas burner had warmed the crypt, even though the door curtain was still drawn back. I had blown out two of the candles, to save them, but there was still enough light for us to see each other. I felt happy, telling the story, even though I probably didn't tell it well, and Jos sat hunched on the bed, his mug clutched between his hands, and listened carefully, occasionally exclaiming or asking questions.

'So! All is well!' I finished. 'And are you convinced now that I'm all right?'

He smiled slightly, and nodded.

'It's okay. You've obviously thought it out carefully. And I've said before that you're very practical.'

'That sounds terribly condescending, young Jos! As though you can't believe that a woman could be so well-organised!'

But I smiled, too, to lessen the sharpness of what I needed to say.

'The last thing I want is for you to feel any sense of responsibility, Jos. I don't need you. I'm not dependent on anybody. Come and visit if you wish, but you can also completely ignore me if you prefer. I know exactly what I'm doing.'

He stood up, handing me his mug.

'I see that now. I'd like to visit now and again, if that would suit you.'

'There'll be improvements and innovations each time you come. This is just the beginning. And now and again, if I find myself up your way, I may come and see the seals. And you.'

'Yeah. That'd be good.'

He ran his fingers through his hair so that it stuck up on end, and snorted gently. 'You know, I can't really believe this. This weird set-up, and you sitting there, Harriet, handing me tea like the lady of the house. And looking so normal. I'll say one thing, no one could ever take you for granted.'

I followed him out, reminding him to watch his head, and we

both turned and looked down at the mausoleum, stark against the sea.

'Thanks for the agate. I'll find a special place to put it, near a candle, perhaps.'

'An offering to the dragon!'

Jos turned towards me and stuck out his hand. Surprised, I put out mine, and he shook it, very formally.

'Thank you, Harriet,' he said, and his glance was very direct and penetrating. As he walked away, I remembered a final, important message, and called after him.

'Don't tell anyone where I'm living. Please. But tell them I'm all right.'

He raised his hand in acknowledgement, and I was left, rubbing the agate that was in my pocket, like a worry-bead.

Thirteen

I could see what Jos meant, about the seal. Even without the binoculars, I could see that she was lying differently from the other cows; she gave the impression that her insides hurt and that she wanted to curl up on herself and keep warm. I nearly said as much to Jos, but I could imagine his response ('You'll be telling me next that she ought to be tucked up in bed with a nice hot water bottle!') so I kept quiet. Jos was pointing out the seal's damaged flipper, handing me his binoculars.

'I reckon she must have been smashed against a rock in the storm. She's hardly moved for the past three days. My guess is that something inside is damaged, like her gut or liver.'

'Poor thing! She'll just starve. The others won't help her, will they? Not like elephants?'

'No, they're pretty much ignoring her, actually. But she may not feel like eating, anyway.'

'What are you going to do?'

'Nothing. What can I do, except watch? It's interesting, watching how the others behave towards her, anyway.'

'But you can't just sit here, day after day, and watch her die!'

His apparent callousness shocked me; a beautiful, finely-adapted animal was probably dying in front of him, and all he could do was write notes in his field diary. There were several other seals on the rocks but (as far as I could tell, looking at their inert and silent bodies) they seemed to be paying no attention to their wounded friend. She might even be a half-sister to several of the other cows, but a sense of family unity was not apparent. The thought of her dark eyes, shrunken and filmy with pain, was not easy to tolerate.

'Do you see those three cows there, on the right? The two lying parallel with each other, and the third one in between, lying at an angle – like a Z? I can recognise all those three, now. Look at the markings on their heads and necks. The one on the left has got two scars by her ear. Can you see?'

I found it hard to see much difference between the three females, but then, I hadn't spent as many hours as Jos had, intensively watching hauled-out seals; and, anyway, I was rather more interested in examining the hurt seal. I could imagine her lonely aching body so clearly and felt such empathy with her that it seemed to me that, just by the touch of my hand upon her smooth head, I would be able to soothe and comfort her. Surely, we would have such confidence in each other, and faith, that she would be healed? If I could somehow move her round to Death Bay, I would be able to look after her, and feed her back to glistening, blubbery health. It did occur to me that Jos might not be completely enthusiastic about my removing one of his study animals, but I could possibly come to some arrangement with him when the opportunity arose. We had a slightly better understanding of each other now, after all. But first, I needed his help.

'I'm impressed. Have you given them names? Or do you use numbers?'

'Numbers, it's less emotive. And it's quite difficult to tell, if they're lying on their bellies, which sex they are, so I can't always say "Female One", "Male One" and so on.'

'How many seals are there, in the colony?'

'Well, last autumn I think there were about thirty. But I haven't seen that number all hauled out together. I won't be certain until I can identify every single one. I'm getting there, though.'

'Would it help to go out in the boat? To have a closer look? You might pick up some other markers that would be useful, and you can probably sex them better from close to. You could have a look at that wounded cow, too.'

'Hey, that would be really great, Harriet.'

Jos dropped the binoculars from his eyes and swung round to grin delightedly.

'Terrific. Are you sure you wouldn't mind? But hang on! I thought you didn't have any oars? And that the motor was done for?'

'I've mended the cracked oar. And now I've found the other. But I need your help to get it – that's why I'm here.'

'And I thought you'd come for the pleasure of my company! More fool me! What have I got to do? Scale a fifty-foot cliff? Dive down twenty fathoms? Tell me the worst!' He raised his eyebrows briefly in mock despair.

'Nothing too dangerous. Basically, the oar's jammed in a crack and I can't move the boulders and pull it out at the same time.'

Jos's left eyebrow rose this time, in that mocking expression that had so unnerved me at our first meeting.

'I'm surprised at you, Harriet. Giving up! I'm even more surprised at you coming to ask me for help. I bet if I wasn't here you'd have thought of a way of doing it on your own. You know what you're suffering from? It's the "Sauce Bottle Syndrome".'

'The what?'

'A friend of mine told me all about it. She was feeling disgusted with her fellow females at the time, her "sisters", so-called. She said that women could do anything if they put their minds and muscles to it. But if a man appeared among them, they immediately – unconsciously – became subservient, and could no longer perform the simplest physical task, such as unscrewing the lid of a bottle of tomato sauce. The bottle would have to be passed along the table to be dealt with by the male.'

'Oh, very clever.' My sarcasm was childish. 'But, as regards the oar, another woman or even a well-behaved monkey would do as well. I just don't have three hands, that's all, and you just happen to be the nearest person, whatever your sex.'

I had found the oar this morning, jammed handle upwards between three boulders. It wasn't far from Camus Beag, and must have been sucked out by the stormy tide, then swept in later that same day. The heavy seas and high tide had cast it up high amongst the rocks, and had pushed and rolled the stones and boulders until the oar was wedged tight inside a cleft. The sea had been teasing me again; the oar was arranged conspicuously, but was inextricable. I had pushed and rocked the stones. I lay on my stomach and tried to pull out the tightly-wedged pebbles. I pulled and I shoved, and I braced my back against one rock and pushed with my feet. But the oar had remained tantalisingly stuck. All I needed was a second person, to stand in the right place, just to the left of the cleft, to pull the oar out while I rocked the stones apart. Nevertheless, Jos's jibe upset me, and I wondered if I had, without being aware of it, been insidiously weakened by the knowledge that potential help was nearby.

'Oh, I'll come, Harriet. Of course I'll help. Just this once, though, since it's in my own interest. I wouldn't like to think you were becoming dependent.'

He stretched and grinned, turning to look once more at the seals. And then his grin disappeared.

'Oh no! It's that seal, isn't it? I wondered why you were being so helpful. You don't really want to help me at all, do you? You've got some idea about saving that seal. You're crazy – she's as good as dead. And,' unaware of his contradiction, 'how am I going to explain in my thesis that a woman came and took away one of my seals and turned it into a circus pet? The whole point of this type of study is that it's not intrusive. The subjects should scarcely know you're there, because otherwise – if you intrude conspicuously – their behaviour changes. And then you're studying a false situation.'

'Let Nature take its course, and all that! On that basis, if you were in a city and saw someone being mugged, you should just stand in a doorway and watch. And explain to the police that you were studying "Survival of the Fittest".'

'That's totally illogical, and you know it! *Please* don't interfere with the seals, not again. Look – I'll help you get the oar out, but not now. In two days. That cow will be dead by then. And we can row out near the rocks and study the colony from a distance. If you'd still like to. You can help me to try to identify them, I'd very much like you to be involved.'

Now it was my turn to look sceptical.

'Involved in that sort of activity, anyway. If you think you'd find it interesting. And if you're still prepared to take me in the boat. But I'm not going to help you get the oar now, just so that you can go out there and disturb the colony.'

There didn't seem to be much more to say. I looked down to where the dying seal lay, occasionally splashed with spray. I didn't feel angry with Jos, and the idea of photographing and observing the colony from close quarters, guided by Jos's increasingly knowledgeable comments, was, undeniably, interesting.

'All right then. Come and tell me as soon as it's over.' I gestured at the haul-out rocks. 'If I'm not at the crypt, I'll be on the croft.'

He was clearly amazed at my capitulation, but I wasn't going to leave him time for further argument.

'See you soon.'

'Oh. Right. I'll be in touch.'

I'm not used to arguing with young men. I haven't been used to arguing with anybody for a decade or so, apart from myself – and my conscience. I don't count the imaginary arguments that I hold with Graham, because they run to my own script and choreography. It's so easy to dismiss Jos as a boy, a bearded boy admittedly, but nevertheless a fairly junior member of the human species, enjoying a bit of freedom and adventure, and messing around with tents and marine mammals. But, when his one-sided interaction with the seals is under threat, he becomes utterly strong-willed in his protectiveness. Then, I'm reminded that he is an adult, has been legally an adult for several years, and is very much entitled to guard against intervention, whether on his own territory or the seals'. Sometime, perhaps, we could discuss further this concept of the non-intrusive study, because it also relates to us and our relations with the outside world, our own behaviours. There are so few places where humans don't intrude. I suppose this island must have a low 'intrusion quotient' (what a good term that is! I just thought it up at this moment; I must tell it to Jos, sometime). But despite that, there *are* human intruders on my territory, and my behaviour changes accordingly, doesn't it! Oh yes, Harriet, just think about some of those embarrassing behavioural changes! It would probably be safest not to think about them, wouldn't it, for the sake of mental stability! And now the tomato ketchup – the 'Sauce Bottle Syndrome'. I'm glad he told me about that. Very percipient! Of course I'll get that oar free on my own, how could I have imagined otherwise?

As I walked back along the cliff path, I thought about the seal. She had already become 'my seal' in my imagination. She would soon be fit and well again, and I imagined her swimming around the boat, disappearing to hunt fish then reappearing with a snort, her round head turning from side to side as she looked around to find the boat. I imagined her at Death Bay and Camus Beag, lazing fatly on the rocks or just wallowing in shallow water, keeping an indolent eye on my activities. I had no plan; I felt certain that I would be shown the way and everything would work out as expected. I didn't even consider Jos. The outcome was clear.

But that damned oar would not shift! I returned to it, confidently, like young Arthur to the sword in the stone, but there was no magic there and I was completely defeated. Half an hour later as, sweating and furious, I was searching for wood to act as wedges, Jos appeared. He came straight across the rocks to where I was attempting to hide my red eyes and redder face.

'Harriet, I'm sorry. She's dead already. I thought we saw her move a little, didn't we? But she must have died then, I think. I'm so sorry. The gulls gave it away, otherwise I mightn't have realised. They must have been cruising around, keeping an eye on her, and then one came down about fifteen minutes after you left. So then I knew.'

He didn't say what the gull had done, he knew I'd understand.

I'm ashamed of myself, but I cried; for the seal and for my loss. I sat down by the cold grey waters of the Atlantic, and I wept. Jos, embarrassed, left me alone, and leapt away across the rocks. I saw him struggling with the oar. Eventually, I wiped my no-doubt blotchy face and climbed over to join him.

'You've every right to squirt tomato ketchup all over my face,' he said cheerily. 'It'll definitely have to be a team effort. You pull and I'll push.'

'There doesn't seem much point, now.'

'Of course there is. You'll always need the boat. And anyway, I thought you were going to take me over to help with the identification.'

I sighed. 'How about next week?'

'No, now would be perfect. If we can get this thing free. They'll all be gone later in the day – well, the corpse won't – but the others will be going when the tide starts to come in. Come on, Harriet. Let's go.'

'I'll see. It depends on the state of this oar.'

But the extraction was simple, with two of us. The oar was abraded and the wood was furry, but I would be able to sort that out with some sandpaper and varnish. It would still work, as an oar; it would work today.

So, we stopped off at the crypt to pick up biscuits and warmer clothes for me, and at the outhouse of the cottage to collect waterproofs. I hadn't had the boat out on the water since the storm and there hadn't yet been an opportunity to clean it. Jos helped me to carry it down to the water, and was astonished when I showed him how high up the beach the boat had been driven before it was engulfed.

'It's a miracle it wasn't completely wrecked.'

'Yes. I hope it's still waterproof. We'll find out, won't we? You may need to use the bailer!'

Although the sky was grey and dull, the outer islands and

northern headlands were startlingly clear and close. The sea was choppy in the cold breeze, and we took turns at the rowing. Jos was a strong oarsman, but erratic, and our bow yawed in one direction then the other. It was obvious that, as he himself explained, he had rowed only on quiet inland waters where waves didn't push one around. I took over again as we passed Death Bay; the mausoleum was an uncompromising pattern of lines and right-angles.

'Why don't you keep the boat there?' Jos asked.

'I've still got a lot of work to do on it and the tools are at the cottage. Anyway, this shore's too exposed, it would be battered to pieces in the first small gale. It's safer where it is.'

I couldn't possibly move it; the boat was protected in a special way in the bay beneath the croft.

Every surface of the boat was sticky and rough with salt, and a small pool of sandy water sloshed between my feet. But we were alive, my boat and I, and out once more upon the sea.

Jos pointed as a seal bobbed up a hundred yards away.

'Oh yes. That's Matilda.'

'No, it's Number Seven,' he corrected. 'You can tell by the gleam in her eye. Wish I had as much blubber as her. It's cold out here!'

'Aye, laddie, you need fattening up. Put a bit of flesh on those bones and colour in your cheeks.'

'You can talk. Biscuits, indeed. Not even chocolate ones, either.'

But we were rounding the corner to the seal rocks. As we moved into the lee of the headland, I swung the boat broadside and steadied it with the oars, so that Jos could look through his binoculars. He was counting bodies.

'Sixteen, including the corpse,' he said and, handing me the glasses, held the oar handles so that I could look.

My seal lay dead and bloated, surrounded by the sleeping bodies of her group. Even as I watched, a greater black-backed gull swooped down, settled its wings with a flurry, and determinedly stabbed at the dead seal's eyes.

'Doesn't it bother the others? Will they keep coming to lie here as she rots?'

'What else can they do?'

'Well, couldn't they push her body into the sea, like giving her a proper burial? Imagine watching birds peck her to pieces. It's such a waste, Jos.'

And what happens to the souls of seals? Is there a watery limbo for marine animals?

'What's wasted? Look at the gulls! Okay, it's unpleasant to watch, but the gulls are getting food, there'll be food for the fish as the remains get washed off into the sea. There are nutrients for bacteria, and for plankton. Think of the whole food chain – that corpse is providing food for thousands of other organisms. Nothing like as many benefited when she was alive – and think of all the fish and crabs she ate! It's just one big recycling factory. Fantastic! That cow should be flattered to think how many others benefit by her death!'

The argument was startling, and I looked at Jos with respect.

'I hadn't thought of that.'

'Well, you haven't been trained to think that way, that's all. French doesn't help. "*Après moi, la deluge*" doesn't apply to dead seals.'

'An indirect corollary is that it would have been selfish of me to have kept her alive as a pet.'

'That's extremely indirect, if not tortuous, but if you want to look at it from your non-global viewpoint, yes, that would be correct! However, I never even considered that as a real possibility. And neither did you, really. If you're honest, you'll know there was no way you could have made that happen.' He paused. 'You really should get a dog, Harriet.'

'You know my arguments against that.'

'Well, perhaps you'll find another hurt animal. Not that you've much room at the moment. How about a mole?'

I merely grunted in reply.

'Anyway, shall we get a bit closer and have a go at sorting out these beasts? Unobtrusively. Do you mind?'

I rowed slowly round the rocks, keeping my distance, while Jos wielded binoculars, camera and notepad. Differences were apparent between the animals, but it was a difficult and cold task. Two or three found our presence too intimidating and waddled and splashed into the water, but the others lay still for their examination. The dead one lay even stiller.

Jos pointed out how her body was swelling, presumably as bacteria from her gut swarmed into her dead tissues and produced their stinking gases. Jos said that the insides of dead whales cooked in the heat released by decomposition; their insulating blubber worked in both directions. Jos also said that the Eskimos (or the Inuit, as he called them; names and fashions change) stuffed a fresh sealskin with freshly-killed little auks, and buried it, so that the little birds fermented; a delicacy, he said, but he'd never tried it as lickle piddled auks weren't sold in British delicatessens. And an old memory, that I must have been trying to suppress, resurfaced; of something pale flopping backwards and forwards as the waves advanced and receded at the edge of the sea. The empty body of a dead seal pup, its organs and flesh eaten away so that only the thick sac of blubbery skin remained, tough like rubber. A perfect body-bag for little auks.

I enjoyed studying Jos and I tried not to be intrusive. He muttered and hummed, exclaiming with delight, electric with enthusiasm; his whole body seemed to burn with excitement and he kept repeating how glad he was, how pleased, that I had brought him here. The gain from watching and hearing him far outweighed my supposed loss. And that, in any case, was a loss that existed only in my mind. The sea bumped and slapped against the hull, and I leant over to trail my fingers in the water, and licked the salt from my fingertips.

It was impossible to put Jos ashore in the bay of the seals, so I dropped him off by the mausoleum and completed the trip to Camus Beag on my own. It was a pity that his jeans got so wet when he jumped out, but at least he didn't drop the camera. I was tired and my hands were blistered from the rough wood, but I smiled to myself as I watched his long dark figure lope swiftly towards the moor. It was a very long time since I had been of use to anyone.

Fourteen

I long to take handfuls of this beautiful spring light into the crypt with me. There is a gentleness in the light of a late May evening that should not be trapped outside and forbidden to enter. Last night, I sat outside by my fire of peat blocks until the darkness fell, and felt the breath of spring stirring the young leaves. I heard the curlew call again, and my body shattered into thousands of twinkling fragments that blew across the moor and sea. The thin smoke from the fire drifted down towards the shore in the cooling air, and peace and quiet optimism nestled close against the earth. I am so fortunate; and I give thanks. Hear my thanks, O Lord, and believe me.

I woke early this morning with the sweet acridity of peat smoke on my hair and pillow, and I suddenly needed space and empty air. A satin sea embraced the shore, and everything held its breath in sweet delight. Verticality was not the key to understanding, and I lay, at peace, upon a tomb; my eyes were closed and my arms were limp by my side, so that my sense of hearing was saturated with the hiss and suck of the sea. Even the bird calls were muted as every living thing absorbed the sensitivities of the morning. It was as though my body relaxed and lay so limp and flat that it merged with the stone, and my mind expanded and spread to the edges of the horizon. It became part of every stalk and twig and boulder, and glided over the sensuous surface of the sea, touching with self-conscious tendrils the consciousness of the benthic brain.

And thus bonded, I lay at peace, and felt my body quiver with the extension of my personal universe.

I was thus positioned when Jos found me. He called me, softly, from the chain perimeter of the mausoleum, and, with admirable control on my part, I managed not to flounder like a flatfish on the tomb, but merely raised a hand and beckoned. Before he could ask me what I was doing, I suggested that he should climb on to the adjacent tomb and do as I had been doing, relax and listen to the sea. Jos, too, is sometimes unpredictable, for immediately, without even speaking, he climbed up and lay as I suggested. I should explain that one must indeed climb and pull oneself by brute force on to the top of these tombs, because they appear to have been built to accommodate eight-foot giants of enormous girth. The enormity of the tombs is, in some ways, disturbing, creating an image of each body lying inside like a solitary match in a matchbox. What do they do with all that space?

When he had arranged his body with propriety upon the shining speckled granite, he asked what he should do now, and I told him to close his eyes and listen to the echo. I had discovered this curious phenomenon some years ago: the roof of the mausoleum is pitched in such a way that the noises of the sea reverberate and are bounced about the listener's head to form a bowl of sea-sound, that obliterates all other. Occasionally, the cry of a gull or oyster-catcher is caught and trapped, so that a flock of birds swirls and dives around one's head.

'Do you need to lie down to get the full effect?' Jos sat up, and turned his head this way and that.

'No. But I was feeling lazy because I got up early. And those steps are hard to sit on.'

'I got up early, too, but for a specific purpose. I'll tell you about that in a minute.'

He continued to turn his head, looking up at the roof and then at the lie of the land around us.

'There must be a kind of funnel effect – you see where the burn goes down to the beach? How its bed is sort of U-shaped? Hang on a minute and let me test it.'

He swung his legs over the edge and dropped off the tomb, then walked away from the mausoleum in a direct line towards the beach. After twenty or thirty yards he stopped and called. I think he called 'Harriet!', but his words were drowned in sea-noise. I shook my head and shrugged my outspread hands, so he walked further away and tried again: but I heard nothing. Then he crossed towards the shallow gully, and turned. I couldn't see what he was doing, but the whistled notes of a jerky tune, *'dumty-dumty-dumty-dahdahdah, dumty-dumty-dumty-dahdahdah'* mingled with the wave-song and criss-crossed contrapuntally to a *tutti* of jumbled notes. I waved my arms over my head, and I could see now that Jos was laughing. As a final test, he crossed the burn and moved away across the grass, and his man-made sounds were once more lost.

'You're determined to cast me as a witch, aren't you?' I said when he returned.

'I remembered it just in time! I was racking my brains for something relevant. Was it clear?'

'Perfect. It's instructive to see – and hear – the scientific mind at work. Do you want me to go and shout something edifying at you, so that you can study the effect up here?'

'No. Let's leave it for now. I really came to ask if you'd like to come on an expedition with me, down to the south coast. There's a big sandy bay marked on the west of that promontory that sticks out to the south, and I was just thinking that I'd like to see some different scenery for a change. I could do with a day off.'

'That's the bay that's called Red Sand, isn't it? Yes, I'd love to come. I haven't been down that way for years. When are you going to go?'

'Well, now, actually.'

'Now!'

'If you've nothing else pressing to do. The weather looks set fair for the day, I should think.'

'Well, why not? I'll need to get some food and drink, and put a few things in a rucksack. Am I allowed ten minutes or so to organise myself?'

'You'll need to pack a biscuit or two, because I don't want to have to share my egg sandwich with you.'

'That would be stretching neighbourliness too far,' I agreed, and we exchanged smiles.

Although the tide was going out, we decided to keep to the easy turf of the raised beach for as long as possible, and to cut over the westerly shoulder of Sgurr Mor. At first, it felt strange to be walking with a companion, along my well-known trails; to be setting off for the purpose of spending a whole day in someone else's company, of showing him the easy way across the burn, and the decaying stalker's track across the hill. But Jos's obvious happiness at the realisation of a holiday and new territory to explore bubbled out of him in unending conversation, so much so that he occasionally had to stop to catch his breath. Our progress was, in any case, slow, because we halted frequently to examine signs of other life: a clump of primroses on a warm, damp bank, perforated galls on the twigs of a stunted oak, catkins on the birches, and the cracked skeletons of sea-urchins that had been dropped by gulls. He was better at birds, and, with the tuition of my flower books and herbals, I was better at flowers; neither of us knew anything about rocks, but that didn't stop us picking up pebbles or examining the twisted contours of boulders. We sat to watch an eagle, and our binoculars swept across the sky as it swooped on still wings from the mountain slopes across the moors. We ate several of my biscuits, and watched the deer browsing in the southern sun. Jos appeared not to mind that the conversation was one-sided, and that my replies were spare and sparse. I've forgotten how to converse and conduct a dialogue, and even today, I'm still constrained by my prohibition on asking personal questions. But my deficiencies no longer made me anxious for we were, for that day, companions with a common goal, and our interests in the earth around us were complementary, and thus enlivening and enlightening.

I suppose it's a damning measure of my self-absorption that it hasn't previously occurred to me that Jos might often feel lonely for very long periods of time. While we were walking, he had been telling me about a camping trip with a group of friends, and a pub in which they had all spent a rainy day. It struck me then that he must, at least occasionally, miss such companionship.

'Have you camped on your own before? Have you ever been on your own for such long periods?'

'No, never, actually. I've known for a long time that I wanted to do field work – I like the work and I know I've got the necessary self-discipline. But I hadn't really imagined what it would be like to be working on my own, completely on my own, in the field. I suppose I'd always imagined that my supervisor would be nearby, at least, to call on, or that there'd be others on the same project. It takes a bit of getting used to.'

'It must do. Will your supervisor come over to see how you're getting on?'

'Oh, I expect so. But getting back to being alone – *you* manage. You seem to be entirely independent, and there must be weeks on end when you hardly see or speak to anyone.'

'I generally try to avoid people, yes. But don't forget that I wanted to be on my own. It was necessary for me and I've had a long time to get used to it. Even though you do think I'm a bit peculiar as a result. Probably with reason!'

'You know, I'm really glad you agreed to come with me. I thought I was going to crack up last night, with no one to talk to. I don't know, it all just got to me. This is great. And I'm glad I'm not scared of you any more – even when I saw you lying on that tomb!'

'Well, I suspect we can learn a lot from each other, Jos. You'll be relieved to hear that I'm no longer scared of you, either. And you should realise that I have never, since I came here, talked to anyone like this, let alone walked around the island with anyone. That, for me, takes some getting used to, but I'm not sure I could cope with it on a frequent basis!'

'I'm honoured! Are you coping with it now?'

'I'm thoroughly enjoying it.' ('It' depersonalised this strange situation; I couldn't bring myself to say 'being with you' because that would imply intimacy, where there was none.)

'We're of mutual benefit to each other. And – changing the subject—'

'You always do!'

'—it's a perfect day for an expedition, isn't it? Do you see the peninsula sticking out? We'll probably be able to see Red Sand when we get around that corner.'

We ate more biscuits to replenish our energy, and then ran down the dunes on to the beach in time for a very late lunch. We had collected firewood as we walked the last mile, and now we lit a small fire and boiled water in the billycan that Jos had carried in his pack. We feasted; tucked in among the low dunes and hissing marram grass, breathing the scent of burning wood and dried black kelp, we drank hot coffee and shared our meals of buttered sliced bread, sliced boiled eggs and sliced tinned meat. Sand in the sandwiches and salt on one's lips! The sight of so much flat sand invited artistry, and Jos wrote 'Jos and Harriet were here', and shuffled in circles, dragging his toes to make patterns. I told him how, when I was young ('Oh, of course. You wouldn't dream of doing it now!' 'Certainly not. Not while you're here, anyway!') sandy beaches inspired me to run and run in circles, yapping noisily, like an excited dog.

We scuffed our boots along the tideline, searching for treasure, and found the delicate grey skeleton of a heart urchin, and thin, pink, crabs' claws. Jos showed me a pale, flat shell, through which a hole, with neatly bevelled edges, had been drilled, and he told me that a snail had then sucked out the bivalve's body. At the side of the bay, where the sand met the rocks and a shallow stream of brackish water trickled seawards, we built a dam, and then another and another, all linked by narrow channels. Why had I never built dams with Tom? On the few occasions that we had been to the coast, it had always been Graham who constructed dams and castles for Tom to decorate with shells and pebbles covered in red weed. Sweet, clumsy Tom, uncoordinated and careless of his strength! Had I been left to organise the towels and food, to shake the sand from the swimming costumes, conceding our separate roles? Or had I willingly, for one day, renounced motherhood to let Graham entertain our child, and wandered lonely as a summer cloud, along the sea-washed shore? I no longer remembered, but today I discovered the uncertain delights of sand construction; how much more skilful to build a house of sand. . . .

Rockpools cradled still more treasures within their pink-encrusted walls; anemones, and coloured weed, and chitons plastered flat to stones. Hermit crabs inside winkle shells skirmished over territory, and we watched as a crab rolled a larger, empty shell between its claws, turning it and testing it for size. Then, hastily, it left its present bungalow, and twisted its soft, vulnerable body backwards into the new, unoccupied villa. Safe again, it slammed its claw sideways across the entrance, like a sliding door.

The waves were rushing in across the flat sands as we stoked the charcoal of our fire for a final brew before returning home, and we emptied our pockets and compared our hoards of shells and pebbles, bones and sea-urchins. The low dark hull of a tanker steamed along the western horizon but, apart from that, we had seen no sign of human life all day.

Yet, humans had once lived here, for, tucked at the edge of the finger of land that formed the bar, were the stone gable-ends of two small cottages. We walked over to look at the sad, derelict shrines that were dedicated to human endeavour, where families had lived and slept and worked the land and sea. Low walls remained, and the front wall of one cottage; all timber had long since rotted, and nettles and brambles filled the rooms. But the associated sadness was a product of human memory, not of the stones themselves. The crumbled cottages had opened their hearts to their surroundings, and their surroundings had climbed and tumbled in, appropriating every cranny and free corner, restoring the stone to natural, lived-in splendour. Golden lichens, feathery mosses and the delicate trefoils of wood sorrel decorated the walls, and there was thrift clinging to the sandy mortar, and a collapsed bird's nest by the door.

Do the walls of dead cottages shrink, like a dehydrated corpse? It seemed impossible that this one small area could have contained chairs and a table; and could a double bed and press have squeezed into there? How could so many human thoughts, activities and artefacts have occupied so small a space?

At the head of many west-coast bays and in otherwise-deserted glens, such derelict remains are found: monuments to disease, the magnetism of the cities, and to the long-legged haughty sheep. How could one's heart not be moved at this evidence of the ephemeral constructs of living people? (And, in contrast, the construct of the dead at Death Bay would out-survive many generations.) But now, I saw the beauty, the rightness of the living ruins, the demesne's demise; my human sadness was an anthropocentric irrelevance, for did not wasps and birds build new nests and voles dig new burrows? But Jos was saddened and bitter at the loss, and although my own acceptance surprised me, that I could so dispassionately rationalise away my own sadness, I tried to persuade him of his previous argument, that each dead thing bestowed new life. However, he remained too concerned with the human element to be convinced.

As we were leaving, he stopped to clear composted vegetation from a low bench by the wall; a scrape of his boot brought a dark gleam from the stone, and I returned to help him. There was a thick chunk of polished slate beneath the crust of plants and insects, and its ragged edges showed where it had been cracked to make a seat. From a table for the dead to a life-supporting bench! Fantasy and reality blurred together as I explained the supposed origin of the stone. The story cheered and delighted him, and we mused on the difficulties of transporting such a large lump of stolen stone.

I stopped before we left the bay, and looked back at the deserted crofts. The late afternoon sun was still bright, and the ruins on the far side of the valley were not yet in shadow. My crypt and these crofts were now linked, and the significance of the ruins whispered across the bay.

'You can scarcely see the ruins now, Jos. Look how they blend in. Merge. It hasn't taken long, has it, for those cottages to revert, and now they're part of the natural landscape.'

'That's what will happen to yours if you don't get on and mend it. I keep trying to tell you that.'

'I know. That's what I'm saying. It won't take long, a couple of winters and growing seasons, perhaps, for the cottage to become less offensive.'

With a little help from its friend; the cottage was not yet self-sufficient, and our symbiotic association hadn't yet ended.

Jos stopped and gripped me by the arm; he shook it slightly.

'You *can't* mean that you want it to fall down entirely, and decay! I don't believe you! How can you wish for your own home to collapse?'

I put my hand over his, to reassure him. He stared at me, strangely, then sharply pulled his hand away.

'I don't need it any longer, Jos. My new home is all I need. I'm just a hermit crab in reverse – you only have to consider that people shrink as they get older!'

'But you haven't even got a toilet! What will you do when you get sick, or old?'

'I shall have to manage, won't I? For Heaven's sake, tens of millions of people in this world don't have toilets, and there are thousands of people who don't have a permanent home. By choice! Anyway, I was thinking this morning about improving the lighting, by digging out the other door. Do you think I should buy some clear corrugated sheeting to use as a cover?'

'I'm not even going to think about it, Harriet. The fact that your cottage is a blot on the landscape is because it's damaged. It needs repairing, or else it's a complete and utter waste. Of everything. Money, effort, your life, your belongings.'

He stopped, as an idea struck him.

'Look, I've already offered to help you with the labouring. And

I'm sure you can pick up roofing materials cheaply, or second-hand, or something. I could try to find out next time I'm on the mainland.'

'Jos, you're very kind and thoughtful. And I do appreciate that. But no. I'm not held up for lack of money, either, you needn't worry. It's my determined intention to live in that crypt, and I shall see that the cottage grows old gracefully.'

Religious intolerance had driven me from my husband's house, back to my mother, and she left her house to me: but I sold it when she died. Tom was gone; nothing but confusion remained, and I left, to wander in the wilderness. The profits bought me the croft, and the remainder was more than adequate for my trivial financial needs. And now I needed even less, only food and drink and little else. Physical simplicity; but the mental complexity of this step was enormous as I struggled inwardly to undo the knot and find the thread.

'Jos! Think no more on't, and enjoy your day. Take life as it comes.'

I reached up and smoothed the side of his head, as one would comfort a child; a long-lost and quickly re-found gesture. His frown deepened, and he puffed out his upper lip so that the moustache bristled, but then the clouds lifted and he smiled.

'You're right, as usual. Why should I worry? It's nothing to do with me, is it, where you choose to live! Let's forget about all that. It's been a good day today, hasn't it? We must come here again.'

'Oh, there are plenty of other places to explore. But this has been special – and will continue to be for a few hours yet. We've a fair way to go!'

We didn't stop again, but nevertheless dusk was settling over the moors when we reached the crypt, and Jos had another half-hour's walk ahead of him. From the moor we watched as the corrugations of the sea turned pink in the setting sun, and then we parted and I went home to light my candles and to sleep.

Fifteen

I don't know what to do.
I no longer believe in God.

Something happened to me at the cottage yesterday. I can't remember, I can't remember why I was there. The sea was so loud, but I couldn't understand its words. I hadn't been hiding from the sea, that's not why I had been hiding, because when I heard the sea I needed to touch it. I washed and washed and washed myself. I think there may have been a boat, but I didn't care. Perhaps someone saw me but I only saw the sea.

What happened to me there? Why was I at the cottage? Was I looking for hooks? There was a red packet of mackerel hooks by the door. I can't remember, and I came home and slept.

And now, this morning, I don't know what to do.

Because I don't believe in God.

See, I have to whisper it quietly, in the darkness of the crypt. Can you hear me, Lord? Can you see me hidden here inside this crypt, into whose care I thought *you* had committed my soul and mortal frame?

I hope you don't know what I just whispered. I hope you can't read my thoughts. I hope, by denying you thus (I don't believe in God, I don't believe in God. There I have whispered it twice more, I have denied you thrice – and no cock crew) that I can switch you off, so that you will not punish me for this, the greatest sin of all. Clouds of negativities, intermingling and coalescing like the wavering ribbons of smoke from the candle, joining and spreading until the dark air is redolent of pain.

I'm not a theologian, I've never studied the intricacies and subtleties of my dead faith. I've merely tried to do as I was told, and not to question. Four decades of life and the rosary. Lost years! The love and wisdom and infinite patience and kindness of the Lord; the infinite superiority, and hard, unyielding righteousness; the capacity to forgive that was immeasurably vast, and yet the facility to punish that is frighteningly unintelligible. What sort of a being are you? No being at all, no person, nor yet people, but three nebulous strangers, conjoined as triplets, yet individual entities from whom there was no escape. And for what purpose? Must pain, guilt and struggling all predominate? Where is the beauty, where's the space and freedom to shout aloud a hymn of praise? Who decreed that we should suffer for our sins? For our faults, for our faults, for our most grievous faults.

We have all been missing the point!

By denying you, can I whisk you away from my consciousness with the flick of a handkerchief? You no longer exist; therefore I should not be afraid of reprisals. I should feel only wonder and elation, as I embrace the new truth and understanding. I should have no fear.

I wish I had no fear.

For what sort of a god is it, that reaches down and plucks innocent animals and offspring from their natural lives? Where is the reasoning in taking the best to yourselves, and condemning those of us that remain to earthly misery and eternal terror? Heaven must be cluttered with animate niceness – and for what purpose? What use? A one-way process, that leaves emptiness in its place, so that the earth's quota of spiritual resource is continuously depleted, the continuous drain leading ultimately to implosion and collapse. The earth, thus uncontrolled, would become a black hole of heavy nothingness. It is not the earth's physical laws that define the equation of collapse, but the indefinable constant of the loss of empathy.

That is not the way to Truth. And I see, at last, that the reality is multidimensional, pointing to every corner of infinity. Until now, it had been instilled in me, my mind had been enclosed and fettered, that the road was two-dimensional that led the soul between Heaven and Hell. The road was dotted with snake-pits and ladders, and misleading clues to short-cuts. The rules maintained their anarchic hold, my thoughts and movements were checked. It was ensured that self-analysis became voluntary and mandatory. Lines of escape were barred with altar rails and the flashing red lights of the sacristy, exclamation marks that indicated warnings and commands. Thou shalt; thou shalt not. Will you, won't you, will you, won't you? You *will* join the dance.

My soul's been enclosed in a spiritual box: and it's a fine irony that this *physical* box, my burrow, my shell, has suddenly shown me the exit to the clearer path. Through its confines, it releases me. The iron fetters are broken. I can reach out in all directions, seeking and finding. Help and companionship are palpable, warm, subtle and subterranean, and of the earth; I needn't be alone or frightened any more.

Why has it taken me so long?

How does one tell someone, hitherto real and all-pervasive, to whom one has spoken every day, someone who bestrode the world like a mighty colossus – how do I tell him I don't believe in him? That I don't believe he exists? I don't believe in him, or his colleagues. I can't tell him; there's nothing – no one – to tell, there's nobody there any more. They have all gone, vanished from my personal space, leaving a terrifying forty-five-year void. It has taken me all my life to start my life. Why was my age of enlightenment so late!

All my life. For all my life I have been shepherded and guided, there have always been an instruction manual and written rules, and someone to ask. Can I really, after all this time, throw all that away? Dare I abandon the strict codes and beliefs, to share myself with this unknown entity? O Lord, I'm scared. Mary, forgive me and pray for me as I leave you. Please leave me alone. Don't

chastise me and persecute me. Please leave me in everlasting peace.
Visions of Hell-fire burning, and the candle wafts up a votive prayer; see how my small, solid world flickers in the flames. It sparkles like tiny mosaics in my tears. I am entering the unknown. Help me!

The flame wobbles in the breeze as the sea-sound enters. The sound fills my ears where I kneel against the bed. My skull sings with the sound. I am healed. In the night I suffered a sea-change and I tremble with the susurrations on the shingle. God is there no more. Listen! The whispering guilt is gone, I am made whole and fragmented. *Each stone, each bead of moisture is me.* The air touches us all, we are linked by the air. The earth and waters lift up their voices and the air carries their songs. The water that gives life to living things, and rushes to the sea; the sea that gives off water to the air, water that moves and carves the very shape of the earth. And within and upon them all, life, feeding and being fed upon, living, dying. Dust to dust and ashes to ashes, and all of us enmeshed in love and continuity. The simple beauty of perfect harmony and unity.

I woke this morning, and knew that it was so. The pieces have fallen into place, and at last I comprehend. That ecstasy was there, waiting to be released, and now, at last, I can close my eyes and reach out my arms in welcome and surrender.

There! I bow my head to the floor and touch the earth with my lips. I swell my chest so that air floods in, and I blow the air out gently, through my mouth, feeling the warm dampness that it gains from me. My moisture soars into the atmosphere and will fall, as rain, upon the land and sea. The intuitive feeling of belonging, the exhilarating oneness, must be my guide, because I don't know the moral code and there are no obvious rules. And who, experiencing this, could be afraid of dying, the eternal perpetuation of one's being and perception. The implications are unknowably enormous. To be free of guilt, to experience true freedom, to be alone in bliss and unhampered, no longer watched, and yet part of a mighty, living whole. Abstract and intangible;

yet I must touch it, feel it, and be felt.

I must go down to the sea again, to the sensate sea and the sky.

The straight line of the horizon bisects these two great, unencumbered spaces. Here on the shoreline is simplicity. Here at the edge of the land, I can see the three great components, stacked one upon the other, the sky upon the sea upon the land. The air is the highest and the sea is the greatest. The sea proposes: the sea disposes. It is the dominant force here at the extremity of the land.

Once, mighty sea, you brought me a crab, a big, deep-water edible crab, pink and brown, and white-fleshed. Oarweed was attached to his shell, a flat frilly frond like a banner that advertised his presence. The storm currents had whisked and spun him to the surface, and the sea threw him, perplexed and helpless, on to my shore. And there have been other gifts: plastic plates, potatoes, a quarter-bottle of vodka, fine wooden boxes and a yellow oilskin. Gifts, teasingly hidden along the shore, but there for the taking. And I thanked you, but I didn't understand.

Forgive me, sea; I understand now – take me and make me whole.

I offer myself. Naked, I walk into the grey waves that are cold as meltwater. The cold is so intense that my legs ache, and I can't move. But I need to do penance. I think my heart has stopped – my lungs contract and force the breath from my body. The cold mortifies my flesh, it's dead and crinkled. But I submit to the pain. I stand and confess, and pray to the sea for forgiveness that my eyes were opened late. I immerse myself, I beg it to cleanse me. It embraces and enfolds me, explores my body, presses my breasts with its cold hands, so that my skin puckers and responds. I brace myself against its thrust with spread thighs, then I cup my hands and drink. I place a flat frond of fresh green weed upon my tongue, and swallow, and salt spray baptises my forehead.

The seventh wave lifts me and explodes on the shore behind me. It is a Sign: we are all One, flesh and plant and water.

Sixteen

The pea seedlings were four inches high and bushy, and I had to separate their delicate tendrils. A line of holes was waiting to receive them; the earth had been dug and mulched with compost, then raked and cleared of stones. Wire netting and black thread lay ready for the contest with the birds, and there were several jars half-filled with sea-water that would be sunk into the earth to trap hungry slugs and snails. The annual war between those of us for whom garden peas were a favoured vegetable was about to begin. It was a tense moment, and my nose began to drip as I patted another seedling into place.

'Fresh peas! Those seedlings look good!'

I'd heard Jos approaching so I had kept my head down, but he'd obviously seen my face.

'Oh, but *you* don't! I wondered why you were all muffled up—'

'—like an old woman? Thank you. You're not making me feel any better.'

I sat back on my heels, blew my red, raw nose for the hundredth time, and blinked the persistent water from my eyes. I was feeling very sorry for myself.

'I've got a cold.'

He laughed: unsympathetic bastard.

'Well, if you will go swimming in the sea, what do you expect? What, in God's name, were you thinking of?'

'It wasn't in God's name. And anyway, you don't catch colds

from the sea. I got it from MacGregor – and I suppose he got it from some damned tourist or other.'

I tucked my head down into my collar, grumpily, then the full implication of what Jos had said penetrated the pot of damp cotton-wool and mucus that was my head. I felt my cheeks burn with embarrassment. (When did I last blush?)

'Have you been spying on me?'

'Of course not. Wouldn't dream of it. People don't do things like that round here, do they? No, I was miles away on the headland and just happened to catch a movement in the water. A strange pale object thrashing around in the sea. They're strong binoculars, though – high magnification.'

'Jos!'

'I hoped it was a mermaid, but she didn't have a tail. Just a pale pink swimming costume . . . I suppose. Or were you naked?'

He spoke the last word in a hoarse whisper, thrusting his beard towards me. The skin round his dark eyes crinkled as he grinned.

'I was just having a wash, that's all. What were you doing on that headland, anyway? Peeping Tom. It's bad enough you coming here and standing on my carrots . . .'

He looked down, parodying guilt with a down-turned mouth and upraised eyebrow, and bent to straighten the thin green blades that he had flattened into the soil.

'Sorry. Here, let me put in the peas for you. You look awful. Isn't there a chair or something that you can sit on the sun, and recuperate?'

'No. But you can put the peas in, if you want. Bending down makes my nose run. Do you know what to do?'

'Nope. My parents used to buy their veg.'

'What a luxury. You need to feel around in the potting compost and unravel the roots, so that you can take out one plant at a time. Then put it – with some of that good soft compost – into the hole, and scrape some soil around it. That's right, keep it upright. Then press the soil around it. Good. Carry on!'

'What's this compost in the tray, then? You don't have it sent over from the mainland, surely?'

'No, it's my own special "Falmer's mixture". That has a good agricultural sound, doesn't it? Soil, river sand, and composted seaweed and garden rubbish, from that pile over there.'

'You should patent it, set up a cottage industry . . .'

'And you should train your seals to transport it to the mainland. A wonderfully clever idea, Jos. Why don't you just plant the peas?'

I sat on the wall and closed my burning eyes, feeling the sun hot on my face, and willing it to kill the virus. The thought of Falmer's mixture had given me the first prickings of an idea, a means of saving myself from a potentially damaging experience that was being set up to ensnare me. The shepherd was hunting out his strays, and this particular sheep had turned feral; this tough flesh was mutton, not sacrificial lamb.

When I was at the shop, purchasing food and obtaining a cold as this week's free gift, John MacGregor had also handed me a letter. In return, I handed him my list, explaining that there was no urgency, I'd probably come back in a fortnight.

'And what about Calor, Harriet? Or will you not be needing it now?'

I realised that he knew. We had each, so far, carefully avoided reference to the state of the cottage. The problem of the Calor gas had been much on my mind, for it had run out a month ago, and I had been making do with my outdoor peat fire. But although the track had been repaired, I had been worrying how I could transport the cylinder that extra distance to the crypt. But if John MacGregor knew that I now lived at Death Bay . . .

'As a matter of fact, I do need a new cylinder.' I was cautious.

'I could leave it at the usual place. Or further up the track, if that would be easier.'

Closer to the start of the path to Death Bay was the gracefully unspoken implication.

'Yes, further up the track by the first path across the moor. That would be a great help. Thank you.' I smiled at him. 'How did you know?'

'Did you think I wouldn't?' He was amused. 'If you were not at the cottage . . . There's the bothy, right enough, but that wouldn't be – suitable, shall we say? And when a person moves to a new place, a person soon makes tracks on the ground, and leaves signs, sledges, smoke, that sort of thing. That could only be seen from the sea, of course,' he added hastily. 'It's unlikely anyone much would be walking that way, now.'

I sighed, and nodded. 'Ah well. So everyone knows.'

'The few folk here on the island, aye. But it's no one else's business, is it, Harriet? And as far as I'm concerned—' he leant over the counter, '—it will stay that way. You'll get your own place set to rights one of these days.'

'Yes. There's no rush. I'm busy with the garden just now.'

'Aye. No rush. But I'll bring the Calor across later this week. Now then, don't forget your letter.'

He pointed to where I'd left it on the counter; I hadn't wanted to pick it up. I put it in my pocket, shouldered my pack, and nodded goodbye.

From the postmark and the style of its printed address label, I knew the envelope was from the parish office. I was rather afraid that I knew what it was going to say. I was right.

'Dear Miss Falmer, May I introduce myself as your new parish priest. I believe we have met once before, briefly, at the church, and I have been looking forward to meeting you again and talking to you. I know there are often unavoidable difficulties in reaching St Thomas's from the islands, and I have been wondering if I might, instead, visit you? I am planning to visit the island in mid-July and would greatly enjoy the opportunity of meeting you again. I hope this will be convenient . . .'

There was no escape. It was no good my writing and saying that I'm sorry, you're wasting your time, I don't believe in God. It was also futile not to reply. He would come here anyway and, in the former case, with even greater haste and vigour, prepared to exorcise the demon of unbelief. Father Peters, striding along the track with his black robe flapping like the avenging angel! Turbulent priest! I cannot believe that I once hoped for his visit, longed for the mutual exchange of gifts, tea and biscuits for gentle benediction; that (profanity!) I lay in the doorway of my future home and fantasised about his coming, with reverential bliss.

Who was I then? I was a stranger, unawakened, unevolved, and now extinct. I thought I was Mrs Harriet Falmer, a woman who was misled into believing that hers was a marriage that was made in Heaven, and therefore could not be unmade. A woman whose burden of guilt so crushed her that she was trapped inextricably in uxoriousness, and refused to admit the obvious truth. What fantastical conditioned reflex and hysterical contortions had led me to retain my husband's name, yet single title? Had I, Harriet Longmore, really believed that the legal severance from my husband was disallowed by God? And that we were condemned to be for ever united by an unbreakable bond? I know that I had long ago ceased to question the mental convolutions that had embedded this idea in my consciousness; they had been the ravings of a sick mind. The idea and its consequences had become so much a part of my being and my daily behaviour that they no longer existed as separate entities, to be picked up and queried. The Lord had joined us; and although Graham and I lived apart, I considered that our separation was merely geographical.

As I sat there, sniffing, in the sun, I realised that the truth had been rejected and buried beneath layers of inherited and mindless ritual. There is no God: I am free! Twice free! I've been unmarried for ten years. I'm Miss Harriet Longmore. I am me! Harriet Falmer exists no more!

'What are you smiling at? Can you see how inefficient I'm being, even with your eyes closed?'

I opened my eyes in shock. I'd forgotten Jos was there. He was sitting back on his heels, looking up at me. His face and arms were tanned, and his tangled dark hair shone in the sun.

'I didn't know summer colds made one happy. Or are you delirious?'

'Probably! No, I'm very happy. So you've finished! You've done that well for a beginner. That's a very orderly row of peas.'

'I finished about five minutes ago, but you looked so peaceful that I just left you to it.'

'Despite this cold, I feel peaceful, and happy, and very – free.'

'But you've always been totally liberated, as far as I can see. Why the sudden revelation?'

'Falmer's mixture! Throw it away! It's now Longmore's mixture. Not quite so evocative, but full of magical growth factors.'

'What *are* you talking about?'

'Jos, listen! I want you to do something for me. No, not more planting. I want you to write a letter for me. To say that Harriet Falmer doesn't live here any more.'

'But why? I can't do that, you do live here.'

'Yes, but I'm Harriet Longmore. I'm no longer Harriet Falmer. Don't worry, I'm not feverish or suffering from dementia. Just give me time to explain.'

It wasn't going to be very easy. We put the bird-deterrents and slug traps in place, then I let him into the cottage to wash his hands at the sink. He looked around at the growing decay in obvious distress, but without comment, then we walked slowly back towards the crypt. I noticed that he had brought nothing with him, no binoculars or rucksack, not even a pullover, and I wondered vaguely why he'd come, but I was too preoccupied with thinking how to explain my change of name.

Necessarily, when I did, I omitted much, and I told him merely that I had been married and was now divorced. I made it seem a recent severance as, indeed, it was; psychologically, it had occurred within the last half-hour.

Jos looked at me strangely, and was less surprised than I expected. But then he reminded me of our first, awkward meeting, of which the sole aim and basis had been the delivery of the letter to 'Mrs G. Falmer'.

'But why did you have to pretend to me and to everyone else that you were not married, when you were? And now you're not. Married, that is.'

'It's too complicated to explain. And it's my private business, anyway. You will keep referring to me at the shop as Miss Falmer, won't you? I don't want to have to explain to anyone else.'

'So I'm the only one to know? Well, well, I'm honoured! Okay, Harriet Longmore, merry divorcée. What now? What's this peculiar letter you want me to write?'

'It's difficult to tell you this. I recently abandoned Catholicism.' That sounded pompous, but I had to get this explanation finished. 'The priest on the mainland wants to interrogate me and persuade me to return to the Church, but I don't want to see him. Unfortunately, I know he'll come here anyway, whatever I say.'

'Can't you hide? That's something you've been always been good at, and he surely won't find you at the crypt.'

'Yes he would. He would find me at the crypt, that's probably the first place he'd look. So the safest way of escape is for you, please, to write a nice, polite, formal note, explaining that Miss Falmer has left the island, and has left no forwarding address. You don't need to sign it with your own name, if you don't want to. And post it on the mainland, don't hand it in at the shop. Or enclose the envelope in a letter to a friend, ask them to post it. Please, Jos.'

Jos thought about the proposition, frowning slightly. He clearly disapproved of the task, but he could see its harmless logic. He followed me into the crypt as I looked for paper and envelopes in a cardboard box.

'It smells better now, no longer like a damp dungeon.'

'Joss-sticks! I use them sometimes in the evening.'

His eyebrows shot up and his eyes widened, then I distinctly, despite the dim light, saw him flush. He looked downwards, seemingly avoiding my eyes.

'Where did you get . . . them?' The last word was slightly stressed.

I blushed for the second time that day (that year? that decade?) and then started to giggle.

'I found them in the attic. Luckily the mice hadn't touched them. I bought them years ago, long before I knew you!'

'Lucky for me! I hope you don't run out.'

He snorted, and then we both laughed self-consciously, like children sniggering quietly at a dirty joke, hoping that an adult wouldn't overhear.

But I sensed a sudden tenseness in him, and his eyes glittered blankly in the candlelight, so that I was flustered and turned away, and blew my nose. The sheep rolled her yellow eye, and I swear the dragon leered.

'Come and sit outside, and I'll dictate.'

I handed him the paper, and a book on which to rest, and showed him the most comfortable rock as a seat.

'I don't like doing this, Harriet. What if this priest comes over anyway, to make enquiries? And asks what the Hell – or whatever priests ask – I was doing with your mail?'

'It will be all right, don't worry. You don't have to give him an address. I will still be here, in any case, and if necessary I will just have to own up and face the music. Now – *'Dear Father, your letter for Miss Falmer arrived the other day. However, she no longer lives here'* – got that? – *'and hasn't left a forwarding address. I thought you should know, to spare you an unnecessary visit. Yours sincerely . . .'* etcetera.'

I watched as he wrote, repeating the phrases where necessary.

' *"Joseph Allen."* So that's what it stands for. I'd wondered. Very biblical.'

'I was named after my great-grandfather, so there's no great significance in it. But what do you have to do with biblical things now? You've just told me that you've abandoned all that. Or have you merely switched from one sect to another, Catholicism to strict Methodism, perhaps? No booze, no swearing, no fun. No sex.'

'No! Not at all! I . . . Oh Hell, Jos, that's one of those "Have you stopped beating your husband?" questions.'

'Is that why you just got divorced? Because your old man wasn't here to beat you up?' He was abruptly sneering, vicious. 'Or do you go in for self-flagellation? You need to be a masochist to live like this, Harriet!'

'Stop it, Jos!'

But he couldn't, the destructive urge was driving him on. He leapt to his feet, throwing the writing paper on the ground. His face and words were ugly.

'This stinking, scented hole! Cold baths! Lying on top of tombs to get your kicks! What is this? Necrophilia? Black magic? Is this why you don't want the priest to come? Do you dance naked in the moonlight, too? Fuck with the fishes?'

He stepped towards me, and I stood back quickly to give him room to leave, but I stumbled on the low stones and, staggering, dropped my rolled-up handkerchief. The blue agate that I had been holding, smoothing and rubbing with my thumb, fell and rolled at Jos's feet. He saw it, and I thought for a moment that he would grind it into the earth, but he suddenly stood still. His shoulders slumped and the anger left his face. Wearily, he bent down and picked up the agate, and held it out to me.

He was too close and the hurt was too great. We needed space.

'Why don't you take a few days off, and go back to the university, or visit your family? You need to get away from here for a bit. It's too . . . limiting, here.'

He was silent.

'Go on, Jos.' I was gentle, persuasive. The pain had numbed me. 'It's what you need. Nothing much is happening with the seals – you've got a couple of weeks before the pups arrive, haven't you? You can afford the time.'

'Yes.'

The letter lay on the ground. The risk was enormous, but I, too, had to survive.

'And please take the letter with you. I'm sorry. But it's necessary. Please.'

'All right. I need the envelope.'

His hands were trembling, and the address was barely legible, but he put the letter inside and licked the flap. His voice and expression were grey and dull.

'I'll get tomorrow's boat.'

I nodded, and he turned away without another word. I went

into my cave and closed the makeshift door.

The fever brought strange lurid dreams and I woke, sweating, hot blood pounding behind my eyeballs. I had been dreaming of Graham, screaming at Graham, with the exhilaration of a shouted argument. I think I had woken myself with shouting. Only two or three times during our marriage had we screamed at each other in fury (Graham, as I have mentioned before, preferred weak diplomacy to outrage) but the fights had stimulated us, sweeping us along with their increasing intensity, so that we scarcely knew what we did: and revelled in it. It was a different measure of our mutual lust, and the post-bellum concessions were climactic. And now Graham was no more. Throughout all these years of my self-imposed exile, I'd believed he was there; I hadn't wanted to see him, nor had he wanted me, but he was mine and I was his. He'd been there, in my head, to argue with in cold logic and cool irritation. The passion was necessarily gone, but I'd still thought him mine, and had tried to remain true in thought and mind, to the matrimonial vow. I had been cast out; the weight of guilt and oppression crushed my family ties. I had left my husband and my Catholic child. My mother had cared for me and, throughout the mad torment, I had still believed him mine. Divorce by law was an unacceptable irrelevance, a paper-thin document that floated away lightly on the wind of madness. The law of God had been engraved on stone, and what had been said could not be unsaid.

And now, I was quite alone. I supposed that my ex-husband was living a normal, middle-class life with a normal middle-class wife; perhaps they also had normal middle-class children, and they all attended that golden sandstone church, that had been renovated and cleaned, paid for by its worthy parishioners. Perhaps they all shook the Provost's hand on the steps after the service. But I was not curious. I lived my apparently abnormal life that was necessarily class-less because I was alone. Was I abnormal? I supposed so; but I was not mad. From what deep pit of fear had Jos's words welled up? Those words, too, cannot be unsaid. But he is wrong; he doesn't understand.

A black chasm has been opened, and yet the distance between us was so reduced that one light touch might have discharged a spark. The danger, for both of us, would have been immense. Oh, Jos Allen! Haste ye away!

Seventeen

'Sorry! J.'

That was all it said. In the space was written 'Harriet Longmore', but the card had been sent inside an envelope that was addressed, in type, to 'Miss Harriet Falmer'. Very discreet.

I turned the card over, expecting one of those striking photographs of wildlife – an otter, an eagle, or even a wistful seal pup – that are found in every newsagent. Two nude women stood knee-deep in water. One, full-buttocked, had turned away to scoop water over her arms, but the other flaunted her white voluptuousness *en face*, as she lifted one arm to catch up her hair. Pastel pinks, blue-grey and green, dusky, delicate pointilliste dabs: relaxed and tender, warm-water *baigneuses*, conjured by the painter's touch.

Eighteen

I stand on the edge of the world.

The globe turns, and we (the land, the sea and I) move into darkness. Pale darkness, defeating the stars. Midnight darkness. Midsummer silence, that hums below the threshold of hearing with noisy energy, and saturates the senses.

Midsummer madness, midsummer gladness, midsummer sadness; post-vernal tristesse. Poor mad, glad Harriet, who dreamed of schoolboy love-letters, and was chased around her *Lebensraum* by a figment of her imagination. Who was frightened to remove her fig-leaf, for fear of the young Allen, who coiled like a dark serpent, with glinting binocular vision, at the edges of her sea-damp eyes.

I stand here alone, on the horizon of the turning Earth, like a dark pillar reaching up towards the strengthening stars. I pour a libation on to the mountain top; the alcohol evaporates into the sky and the peat-flavoured water trickles to the sea.

Is the seal-watcher asleep? Or is he sitting outside his tent, drinking the intoxicating midsummer air? He'd had a great time, he said, spent most evenings in the pub with his friends. Catching up, he said.

'You'll be coming back here to give your hangover a rest, then,' John MacGregor said, and they all laughed.

'You'd better give the lad a can to take across with him,' said Robbie. 'It's lonely over there. Maybe you should take a couple.'

He tilted his head towards me, and grinned.

I'd wanted to shut the door quietly, unobserved, and to tiptoe away and hide until they'd gone, but the clanging bell had shouted my arrival. Their heads had turned, and the enormity of Jos's presence had filled the shop. I was gauche and speechless. He didn't flush or look in any way abashed.

'Hi, Harriet! I'm back.' Casually, unconcerned.

'Oh. Hallo.'

I tried to sound non-committal, as though I hadn't really been aware that he had left, but the brisk walk and my embarrassment made me damp with sweat.

'Morning, Harriet. Nice to see you looking well. Island life suits some better than others, doesn't it, Jos? Jos here's been living it up in the city, by the sound of it. Wild parties every night.'

'Nice to get back, though, isn't it?' Robbie Ferguson had been watching me all this time, and now he picked up his cigarettes from the counter. 'Well, I'll be away, then. See you tomorrow, John.'

He brushed past me, where I stood at the door, and I forced myself to say goodbye.

Jos was picking up his purchases, and he waited while I bought mine. I willed him to leave, but he leant against the counter, chatting light-heartedly, asking how the weather had been, and telling us about the porpoises he'd seen from the boat.

'I'll walk over with you. I'm finished here.'

'All right.'

How could I refuse? But my body wanted to twist and curl with rejection. We left the shop together.

'Jos, I don't want to walk up through the village with you. Everyone will see us and gossip. You go on alone.'

'What? Whatever do you mean?'

'Oh, you know how they talk, it's not right.'

'But we're neighbours, Harriet. And where would you go, meanwhile? It's not as though there are any other shops, and you can't go and sit in full view on the bridge until I'm out of sight. It's only to be expected that we'd walk up the track together. What's the matter with you?'

He seemed genuinely exasperated. He was right, of course. And our standing there in public, arguing intently, was much more revealing than any casual walk between neighbours. I looked back, and saw Robbie Ferguson sitting on the wall by the shore, looking up towards us. I set off quickly, and Jos strode beside me.

'Slow down a bit! I'm really unfit after last week. Oh – I posted your letter, by the way.'

I'd almost forgotten about the letter; the postcard had dominated my thoughts.

'You know, I'd forgotten how fantastic it was to have proper food, food that was prepared for you and set down on a table with proper cutlery and glasses. And people! It all seemed so crowded. But it was great to be back. Beer! Curries! Even music!' He laughed. 'It was hard to believe that this island even existed, when I was over there. Life's a lot simpler in the city.'

I heard the unspoken counterstatement in his words, the allusion to the complexity of our life here, and I nodded, scared, yet relieved, that we were now to talk about ourselves.

'I suppose you mean simpler because there are so many people. Thus one's relationships with other people are too . . . diffuse, I suppose. Less concentrated.'

'What do you know about it, Harriet? You haven't lived anywhere else for years. You don't know what people get up to in normal life, do you?'

We were out of sight of the village, and I had stopped, hoping that we might sit down to discuss this matter rather than pacing along with heavy packs, short of breath for rational conversation. But Jos had carried on, and his curtness had instantly snipped the thread. He waited for me to catch up, and we walked on in silence. After a few moments he looked at me.

'Harriet, are you still cross with me? About the shitty things I said? I'm really sorry. I guess this place had just got to me. I needed a break, you were right. Incidentally, you did get my card, didn't you?'

'Yes.'

Oh yes, I received your card. Can't you tell, merely by looking at me, that I received its message, and I don't know how to respond?

'As soon as I saw it, I wanted to sent it to you! A friend of mine had come up for the day, and we went to the museum because it was raining. He was looking for a picture of the Viking longship, for some project or other, when I saw that card. I'm sorry there wasn't one of a single woman in the sea – but that was the best I could do!'

His voice was light, amused, almost indifferent.

'How did you explain it to your friend?'

(Had they laughed about me, dismissively?)

'Oh, I don't know. I told him some tale about nudist colonies and mermaids! Actually, I fancied the woman in the painting. Did you know, by the way, that sailors used to think that sea cows were mermaids? Not very flattering, was it?'

'No. Thank you for the card. And for the apology. I'm glad you had a good break.'

Poor cow. Poor silly Harriet. I let him tell me about a film he'd seen, and we talked in airy bursts, small bubbles of sound. Then we reached the upward climb towards the pass, and there was no need to talk. I was tired and empty, and I walked too slowly, so I told Jos not to wait for me, for he had a longer walk.

'Are you sure you don't mind? I hope the tent's still there. I left it full of boulders in case there was a storm!'

I know, Jos, I know. I went there when the boat had gone, to find and exorcise our demons. All right, I lie; I went there to pry and spy. I wanted to find out more about you. I examined your tins of food and your cooking pots, I smelt the stale smell of your abandoned clothes. And, Jos, I lay inside your cold, damp sleeping bag, smelling your sweat, and trying to see my nakedness through your lonely eyes. I lay in your bag and watched the sea, I saw a mermaid on a dolphin's back, but the vision of my thin, pale body filled my eyes with blind disgust, so that I saw myself as crazy and perverted. I saw what you saw, Jos; but I also thought that I felt the heat of curiosity, a heat that was fuelled further by the impressions of bathing belles. *Belle lettre*! But no, I was wrong. It was merely a hastily apologetic postcard.

Poor silly cow, lying wounded upon her rock, victim of an emotional storm.

So, I sit here alone, waiting for the midsummer dawn. It's cold on the mountain top, but the sea is a black silk blanket and the stars send down light that is thousands of years old, light that carries ancient unreadable stories that still seem to us as new. And the warm blue agate in my hands sings stories of the land and sea.

Nineteen

'But when do you think they'll come?'

'Late evening, I should think. They'll surely wait until dusk at least, they'll want you to be inside, even in bed.'

'Why don't I go over to the bothy? We could barricade the crypt somehow, so they can't get in and do any damage, and then we can go away. They won't wait around, I don't suppose, if I'm not here.'

'I don't know, Harriet. I think they'll just come and look for you. They'll come over to my tent – if they're not totally legless – and they can get most of the way to the bothy by Land Rover if they really want to.'

'Are they after you, too, then, that you think they'd bother to go all that way?'

'No. I don't think so. Harriet, I'm sorry, but from things that they said, they obviously expect us to be together. If you're not here they'll expect you, well, to be with me.'

Jos looked away, embarrassed.

'Oh. I see.'

'So I don't think our absence is going to help. We've got to do something positive to stop them.'

We were standing on the moorland that overlooked both Camus Beag and Death Bay. I'd been gathering crowberries, the small, reddish-black berries that are so bitter uncooked but which, stewed, liven up even cold, tinned meat. I was working my way down towards the sea, so hadn't noticed Jos as he came pounding over the moor. He had shouted, urgently, and had arrived dripping sweat and angst.

'Ferguson and the sheep-shearers are coming over,' he gasped. 'I came straight to warn you.'

Droplets of sweat trickled down his temples and caught in the edges of his beard.

'Why to warn me? What are they going to do?'

'I don't know. They just want to give you a fright, I think.' He took a deep lungful of air and tried to control his voice. 'Ah. God! I'm exhausted, I've never walked so fast in my life . . . Phoo! Let me sit down a minute and I'll tell you.'

He collapsed on to the ground, and I waited while he caught his breath. I hadn't seen him since he had returned from the mainland, when we had walked back together for part of the way. On that occasion we had parted amicably enough, on a superficial level, but we had thereafter kept out of each other's way.

'Where are they, though? There's no one on the track.'

'No. It's okay. For a while anyway, I think. They've still got some shearing to do. I overheard them talking.'

'Where? In the village? Start at the beginning.'

'I had to go in this morning because I wanted to collect the post – I was expecting a parcel. Okay? Anyway, as I was walking in, I had just passed the bridge, and there's that old stone seat – you know the one? Well, Robbie Ferguson was sitting there with a couple of mates, rough-looking characters. They were pretty loud, passing round a bottle, having a good time. Anyway, I just sort of nodded and went on to the shop, and I asked John who the two blokes were, and he said they were the shearers. They'd come over on the boat yesterday. I made some comment about them looking pretty well away, and he laughed and said, "Aye, they like to have a good time. No doubt Robbie's entertaining them while they wait for the ewes to be gathered." We talked about them for a bit. They come over each year, apparently, but since there aren't too many sheep any more, they just have a good time, socially. Out of their minds, most of the time, I should think.'

'Go on. How do you know they're coming here?'

'Well, of course I had to come back past them again, and I suppose I was walking fairly fast, as usual. Ferguson called out something daft—'

'What?'

'I can't remember, Harriet. Something silly.'

'Tell me!'

'If you really want to know, he said: "Rushing back to your fancy woman, are you?" Not very original. And something about why didn't you, Harriet, make a spell that . . . Oh Hell, Harriet. I can't remember. I don't want to remember. It was just stupid. Drunken talk. And anyway, it was just words, it doesn't matter. It isn't as though it's true, anyway, is it?'

Jos was upset, impatient, and cold nausea tugged at my throat.

'I just tried to laugh, and sort of waved, and carried on. But I knew they were still talking about me, because when I looked back they were still watching me and had their heads together. I didn't like that, really, because I'd thought that I had been getting on all right with Ferguson. I couldn't stand not knowing what they were saying, so I went round the corner into the wood, and doubled back so that I could hear.'

'That was risky. What if they'd seen you?'

'I know! I was dead scared! But I did it, anyway. They were all talking and laughing, their voices were getting louder again, and I could hear Ferguson going on about you living in a cave, and being a witch. And how he'd seen you . . .'

'Go on.'

There was a taste of vomit in my mouth, and Jos's face was suddenly lined and pale.

'Christ, Harriet! What do you get up to? He was going on about your *tits*, if you must know. And then your fox. It was disgusting, Harriet, I could hardly bear to come here, after that. I was so ashamed.'

'He must have been drunk! You *can't* have believed him? No, Jos!'

'They were very drunk. When they were all talking it was crazy, all slurring and whispering and then shouting. They were getting very excited about foxes, but I couldn't understand why, it was very confused. I was going to leave, but then one of the shearers said he wanted to see this witch, and that got them excited all over again. The gist of it seemed to be that they'd drive over this evening, after the shearing, and, presumably, after a good few more drams, give us both a good scaring.'

He sat silently, then, looking at his hands, which were clasped around his knees. I closed my eyes, and willed my body to shrink away. Not Ferguson; Ferguson talking, destroying . . .

'They were very drunk even then. It was – what? – nearly midday when I left. They'll probably never get here, they'll be too pissed by tonight.'

'They have hard heads. John MacGregor once told me he'd seen them get through a bottle each in one day. I'm sorry you're caught up in this, Jos.'

'What's it all about, though? Why does Ferguson have this thing about you?'

'I don't know.' (Why *does* he? I don't know what to do.) 'He's just bored, I suppose, and I don't fit in with the normal pattern. And I played a trick on him and his father once – but it was entirely harmless.'

I explained about my performance. It had been several years ago: the Fergusons had tried to drop their pots off Camus Beag. They'd brought the boat in close, and wallowed, staring at the croft.

'I couldn't stand it. I went outside, and stood there, in the wind, with that long black skirt blowing round my legs. Finn was just a cub, standing at my heels – that gave me the idea, really. I raised my arms and spread my fingers – like this – and pointed at the boat. And then – it was an incredible coincidence! – there was an awful shriek behind me and Connan, my herring-gull, flew down towards us. He skimmed round my head and arms, I suppose he thought I had food for him. I waved him towards the boat, pretending to throw food, and he screamed and spun out towards the sea. It was like sending a missile towards the boat.'

I was a witch, dressed in black, in blowing robes, surrounded by my familiars: a stark untruth in black and white.

'And?'

'The Fergusons left, actually.'

'Hmm. I can see that Robbie wouldn't easily forget a thing like that. What about . . . all the rest of it?'

'Entirely his own sick imagination, alcohol, and the need to make a good story. Please forget it, Jos.'

He nodded, but his eyes shifted away from mine.

'Anyway, we need to think what to do.'

We discussed it, and agreed that merely running away and hiding would not be a good strategy. Jos was vehement that we must do something positive to dissuade the invaders from investigating either the crypt or his tent.

'A performance along the lines of your witch act, that would really scare them away.'

'Thereby reinforcing the idea of my unnatural behaviour, so that they return persistently and with an augmented army. Jos, I have to live here, for the rest of my life. Unlike you!'

'Well, look, it doesn't have to be an act that's specifically associated with you. This place is pretty ghoulish, anyway, isn't it, with the mausoleum? We'll have to use that in a general sort of way.'

'Enlarge upon the existing atmosphere. Yes! A supernatural occurrence, associated with the mausoleum, rather than me. Yes!'

Suddenly we were both beaming at each other, caught up in the idea of play-acting; that we would be dealing with real people, in a potentially threatening situation, was temporarily forgotten.

'I think that somehow we have to lure them down to the mausoleum, and give them a good fright.'

We tossed various ideas back and forth, exaggerating and elaborating and rejecting, until finally we devised a plan.

'Yet we can't just sit and wait all evening. What if they don't come? And how will we know when to start?'

'Look. We can see the track from up here. We'll prepare everything, then we'll keep watch. The Land Rover will probably have its lights on, and even if it hasn't, we'll be able to pick it out through the binoculars. They're as good as night-glasses, at dusk.'

We went down to the crypt to gather together the few 'props' that we would require. As usual, I made tea, and when the air cooled in the early evening, I lent Jos a large pullover; he had left his parcel and his rucksack in the copse by the pass, so that he might get here more quickly. He hadn't been here, to the crypt, since the day that he wrote the letter that severed my connection with Father Peters and the Catholic church. Had Jos really said those cruel things before he left? And Robbie Ferguson? Such foul-mouthed allusions. Was I a victim of my own harmless nakedness? If I were a man, my behaviour might have been dismissed as mere eccentricity. As Jos sat there, wearing my pullover, drinking my tea, his gaze blank and inward-looking as he stared out to sea, I longed to enlighten him, and explain. But the time was wrong.

Even if we had not been forewarned by the sight of the Land Rover on the distant track, we would have been alerted by the noise of Robbie's gang as they staggered over the moor towards Death Bay. It was only ten o'clock, but although the sky was still light, the shadows in the valley were deep and undefined.

We had barricaded the crypt door as best we could, with driftwood and old fencing wire. I had doused the fire with water, and had removed the wet peat-blocks so that only cold ashes remained. They would not be allowed to think that I was nearby and hiding. My heart was thudding and my hands were cold and damp when I heard the men's hoarse whispers as their heads rose up upon the skyline. They stood still for a moment, staring and searching, before they would commit themselves to the bowl of darkness that lay below them. Their hushed voices were clear and rough in the still evening air.

'There it is. See those stones over there, that's the entrance. I cannot see a fire.'

'Does she live *there*, then? In that hole?'

'Nobody stirring there, you're right.'

'She'll be inside, most likely. 'Less she's out on her broomstick.'

There were cackles of laughter, abruptly hushed.

'Hush, man, you'll be waking the dead with your noise.'

'Aye, right enough. There's the three of them down there, in the tombs. They'll hear you, Angus, with your great loud mouth!'

Robbie waved his arm, swaying, towards the mausoleum, and they all sniggered and moved close together. Then they came skidding and snorting down the hillside, slipping and grabbing at each other's arms. They wandered around, a shifting, indefinite group, on the flat turf below the crypt, and stood looking up towards the entrance. One man was strangely hump-backed, until he dropped his sack.

At that point, I lit the candle that was sheltering at the base of one of the tombs; its flickering light could only have been a pin-prick at the edges of their vision, but it would delicately jab until it snared them. I slipped away, crouching, towards the sea. My hands were shaking and I could hardly breathe. If the men were not attracted towards the mausoleum, they would continue onwards towards the crypt and our plan would fail. They would burst in and invade my home. And I was also terrified lest they were not duped, and they searched for us and found us. There would be no laughter in them then; the joke would be turned bitterly against us, if they found us, dark-clothed with blackened faces, co-scripting this play upon their superstitions. I was suddenly, inexplicably, terrified – but at least Jos was here.

Jos was alone and exposed upon the sacrificial slab, alone to play his role of resurrection. The men were still muttering and havering, but now one of them broke away and moved quickly up the slope towards the crypt. He crouched and ran, like a boy playing cowboys and Indians with his friends, and within seconds he had reached the rocks. He stooped to one side of the entrance; I could see him reach down and touch the ground.

'It's closed up. She's away!' he shouted, not whispering at all.

But even as he called, there was a loud, deep knocking from the mausoleum.

'Look! A light! By the tombs. Robbie, come down here, man. Quick!'

Robbie ran back down the slope towards his friends, and I saw the pale moons of their faces as they turned towards the sound and the dying sunset.

'It must be her. She's down there!'

The candle-flame danced like a will-o'-the-wisp, and the knocking was repeated, slowly, evenly, three times more.

'What's she doing, she's in the tombs!'

'No, it's not her. She's not here. The fire's cold and the place is all shut up.'

'Come on. We'll look, then. Come on.'

Bunched together, they started to approach the mausoleum, cautiously, uncertainly, none of them wanting to hang back and be taken for a coward. When they were within about twenty yards of the steps I tugged hard on my rope, and the spiked iron chain that made a token fence swayed and clanked and rattled. At the same moment, Jos, who had been lying flat on top of the middle tomb, sat up; he had his back to the men and he sat bolt upright, his legs straight out in front of him. The mausoleum was a black mass of shadow, and his upper body was a dark pillar appearing from the tomb.

There were heavy oaths, and a man cried out, chokingly. But one of them, braver, called:

'No, it's just the woman, having us on. Here, Harriet! We're coming in there after you.'

'No, Lachie, come away! It's not her – it's going back into its coffin. Oh God. No!'

The voice began moaning.

Somehow, Jos had contrived to shift his body along the tomb to the edge that was furthest from them. I could just see that his legs dangled over the edge that was towards me. He must have inched forward on his thighs, because his legless torso appeared not to have moved. Now he groaned loudly, and slowly lowered himself on to the ground, so that, from the men's point of view, he disappeared. No humped corpse lay upon the slab, which gleamed emptily in the pale remaining light of the sky.

As Jos crawled towards me where I lay in the gully of the stream bed, I saw that one of the men, Lachlan the brave, had climbed over the chain to get a better view of the shining stone. I blew softly into my penny whistle, sliding quickly up and down the scales and, in my imagination, I followed the silver trail of the thin chromatic sounds as they funnelled upwards from the sea, bubbling into the mausoleum roof, and spilling out again, tumbling and echoing, twisting their cold, precise fingers into the guts and faint hearts of the three mighty warriors, so that the men were temporarily turned to stone. They were transfixed by the ghostly tune.

Jos threw a pebble at the mausoleum roof and its sharp 'ping' acted like a trigger, releasing the statues so that, with ugly yells and moans, they leapt crazily and drunkenly across the valley floor. The hillside was too dark to see their progress, but soon three figures, one carrying a bundle on his back, were seen briefly on the skyline, before sinking down towards the east.

We lay where we were, quite silent, knowing that if they, and their whisky-stimulated courage, returned, we would have no escape. But the valley was quiet, save for the sleepy evening cries of sea-birds and the shushing of the sea. Eventually, Jos climbed up to the ridge and, when he returned, reported that he had seen the lights of the Land Rover heading back towards the pass.

There had been something frighteningly ugly about the show, and we didn't feel inclined to discuss it further. There was also an uneasiness between us, associated with anticlimax, and with future uncertainties.

'We could light a fire on the beach, and have a brew-up there,' Jos suggested, and I was grateful for his quiet diplomacy, because I had no wish to go home yet.

We went back to the crypt and collected food and drink. The

small candle-flame still trembled by the tomb and I pinched it out, and patted the tombs, thanking them and asking their forgiveness for disturbing their summer dreams. Then we lit our fire amongst the boulders, and we watched the stars and the pale, shifting lines of foam. The heat warmed our fronts and faces, and we ate and drank, and dozed, and talked inconsequentially of this and that; no dissection of events or wondering mention of 'What if . . .?' I would have liked to be at sea, safely buffered by its strength, but I was indolent with aftermath, and could not move.

With the dawn came cold, and a renewal of courage as the world came back to life around us. Jos had saved me, and I hope he understood that I didn't know what to say. He helped me remove the barricade once more and I touched his arm in gratitude before he left. The dragon yawned and grinned, and the crypt was inviolate as I lay down, at last, to sleep.

Twenty

'I eat foxes for breakfast.' It was a plain statement; he was quite matter-of-fact.

'What did you say?'

'I can't catch that sheep. But a fox would fuel my flames very nicely.'

'Are your flames going out?' I looked up in alarm.

'We need them to be bigger for the winter, to keep us warm.'

'But it's still summer!'

'I know! But we need to plan ahead, Harriet.'

'I don't seem to be able to do that just yet. Tell me, dragon, why are you here? A phoenix in a tomb I could understand. Why you?'

'We're creatures of the earth and sky. Had you forgotten that dragons live in caves. Be thankful you're not a virgin, Miss Longmore, or I would have eaten you!' He licked his lips and winked, salaciously.

I blinked the sleep from my eyes and got out of bed, to push the makeshift door aside. The mausoleum slept in shadow below me, and the clear air sucked up sounds and swallowed them. Stillness lay over the land, knee-deep, and I needed to wade within it.

I dressed, and made tea on the gas-ring, then went out into the fresh morning. I crossed the valley and walked up on to the moor. Below me lay the ruined cottage; I could see neat green rows of vegetables in the garden, and the top of the rowan tree outside the front door. Ahead of me rose the hills, massive and welcoming, their near flanks shadowy with the promise of freedom. The peace of perfection was treacle-thick around me; it was not an illusion or a dream, but real, tangible, intimate. My boots scraped through the heather as I passed the cottage. I crossed the shore above the beach and felt the turf crisp beneath my feet. I trod on thyme and the scent made me pause and reach down into the stillness to feel its small pink flowers. I stopped again to watch a heron that stood motionless above the soft swell of the sea, where brown weed was lifted by the full, smooth tide. The heron stood and stared at his minutely moving world, but the morning stood still around him. I felt his concentration, the blankness of his mind, and his quietude wrapped itself around me like a blanket. I was cocooned in timelessness, and felt the land-mass drift and buckle on the dragon-hot lava of the earth; the mountains pushed up into the sky and the sea licked and cooled their toes. My own life was merely a millisecond's duration, and its transient dramas almost non-existent. Yet the heron persisted eternally.

The line of the hills rose above me, and I climbed upwards towards my viewpoint. The sun was creeping round the mountain's shoulder, my rocky seat was warm and sheltered, and I lay and stared at the sea, unthinking, dazzled by its shifting light, its numinous glow, until my eyes were blurry from lack of blinking, and I closed them and slept.

The clink of rock on rock woke me from dreamless sleep. I was sun-dazed and soporific, and I expected deer. But Jos, breathless, stood above me. Jos, breathless, pursued me, every day! But he was distraught, and fell on his knees next to me and tried to speak. His shirt was dark with sweat, and he gulped in air.

'Harriet! Harriet, they killed Finn!'

I couldn't understand. How had Jos found me? What was he talking about?

'Your fox. They shot him. And they dumped him in my tent!'

The memory of the shock was in his voice, and he was suddenly overwrought, so that a long chain of sobs bent him against me. Poor frightened child. Finn's death was a not-yet-clear event, a numbness, but the sight of Jos crying tore at old memories and I reached out and held his head against my shoulder, stroking his hair. I pulled him to me and cradled him against my breast, kissing his poor wet cheeks and smoothing his hot head. I rocked him gently and kissed my poor hurt child. His hands held me tightly and I opened my shirt so that he could find comfort. Oh my beloved, stay with me, my beloved, darling boy. I lifted my breast to his mouth. I pressed his head against me, and the warm wetness of his tongue and lips caressed me. In a dream, I held my hurt boy close against me, and my tears fell on his face. Oh my love, my sweeting, my dearest heart; come back to me now. His warm hand slid against my skin and clutched me as he suckled, and then a fiery heat engulfed me and I groaned with longing. Then Jos's lips were on my neck and face, it was Jos who licked my tears, and his moustache pricked me as we kissed. And I wanted Jos Allen, oh how I wanted him; and the wonder was, he also wanted me. We struggled to undo our clothing, moaning and half-laughing in our haste, until we lay naked in the sun, and our bodies kissed and intertwined.

Afterwards, I held him tightly to me, full of the ache of love and desperation. He was all I had; for my son was dead. Jos, my love, my child-bridegroom, let me hold and love you. Grass stubble spiked my skin, and a light breeze cooled our sweat, but his body was hot against me, and I revelled in the smooth softness of skin against skin.

He pulled away, and looked at me, and I was suddenly shy, ashamed of my ageing body, but his fingers whispered lightly over me, like the edge of the sea on the pale sand. I tangled my fingers in the dark hair on his chest, and traced the edges of the tanned V below his neck. I stroked his temples and his cheeks; he kissed the palm of my hand, and we regarded each other, unsmiling. There was a hard knot of fear inside me and I didn't want to contemplate the past or future; but that tense knot trembled with excitement, too. My turbulent present was Jos. I pulled him towards me again and our mouths and bodies were hard against each other, squirming, shifting to find new points of contact. I felt my breasts flattened against his rough, hard chest, my thighs against his thighs, and the pleasure was unbearable, so that I rolled astride him, now starkly unashamed. And we cried aloud the intensity of our pleasure to the watching sky.

Later, we sat, half-dressed, with our backs against the rock, like a young couple on a park bench. Jos's arm was round my shoulders and I thought, fleetingly, how a son might thus, protectively, hug his mother. Jos was gently amazed, trying, hesitantly, to express – what? – his happiness, his astonishment, his hopes. His jejune pride in our coincidental climax was touching, but devaluing, because, for me, the experience was too intense for verbal rhapsody.

'It's a bit like riding a bicycle, Jos. One doesn't forget!'

The image, and its echoes, made him laugh.

'You know, you surprise me every time I'm with you, Harriet. I think I'm beginning to understand you slightly, and then you say something that is so... completely unexpected, that I'm lost again!' He was perplexed, frank. 'I've wanted this for weeks, months, even. I didn't think it was possible, I can't believe it's happening.'

What had happened could never be undone; our relationship could never again be neutral. I didn't want him to be frank; I slid my hand up the inside of his bare thigh.

'You incense me!' I applied light pressure, waiting. 'Go on – think about it!'

It took a while for him to make the connection that time, then he pressed my hand against him and murmured his longing; but there was another urgent matter that we had ignored.

'Tell me about Finnghail. And how you found me here.'

'I think I should thank Ferguson and his cronies, don't you? Not many couples are brought together by a dead fox!'

But he was only half-joking, and he rubbed his cheek against mine and squeezed my shoulder.

'They left him in a sack. Do you remember, one of the shearers was carrying a bundle of some sort?'

I nodded. 'I didn't even think about it at the time.'

'Well, after I left you, I wandered back towards the tent. But I didn't want to go to bed. I couldn't stop thinking about you. Sounds corny, doesn't it? Didn't you realise, Harriet? I didn't want to sit on the beach with you all night, I wanted to make love to you. God, Harriet, I've longed for this. All this time!'

'Lust. It destroys your reasoning!'

'No! It's not just—'

'Sssh! Tell me about Finn. *Finn.*'

'Okay. Anyway, I couldn't face going back to the tent, I didn't know what to do. I thought I'd go and look at the seals, see what they did at dawn, or something. Seals, for God's sake! So I went and sat on the headland, and tried to plan out what I'd do today. I just kept thinking of you, though, in that crypt. Pathetic, really; going over bits of conversations, thinking about you being married . . .'

'Finn, Jos. Please. It's important.'

'The bastards dumped him on my sleeping bag. I went back to the tent eventually, seven or eight o'clock or so, and I saw that the fly-sheet was undone. I had an awful feeling that someone was in there, lying in wait, so I crept up to the back end and listened. There wasn't any sound, of course, and when I looked in, there was a dirty fertiliser sack on top of my bag. I dragged it out and cut the twine – and there was this dead fox inside. It really stank! I tipped it out, and you could see it had been shot through the head. I just wanted to be sick. I couldn't understand why it had been dumped on me. And then of course I remembered your fox, and how you'd said it was lame. I couldn't remember which leg, but it definitely has one leg that's slightly twisted-looking.'

'Back left?'

'Yes, it was the left.'

'They must have come back later in the night, after all.' I felt ill again. 'I suppose they thought I was with you and came to look for us.'

'I wish you *had* been there with me, all night. I don't think they'd actually have done anything, you know, if they'd seen us together. They'd probably have gone away. Sniggers, perhaps, but it's what they expect, it would be more normal, Harriet.'

I thought about that for a minute, and was again stirred by his unsuspected perceptiveness; there probably had been no harm intended – to us. But Finn was dead.

'You heard them muttering about foxes, didn't you, in the village?'

'Mmm. I guess Finn, or another fox, had been making a nuisance of himself with the lambs. I suppose they must have shot him a few days ago, by the smell of him – sorry! – and then got around to thinking about you. The three of them together, and the whisky . . . well . . . Harriet, I was scared. I felt so alone, and as though they were getting at me personally. I was irrational.'

'How did you know to come up here?'

'It's silly now, looking back on it. But I was so strung up about you, and not knowing what to do. I was almost thinking of leaving the island for good, and giving up the job. It was getting intolerable, this wanting to be with you and yet knowing, logically, it was wrong, hopeless . . .' He shrugged. 'I'm not sure what we're going to do.'

My throat was tight as I kissed him, and held his head to mine. I'm not sure either, Jos, I'm not sure.

'But if you'd left, then someone else would have come to watch seals in your place.'

'I know. I couldn't bear that, either. I don't want anyone else to know about you! Anyway, when I realised the meaning of Finn, I could only think of telling you. I ran all the way to the crypt, and you weren't there, so I ran over to the croft. And I saw you climbing up the hill. You'd almost reached this place. I shouted, yelled at you to wait. You didn't hear me, Harriet, you didn't hear! I just felt desperate. It was weird, I think I was quite out of control. So I just started running across the beach, and then came up here after you. It nearly killed me, actually. I didn't even think what I was going to do or say, I just needed you so much. But it's all right, isn't it?'

He smiled thinly, shame-faced. But as he spoke, my uncertainty had lifted, and was replaced by elation.

'The meaning of Finn. Of course! I'm such a fool. The dragon told me – no, I dreamt the dragon told me that he ate foxes for breakfast. He needed a fox to fuel his flames, I think that's what he said. Don't look so puzzled! It's obvious now, it's part of the pattern. Finn's death was meant to bring us together.'

And my lost son is laid to rest, where he belongs; it's part of the intrinsic pattern, predestined, hitherto unknown but now revealed, coincidences that concatenate and communicate! Hail *mare*! O, blessed art thou amongst waters, your blue robe glistening in the light of the sun.

Light and love seared my eyes, my gaze turned inwards so that I was enchanted and ensnared in the swirling, widening spiral of events. Kaleidoscopic patterns emerging, submerging, only to re-emerge according to pre-calculated rules. And I was intimidated by the carefully-woven exactitude of the threads, and by my powerless and willing acquiescence.

'It was almost as though you were expecting this to happen. I still can't believe it.'

I opened my eyes. Jos was looking down at me.

'Had you – you know – hoped for this?'

I thought hard before I answered; I was confused. I thought I'd guessed at Jos's fantasies and then, seemingly, had had my guesses dismissed for their laughable inaccuracy, products of my own fantastic invention. 'This' I had not, seriously, desired, this juxtaposition and merging of territories and bodies – and not yet of souls. But if I had been prescient, I would have recognised that our relationship was natural (as Jos had pointed out) and, moreover, an inescapable fate. Not a fate worse than death, but a fate better than life itself!

'No, Jos. I'll be honest. I hadn't hoped for this. I suspected that you had, that day I told you about my divorce – and I was unable to accept what you seemed to want. I neither desired nor needed this. I thought. But I was very wrong, because I see now that it was inevitable. And I am glad, believe me. It will be difficult, though!'

'For both of us, I think! But I always thought it was hopeless, anyway. I thought you were so strange, wild, untouchable. Almost supernatural. Then when you told me you'd had a husband, it made you seem much more normal, more human. I thought I'd go crazy with jealousy!'

'I know. The postcard . . . I wasn't unmoved, Jos.'

'If you knew the worry I went through to get it . . .! I saw you in the sea – did you know I've watched you several times? You're not as fat as the woman in the painting, are you?'

His beard tickled me as he told me of his search for the perfect picture.

'But I regretted it the instant I posted the letter. I wanted to lie in wait for the postie and get it back, and I was really nervous about seeing you again, afterwards. It was so *obvious*, wasn't it? But you are happy, though, Harriet, aren't you? You're not going to turn round and tell me to go away?'

I touched his eyelids and his lips, and the sparks of protective desire that had been fanned within me blazed out hotly over this, my lover.

'I've told you. This is right. It's what we must do. Dear Jos, we have no choice.'

'But that's so abstract. Do you love me? I love you so much, I've loved you for ages.'

'Oh yes, my fox-cub, my frustrated friend. I need you. Can you doubt it? Now I see that I must also love you.'

And thus dies Tom again. Was there meaning, after all, in Tom's death? Was this it, that he should be incorporated and transsubstantiated, to be resurrected in a new persona? To be translated from dependent, unwhole child, to questing, thirsting, needing lover? Fanciful rationalisation! Obscene absurdity! Tom dead; Tom cremated in his small white coffin, his soul speeding upwards, flying from the black wings of muttering priests, to hover, unused, in limbo. He reached out and held me as he died; our fingers linked and I could not let go. Dear heart, beloved; I recall your loving trust and unwary smile. I see you now, your long eyelids creased as though from perpetual mirth, and I hear your rough, dear laughter. But you are gone, my Tom: I mourned your birth, uncomprehending, but I dared not mourn your death. You lived on for me, in my thoughts and dreams; I dared not let you go. I held your hand tightly, but they took me, weeping, from the room. Your Bible lay beside you on the bed, they had to allow the priest to see you, they had to – but the walls dripped venom and hate. And my own son lay dead. For what, Tom? For what purpose? To send me into exile, so that I might be chastised and castigated and that I might, finally, comprehend? If you had not been born thus, and had not died, I would not be here. Were you, then, the key? Without you, I would not have the sea in my ears and eyes, nor Jos's hand around my heart. Without you, I would be the childless wife of a middle-aged accountant, attending Mass on my own, dancing attendance on my husband at dinner parties, and sending cakes to the charity bazaar. Without you, I would have been lost; and now, without you, I am renewed. Dead, cremated, carbonised, you have moved full cycle, revivified from the air. United once *in utero*, we are once again united, by infinitesimally small threads. Tom, I didn't want you to die; I have to see some purpose in that useless waste. My love, I welcome you and thank you.

'I'm not going to go away. Why are you holding me so tightly?'

'Do you know, I'm old enough to be your mother?'

'Not unless you started very young, surely? How old are you, then?'

'Forty-five.'

Pause.

'Hmm. Interesting. Jocasta, turn me on!'

'Hah!'

Pause.

'Did you have any children?'

'One. He died.'

'Oh.'

Pause.

'Were you married for a long time?'

'Jos, stop! That's not your concern.'

'But I want to know about you. I'm not going to tell anyone else. I can't help wanting to know.'

'None of that is any longer relevant. You would know nothing about me, by knowing about my married life. We exist here and now.'

'Don't we exist elsewhere? Can I never leave this island?'

Silence.

Twenty-one

Jos once told me that, with most animals, pairing of the sexes provokes conflict between the sexual urges and the instinctive need to maintain individual territory. In some species, he said, the second factor remains dominant, and there is a tremendous risk that one of the partners will fall victim to the other's territorial aggression. In others, the desire to form a partnership that balances sexual needs and mutual dependency is apparently overwhelming. (But here I'm interposing my own anthropocentric interpretation; Jos's description was factual, merely emphasising the contrasts from the point of view of the comparative ethologist). There is a scale of gradation between the two opposing forces (why else would one mention the extremes unless there was a range of intermediates!), and somewhere along that scale is a state of apparently complete indifference ('What a bore! Hurry up, I'm eating!') and a state of mutually wounding excitement (I've watched garden snails sticking each other with love-darts like sado-masochistic picadors).

What is the position of Harriet and Jos on this scale? The student of animal behaviour, stumbling upon us a few weeks ago, would have observed two apparently independent and solitary individuals, both living in makeshift tunnel-shaped dwellings, one below ground and the other above. The female of the species is apparently the hunter-gatherer; her agrarian instincts are well-developed although technologically primitive, and she lays traps, successfully, to gather marine animals. She also labours to gather burning materials for the fire, in order to provide heat for cooking and for warmth. When not working, she patrols her territory or spends long periods sitting and watching. 'Aha,' says the student, 'the female is obviously preparing her territory for a mate, setting out her wares clearly to show that she is an industrious home-maker. And see how she wanders through her territory, placing herself conspicuously at vantage points in order to be seen by a potential mate in his searching.'

And what of the male of the species? His self-sufficiency is less highly developed, in that he collects prepared food from a pre-arranged location (an artificial feeding-station?); he is neither a hunter-gatherer, nor industrious in the preparation of his territory, he is a consumer. He spends most of his waking hours walking, searching and staring through binoculars. It may seem to the student that the male exhibits some confusion about the nature of his potential mate, for he often spends more hours searching for common seals rather than for a human female. (There is, unfortunately, the possibility that the male was hand-reared, in that he displays such conflicting search-patterns, and is dependent on the feeding-station; such a background would thus invalidate the use of this individual in the study of mating-behaviour). However, it seems clear to the observer that the female is preparing herself and her territory, displaying herself to her best advantage (even though she does not possess the beauty of the type-specimen, whose perfection glows from the pages of the identification handbook) in order to attract the attention of the searching male.

And what, then, of the courtship rituals? The student notices periods of verbal intercourse, when signals are exchanged; the interactions appear amicable and unexcited, but there are occasional outbursts of aggression, when the territorial conflict becomes dominant and the individuals separate and disperse. But, Harriet, think carefully: there were also occasions when the female, briefly, so very briefly but distinctly, reached out and touched the male. And did he not, once, briefly smooth the hair upon her head? Such small signals, subtle invitations, are at once noted and marked down and *underlined* by our invisible watcher, perhaps followed on the page by unscientific exclamation marks.

Let us now examine the incidents at Red Sand. The male visits the female, and they become involved in a short courtship ritual whereby they both lie down within a pseudo-tunnel; thereafter, their verbal interactions are amicable.

Then we spent the day together. Oh no! I can't go on with this! The analysis started as a joke; I don't know the jargon and the terminology, I was only following through Jos's thesis for my own amusement, in my own, untrained manner. Oh no! How that student must have danced that day! We then completely removed the threat of territorial conflict by leaving both our territories and continuing the ritual on neutral ground. Both male and female cooperated in complex building and decorative rituals upon the sand and, together, examined other dwellings.

'The ritual progresses well,' the student noted, with a complete lack of objectiveness. (I don't think I can bring myself to discuss the culminating steps. Viewed in these terms, the outcome has a crude inevitability. But I can't stop.) The female ritually purifies herself in the sea and is studied from well outside her territory by the male. He comes closer to the female's territory, but he moves too quickly because it seems that he briefly usurps the female's agrarian role. A violent outburst of aggression results (the observer does not know the real reason and can only interpret what he or she sees) and the male disappears from the area altogether. And now – now the female apparently searches for the male. She visits his territory in his absence and . . . and – oh yes, Harriet, come on! Use the proper language! – enters his tunnel and displays her sexual organs.

The student of animal behaviour is overjoyed; this is a major breakthrough! (But now I can't stop laughing; thank goodness for the absurdity, to laugh is to release the tension! Right! Continue! What next?) The male finally returns, amicable verbal intercourse, etcetera; interesting, no signs of either aggression or sexual attraction after this interlude. But the sequel is beautiful in its perfection! The two individuals are then united in aggression against other searching males and drive them off! The pair-bonding is almost complete. (Jos would be pleased that I pick up his snappy jargon!) The next few steps in the courtship are enigmatic. The male returns to his territory and starts his searching once again, this time for seals; is this a sign of last-minute uncertainty? Then he drags something out of his tunnel; ah yes, it's food. He must have prepared a gift of food for his future mate. But then apparently he no longer considers it to be suitable, for he sniffs at it, pulls it around, and then starts running with great speed and determination towards the female's territory. Again, apparently to avoid conflict (I think I'm enjoying this!) she has moved to the very limits of the territory, and there she lies, waiting. When he arrives, there is almost no verbal exchange, and physical contact occurs immediately, followed quickly by repeated copulation.

That certainly de-mystifies the process, doesn't it, reduces it merely to the reiteration of a textbook hypothesis, illustrating the complex interplay and balance between animals' primal urges. The student should be well pleased; he can write a paper, present his work at conferences (with slides?) and, if he's lucky, his results and conclusions should be quoted frequently for years to come. Excellent piece of work. Well done. That's that sorted out, then.

So where, Harriet, *is* your mate? Here you are, in the prepared tunnel-home, with your cooking-fire lit. Why aren't you and your mate snuggled up together, indulging in mutual grooming, feeding each other, or repeatedly copulating? Why has your mate returned, on his own, to his tunnel?

Because, dear student, you can only interpret what you see, and the ideas and philosophies of the animals that you study are invisible, hence unknown; they are variables that are missing from the equation, the missing factors I, U and Y. I'm quite keen on the idea of repeated copulation, but unfortunately there are other, less instinctive, forces that must be included; and there is also the factor of Time. The expected result was based on the premise that Jos and I were very similar animals, but, you see, the rationales for our individual existences are too different; solitude and territoriality have been my *raisons d'être* for too long to be instantly abandoned in favour of commonality. I don't regret our mating, if I must use that term, I rejoice in it and accept, now, its inevitability; but it was inevitable for reasons very different from those of basic animal urges. It was not a desired outcome on my part, I swear it was not. We evolved slowly from antipathy to companionship and help, but no further. It's going to take me time to compromise; I recognise that this may be a selfish and egocentric point of view, but I think he understands. It's because his understanding is implicit that I care for him. He understands about other people and about sharing, but I've forgotten. It's too soon for me to take or give, full-time.

I sat in my lair like a female spider, alone and strange, and he slipped in quickly under my defences with his helpless tears. The Plan had been devised with complicated elegance, so that even Jos was unaware, and now we have both become entangled in the web, bound helplessly by our own secretions.

Jos and I came down from the mountain, and we 'buried' Finn. Whoever had killed him had shot skilfully and cleanly, right through the skull, and for that I was grateful. But I wished they had not cut off his tail. He had been a fine animal, despite his crooked leg, and I hoped he left fine cubs behind; perhaps they were already learning the taste of lamb, on the far side of the island, and preparing to avenge their father's death.

We both were tired, but I wanted to leave Finn below the gorge where I had found him. Jos put the crumpled body in the sack and we walked up the valley behind Death Bay. I showed Jos the foxes' old den, and explained to him, as I had once explained to Tom, where Finn had fallen; but the difference was not only in the telling, for Jos was alive and warm, my lover not my son, and his arms were around me and he held me close. We laid Finnghail on a boulder amongst the bracken, within sight and sound of the water. Soon he would be gone, food for insects, hoodie crows and gulls. My clever fox, wild and playful companion and friend, had served his purpose in life and death, and would now live on. His body was laid to rest, as was my son's memory, two losses to make one gain. I didn't yet know if Jos's worth was equivalent to the two of them, but his presence enfolded me, as the noise of the river enfolded the valley. We stood silently together and listened. He ran his hand through my greying hair, and I smoothed his cheeks with kisses. And I was weak with love and sadness at the wonder of it all.

But I'd forgotten, dear dragon, how sex changes a relationship. An awkwardness creeps in, silences prickle with tension, and comfortable companionship and easy conversation are replaced by statements that are replete with significance, pauses pregnant with private jokes. A relationship previously valued for its easy compatibility is suddenly transformed to a subdued duel between strangers, as we each re-assess our relative positions. No, I'm not talking about those kinds of positions! Your breath, dragon, reeks of innuendo and *double entendre*, and your imagination is doubtless overheated by your glowing flames. You have eaten your fox. Is that really your tail that curls beneath your belly?

I am merely trying to understand why I am here in my tunnel without my mate, and my reasoning is doubtless naive and incorrect. Where platonic friendship allows for equal status, sexual intercourse does not. Yet sex and friendship must learn to co-exist. I will be re-educated, I'll be both teacher and pupil. It's merely that I don't want to be helped across the burn, I don't want to be offered a proprietorial arm; I haven't suddenly become an osteomyelitic patient or a bone-china plate.

'Petulant pig-headed woman! Always protesting.'

'Is there to be no peace, dragon, even in my home?'

'Do not forget that it is my home, too. We share it, you and I, and you can learn much from me.'

'But there mustn't be a take-over bid for my independence!

Surely you can understand? Ah, but I'm tired, and tiredness breeds misapprehensions and irrationality.'

'Your place or mine?' Jos had asked, half-joking.

The present had shivered and disappeared, and the unknown future rushed alarmingly towards us and threw down its gauntlet, demanding sensible decisions. Neither of us was ready to accept the challenge, and the empty question lay there on the ground.

I went to his tent in the morning, early, because I wanted him to be asleep. I wanted to be there when he woke. I washed, and dressed carefully in a skirt (a loose, cotton flowery thing that I hadn't worn for years) and a short-sleeved blouse that had faded, through years of washing and drying in the salty air, to pale cornflower blue.

'Look at you! When did you last dress up for a man?' the dragon jeered.

'It's nice to see you taking a bit more care with your appearance,' said the sheep, like anybody's mother.

I was embarrassed, and turned my back on them as I buttoned up my blouse. The clothes were slightly creased from storage, but the creases would fall out as I walked.

There were seals on the rocks, and the pure white backs of the gannets that beat slowly over the water dazzled like a dream. Jos's tent was an orange limpet that clung tightly to the turf. It was closed and silent, surrounded by a paraphernalia of equipment. Now that I had reached the camp-site, I didn't know what to do, so that a nervous yawn billowed up and surprised me, making my eyes water. What had seemed a good idea in the safety of the crypt now seemed foolish and contrived. Why was a woman of my age chasing off across the clifftop after a young man? It was undignified, committing. Who are you fooling, Harriet? There are very few people who looked dignified when they are naked! And Jos appears to have committed himself; to what, we haven't yet discussed, we haven't dared discuss. Should I, too, make some commitment? I should, but I'm terrified by the implications. I'm immobilising myself within a web of words, instead of allowing spontaneity to guide me.

I went quietly down the path towards the tent. The flysheet was zipped closed. I remembered how the zip made a loud rasping sound when it was undone, and, kneeling on the ground, I moved the fastener, carefully, slowly, ratchet by ratchet. Now I could hear Jos breathing, deeply, evenly, and the soft slitherings of his bag as he moved slightly in his sleep. I had opened the zip six inches, and I could see that the tent's inner door was tied open. The inside surface of the flysheet was beaded with condensation, and small droplets spattered on my hand as I leant forward to support my weight. Jos's sleeping bag was half-undone; he must have been warm because he had pushed down the cover so that his upper half, dressed in a dark T-shirt, was exposed. His face was turned towards me; sleeping, it had lost some indefinable protective characteristic, and was calm and defenceless, revealing the youthful vulnerability of the man. He lay on one side, with his cheek upon his hand; his beard was crumpled against his palm, and the veins on the inside of his arm were dark tracery in the orange light. I felt amazement, tenderness, that this boy-man wanted to link his life with mine, and I held my breath lest I wake him and destroy the feeling of sweet sadness that welled up inside me. But he must have felt the pressure of my eyes, for he stirred. Hastily, I tried to back out before he saw me spying on his private soul, but the hem of my skirt caught on the handle of the billycan, and the small clatter woke him. His eyes opened in panic, then were briefly puzzled; but then he murmured, 'Harriet!': and remembered. An ineffably sweet smile lit every angle of his face. I shall never forget that smile; the memory of it has lit the crypt and warmed the air around me, on cold winter nights.

'Are you really there?'

Then he sat up quickly, worried, holding out his hand.

'What's wrong? Have you come to tell me—?'

I took his hand in mine, reaching through the doorway,

'It's all right, Jos. It's still all right. I just wanted to say good morning.'

'Are you sure?'

He was anxious and unsmiling, holding my hand tightly, so that I crouched, awkwardly unbalanced.

'I had this awful thought that you had come to tell me to go away and leave you alone. That you never wanted me to interfere with you again.'

' "Interfere with me." What a lovely expression. It sounds like old men, fumbling with one's skirts under the table. Or accidentally pressing one's breast while they help you on with your coat!'

The picture made him smile, and he gave my hand a disbelieving shake, and looped towards me in his sleeping bag, like a caterpillar.

'Did old men do that to you?'

'No. And perhaps they never do. But I wanted to see you, Jos. And it really is all right. I'm getting used to the idea, slowly. Don't worry – I don't want you to go away.'

I touched his cheek, trying to smooth the smile back on to his face.

'Not exactly bursting with enthusiasm!' He was rueful. 'But I suppose I should be grateful, given the strange circumstances.' He caught my hand again and kissed the palm. 'Harriet. Harriet Longmore. I still can't believe it!'

I gently freed my hand, and stood up, because my knees were aching.

'Get dressed and come out and look at the sea with me.'

'I'd rather look at you.'

'Don't be trite!'

'I don't care! I wish I could wake up every morning and see you, you look wonderful. Although a little crumpled!'

I looked at him, surprised, and then down at my clothes; the creases were stark and ironed-in. I could only shrug, and then moved back to let Jos push himself upright through the opened door. But he walked over to me, bare-footed, in his underpants and T-shirt, and caught hold of me by the shoulders. I was unprepared, and resisted slightly.

'There! Good morning, Harriet!'

He kissed me, gently, and his sleepy smell was warm in my

nostrils. Then he was pressing himself against me, and his lips were hard.

'I want to interfere with you. Let's interfere!'

'No. Not now.' I turned my head away, shaking it slightly.

'You can't come and wake a man in his bed just in order to talk! You can't do this to me!'

I could feel what I was doing to him, as he bunched my skirt and put his hands over my buttocks, pulling our bodies together. I hadn't wanted this, and I was aghast that I had not imagined this to be the natural consequence of my hesitant spontaneity. I brought my arms up and pushed lightly, placing a physical barrier between us, smiling, placatory, turning a cheek, pushing, applying pressure, until there was space between us.

'Jos, I came to talk. Please, be patient, we do need to talk. To sort this out. Stop! Listen. We must discuss what we're going to do.'

'But I know what I want to do!'

He played at being petulant, a little sulky, but he moved away and pulled off his T-shirt and draped it over the ridge pole before crawling back into the tent. He muttered and grumbled as he lay flat to pull on his jeans, and there were melodramatic oaths and exclamations as he searched noisily for a clean shirt. He crawled out again, and dribbled water from a container into one hand, then rubbed it over his face. He poured more water into a mug, scraped a thin layer of toothpaste on to his toothbrush, and walked a few yards away towards a rock to clean his teeth, spitting loudly, then whisking his toothbrush in the mug to clean it.

'Right! I'm ready!'

His hair was tousled, but his beard shone in the sunlight, and I wanted to reach out and stroke it, but the intimacy would have introduced another diversion.

'Let's go over that way, down towards the sea.'

I didn't want to be near the tent, there was a need to be uncluttered by associations.

'Okay. There's a big stone down there, a good conference table.

Will you chair the discussion? Perhaps we should call this a workshop, like at conferences, where everyone gets together to thrash out problems.'

Jos's manner was jaunty but febrile, and when he held out his hand I couldn't refuse him; I could feel a faint vibration, a tremor faster than his rapid breathing. As we walked down the steep grassy slope towards the stone, our hands clasped more tightly. Gradually, all feeling became concentrated in that clasp, and a liquid, red-hot current seemed to run down my arm and join with his, so that our fingers throbbed with its intensity, and were inseparable. When we reached the stone, we stood together, locked together, indivisible in the flames, both shocked into stillness, encapsulated in silence of our own making, and united by the power within our hands. I scarcely breathed, for to breathe would be to disturb the air; the world was out of focus, except for Jos.

Then Jos sat down suddenly and closed his eyes. His grip loosened, and he rested his arms on the stone and laid his head upon them.

It's curious how one can stop thinking; one's body continues to run itself, but the mind is oblivious and closed down. It was as though the white-hot heat of recognition had blasted me into immobility. Five minutes (ten? fifteen?) later, Jos raised his head and looked at me; he was dazed and puzzled.

'There's not much to say, is there?'

'I suppose not. Some practicalities, perhaps.'

Our discussion was desultory, halting, with long silences, pauses while we searched for words or meanings; circumlocutions, muddles, soft apologies and suddenly blurted explanations. We both trod warily around each other, trying to rationalise and contain the situation. We were chaste, abstaining from physical contact, caressing each other with words as we luxuriated in exposing our feelings for each other; perhaps we had never been so frank. Jos's need was to explore the beginnings and development of his love, and he was agitated, excitedly stumbling through a maze of conflict and contact.

'There seemed to be a pattern of two steps forward, then one step back. If something good happened, so that I thought we were getting closer, then the next time, at even the next minute, something would happen that convinced me you still hated me. Like – oh, you'd hold my arm, and then next moment you'd be going on about my invading your privacy. I didn't know where I was!'

'It was an obsession. You've had nothing to do but analyse the only human interaction you've experienced on this island, or at least, the only interaction with a female.'

'You know, I hated you at first! And I hated you again after that divorce business. I'm still sorry about what I said.'

'I know.'

'But that was because the picture I'd built up of you had instantly changed. You'd been cheating me!'

'I'd been cheating myself, too, and I only realised it that day. It is possible . . . I don't know, it's a difficult situation to reconstruct . . . but if you'd made a move, then . . . your feelings were very obvious, I think. I understood your motivation but I didn't want to acknowledge it.'

'If I'd made a move . . .? What would have happened, Harriet? You'd have barricaded yourself in the crypt and never come out.'

'I don't know, Jos. I was very happy at that moment – despite my cold! I wasn't very desirable, anyway, was I, with my streaming nose and red eyes? I was just wondering if I'd have, well, succumbed, if you like. But it would have been disastrous, then, we'd have regretted it. I would have, especially. No, it had to happen the way it did.'

'It was so amazing, the way it happened. The way you just took me to you . . .' He blushed.

I was excited, and perhaps appalled, at the memory, how I had taken Jos to my breast like a suckling child; and I was briefly saddened, too, that it had been impossible to arrange for my breasts to be heavy with milk. Our union would thus have reached the ultimate exquisite perfection, and the circle would have been complete. The beauty of the image made me ache at the lost opportunity.

'It was meant to happen then, Jos, so it was natural and right that it should happen that way.'

'What is "it", Harriet? And why was it "meant"? You keep using that word. As though it – there it is again! – is our destiny. As though some strange god has decreed that we should be together.'

'In a way, yes.'

'But what has happened to us is quite normal, people fall in love all the time, don't they? You presumably did, once before. I don't like to think that someone, some thing, has arranged for this to happen. As though we're puppets. It's love, my love. Love what makes the world go round. Isn't it?'

We didn't even know why we were arguing. There was a prickly excitement between us, a challenge. We were both stimulated, both half-smiling, half-annoyed, slightly breathless. If one of us made a gesture as though to make contact, the other recoiled, and the space between us seemed to sparkle, forbidding yet daring us to cross it.

'Love! I don't understand you, Jos, why you should *love* me. You're deluding yourself. I'm old, I have grey hairs. You've even said I'm crazy!'

'And you're fishing for compliments. But I'll tell you why – you're warm, and funny, and intelligent, and . . . strong.'

'You just want me to look after you! The classic seeking for a mother-figure!'

'No! Despite earlier remarks, I'm much too inhibited to have sex with a mother-figure. Oedipus was a mother-fucker. In the true sense of the word! And what about me, then? What do you see in me?'

'Well . . .' I frowned, deliberately teasing, wondering what it was about Jos that provoked this strong feeling of unity. 'That's difficult. You have a gorgeous body. And I like your eyes.'

'Seriously, Harriet. Forget about my body. Or is that all there is, when it comes down to it? Sex and the single woman?'

He was suddenly no longer joking, but distant and helpless. I had to be specific, or I could lose him.

'You're thoughtful, and generous. There's a strength, but also a delicacy, about you. I can't really explain – it's in the way you treat people – me. We could like the same things, I think. You need me. I need you, Jos – we both felt that, as we came down to this stone, this workshop table.' I tried to smile. 'Who could doubt it?'

He was part of me, of us, of everything; I couldn't lose him. He was sitting absolutely still, and I could sense that he was terrified, still waiting. The lie slipped out easily, because it was necessary; without the lie, he would be destitute, and how else could we be bound together?

'And I love you, Jos. No other explanation is necessary.'

His face went white, and he let out his breath in a long, sobbing sigh.

'Are you sure? Can you be sure, so soon?'

I reached across the table and took his hand, straightening the clenched fingers. I felt a traitor, but our mutual dependence was now insuperable.

'Oh God, Harriet! Harriet, my love. I love you so much. You've made me cry!'

He rubbed the heel of his free hand against his eyes, and smiled. We sat and held hands. Although the sun blessed us, the sea, stirred by far-distant, unseen storms, bulged and sank below us, in a heavy, soundless swell.

'You do realise, don't you, that to be in love on a desert island is easy. We're isolated, we have no one else, or what they're thinking, to concern us. But what happens when you have to go back to the university, and your friends and family?'

'I'll come back. I won't be away for long. You could come with me, if you liked – for some of the time. We could visit some of your old haunts, and I could show you mine.'

'And your friends. And family. What are they going to think when you introduce this untidy woman who's almost twice your age?'

'They can think what they like! They'll just have to get used to the idea, won't they?'

'Can you really see me coming with you, and fitting in? And another thing – if you'd met me in that sort of environment, you wouldn't have given me a second's thought, would you? It's the island that's important in our relationship, and the fact is that I live here. I'm me because of this environment. The island and I are integral to each other. Do you see what I'm saying?'

'Yes, of course I see. I've been trying not to. Do you think I haven't worried about this? That's the reason why I kept trying to avoid getting involved, why I thought about leaving. Because I can't see what we're to do! Harriet, there has to be a solution, or else the whole thing becomes unbearable.'

'There will be. I'm sure the situation, for want of a better word, will sort itself out. We'll be shown what to do.'

'There you go again, as though we're part of some master plan.'

'I'm sorry. But I'm hopeful, because I've found that events do usually seem to make sense, in the long term. It's probably not worth wasting energy in worrying, especially since I have scarcely had time to come to terms with the present!'

'I wish I had your faith. There doesn't seem to be any room for compromise, though. Are we just to sit around, to "wait and see"?'

'I don't think we need to sit around, do you? I'm surprised that you're not more inventive. And we haven't even had breakfast yet!'

Jos lies here beside me; his chest is slick with sweat, as the midday sun beats down upon the tent. Is there, within the animal world, a correlate of our present situation? One of these days I must ask Jos. For this male did not, like the bower-bird, create an artistic Eden, wherein I might be enticed to copulate. Nor did he, like the stickleback, flaunt his glowing colours and show me an artfully constructed love-nest in which we might perform our sexual slitherings. I have been snared within one man's territory, a one-man tent, stocked with the plethora of possessions for one man's daily life.

I hear a boat, and crouch forward to look out of the flap. I am cautious, rightly, for I see Robbie Ferguson at the helm, his binoculars to his eyes. He cannot see me, except in his imaginings, for I am hidden by the flysheet.

'What's that?' Jos stirs.

'The Fergusons' boat.'

'The nerve of them! They'll disturb the seals.'

(And what about us? Do they not disturb us? Am I thus instantly dismissed? Have you also forgotten Finnghail, so soon?)

Jos crawls to the entrance, displacing me, and, even as I move, I see two seals plop into the water. Jos's rump gleams orange-white beside me, and I slap it lightly, so that he shouts and laughs, and I urge him to be quiet, nervous lest the Fergusons hear.

'Damn them! Wouldn't Ferguson be amazed if he knew what this tent concealed? Shall we leap out and dance naked on the grass? That would give him something to gossip about.'

'You're so obscene.'

I'm sickened at the thought of island gossip and Ferguson's knowing leer; but I try to be amused at Jos's juvenile bravado and need to boast.

'Well, I suppose they'll find out soon enough.'

It sounded as though he hoped that our liaison would soon become common knowledge and part of the tradition of local folklore. Would he be considered as the vanquished rather than the victor, the poor innocent boy who fell under the witch's spell? Or would he be hailed, in private conversations, as the man who awakened the sleeping spinster? Ah, the spicy secretions of titillating tongues! But perhaps I flatter myself: ultimately, who really cares?

'I must leave soon, as soon as the boat has gone.'

(They have lines out, fishing for mackerel. I, too, have mackerel hooks.)

'You can't go yet. What's wrong?'

'Nothing. But I have work to do – and so have you, dear Jos. You haven't done anything for several days, have you?'

'No.' He was serious, thoughtful. 'No, I haven't. Oh Hell! You're so distracting, I just want to spend all the time with you, at the moment. Shall I come over this evening?'

'I don't think so. Perhaps this sounds selfish, but I'm not sure that I'm ready for you to stay with me overnight.'

'I know. I am trying to imagine what it's like for you. I think I'm just jealous of the time you spend on your own, it's difficult to accept that you are still a complete person without me.' He looked up at me, from where he lay. 'I'd like to know you well enough so that, when we're not together, I can imagine what you might be doing. It would make you seem closer, and make me feel as though I'm more a part of you, somehow. How terribly romantic – I'm quite embarrassed!'

'You say the most extraordinarily nice things. And I'm sorry to be so selfish about wanting to be on my own. You'll soon find out how boring my life is. There's nothing much to imagine – gardening, fishing, walking . . .'

'It sounds idyllic. A sort of paradise. I wish my life were like that, too.'

'No, you don't. And we'd run out of things to talk about if we spent all our time together.'

'Never! We've hardly started.'

'Anyway, I'm only just remembering how to talk to other people. Another person. But we certainly can't sit hunched in here all the time.'

I gestured at the clutter of clothes and notebooks.

'I'll tidy it up. I didn't expect you to come and visit me. Do you realise that, that you came to visit me!'

'It would never stay tidy, especially with two of us occupying the space. I remember when—'

I stopped. I'd been going to add 'when Graham used to stay for a weekend.' Before we were married, when he'd stayed with me in my bedsit, the small room would become a turmoil of coffee mugs, papers, records and untidy clothes and bedclothes, and the air would be stale with talk and love-making.

'What were you going to say?'

'It was irrelevant. An ancient memory of premarital cohabitation. Jos, I know I have no right to ask, but do you have any attachment – I mean – a girlfriend – on the mainland?' (What am I saying? Why do I want to know? And what if he says 'Yes'?)

'You don't have a right to ask, no, since you won't let me ask you about your ex-husband. But, that apart, you do have every right to ask. Though how you could imagine I could have someone else, I really don't know. There's no room for anyone else!'

' "This thing is bigger than both of us", you mean? Don't joke.'

'And you mind what you're doing! No, I did have a girlfriend, but we broke up just before last Christmas. Fieldwork isn't very user-friendly.'

'What does that mean?'

'Sorry, computer jargon. After your time, I suppose! Basically, our magnificent love for each other wasn't strong enough to support our absences. Out of sight, out of mind, in her case, I'm afraid. It's a common problem for field ecologists.'

'I'm sorry.'

'I hope you're not. Don't be insincere! And I'm not sorry, now.'

'So you fell in love with me as an antidote. Very dangerous. During a time of unstable emotions and feverish illusions. Have you deluded yourself, do you think? Will our magnificent love, etcetera, survive during your absences?'

I was not entirely joking, tracing patterns on his thigh with my fingernail, making white lines that were quickly blotted out. He shivered, then laughed, his head thrown back so that I could see his red upper lip below his moustache.

'Ouch, don't! I can't concentrate. I'm not going to answer.'

'No, I'm going. You are just a young lecher.'

'Yep. Great, isn't it?' He spread his arms around me, nuzzling his beard against my neck. 'Thank God we're not both virgins. Wouldn't that have been a bore?'

'You are incorrigibly cheeky. Show some respect.' I caught at his hands, and pulled them away. 'I must go. Please.'

'Your clothes are outside – some of them. You'll have to wait until the Fergusons have gone, because I'm not going outside to get them.'

'The boat has gone. The coast is clear – literally!'

We dressed outside, where there was more room. Jos passed me my blouse from the ridge of the tent, and shook it.

'I could look out for an old-fashioned flat-iron for you, if you would like one.'

'Actually, I have one already—'

'My practical Harriet!'

'—I just didn't get time to use it, in my haste to see you.'

'It looks good, crumpled or not! Can I see you tomorrow, then? Where shall we meet?'

'No, let's not plan anything. Our meeting will just happen, and as a result will be even more exciting!'

'Why are you laughing?'

'What you said, it made me think of the cow with the crumpled horn, and that suddenly took on a new meaning. An androgynous animal! I'm the crumpled cow, but you've got the crumpled horn. And the gods send a curst cow short horns!'

Twenty-two

A shifting cloud of gulls glittered around the stern of the Fergusons' boat, stationed off the headland. Watching it, I nearly trod on a dungbeetle that was trundling across the path. Flies sat on rocks to sun their iridescent wings, and rose from the bracken in buzzing clouds as my shadow swept over them. The harsh cries of nesting gulls echoed along the cliffs and a kestrel plunged to earth then swooped upwards with its struggling prey. And I hummed to the beat of my footsteps as I rushed to Camus Beag to tend my garden.

First, however, I went home to the crypt. The sun was glancing in at the entrance hole, and the place welcomed me like a friend. Radiating paths had been worn into the ground around the entrance rocks, guiding me towards the door. Peat blocks and firewood were stacked at one side of the entrance, and I had laid dried bracken fronds on top of the worn turf around the fire. My water container was by the door, and cooking utensils and a plastic bowl were piled beneath the rock wall. The place no longer looked like a hole in the ground, but was a home.

It was nearly four months since I'd moved in, and I'd gradually discovered what I needed and what I could live without. I had adapted my new life to reduce my goods and chattels to a minimum: everything that was superfluous remained at the cottage and would decay with its surroundings. My new home is habitable and comfortable; it's true that it is also dark and damp, and it lacks what are euphemistically referred to as public conveniences, but one can adapt to private inconvenience if one is determined. I was surprised at how relieved I was at my return, after only a brief foray into the other territory. There, all had been new and strange, a tidal rip of conflict, coercion, consent and coitus, and I was weary from the emotional strain. I had been forced to reach back to retrieve old patterns of behaviour. It had been a struggle to understand and then to convince, to show, visibly, liking and affection, to soothe and not to hurt carelessly. I'd been selfish for too many years, and needed practice to take account of another's feelings. I had to remind myself continually that this dramatic step was not merely that, a drama, a piece of play-acting, but was a real event, indelibly written on the sand. This liaison with Jos was still incomprehensible and unbelievable; we were not teenagers, succumbing to transient amatory delusions. This relationship had to survive. Jos could destroy it, for he might become persuaded that his ideal paradise was a fantasy and that Eve was, in fact, the mad serpent; but I also felt that I was the one who could more easily destroy the relationship, by destroying Jos's own fragile confidence. If I were rich, or a famous actress, Jos would be a gold-digger or a gigolo, my own pet poodle, to be stroked and fondled, while he loved and licked me in return, and begged for choice tit-bits.

'Choice tits, did you say?'

'Damn you, dragon! You have a dirty mind.'

'I could make a good poodle, if I tried. Especially if you would let me wear the sheep's coat.'

'Stop tormenting her. And stop listening to my thoughts, or I shall have to cover you, like a parrot on a cage.'

'I'd like to cover *you*! All right, dear lady, I apologise! Have you thought about the headlines, though? "Lonely scientist falls prey to sex-mad divorcée: 'I felt sorry for him,' she said." How about considering that angle for a moment?'

'Take care, dragon, for I will slay thee. Get thee behind me, and stay quiet.'

Reductio ad absurdum. By translating our relationship into these bizarre fictions, the contrast with the reality is enhanced. The reality is the landscape; reality is sexuality; reality is caring, and perhaps not love. But words are not reality. Reality is Jos, and adapting. We can play games with words, convince ourselves then unconvince. We could lie here on the bed, and bind each other in a web of loving words, and we—

'Aha! So I'm to be voyeur as well as poodle?'

'I shall hide you behind the arras, or at least cover up your eyes. And ears.'

'But leave my tongue free, dear Harriet, that I may serenade you. And my claws will pound out the beat.'

—and we could use words to make us laugh and question, and probe the limits of each other's depth. I have years of silence to retrieve and to fill up with words. Fishing, walking, sitting, watching: every activity could be defined and entwined in a ribbon of phrases and sentences! Summer is a perfect time to start a relationship, an outdoor time, spontaneous, when it's impossible to imagine the constraints of winter. But what of winter? In the cold gales, will we pace between the bothy and the crypt, arriving dripping and disconsolate, ardour dampened, to talk drearily of brighter days? Will conversation turn grey with the skies, and be subsumed within dark silences?

I need more light in here! There must be light! Even today there are dark corners. Yet I love this place – the books are bright against the stone, the floor is thickly covered with dry grasses. I don't mind the dampness because it arises from the earth and sea. There *is* space, there could be space enough for two – just occasionally – if it were really necessary.

'As a special treat? Like after-dinner chocolate? Oh, lucky man!'

But not often. It's my home, my final bolt-hole, the only place where I may hide. The cottage was violated but the crypt must remain intact.

'You let him into your body, think how much easier it would be to let him come inside your house. The former is but the microcosmic image of the latter, and therefore merely practice for the raping of the latter, I would have thought. But then, I'm not a philosopher.'

'Pseuo-Freudian drivel! You sound exactly like Graham. No, you sound as Graham sounded in my head, so I suppose you both must sound like me. I can't remember the reality of Graham . . . My microcosmographic mould is topologically and geographically mobile, and may therefore prostrate itself at distant places, at neutral points or even on ley lines if I so wish. My home, however, remains mine, and my body can retreat into it. But why do I bother to sit here on the bed arguing with you? Unlike you, I have to go outside and work.'

'I would like to come with you. I've never been outside.'

'Poor dragon.' I stood up and went over to look at him and smooth his scales. 'I'm sorry to leave you.'

His flames curled around my wrist like warm, damp tendrils, and I put my lips against his cold cheek, and promised to return.

Were there peas in the Garden of Eden? Possibly not, because otherwise Adam would not have had to wait for Eve to point out the benefits and dietary advantages of the daily apple – one sight of the serried ranks of bright green spheres, nestling inside their satin pod, would have driven him into a feeding frenzy. He would have run from vine to vine, plucking forbidden fruits, popping pods, running his thumbnail along the hollow so that peas plopped into his palm. He would have gorged himself on the sweet crisp seeds until he lay groaning, flatulently over-filled, atop a pile of gaping bivalved shells. Leguminously lugubrious, he would have lain where he Fell, and Eve, dribbling apple-juice down her chin, would have massaged his aching stomach and offered him the sweet roughage of her apple-skin.

My bird-scarers would have had no effect against such gluttonous desire for the sweetness of fresh, green peas. They have had very little effect here, and the local herbivorous fauna has enjoyed a feast; but enough remain for the gardener to enjoy, and there are more to come, a special plenitude of peas. I wander slowly through the garden, squeezing a pea-pod here, pulling up a small carrot there, emptying the slug traps, examining the leeks and onions. Every year, it seems like a miracle that a small, dry seed should germinate and grow to perhaps hundreds of times it size, becoming fresh and moist, bright-coloured; a miracle, that dark stony earth should be transformed by a burgeoning flourish of vegetation, that provides food – and future compost. I have here the ingredients for a fine salad – small lettuces, young peas, a few pencil-slim carrots, parsley and syboes. Such sweet purity, that would be sullied by tinned meat. But crab, fresh crab, would provide us with a feast!

The thought of laying crab-pots, and of an outing in the boat, is exciting, and I hurry to gather together the tackle. It takes several trips to transfer everything to the shore, but I find that I'm singing, as though on holiday. I wish I had some good stinking meat for bait but there's nothing suitable, so I kick limpets off the rocks and hang them in nylon net bags (from apples and oranges) inside the pots. I run my hands along the smooth varnish of the boat and greet it like an old friend. Fine, sturdy creature! I've spent hours sanding and re-varnishing it, and re-binding the oars. The red bailer is tied firmly to the thwart with cord.

The bank of shingle has been dispersed, and the pebbles roll and slip underfoot as I push the boat out into the waves. The sun dries salt droplets to shining crystals on the seat. As we leave the shelter of the bay, the long, rolling swell lifts and drops us, lifts and drops, so that we slide down the back of each wave and my oars take shallow bites. Because I face the land, I see that the rowan tree, in full leaf, breaks up the outlines of the shattered cottage, and I'm happy. I row south, parallel to the raised beach, to where the foot of Sgurr Mor juts out into the sea; here is deep water and oar-weed, interspersed with patches of pale sand. I imagine the large crabs lurking in the submarine forest, eyeballs swivelling, feelers twitching at the scent of meat, one leg moving, then another, a quick lateral dash, a pause, a scurry, and then a slow, steady pacing towards the pot; huge crabs, black-eyed and barnacle-encrusted, with large, fat claws. One can only be optimistic when one fishes. I choose a place to lay the first pot, and stare down into the clear water. The kelp forest is stirred and swayed by the swell, like a dark, many-tentacled animal; a sea-urchin, pale and spiky, is clamped tightly to a frond, and a small fish skitters rapidly across a clearing in the forest, raising puffs of sand. As the heavy pot sinks down through the water, I kiss my fingertips and touch the surface of the sea, praying for good fortune. The tide is low, and the coils of blue rope follow the pot lazily, curving away from the orange float. But as I swing the boat round, I see that the Fergusons' boat has just rounded the point between Death Bay and Camus Beag; I was so absorbed in dreams of crabs that I'd forgotten that the Fergusons were along the coast. There's a nervous pricking in my armpits, but I feel sure that they'll keep away. They won't drop their pots in Camus Beag. But perhaps I'm not so sure, and the prickling is a warning, because the territorial taboo has been broken so dramatically. I row further along the coast, seeking a place for the second crab-pot, and keeping an eye on the Fergusons' boat. They had stopped just off the point, but now the boat's profile changes, narrows, and white foam glints at the bow as it turns and moves fast in my direction. It's still a long way off, and I cannot believe that Robbie will seek a confrontation, so I turn my back and lift the second pot on to the side. Despite my nervousness, I don't forget to ask for the sea's beneficence. The boat pitches in the swell, and lists as I lean overboard to drop the pot, then it rights itself as the weight is freed. Dear sea, please give us a good catch. And please protect me from the Fergusons.

Their boat ploughs onwards, but there's no suitable place between us where they could lay their pots, and I know now that they plan to meet me. I've lost enthusiasm for my work, and the sun seems cooler and the blue sky pales to grey as I spin the boat and row back towards Camus Beag; looking over my shoulder, I can see where our courses will intersect, and I row resignedly and steadily. The noise of the engine echoes back from the shore, and I stop, shipping the oars, to let them take the initiative.

'Hallo there!'

I look up, unspeaking, at Robbie Ferguson. He cuts the engine, and the silence hurts. He is alone.

'Morning, Harriet.'

I nod. And wait. Perhaps it's true that murderers and arsonists and . . . others, return to the scene of their crimes, in order to measure the response, and gloat.

I realise that I mustn't let him know that I know about Finnghail, because then he will know that Jos and I . . . communicate. He'll know no more than that (and that in itself would be too much). Yet I'm certain that my new relationship must be obvious to anyone who looks at me.

'I'm surprised to see you out here – thought I saw you away over there, past Camus Dubh,' Robbie shouts across the water, jerking his head in the direction of the headland (and Jos's tent), 'not so long ago. You must have moved fast! It was your fine blue shirt that caught my eye!' His boat glides closer, and he peers down. 'Laying your pots, are you?'

'Uh-huh.'

I look at his curiously intent expression, and I see myself in my blue blouse, striding and skipping along the path. And I see Robbie's binoculars, and my blue blouse thrown over the ridge of Jos's tent. The two boats rise and fall in the swell, tipping towards each other, then away. I pull down the sleeves of my pullover, because Robbie's boat hides the sun, but perhaps it's really because I want to cover up my blue cuffs, to cover myself. And now I see, also, that I must know about dead, dumped Finn; yet I needn't know how he came to be there, for neither Jos nor I were there. It's important to be calm, dispassionate, even, when one has to talk loudly over the slap of the water.

'Somebody killed my fox. Do you have any idea who did it? Or why?'

'Ah.' He, too, is cool. 'Why should I be knowing a thing like that? *Your* fox, was it, then? Why would it be yours?'

'My fox. The one with the lame back leg, that I hand-reared. I believe you've seen him with me.'

'Aye. Aye, I do now recall a fox. Where were you finding your dead fox, then?'

I was not going to be forced to answer, so I continued staring up at him, waiting, and he finally gave in.

'Well now, I'm thinking the shearers said something about a fox. A big fox with a limp. Aye, I do seem to think that they said something about a fox, being at the sheep a wee while back. It was Jimmy Donaldson – you know him, the shepherd? – he had been after it, and he had shot it. Just the other day, it was, that he had shot it.'

'Did he shoot it over here, then, on this side of the island?'

'No. I was hearing that it was over in the glen behind the farm.' He waved an arm vaguely towards the far side of the island.

'So how did my dead fox come to be – over here? He didn't walk here on his own, that's for sure, especially not inside a sack.'

The memory of that lumpy bag, and of Jos's horror – and of Jos, weeping, breathless, suckling Jos – made me catch my breath, and because Robbie, for once, was not mocking and supercilious, I couldn't help myself.

'Oh, dammit, Robbie. Why did they have to do that? It was foul, and unkind. Dumping it there. And that poor bloody fox – he was just trying to survive.'

A large, rolling swell passed under us, and the boats rolled towards each other, so that Robbie overbalanced from his straddled pose, and held the side.

'Aye, well.' He was mumbling, and his eyes slid sideways and looked towards the shore. 'They'd had a few, most likely. And a bit of a fright, too. It seemed like a good idea at the time . . . a wee bit of fun, maybe. I reckon you're right, it looks a bit nasty, now . . . But I don't know anything about it, myself,' he added hastily, a defiant afterthought.

It was the nearest to an apology or explanation that I would ever get, and I didn't dare (or wish) to pursue it further. We both were silent for a few minutes, and the boats continued rocking, the sea bumping against their sides. Then, just as the silence began to develop into tension and awkwardness, Robbie pointed to the crab-pot that remained in the bottom of my boat.

'Have you no better bait than that? You will not catch a fine crab with that rubbish.'

'No. I haven't had time to go fishing.'

I wished, then, that I hadn't said that. He stared at me, unsmilingly, and eventually asked, 'The lad would have been a bit upset, then?'

Why does my face insist on revealing the truth? The hot blushes turned me into a scarlet woman. I couldn't think of any reply, but shrugged, and avoided Robbie's speculative stare. I could feel him watching me, but then he went over to a plastic barrel on the far side of his boat, and reached down inside, returning with two crumpled, silver-and-grey fish in his hand. The smell of decomposing salted fish caught in my nostrils and made my eyes water.

'Here,' he said. 'These will do a better job.'

He threw the slippery bodies across into the bottom of the boat, where they slithered down and caught against the keel. He gave me a strange smile as he leant over the side and washed his hand, and he had taken me by surprise, so that I blurted out, 'Oh! Thanks! That will be marvellous!'

'Aye, it "will be marvellous" indeed if you catch anything around here. You need to be away from this bay, there's not many crabs to be caught off Camus Beag.'

I couldn't resist the impulse; this was a different Robbie Ferguson. I waggled my outstretched fingers and narrowed my eyes.

'I put a spell on them. It depends whose pots are down.'

But instead of laughter, there was a shock on his face, as his pale blue eyes looked into mine, and for a moment he was motionless, half-stooping over the side. He seemed to shrink back into himself, it was as though an opaque shutter came down over his eyes, so that the ebullience and sarcasm of his character was hidden. Then he straightened up, holding the roof of the half-cabin, and looked quickly over his shoulder.

'Doubtless there's good fishing off Camus Dubh, though. You should try round there,' I continued, as I guessed the direction of his gaze.

'No! I'll not do that!'

'Why not? Don't tell me you believe all those tales about the spirits of the dead?'

'That is not a good place. You should know, that people think you strange for staying there. People have – seen things.' He'd thrust his left hand into his pocket, and I wondered if his fingers were crossed.

'Surely not. Perhaps it's a consequence of too much whisky, people can see all nature of things if they themselves are full of spirits!'

But he was not ready to joke about Death Bay, and I knew that the bay would hold a special threat for him hereafter. I was glad, if it would keep him away, but I was also sorry because he had shown me an unsuspected side to his character. I realised that I had managed not to look closely at him before. With his red hair, and ageless, sandy complexion, I had thought him younger, but now I could see that he was probably my age. He was not a wild young man, but merely an ageing roustabout, who had been trying to have a good time with the lads, and who had been thoroughly scared in the process. (Earlier I, too, had been terrified – but I can't remember why.)

'Perhaps you have some special protection, then?' he asked, distantly, and I instantly regretted having brought up the topic of the supernatural.

I was sure, this time, that he did not refer to Jos, it was the witch aspect that continued to fascinate him, to repel and attract, but the only solution that I could see, at that moment, was to play at being one of the lads; it was a lesser evil, since my liaison was obviously a known, but as yet unacknowledged, fact.

'Well, it's nice to have a man about the place now and again,' I said, demurely; and was puzzled by the look of relief on his face.

'I wonder you didn't think of it sooner. I'm always happy to help out, Harriet.'

'Oh, you have already, Robbie. With the bait.'

'Look, then.' The boats were nudging each other, and he reached across and pulled them closer together. 'A sea-faring woman like yourself, who knows a thing or two about crabbing—'

'Not much.'

'How about joining up with me? I'm single-handed, and looking for a crew. A great opportunity, Harriet – employment, crabs, my company. We can forget what happened before, can't we?'

'What's happened to your father, then?'

'Ach, it was his birthday, and he's still got a sore head. He hasn't been out for a wee while, anyway, says he can't take it any more, he's going to retire.'

'Surely not! He'd never give up the boat?'

'No, he'll come round to it again, right enough. But you're a Hell of a lot better-looking than the old man.'

The red-gold stubble on his cheeks glittered, and there was a masculine smell of cigarettes and alcohol, mixed with the smell of dead fish, as the wind blew his sudden laughter towards me; an outspoken, uncompromising man, rough in his passions and quick to respond to the realities of living. I don't know why he'd frightened me before. Jos had been right; there would be no further threat from Robbie Ferguson, for he had met a situation that he could understand and that was natural. It was the unnatural, the supernatural, that disturbed him and brought out his sly and brooding sarcasm. I imagined myself as Robbie's deckhand, attempting to avoid the long-armed attacks of the skipper and his catch, and I laughed, too.

'No thanks, Robbie. I don't think I'd be strong enough! But thanks for the bait!'

He showed no sign of letting go, so I took up an oar and pushed hard against the side of his boat so that the gap widened and he had to release his grip. He was still grinning as we separated.

'By the way, you're right. You'll never get good crabs here. But they're good down towards Red Sand!'

He lifted a hand in acknowledgement. I had no idea what the fishing would be like that far south, but I fervently hoped that my prophecy would be true, and that he wouldn't feel free to intrude here again, on sea or land. I might no longer fear him, but spies and interlopers are inhibitory. Only God spied on Eden, and here the gods are more benign. The agate in my pocket dug into my thigh and reminded me of its presence as I bent my knees and began to row.

Twenty-three

'A tramp was sometimes seen on the roads around the village. Georgette was sure that he would have referred to himself as a tramp, rather than by that euphemism "gentleman of the road", and he certainly wasn't a tinker. But that was another of the questions, full of insight and empathy, that she failed to ask him.

'He was called Andrew. People who thought they knew him would address him as "Andy", for, after all, why should a tramp have a fine name like Andrew when everybody knew that tramps went by such names as Jimmy, Joe, old Bill, and the like? But Andrew would quietly and firmly put them right. "My name is Andrew," he'd say. And the person who had spoken with too much familiarity would feel put down, and slightly aggrieved, and perhaps no longer disposed to talk to the tramp. Some of the people, including the children, avoided him or pretended they were not at home if he came knocking at their door, because they thought he was a wee bit odd and had some strange ways about him. There were even those who were frightened of him, but gave him food, hastily, lest something unpleasant should happen to them. But, in general, people neither thought much about him, nor were bothered about him; he only rarely impinged upon the existence of the house-dwelling population. He would occasionally be seen along the lanes, and whoever saw him might mention it, in passing, to a friend, and both would nod and murmur "Aye," and secretly would be relieved that he was still alive and mobile, and would give no cause for concern.

'One day, Georgette—'

'Strange name.'

'Never heard of Georgette Heyer? No? I suppose not. Well, anyway, one day Georgette discovered where Andrew lived. Doubtless everyone else had known for months, but with the unobservant, inward gaze of a girl in her late teens, she had been oblivious. She was with her parents, driving up the steep narrow hill that was on the road to the village. It was late afternoon in autumn, the air was mild and soggy, and they drove suddenly, without warning, into a solid band of mist, that emanated, like ectoplasm from a medium's mouth—'

'Ugh!'

'—from a gap in the deep rock cutting through which the road climbed. The car filled with the tingling-sweet scent of woodsmoke, and as they drove by, Georgette saw a grey figure standing by a smoking fire. The picture moved past so quickly that it was almost subliminal and was implanted permanently in the girl's mind. In the days that followed, its significance and detail grew disproportionately large in relation to her daily life.

'For Georgette was bored. She was floating lethargically on the sluggish river between school and university, idly querying the meaning of life, the universe and her previous boyfriend's final kiss.

'The lone grey figure of the tramp, hunched over the embers of his fire, in the dusky light of the dying day! What a strangely romantic figure! What wondrous tales he could surely tell. Georgette had a camera, and she liked to write, long poems with neither rhyme nor metre, and short articles for her own amusement. She began to imagine herself talking to this man, this Andrew (a name, surely, that indicated remembrance of good times past?), gaining his confidence, gently probing. She visualised the starkly simple photograph that she would take, the tramp set against the plain backdrop of the sky, his face subtly betraying the story of his past. She longed to interview him, to reveal him and show the world her skill.

'One day, she realised that this day-dreaming was consuming time and energy and emotion, and that she must turn the idea into reality, or die frustrated. She planned the logistics of her expedition, how she might manage to borrow the car, and where she would park it. Then, when the time was ready, she bought a packet of biscuits and a half-pound of best back bacon with her savings, and put her gifts and her camera, notebook and pencil in a bag, and set out on her voyage of discovery.'

'It was a bit risky, wasn't it, going off to talk to some weirdo on her own, without telling anyone? What if he'd attacked her?'

'It never occurred to her that it could be dangerous. Don't forget that this happened a long time ago, in a quiet rural environment. Attacks like that were uncommon – or perhaps unreported – then. It wasn't a likelihood that people worried about. Are you getting bored? Do you want to make some more tea?'

'No. And no. You could lean back against me, though, and keep me warm.'

'You're supposed to be tough and not feel the cold. Right! So, Georgette parked her car at the top of the hill, inside an open gate where no one would see it, and walked down to Andrew's shelter. A few words about the shelter – it was a small quarry, that had been blasted out of the rock face to form a semicircular indentation. The opening from the road was narrow, but the quarry itself was ten or fifteen feet across. The sides sloped and overhung the base, and the branches of trees that grew on top of the cliff were interlaced above the gap, so that the shelter appeared to have a living roof. The walls were dark, and long straight stalks of ivy reached down from the mat of vegetation like snakes with anchored tails. Dark gloom pervaded the air—'

'The *very* air.'

'You're right. The very air.'

'Why are you describing the shelter now, at this point. Surely Georgina – Georgette – would have noticed all this later?'

'You need to understand the atmosphere of the place. And Georgette has, in any case, just arrived at the entrance. She "took it all in, in a flash." Now please don't interrupt any more, I happen to know that Georgette treated the whole incident very seriously. Just try to imagine what it was like. She was standing at the entrance, holding her gifts, with her bag slung over her shoulder. She would have appeared suddenly, silently, because she had walked the last few yards very quietly and nervously, ready to turn instantly and leave. As she stood at the entrance, she would have been lit by the daylight in the cutting. At first, she would have been unable to see Andrew clearly, for he was sitting in the gloom of his shelter, but the light from the fire would have lit his face from below. He was burning small sticks, that crackled and sent up sparks, and his eyes gleamed with orange reflections as he raised his head to look at her.

' "Hallo," said Georgette. "I've brought you one or two things."

'She held them out.

'Andrew continued to stare at her. Eventually, he nodded.

' "Aye."

' "I'm sorry to bother you. Shall I put them here?"

'She suddenly wanted to leave the food, and run. She took a step inside the entrance, and leant forward to place the gifts on a mound of earth, but Andrew stood up quickly and gestured for her to enter.

' "Oh, no, I'm sorry. I can't stay. I have to get home!"

'But he beckoned again.

' "Come on, come on in and sit down so I can see what you've got."

'He had a deep, hoarse voice, as though he had a sore throat, but she thought that he was smiling, through his bush of facial hair. He stepped back and waved his hand towards the single seat, a rickety wooden chair by the fire. She couldn't refuse, she was committed. She handed him the bacon and biscuits, then she sat down and watched as he put the blackened kettle on the fire. He examined the food she had brought, and grunted, then put the bacon inside an empty saucepan and weighted its lid with a stone. He placed the packet of biscuits on a box. Georgette didn't know whether he was pleased or offended, because he never referred to the food again; she wished now she hadn't used quite so much of her money. Andrew didn't speak to her, but continued pottering around amongst his few possessions. She didn't know what to do, and was hoping, by now rather desperately, that their interesting conversation would soon begin. Eventually, trying to please him, she said: "This is a nice place you've got here."

'Andrew stopped whatever it was that he had been doing, and straightened up. He looked at her, his expression was partly hidden by the long brown tangle of his hair and beard, but his face was a pattern of horizontal lines – his eyebrows, the creases round his eyes, his moustache and the gap of his mouth. The lines moved closer together as he screwed up his face. Then he smiled, and the smile was made wider by dark, toothless gaps.

' "You think so," he said, a statement not a question. "You think it's a nice place."

'Georgette looked around. The place was littered with oddments, dumped here and there without order or logic. There were pans, wooden fruit crates, a transistor radio, oddments of clothing – a dark overcoat, an incongruously bright red woollen pullover – empty fertiliser sacks and a pile of old curtains. Around the fire were miscellaneous items of crockery, and steel cutlery, empty jars and blackened tins. Andrew watched her as she glanced around and then, without a word, took the steaming kettle from the fire. He lifted the lid and dropped in two pinches of tea, then, after a minute, poured the brew into a tin mug and a china cup.

' "There's no sugar, but you can have milk," he said and, when she nodded, tipped milk from a bottle into the cup and handed it to her. Clots of thick yellow oil swirled on the surface, and Georgette caught her breath at the sour smell as she lifted the cup towards her mouth. Andrew squatted on his heels and stared at the fire. She couldn't tell his age, he might have been anything from mid-thirties to mid-fifties.

' "Have you lived here long?" she asked, shifting slightly on the seat, and wondering if she could tip the tea on the ground without him noticing.

'He merely grunted. She tried again.

' "It must be quite a hard life, especially when the weather's cold."

'He continued to stare at the fire, holding his tin mug towards the blaze, but he finally nodded, and said: "Aye."

'Georgette took another sip of tea.

' "Have you done this for a long time?" She knew she was being presumptuous and inquisitive, but she had to know! "Is it something you wanted to do – Andrew—" (it required courage to speak his name) "or don't you have anywhere else to go?"

'She was ashamed of herself, at her effrontery, and she dreaded, yet hoped for, an outburst in response. But Andrew merely put down his mug and stood up, pulling down his baggy, beige pullover. He poked at the pile of curtains with his foot, and picked up then put down a stained tweed cap. He muttered to himself and grunted, and then came swiftly towards Georgette, and put an arm around her shoulder. He bent down and smiled into her face. She spilled her tea in shock, and leapt to her feet, slipping sideways underneath his arm. He continued to smile his dark, open smile.

' "Very nice," he said, slowly and deliberately.

'Georgette was backing towards the entrance, clutching her shoulder-bag and the cup.

' "I've really got to go," she said. "Goodbye. And thank you for the tea."

'She put the cup down on the ground, tried to make a slow and dignified exit, and then began to walk very quickly up the hill towards her car. She looked back, once, and saw Andrew standing in the middle of the road, but she couldn't stop.

' "Very nice!" he shouted again, and his laughter echoed back from the smooth cut rock.'

I disentangled myself from Jos's arms, and stood up and stretched.

'What then?' he asked.

'That's it. End of story.'

'So nothing happened. She didn't get her story. And she never went back?'

'No, of course she didn't.' I laughed. 'How could she?'

Jos was puzzled, disappointed.

'You had this tremendous build-up, I was expecting something really dramatic to happen – that he'd turn out to be a duke, or that he enticed her into his pile of curtains. But it was all a bit of a flop, really.'

'Oh, Jos!' I didn't know whether to laugh or to be exasperated. 'Plenty happened, why can't you see? I'm not going to spell it out for you, you'll just have to think about it.'

He pushed himself upright and groaned.

'Well, don't make me sit here to think about it! I'm going to have to build a comfortable bench if we're going to indulge in campfire stories.'

He started to pick up plates and mugs.

'Leave them. I'll worry about them in the morning.'

'I suppose I'd better be going, then. I don't particularly want to fall over the cliff in the dark!'

The fire was low, and there was a light, chill breeze from the sea. An oyster-catcher whistled, sleepily, on the shore. I slipped my hands under Jos's big, patterned pullover and held his warm body against mine.

'Would you stay the night?'

He held me away from him, and looked at me in surprise.

'Do you mean it? Are you sure?'

I nodded, embarrassed that I had capitulated so soon. Jos was so silent that I thought he was going to refuse; then he gave an odd little sigh, and pushed my hair back from my forehead as he stared into my face.

'Strange lady! Sometimes you are so good to me – and other

times . . . I love you so much that you frighten me. See—' he shrugged slightly '—you even frighten me into saying these stupid things.'

The intensity of his bewilderment chilled me for a moment, and I tried to laugh it off.

'Are you saying yes or no? I'm not quite sure.'

'Of course I'm saying yes. I haven't got around to saying it yet, that's all! I think I'm a bit nervous!'

'Of staying the night? Or of sleeping in a cave?'

'Both, probably. I can't believe that I'll be able to wake up in the night and feel that I'm next to you. And you'll be there in the morning when I wake up.'

'It depends how late you wake!'

Strangely, I was nervous, too, and had to resist the need to fill in silences with inanities. I was anxious about the impression the crypt would make, and I was anxious that I shouldn't seem too set in my own rituals of night-time preparation. But I showed Jos how I damped down the fire so that it might survive until morning, and we lit candles and partly closed the door-covering. There was no passion between us, only a polite hesitancy. I was shaking with tension, but we undressed and piled our clothes on boxes, and slid carefully into the narrow bed. It felt chill and damp against my naked skin, and, as we cuddled together for warmth, my teeth chattered with cold and nerves. Jos was kind and understanding; he talked softly, and hugged me to him. There was no haste, for we had all night, and he warmed and slowly, gently, soothed me. He made love to me, with love, and my eyes were full of tears at his kindness.

'What's wrong, my love?' He licked my damp cheek. 'Would you feel safer if we put the mattress on the floor?'

'No, it's not that. Although perhaps I should make the bed stronger.'

'Does that mean you'll ask me back?'

'It's that damn dragon, he puts me off. I can feel him watching us, as though we're experimental animals.'

'You're mad!'

'No. I have to live with him, you don't. I'm going to cover him up.'

It was difficult, because the mosaic was smooth, but in the end I stood the chair upon a box and hung a shirt across its back, so that the dragon's eyes were hidden. He glared furiously at me, but kept quiet.

'What about the ewe?'

'Oh, she's no bother. She dissociates herself from mundane matters, most of the time. She's very single-minded, an essentially herbivorous outlook on life. *"Alles fleisch es ist wie gras"* and so on. Oh! Why didn't I think of that before? Of course! She represents the other part of the cycle. That is quite extraordinary, that it's taken me all this time to see it!'

'Harriet, what on earth are you talking about? You're delirious. Come back to bed. Please.'

I wanted to stand and look at the sheep, and to think about her significance, but Jos was insistent, and I was cold.

'God! You're absolutely freezing, goosepimples everywhere.'

My teeth were chattering again, but with cold, not nervousness, and Jos shivered exaggeratedly as I put my icy hands against his back.

'You're starting to scare me again,' he whispered. 'I'm not sure I shall want to come back if you're going to do this to me. Will you explain what you were talking about?'

'I'm not sure I can, yet, because I still haven't worked it out myself.'

And it was a private matter; I had never imagined explaining this new philosophy, outlook, call it what you will – religion, even? – to anyone else, so I could not articulate the concepts. Philosophy is too precise a word, anyway, for ideas that were as yet vague, unformed, perhaps no more than feelings, linkages half-glimpsed. I needed mental discipline to think the ideas through, and to organise the fragments into a connected whole. I knew that a logical framework was there, if I could commit myself to a holistic approach; the thought was exciting, and I briefly regretted Jos's presence. Yet the excitement bubbled gently in my mind, and I wanted to share a fraction of it with him, for was he not also a part of this complex meshwork of life and death? Surely we would *both* be permitted to hear the hymn of the sea? We had been brought together to share in this wonderful circle, to become integrated within this wild and delicate environment. How petty everything else seemed in comparison, how unimportant. I wanted to experience again that extra acuity and widening of the sensory field, that expanded, questing, beyond the visible horizons; and I wanted Jos to experience it, too.

Then, suddenly, the memory popped into my mind, like a small explosion: Jos on the moor, and the curlew calling; Jos, stating, briefly, that when he heard that sound he wanted to bury himself in the heather. The statement had been ambiguous, but I had thought, hoped, that I had probably understood what he really meant; now, with hindsight, I was almost certain.

'Jos!' I propped myself on an elbow and stared down at the dark shape of his face; I could scarcely see his features because the candle had burnt low, but the damp surface of his eyes shone in the faint light.

'I was beginning to think you were in a sulk, or had gone to sleep. I'm listening.'

'Jos, do you remember how, one time, I can't remember when, we were up on the moor at the back of the croft, and we heard a curlew? It was early in the year, before the spring, I think, because everything was very brown and bare. And there was a lone curlew calling. You said something interesting then—'

'That's not unusual.'

'Something about how that sound made you want to bury yourself in the heather, to lie down in the heather. I can't quite remember how you phrased it. What did you mean?'

'Shall we get up again and get dressed? I'm beginning to suspect that you're a nocturnal animal. Or perhaps it's the effect of the crab salad – isn't crab supposed to give one nightmares?'

'I am sorry – but there's so much to think about. This is all so strange. And wonderful. It's not really nightmarish, is it? I haven't told you, have I, how happy I am, very happy, that you're here? The words were in my head, but I hadn't said them. I need to remind myself to say these things out loud.'

'Are you really happy? I feel such an intruder, I wasn't sure if you really wanted me. It's very strange for me, too, to be sleeping here – no, lying here – with you, in a cave. Making love to you in a cave. I still can't believe this has actually happened, it's only a few days since I was fantasising about this sort of thing! Ah, Harriet!' he sighed. 'Aaaah, Harriet. Forget about curlews. Do with me as you will, you've completely bewitched me.'

I hadn't told Jos about my recent encounter with Robbie Ferguson, either. I was becoming confused, losing track. Jos's influence was starting to spread throughout my body. Lying down in the heather, that was it. I caught hold of his hand and held it.

'It's important. Think back and try to remember the sensation when you—'

'I'm overcome with sensations now!'

'The curlew! Remember what effect that sound had on you. Think of the sound, the single high "whoo-weep", then another, and another.' I whistled, trying to imitate the call. 'That sound, echoing across the moor.'

I stopped, to give him time to imagine it. He lay quite still for a moment, then shivered slightly and hunched his shoulders.

'Yes. There's such an emptiness about it, isn't there? But if you heard a curlew in a zoo, say, it wouldn't have the same effect. Or even in a wood. Both unlikely of course. But it's only really in combination with the empty space that one receives the full effect. I'm trying to think back.' He spoke slowly, hesitantly, trying to analyse his response. 'It makes one very – aware, I think, that's it, very aware of one's surroundings. In that earlier case, the emptiness (I'm excluding you, you see), a sort of wild beauty, untouched. But that you want to touch.' Now he was puzzled. 'Yes, perhaps that's the heart of it. You want to *touch* it?'

'So when you said you wanted to bury yourself in the heather, do you think that was because you wanted to hide from the curlew? Or did you mean something else?'

'Oh no! I didn't want to hide! I wanted to be part of what I could see – and hear.' He was emphatic. 'I felt deliberately excluded, at that moment. But it was so quick, Harriet. The feeling must have been gone in an instant.'

'Yes – I'm sorry to keep probing – but by burying yourself in the heather, you imagined yourself lying down, reaching out, becoming part of the wildness and the beauty. And perhaps also of the curlew's cry, because they were all part of each other.'

'I think that's what I just said, actually. It's strange – well, it's embarrassing, really – I've never been forced to analyse my feelings before. I wouldn't ever have recognised those feelings as my own, if you hadn't made me think about that situation!'

'I'm so happy! I had hoped so much that was what you had meant by burying yourself.'

'Why is it so important? I can't understand. Oh Hell! I seem to be whingeing about not understanding all the time, these days.'

'I know. And I'm sorry to have acted like the Grand Inquisitor. I know it's not considered very masculine for men your age to feel emotional about beautiful views – beautiful women, yes—'

'That's an incredibly sexist thing to say. I didn't think you'd stoop so low.'

'All right. But I'm so happy that you have this feeling of "awareness" – I can't think of a better word. What I'm trying to say, is that I have it, too. And it's the reason why I choose to live here, in the crypt.'

'Oh.'

The silence stretched out, and I wondered which of the many implications of that statement Jos was considering. Or perhaps he was too surprised (or uninterested) to consider the statement at all. I lay tensely beside him, waiting for him to speak, or snore.

'Does that mean, then, that you have taken the opposite approach? You have buried yourself within the heather in order to hide? If so, I'm very surprised. And you'll need to help me to understand the reasons. You'll still have to help me to understand, whatever the interpretation, actually.'

'To bury myself? No, I had not thought of that interpretation at all, in relation to myself. It's certainly not what I meant.'

I was stunned; but, of course, it was an equally valid interpretation, given the preceding discussion. How much could I tell him? How could I explain the inexplicable?

'The morning after the roof of the cottage was damaged, I walked up on to the cliffs, because I needed to get away, to remove myself, from the mess. The noise up there was deafening – the sea charging in, wave after wave, and bursting over the land. And the wind! Explosions of spray! Nothing was still, nothing was at peace, the whole world was in a turmoil. But it wasn't threatening, despite what had happened to the cottage. There was exuberance, and laughter, a carelessness, as though everything had been released from physical constraints. Like a holiday.'

As I remembered, and spoke, my eyes and ears, and even my skin, became alive and sensitive, and I saw how the fretted figures of spray had joined with the trailing skeins of clouds. I heard how the shout of the sea and the booming laughter of the wind had mingled their voices in song, and how the whole world had spun its fine strong web around me, and drawn me in to the edge of its sentient sphere, teasing, beckoning, 'Join us, join us.' And although my body was still beside Jos, my eyes saw again the gannet, shining white like the colour of peace, but not surrender, beating, questing through the turmoil, as the sea and sky paused briefly, locally, to let it pass.

'Go on. Please tell me.'

I sighed. 'Well, basically, although at first I experienced the usual feeling of exclusion – you see, for me, having lived here so long, it's quite a common experience – I suddenly felt that I was accepted. Briefly. And although that feeling lasted only a moment, I was left with the idea that I, too, had been welcomed. It was almost like a blessing, Jos. I can't explain how unbelievably moved and joyous I felt. Oh, I know this sounds like the romanticising of a middle-aged woman – I'm sorry, it must be very off-putting for you. Boring.'

'Go on, though. You still haven't explained why living here should help. I understand now about the awareness – you've made me see something new and rather surprising, perhaps even disturbing, in myself – and I can see how it might be possible to feel involved. But why should it lead you to do something as drastic as this?'

'There was a whole sequence of events that seemed to indicate that this was the correct answer, the key. The key to the mystery, the key that would unlock an incalculable hoard of riches, for what greater wealth could there be than to have the reason for existence revealed? Hah, but I was not so naive! Perhaps part of it *was* to do with feeling safer, inside the earth, after my recent experience. Animals – foxes, voles – use holes, so why don't I? And there was one here, purpose-built, enduring, magnificent, even with a bed whereon I might lie with thee, my love. What could be more natural!'

'You could lie with me, my love, upon the floor! But perhaps you were referring to your cave, your bolt-hole, rather than this unsteady bed. Bolts, and nuts, and screws. I've shot my bolt. You see, everything is linked together!'

But his soft laugh was forced, and I perceived that he twisted away the thread of conversation so that he could give himself space to think.

And throughout our conversation, the sea beat softly in our ears like a heartbeat, a pulse whose strength spelt out life.

'You said you had been a Catholic, but that you had lapsed.'

'It was more positive than that. There was a conscious cessation, a severing.'

'Did that happen as a result of this revelation you had on the clifftop?'

'No, not directly. And, initially, I thought that the felling of the chimney was a consequence of what I see now as my gradual sliding away from organised religion. The chimney was blown down by the Wrath of God, as a punishment. I was very confused at that stage, even terrified, once or twice. My new ideas developed gradually – no, something made me stop believing . . . It was quite recent, really. It suddenly came to me . . . My ideas still aren't clearly defined. Jos – I'm not sure I want to talk about this any more. Somehow it sounds so absurd and trivial when I try to explain it. I can feel that you're being alienated. It needn't matter to you what I believe, it needn't interfere.'

I didn't believe that, but I began to be frightened that he would see me for what, perhaps, I am – a lonely crackpot living in a cave. And that I would disgust him. Without him . . . I lay down against him, and felt how our bodies kissed along their length.

'We should sleep. It must already be after three, look how you can almost see the rocks outside the door.'

'Ach, I think my head will burst, there is so much to think and talk about. How did I ever become entangled with you, my witch-woman. Ancient crone of the crypt! Jesus, Harriet, why do you go on so much about being old and boring? Just feel us together.'

He squirmed, and the feel of his skin against mine was exquisite pleasure.

'I'm so excited, honoured is a better word, that you allow me to have you.'

'What on earth are you saying, Jos? That I allow you!' (It has been pre-ordained.)

'The things we talk about! The things we do! I don't know anyone like this at home – they all seem so, oh—' I felt him shrug, '—superficial. You fascinate me. And I seem to end up saying things like this, that I'd never imagined myself saying to anyone. No inhibitions! What am I doing!'

My heart swelled with dark warmth. Whose heart would not, given such an overflowing of praise and trust? What, indeed, had happened to both of us? How had my protective egg-shell cracked and left me thus so shockingly exposed? But I no longer needed it, for was I not protected by the whole organic and inorganic world? And yet, and yet . . . I knew that Jos's eyes would one day see the ordinariness of me.

'Don't forget Georgette.'

'She can't possibly have anything to do with us. Can she? Another bedtime riddle?'

'Was it Andrew's shelter that lent the mystery? Don't you think she was probably disappointed with the reality? And what did he think of her?'

'Didn't Georgette tell you what she thought? I wonder how true the story is, anyway.'

'Oh, it was mostly true. With considerable hindsight, the episode was far from being a failure. I'm sure she learnt a lot about herself, and other people. How not to expect too much, and how the unexpected may be turned to later advantage. And so on.'

'Georgette being you, I suppose?'

'Well, I suppose I could have called them Harry and Josephine. But Harry would not have laughed.'

'This is too complicated. I'm too tired to think – or talk. Cuddle me.'

'Not tonight, Josephine.'

'Stop giggling, Harriet, you're so childish, I can't believe you're so old! And the bed's going to collapse.'

Twenty-four

I wish now that I'd kept a diary of the summer's events, but I'd ceased doing so when I moved to the crypt. I still have the old exercise books, their pages curled at the edges with damp. I looked through them not long ago and was impressed at the extraordinariness of my isolated life, the almost pathological intensity of my need to be alone, to avoid contact with other people. The skulking, the hiding, the questions that had to be avoided, and the half-lies that had to be given in reply. And yet I had not been unhappy; far from it, for contacts with civilisation had been so few that they had impinged only temporarily upon my solitude. For who could be unhappy when forced to rely on self-reliance, keeping to one's own private schedule, arguing with no one except oneself, supplying one's own conversation, and, above all else, having time to stop and appreciate that which was all around? Who could possibly regret the encircling freedom of solitude?

But I've forgotten, haven't I, that I wasn't truly free? Can I really have forgotten why I came here? The oppressive tyranny of guilt that drove me in madness to this sanctuary? The perpetual apology, and atonement, and submission. Such an unimaginable bequest of imagined guilt. Ah, the wasted years and the wasted self-pitying tears. Dear Tom, with your stumpy limbs and wide, innocent smile; you were not my fault, you just happened. Now, at last, I'm free to accept your life and death for what they were, uncomplicated and sweet. I'm free, Tom! The new freedom is both greater and less: freedom from guilt and stultifying ritual; freedom to love again; freedom, even, to die, to be disseminated into the greatest freedom of all. But less freedom, too, because of Jos; I'm no longer free to be entirely selfish, and that implies an external constraint on the freedom to die. What did I once write? That the fear of death was obviated in the absence of people who might mourn? I don't want to be forced to fear death once more. He would mourn; and yet, surely, he would, in time, recover and return to the familiar comforts of his own world? Here, in the artificiality of our co-existence, it's easy to become obsessive, possessive, over-responsive.

Compromise doesn't arise without diplomacy and perseverance, and both of us have much to learn! As the days pass, there is a mutual improvement, and there are subtle shiftings in the balance of our relationship. Thwarted, Jos becomes outspoken, the old arrogance and disrespect flare briefly. Thwarted, I enclose myself in silence, and seek to be alone. But our need for each other increases; because he *is* needed.

That morning in July, when we both awoke, together for the first time in the crypt, we were both stiff and bleary. A sub-conscious nocturnal awareness must have kept us rigid in our sleep, lest we turn and push each other from the narrow bed. We woke late; the clouds were flat and grey, the crypt was damp, and love, lust and conversation had gone out with the tide and the fire. My bones ached and my face sagged baggily, and I wanted to be left alone, but I lit the Calor stove and boiled water for washing and for tea. We sat quietly and held our mugs tightly to give us warmth. I scattered the scant remains of our supper for the robin and chaffinch that had followed me from the croft, and I collected up the shells and shattered claws of our two fine crabs, putting them into a bucket so that they could be returned to the scavengers on the shore.

The crabs reminded me that I still had not told Jos about Robbie Ferguson. I'd seen Robbie's boat in the distance when I went out to raise the pots, but he hadn't approached Camus Beag again. I mentioned the earlier encounter to Jos, and explained that we had to thank Robbie Ferguson, yet again, for the bait and thus the crabs, and, in consequence, for bringing us together overnight! Jos was angry; he didn't trust the man, he disliked him for his interference. But now it was my turn to disagree, and I reminded Jos of his own words, that there was nothing further to fear from Ferguson, since he was now aware of our relationship. (I suspect that Jos was also, secretly, pleased and proud to have been found out, so that his skill in sexual conquest could be applauded. Who had conquered whom? I neither knew nor cared – I wanted to wash my face.)

We didn't meet again that day; spirit and emotions were drained through over-stimulation and lack of sleep. We rarely, in the days that followed, arranged time or place to meet but, at some particular hour, one of us would walk across to find the other. Then there would be that small jump of the heart, the quickening of breath, the fleeting mixture of dread and anticipation, that comes with the unexpected encounter. Sometimes I experienced the urge to stop, and watch unseen, what Jos was doing. Or else the need to shout and run. Or even, when he came to find me, the wish to appear engrossed in some minor task so that he would think he had surprised me, unaware. What a variety of reactions are available, ready to be plucked off the supermarket shelf and tested, to try unspontaneously to be spontaneous!

Sometimes we shared a meal, sometimes we watched seals or hunted agates. Several times Jos stayed the night with me, and the dragon's burning voyeur's eyes lent a certain spice to our love-making. We fished and we rowed; once, I persuaded Jos to bathe with me in the burn; we took the Herbal and we looked for new plant flavours to vary our diet; I showed him my favourite lochan, and how to stack peat blocks to dry, and he showed me a peregrine's nest and nesting shags in a cave piled high with guano. I learnt the details of his body, and he knew mine, our moles, scars or stretch-marks were familiar to each other's eyes and fingertips.

I learnt his expressions, the raised eyebrow, the furrowed frown, round-faced joy and dark-eyed thoughtful stare, and his changes from sage to raucous boy to tender lover. I trimmed his beard; he cut my hair and, romantic, placed some in a polythene bag inside his notebook. That day, too, he took my photograph, catching me by surprise as I sat with my eyes closed and face towards the sun.

Jos showed me his notes and told me about the seals. He was single-minded in his work, and I was, rightly, excluded. I saw the meticulous detail of his log-book, the daily listings of the sightings, the behaviour and for how long each seal performed a particular activity. It was a busy time of year, and the rocks were more crowded, for the females had produced their young. Now we could hear soft groans and moans as the normally silent animals communicated. Bulls lurched around on the rocks, heads reared, in their search for new mates, and several times we feared for the safety of the tiny pups. Jos sat for hours, and watched and wrote; pages of notes and data, in which, as yet, there seemed to be no pattern. He was engrossed, alternately excited and despondent. His absorption fascinated me, and I dared not admit that sleeping seals, fat and incongruous like balloons filled with water, had begun to bore me. Did the dragon keep notes on us, too, and did we bore the sheep?

The history of the colony also interested him. If, as he assumed, his colony contained survivors of the group that had been observed thirty years earlier, why had that original colony moved south to this unusual and less hospitable location? Short of communicating directly with the seals, there was probably no way of finding out, but the problem was intriguing, and we promised ourselves that we would plan another expedition, this time to the north to find the colony's former site. It was unlikely that it would contain any clues, but the idea of another outing appealed and held the promise of a picnic, and new views and treasures to discover. We made no clear plans but drifted along from day to day, confident that the right day for the expedition would present itself.

I wish I had kept a diary of those days, to chart the perceptible slide: from extreme oscillations, the passion and desire for coupling to the fear of loss of individuality, submersion within that state of duality that describes the bonded human couple. We slid through careful respect (old-fashioned word, that denotes recognition of another's completeness) and cautiousness, towards a quiet complacency and occasional youthful disrespect or the intolerance of one age-group towards another, each of us confident that temporary damage would not be irreparable. There were times of laughter, of boredom, of tension, there were times when we talked and argued, or stayed silent. And thus, in several weeks, we reached a state of acceptance and near-tolerance, and something, on my part, that might perhaps have been stronger than liking. But to describe this transition as a sliding is probably inaccurate, because that necessarily implies descent. Perhaps it is better to think of a slow ascent to the uninterrupted views of a plateau, rising above the turbulent clouds of the early days. Whatever metaphor one chooses, it's fair to say that the relationship between us became more secure, as our sense of ease in each other's company increased.

If only summer could have lasted for ever! The crypt was dry and sweet-smelling with dried herbs and grass, the croft garden was exuberant with vegetables and wild rose. Pale splurges of yellow honeysuckle dotted the scrubby woodland, and I dug up a root and planted it by the cottage gable. I was fit and healthy, and I felt that I wore my body well. The sun and wind tanned my skin, and each day the sea massaged my thighs and made buoyant my sagging breasts. I rejoiced to feel the air against my face and the grass beneath my feet. For now my skin was more sensitive to the touch and feel of things, so that it was no longer visual beauty that whispered its welcome, but the silk of sea-smooth pebbles, the sticky embrace of a sea-anemone, and the feathery softness of cotton grass. I longed to touch and stroke; the polished granite of the mausoleum chilled my cheek, and my fingers were scoured by the river sand. Even the air pressed upon my skin, so that, once, the sensuous pleasure nearly overwhelmed me and I strode, my unbuttoned blouse an open invitation, to meet my lusting but embarrassed lover.

'Someone may see,' he whispered, shocked, but his hands were reaching out towards me.

'But who?' I laughed. 'There's only you!'

'I surrender. Thank God you haven't got a spear.'

But not for me the blatant inhibitionism of Brünnhilde's reinforced cones and leather-thonged thighs! My breast-plate was the air.

Later, Jos asked, 'Do you often walk around like that?'

'Only when I'm warm. Do you like it?'

'Do you do it for Robbie Ferguson, too?'

'What?' I sat up slowly, unbelieving.

'Is that why I heard him talking like that about you to the shearers?'

He looked away, his voice tight, unable to say the words.

'No.' I was careful. 'I think – only think, mind you, I have no proof – I think he once saw me sunbathing, through his binoculars. I was up on Sgurr Mor – you know where, where you found me – after Finn – and the Fergusons' boat was down in the bay. Think how far away that is. He must have had to use his imagination.'

'It's just that he's always hanging around.'

(Was he? I tried to remember, but couldn't.) I made myself smile. 'But he's always out at sea!'

Grudgingly, against his will, Jos smiled too, and once more we pushed the rest of the world aside, and concentrated upon our private summer idyll.

There must have been times when Jos thought about his future and his past, but we were careful not to approach the subject. But there was a day when our fragile, stable structure was roughly shaken. It was an afternoon in late July, and I'd taken the boat out to trail a line and see what was biting. The day was calm, and nothing took the bait, so, on impulse, I decided to row round to the bay below Jos's tent. I would wave to my seal-watcher; we would be able to see each other, but could not talk or touch, sweet torture. As I came round the point, I looked over my shoulder, to set my course, but instead of one tent, there were two. A second tent, identical, bright orange and ridged, was pitched next to Jos's. The boat pitched in the eddies that swirled round the point, as I sat still and stared, uncomprehending. The glossy head of a seal broke through the surface nearby, and its eyes were like round, dark glasses as it looked at me, but I scarcely noticed. The tent drifted in and out of focus, and my eyes were dry with looking. The dull crash and sigh of the sea grew louder, and I watched as each low swell nudged the cliff and broke apart, into bright white cascades of foam, that bubbled and bobbed upon the surface. The boat rocked soothingly as the swell bore us towards the cliff, and I gazed at the bubbles but saw two orange tents. But now the backwash made us pitch and yaw, and my arms awoke and pulled us away from the black teeth that smiled up through the cream, and rowed us back to Camus Beag.

I didn't spy. I kept away from the crypt and the croft for as long as I could each day. I went away on long walks inland and to the south, exploring in minute detail the rocky outcrops on the moors, the beds and banks of burns, and weedy inlets on the shores. I wore dark clothing as camouflage, and I walked, scrambled, slid and peered, and at the end of each day my rucksack and my memory were full of natural treasures.

There was a strange numbness, a shying-away, when I thought of Jos. The old fear of the intruder had returned, as strong as ever, deeply conditioned, and although I didn't fear Jos, it was those whom he brought with him that had frightened me. There was a picture lurking in my mind, of a scuffed wooden wedge, and as my eye travelled upwards from its point I saw one, then two, then three, four, five people, all faceless except two. But it was a distant picture, blurry. Most clearly, and more often, I saw myself, as from outside, wandering alone, timeless, through the seasons and their scents. I was alone, and although I didn't see the colours of the image, the soft warm perfume of infinite peace filled my nostrils.

Overnight, the weather changed. I was woken by the sound of rain splashing into a puddle outside the door, and a cold damp wind blew in through the entrance. The hearth was sodden, and I closed the door-covering and stayed inside, lying on the bed, blank-minded, half-dozing. The dragon had been strangely silent for the past few days, and now it was the sheep who spoke. She was looking at the wild flowers that I had brought home to identify, and she started to tell me which she preferred to eat. I chided her for destroying them, but she pointed out that I had done the same, and then bleated something about 'out of the sweetness came forth strength'. I couldn't be bothered to unravel her enigmas, but, as I drifted in and out of sleep, her voice droned on about lions lying down with lambs, and that she'd warned her lambs to be careful of wolves. Or was it Trojan horses? And what was that about horses' mouths? Listening to her soporific voice was more soothing than counting sheep, and so, when the dragon roared 'Hah!', I leapt upright, stiff with shock.

'Harriet? Harriet, are you there?'

I didn't answer, for I imagined the faceless figure, standing quietly behind him, waiting.

'It's only me – he's gone! Harriet!'

I stood up, indecisive. He had been in contact with the outside world, perhaps contaminated. He was like a stranger, whom I would have to learn to know again.

'Harriet? Are you there?'

'I'm here. Come in.'

I held open the covering, and stood aside. He shone with rain and his beard dripped water. Even in the dim light, with blinded eyes, he must have seen my reticence. We remained standing by the door, and I didn't know what to say because I was mesmerised by our silence.

'He's gone.'

I nodded. Jos's face was pale and his eyes were dark pits in the gloom as he peered at me. Rain continued splashing as the silence stretched.

'Look at me, Harriet. Have you gone, too?'

The empty hopelessness of that quiet question, almost a

statement, was terrifying. The words fell between us, creating an emptiness into which I was sucked, and I hugged his stiff, wet body against mine and held his sodden head. He was quietly unresisting, having slipped, yet again, beneath my defences; his eyes were closed, and he sighed as I murmured that I loved him, for there was no mistaking the tenderness and relief that made me ache to care for him. I helped him take off his wet coat, and we lay down, clothed, upon the bed. We held each other tightly, silently, and soon we slept.

When we woke, Jos had so much to tell: of the shock when his supervisor had arrived, unannounced; of his fear that I might run into them, then his relief when he realised that I must have seen them and had decided to stay away.

'But then I became more and more convinced that you would be angry, and that you were blaming me for Peter's visit. I was certain that you'd never want to see me again, and that you'd fade away like a chameleon so that I would never find you. You nearly did.'

'But what about your supervisor? Didn't he want to know why you were so distracted? He presumably came here to discuss the project with you?'

'I don't think he noticed. I hope not, anyway. We had quite a good time together – he's a nice bloke, we get on really well – and we spent quite a lot of the time just kicking ideas around. He seemed to be really pleased to be out in the field and watching seals – escaping, he called it. He had some good ideas, actually.'

'You sound surprised.'

'Well, I suppose I was beginning to think that I knew more about the project than he did. I'm the one that's here, doing the work after all. But he's pretty clued up.'

'How old is he?'

'Why?'

'He presumably isn't terribly ancient if he brought his tent across and spent several nights lying on the ground.'

'Oh. MacGregor brought him some of the way. He's about your

age, I should think. You'd like him. He was quite keen to meet you, as a matter of fact, but I managed to dissuade him. I didn't think you'd like that.'

'Jos! What on earth have you told him? Why did he want to meet me?'

'I didn't tell him anything, if you mean about us. No, he knew about you living over here – on the croft, I mean – and he made some remarks about you having plenty of opportunity to observe wildlife, or something like that. That you'd probably be very informative. He asked if I'd talked to you.' Jos smiled at the memory.

'And?'

'Oh, I told him that you were a bit of a recluse. Actually—' his smile widened, '—I said that you were a misanthropist and that you positively dissuaded visitors. But it was Ferguson that nearly gave the game away, I almost had to stuff one of his stinking herring into his mouth to shut him up!'

'Robbie? What has he got to do with it?'

'We were out in his boat yesterday. I wished so much that you could have been with us – but without Peter and Robbie!'

'I'm totally bewildered. What has been going on, these past few days?'

'It was Peter's idea, I think he just wanted a jaunt out in the boat, really. It turned out that he'd also had the idea of going to look at the site of Jamieson's old colony, and he'd got on to Ferguson, when he arrived, and arranged for us to be picked up in the boat. That was yesterday.'

'So you've already been to the old haul-out site?'

'Oh, Harriet, yes, I'm sorry. Peter had already arranged it, I couldn't refuse. We'll go again, just the two of us. I promise. It's beautiful, I'd love to show it to you.'

'I've been there before, Jos, this isn't a very big island! But you still haven't explained about Robbie nearly giving the game away.'

'Ah yes. He brought the boat round to that small bay beyond

the bothy – do you know it? There's deep water at one side, and long smooth rocks, so he could get the boat in easily. And he'd also laid some pots around there – he's still hanging around, you see, I told you! Anyway, I helped him pull up one of the pots, and he started asking me how many crabs you'd caught with his bait, and if I'd enjoyed them. Cheeky bugger! Actually, he was a bit nasty about it. I shut him up, quickly. I'm sure Peter didn't hear because he was putting a film in his camera, in the wheelhouse.'

'Hmm.'

'Then, I can't remember how it came up. . . oh, I know, Ferguson and Peter were talking about storms, and Ferguson mentioned that your cottage had been wrecked. Peter was really interested and wanted to know about the cottage, but Ferguson just shut up. But then he said that you seemed to be managing very nicely now. He didn't quite do the "nudge, nudge, wink, wink" bit, but he was staring his bloody head off at me all the time. I just turned away and pretended I hadn't noticed.'

'And Peter?'

'He gave me a funny look. But he didn't mention it – you – again. Nothing definite was said, ever.'

'He'll probably be annoyed if he finds you're wasting your time running around with the local witch. It's more likely, I suppose, that he'll be worried. After all, he is responsible for you. "What would your parents say?" and so on.'

'My parents? Hell, I'm an adult, I'm running my own life, following my own career. I'm twenty-five, Harriet! My parents have nothing to do with it! You're not keeping me here against my will, you haven't raped me! We're nothing to do with anyone else.'

'I know that, Jos, but it's easy for me because my whole life is here. But you have another life, over there. This is analogous to a holiday romance, if you think about it, and soon you'll have no option other than to go back home.'

He buried his head against my neck, and his voice was a mutter that vibrated in my hair.

'I don't want to go back. Even three days without you was awful.'

I lay with my arms around him, and stared at the roof, making patterns in the stones as I wondered what we would do. As the faceless ones assumed identities, would they drive a wedge between us?

A few days later I went across to the village to buy some stores.

'Someone was asking after you the other day, by the way,' John MacGregor said. 'That professor or whatever he was, Mr Metcalfe.'

'Oh? What did he want to know?'

'I think he was maybe of the opinion that you might be staying in a tent. But I am not too sure, because he had a roundabout sort of way of approaching the question.'

I looked at John MacGregor, but he was staring out of the window, and there was a lightening in his face, a crinkling at the corners of his eyes. I waited, knowing that he was seeing Peter Metcalfe's face within his mind.

'And I think, now, that I may have given him a roundabout sort of answer, that was not quite an answer, you will understand.' He looked at me, then, and there was a brightness in his eyes, of half-concealed mirth. 'That you were well-known hereabouts for being an independent, resourceful kind of woman who did not care to interfere with another's business . . .' There was a faint pinkness in his cheeks, and he was staring, once more, out of the window. 'And I'm thinking that young Robbie will have been saying the same . . . if he wants his cigarettes . . .'

Twenty-five

Jos was baptised on a summer afternoon. It was a warm day, yet the sea was still startlingly cold, but there were no medusae. I had waited until the waters were clear and the time was right.

It was Jos, of course, who had told me that they were called medusae, and the name at once transformed them from pale, flaccid jelly, slimy things that crawled with legs upon the slimy sea, into mysterious, pulsating, sentient creatures, strong in form and purpose. They arrive every year in their thousands, perhaps millions; medusae, many-tentacled, yet blindly seeking each other. Jos asked me later if they congregated at a particular phase of the moon, but I hadn't kept a record. I was collecting limpets when I saw them, and I knew that by the evening tide each bay would be massed full of jellyfish. The light wind had begun to drop in the late afternoon, and the conditions would be perfect.

Jos was sitting on the headland, reading. There were photocopies beside him, weighted with a stone, and he was intent on his study. It was two weeks since the death of Finn, and I came up quietly behind him, so that I could stand unobserved and look at his bare back and bent head.

'Hallo.'

He jumped, frowned in irritation, but then his smile was like a beacon, and he caught me by the ankle and slid his right hand up my calf.

'Hallo. You gave me a fright.'

'I won't disturb you.'

'You have. I am. You always will.'

'I'm not going to stay. You're working.'

'No, I've stopped. Look!'

He recklessly threw the photocopy away, but it was caught quickly by a ragged bush, and was saved.

'I merely came to issue an invitation. I want you to come at eight o'clock tonight—'

'I want you to come now.' He moved his hand higher up my leg, but I stepped back.

'At eight o'clock. Meet me on the shore at Camus Beag—'

'Ah! "Meet me on the shore at Camus Beag, at Camus Beag . . ." It's like a song. See! "Meet me on the shore . . ." Music to my ears!'

'Meet me on the shore at Camus Beag, and I will show you—'

I paused, now, grinning.

'All! Show me all! But I can't wait 'til eight!' Jos jumped to his feet; teasing, he caught my upper arms, and his open mouth was dark against his beard. 'Look, I'm showing you half of me already!'

'You must. Wait. At eight, I will show you one of the wonders of the west.'

But his exuberance was overpowering. He smelt of sun and salty skin, and the hair in his armpits was glossy with sweat. I had meant to leave, but the muscles of his back were hard beneath my fingers. We revealed all, at half-past three, to the wonder of the west, and laughter gurgled in my throat at the discomfort of the sloping ground and the pricking of the grass.

You can't see the jellyfish from the clifftop; well, that's not entirely true, it is possible to see a few, but there is too much shine on the water, so that the presence of the secret horde remains undetected. Instead, you need to look obliquely at the surface of the sea, when it is completely calm, neither troubled by waves nor crinkled by cat's-paws. That evening, the weather conditions were, as I had expected, perfect; the breeze dropped and the sea was molten silver. But the still air was thick with midges, and we doused ourselves in jealously-hoarded insect repellent, and buttoned cuffs and collars tightly before we went down to the shore. As we stood there, flapping away insects from our faces and swearing at each stabbing bite, I showed Jos how the surface of the bay was dimpled with spreading circles of ripples, glinting pink and gold in the evening sun, small circles, large circles, dying then reappearing elsewhere, soundless, secret agitations. The silence was heavy, as though the birds, and even the sea itself, were hushed in awe. The keel of the boat rumbled on the shingle, and the sound echoed back from the rocks, so that a turnstone trilled with surprise.

I rowed slowly out towards the ripples, barely disturbing the surface of the water, the boat gliding quietly between each stroke. A pale jellyfish swirled in the whirlpool of an oar. Another jellyfish pulsed by, its back denting the surface, and then suddenly the boat was sliding over a carpet of them, stacked one above the other, layered within the water. Jos took an oar and pushed it down vertically.

'They must be five or six feet deep! Do you think it is the same in every bay?'

I shrugged. 'Possibly. For a large part of the west coast, anyway.'

'There must be millions of them!'

The boat was scarcely moving, and we both leant over the side and watched. Milky umbrellas, marked with purple horseshoes, opened and closed slowly, somnabulistically. They drifted, contracted, subtly avoiding collision. Deep down, flanked by pale moons, a tawny-brown bowler hat trailed thick tentacles, like frilly knickers.

'How do they know? How do they know to come here, where to meet up, and when? To swarm and spawn.'

'Is that what they're doing? Mating?'

'Yes, but not like us, they don't touch. They release their sperm and eggs into the sea, clouds of it, a soup of gametes, all wanting to get paired. And then there will be clouds of planktonic larvae. I wish I had a microscope! What an incredible sight. I've never seen so many jellyfish!'

'Think what they must look like to a seal! Like a cloud of paratroopers, swaying down through the sky!'

'Yes, yes!' His voice rose, and the boat rocked with his excitement. 'Imagine what it's like, though, imagine swimming through this. I wonder if the seals get stung?'

Perfectly cued, a wheezing sigh broke the silence, and we looking up, startled, to see a seal pointing his wet muzzle towards us. He wheezed again, and then his nostrils pinched shut and he sank below the surface; but he did not dive, his back rose and dipped as he porpoised through the surface water, occasionally lifting his head to snort and sigh in complaint against the intrusion.

'I've never seen one do that before. Look at him! Why doesn't he dive and get beneath them, I wonder?'

Then, further out, the seal did dive, and we didn't see him again. Silence returned, and for a while neither of us spoke, as the boat drifted imperceptibly with the tide. The boat might have been floating in the silver evening air, for the sea was silken and insubstantial. I lay back against the bow, and Jos occasionally trailed an oar in the water, to watch the medusae stir. Why, then, was there this faint, anxious buzzing in my mind? Was there something that I had forgotten to do (turn the oven off, put the cat out), something that I regretted having done (the list was enormous), or an unasked question for which I needed an answer? Why was I feeling bothered, on this most perfect of evenings? I slipped my hand into my pocket and felt for the agate, but its smooth surface didn't reassure me; rather, it reminded me of guilt. If it had been a rosary, I would have been guilty of adultery, and staked out alive for the midges; not joyous coupling, not chaste, indifferent spawning, but adultery, fornication. The same act, but different gods. On the one hand: thou shalt not. Thou shalt not commit adultery, nor covet thy neighbour's ass ('But, gee, how can I help it? He has such a beautiful ass!') nor hang out thy washing on a Sunday. Or else. On the other hand: love us! Care for us, experience us, be one with us – or else? Peace, brother, love one another, feel the powers of the flowers, and do the hippy-

hippy shake. Or else? Was that it, the failure to delineate the limits of non-acceptance? Was that the rub, the question? Nebulous, formless words, re-forming and crystallising precisely out of the turbid wash of not-understanding; cloudy medusae, swirling passively in the backwash, yet pulsing forward, determined to communicate. The questions formed, stacking one upon the other, massing together and waiting to burst out.

'Jos?'

He had been staring over the stern, and his eyes were still focused on far-distant seas.

'Mmm?'

I moved back to the middle seat, and water slapped gently against the sides.

'Jos, I think I need your help. Suppose one didn't believe in the idea of a jealous God, Hell, and Divine Retribution – and I'm not, now, talking only about Christianity, although the God of the Jews and the Christians is the one we know best. Suppose, instead, that one believed in – oh, that sounds like "believing in" fairies and Santa Claus, doesn't it? – that one acknowledged and respected other physical, hence more immediately visible, although nevertheless spiritually indefinable, entities as gods.'

Jos sat up straight, frowning. 'Such as?'

'Such as the earth, the air, the sea, for example. And you can, of course, intellectually and by direct inspection, understand and observe how these three entities are linked and interact and change state. They are, I suppose, the Three-in-One, the Trinity, of the natural world. The inanimate world is shaped by their interaction, directly and indirectly. All living things exist upon or within them, and through their agency. And before you object, the circulation between sea water and fresh water is implicit, the sea being dominant and original, and therefore the lesser being subsumed within the greater!'

'Wait a minute, this is getting out of hand! You're going too fast! You're promoting three natural phenomena – the three building-blocks of our world – to the status of gods. Is that right?'

'Yes,' I said, trying not to feel foolish.

'Okay. Go on, then, I'm listening.'

'It's possible that to call them gods is the wrong word. I intended to imply that there are three dominant forces, about which one has the intuitive feeling that they are, in fact, one and indivisible. Everything exists in dynamic cooperation with everything else and, in particular, with the three dominant forces. Once one has grasped that idea – which I've stated in a very unemotional, unexciting way – it's only a short step to see that there is a global companionship. And that it's infinite, everything upon the globe is interlinked, plant, animal, stone, water, for ever. Eternal global companionship!'

'It's quite an attractive idea.' He was being polite. 'But I'm not quite sure what you're getting at – or what it has to do with me. I don't mind being linked to you for ever, but I'm not so certain about them down there.'

'I'm just trying to consider this dispassionately, Jos, without bringing in any personal element. It comes back to what we touched on that night in the crypt, the awareness, the love. I wish you could experience the feeling, too, then perhaps you'd see what I'm trying to get at. But it's not just that, I need help in understanding the . . . the system, no, the means whereby one becomes interlocked with the system. It's all very well appreciating the existence of the possibility, but one needs to be acquainted with the ground-rules, the conventions. Do you see? There have to be right ways and wrong ways of taking part.'

'I don't know, Harriet. Hell, I'm sorry, it's not something I've ever thought about, really.' He rubbed his hand across his face and beard. 'I'm sorry, I know it's important to you. I would need to think about the implications, but I'm not very well-equipped – I was brought up as Church of Scotland Protestant, middle-class, conservative background, don't think too much about religion but turn up at Christmas and Easter and the like. And I had a few lessons in comparative religion at school. But that was it, and I've forgotten any details – if I ever knew them! What you're trying to get at sounds a bit like Buddhism. And isn't there some sort of sect up north . . .?'

'Ah well, never mind. I'll just have to keep on worrying away at the problem on my own. I wish I had some books about other people's ideas. Or that I could talk to someone who could discuss the controlling aspects of similar philosophies. Oh, Jos, I'm sorry – I didn't mean to be dismissive!'

'Would you really like to talk to someone else?' He was astonished, and also upset.

Would I? Perhaps I had also astonished myself. I thought about his question for a moment, then laughed.

'No! I wouldn't! I don't even know why I said that!'

'I can't imagine you talking, talking properly, you know, to anyone else.'

He leaned forward abruptly, so that the boat rocked, and sent back a wake of ripples.

'I think I'd be very jealous. We, you and I, exist *here*. There can't be anyone else, we're the complete entity, it has to be just the two of us. You, of all people, must see that. I can't believe that you, of all people, could think otherwise.'

His intensity was frightening, it trapped me, squeezed me, so that I was stifled.

'Jos, listen. Listen! You've not been listening to what I said. There will never again be just the two of us, and I'm not talking about other humans such as your supervisor. We're part of everything that we see, that's what I'm trying to explain to you. I want you to feel the same absolute contentment and inner peace that I have come to experience. We need nothing more than what we have already. I've been thinking aloud, really. I'm struggling. I need to understand what *penalties* could be imposed for failing to live up to the required standards of action and belief.'

'Ach, it's all so abstract. I can't think in these terms. I cannot see why you have to confuse your thinking with all this talk of penalties for the backslider or unbeliever.'

'But there must be penalties, because otherwise what would be the incentive to keep on believing? If it was equally easy not to believe, then why bother?'

'That's your Catholic upbringing coming out. Though I suppose it's a way of thought that's a product of any punitive religion. But don't you see, it's also the way in which missionaries, crusaders, witch doctors, Stalinism – even McCarthyism – worked. It's a means of subjugating populations and individuals to a way of thinking. Do it – or else!'

'Yes! That's exactly what I had been thinking.'

'Or else you'll die, or go to Hell, or be sent to Siberia, or whatever. To talk of a moral or ethical code that has to be reinforced by threats, whether subtle or brutal, is to talk of a code that has its basis in something that is essentially evil.'

'That's very severe. And it frightens me, because that means that the codes that guide a large proportion of the human race must be based on a misapprehension.'

'Well, do you feel confident about the essential goodness of mankind, when you look around?'

'There's no one here to see.'

'And aren't we lucky! Let's forget about the rest of them – we can, here. Believe in your doctrine of global love and awareness, or however you want to define it. If it's all about appreciation of the natural things around you, if you can find it in you to see good, or beauty, or whatever – what can be wrong with that?'

This was a new Jos that was leaning forward and gripping my knee, inspired, demanding.

'So why do you have to mess it all up with rules, and Doing Wrong? When you die – excuse me, I'll be more personal – when I die, it is fact that my body will decompose – nice word, incidentally, it should appeal to you, suggesting as it does the disintegration of the complete composition – and become part of the environment. Like Finn. And that dead hind that you once told me about. Whether or not I will be able to appreciate that spiritually is a different matter – that would be a *bonus*, if you like. The worst that can happen, if I don't follow the path of the believer, is that I merely die and am no longer sentient. I'm switched off, full stop, end of Jos's tale. So I'm not around to feel miserable that my spirit isn't experiencing that ecstatic reunion with the sea, or a primrose, or a Scots pine, or what you will.'

'It would be a terrible loss, though. What would there be to look forward to? Having already experienced something of that ecstatic feeling – and you were mocking me! – and having experienced what would be possible, I have to know how to attain that state permanently.'

'No, now *you're* not listening. You say you've experienced this feeling once or twice already. Well, I say that you are quite incredibly lucky! The majority of people are astonishingly oblivious to the natural world around them, and are incapable of looking for good in anything.'

'I suppose that's true.'

'You do seem to have developed, recently, I think, a sort of gift for extra awareness or perceptiveness, call it what you like. My point is that you have this new philosophy, and that you are aware that you have the capacity to be happy within it. On a day-to-day basis. Not at some time in the future. Now. Can't you just live with it, within it, take life as it comes?'

I was silent, staring at the planks beneath my feet, noticing, without noting, where the varnish was chipped and scratched. There seemed to be something wrong with what Jos was saying.

'But isn't that an extraordinarily selfish philosophy? That I just carry on with what I'm doing, because it seems to be right. And to Hell, or wherever, with the rest of them? You included?'

'No, I don't think so. If you are made happy by everything that surrounds you, your happiness will be communicated to your surroundings. Won't it? I think that's correct. There'll be a degree of positive feedback – there's a good scientific term for you!'

'Any woolly hypothesis can be validated by a good scientific label!'

'That's the remark I should have made.'

'But implicit in your argument is that the effect of my happiness is to increase the contentment of everything that caused my happiness – so the effect escalates into a glorious explosion of local joy! Even I can't quite believe in that!'

'Okay, that's obviously absurd. Basically, there can only be good in loving and caring and being happy. I'm beginning to sound like a preacher. What are you doing to me? If you can stay like that, though, it has to be good for everyone, everything. And on an entirely selfish note, since we were talking about selfish ideals, if you're happy, I'm happy.'

I smiled, and put my hand over his, but I was not yet convinced. And talking about these ideas reduced them to the personal, and therefore trivial, level. I wished that Jos could understand my own deep conviction. He shifted on his seat, and shivered slightly.

'But you're making a mistake, Harriet, if you try to incorporate these ideas or feelings into something like a religion, because there's a real danger then that you'll start to see that it's the only way of thinking. The Truth, with a capital T. And then you'll feel the need to evangelise and convert. Yes, I can read your mind, Ms Longmore! Don't look at me like that!'

'I won't preach. But I know you already understand a little of what I've been saying.'

'Perhaps. But religion and philosophies don't easily transfer to different locations, either. What you believe in here would be entirely inappropriate in a town.'

'Yes. It could only work in a place where one is in close contact with nature. Perhaps it's special to hermits and recluses.' I smiled again. 'And their mates.'

'Never mind about mating! Have you looked to see where we are? Christ, we're miles out, and it'll soon be dark.'

We had, indeed drifted a long way during our talking, and the light was fading to silvery-grey, so that details on the shore were merging into blackness, shapes becoming indistinguishable. I took up the oars, and the boat sped easily over the silk-smooth water. I imagined the medusae spinning out of control in the vortices, their mute, primitive urges disrupted by dizziness; but

I didn't envy the simplicity of their brief lives.

I think of the event, privately, as a baptism; Jos, of course, is completely unaware of that interpretation for, although he has never attempted to dissuade me from my beliefs and he has been tolerant, and perhaps even amused by our discussions of my 'philosophy of awareness' as he persists in calling it, he remains adamant that he himself has no religion or inner convictions, and that he wishes to remain that way. Convictions, he says, in religion or philosophy, require too much hard work to be maintained.

'What about conviction in love?' I asked him. 'Is that hard work, too?'

He had to think about that, but he finally replied that the conviction, once it arrived, was easy to maintain, but that the relationship itself required hard work, but was challenging and therefore stimulating.

'A good answer,' I replied. 'Your eloquence impresses me.'

'Me too. You see how you influence me. I'm not like this at home.'

'No.'

There was a silence.

'Do you think, Joseph, that your transformation has been brought about by living in a cave?'

He didn't rise to the bait, however, but scowled, and chewed his lip, and his face was furrowed and distant.

'Harriet, I've got to go back next week. For a week or ten days. Probably ten days.'

'Oh.'

'It's a Hellish nuisance, because I ought to be here watching the pups. But I have to go back to analyse some of the data for my end-of-year report. Do you realise it's nearly September? I will have been here for a year!'

'We've been together such a short time. I wish I could imagine you at the university. I like to think of you looking very academic and busy – except that nobody ever did, as far as I remember.

Where do you go to write? Do you have an office, or do you have to do all your writing at home?' My stomach clenched nervously. 'I haven't even asked you where you stay.'

'I share a flat with a couple of others, nothing special but it's comfortable. And I share an office in the department, with some other ecologists. That's a bit of a tip, diving gear, waterproofs and collecting equipment all over the place. But I expect I'll be spending most of my time in the library or on the computer.'

'Do you know how to work a computer?' I was impressed.

He laughed. 'Depends what you mean by "work". Yes – most people do, these days, at one level or another. I use a big one for data analysis and a small one as a word-processor – that's for typing out my report.'

'It's so strange to think that has all passed me by! What do you do with your report, once you've finished it?'

'Peter reads it and criticizes it, and we discuss what else to do. And I have to give a talk in the department, as well. That's really nerve-racking.'

'Are people very critical?'

'They can be. But I guess it's usually quite helpful – and then we all go out and have a couple of beers afterwards.'

'And curries.'

'Those too. Are you envious? Do you want to come, too?'

'I'm envious about the curries. It will be nice when you get back.'

'*Nice*! I may as well stay over there if you only think it will be nice!'

'You know quite well that was an understatement. I just don't want you to become corrupted by the fleshpots. I want you to remain young and sweet and innocent. And mine.'

'So that you can corrupt me instead? I accept. I'll hurry back.'

We were both laughing, light-hearted, but there was a seriousness beneath the banter. Here, Jos had been immersed in island-ness, and had been influenced, but his penetration was as yet a veneer, it had not become structural and supportive. I was certain that the thin coat would be rapidly discarded when he left. How could I protect him? I recognised that I could not, but that the sea would, if asked. That recognition, that certainty, brought peace of mind, and confidence, and so I waited impatiently for a warm day. It was not until the day before Jos was due to leave that suitable weather and a suitable occasion coincided. I had promised to take him round to the haul-out rocks by boat, so that he might attempt to collect faecal samples to take back with him; he hoped that the seals would forget his intrusion during his subsequent absence.

The pups were six to eight weeks old, and mobile, and seals plopped and slithered into the sea as I held the boat close to the rocks and Jos climbed out. One cow with a small pup remained, and moaned softly in annoyance, but she, too, departed, leaving her child, as Jos clambered over the rocks with his plastic pots. Despite his pessimism, and his anxiety at disturbing the colony, he found two piles of droppings, and we then departed hastily.

The auspices were good and, although it was windy on the water, Camus Beag was sun-lit and sheltered. I made Jos row for the last half-mile; the wind was against us, and he soon became red and sweaty from exertion.

'Faster, faster!' I cried. 'See how fast you can go!'

Bless us, O sea, give us your blessing. Please take care of him. Please love him and make him ours.

Gasping and breathless, he rested at last on the oars, and the boat rolled in and crunched against the shingle.

'Right, everyone into the shower now,' I called, in my jolly-hockey-sticks, no-nonsense voice. 'Yes, Mr Allen, that means you, too. Strip off, now, into the sea!'

I started pulling off my clothes, not too fast.

'You can't be serious!' Jos was still laughing.

'Oh, I am. Come and swim with me.'

'But it's freezing. I'll die.'

'Then die in my lap, sweet male. It's our last chance to swim this year, it'll be even colder when you get back.'

He tried to resist, feebly, as I started to undress him, but eventually he stood, naked and shivering, in the boat. I stepped over the side.

'You have to get in quickly, it's the only way,' and I forced myself to stride out to the depth of my thighs then threw myself in.

'I'll splash you if you stay there!' (I would not have done so; I remember from childhood days how being splashed could turn resolve into bad temper.)

'Don't you dare!'

Jos stepped down into the water, and yelled. But then he ran forward in great, splashing leaps, and dived low and flat, coming up again with a roar, his hair plastered darkly over his eyes.

'My heart's stopped. How can you bear to do this?'

'It's for your own good. At least you'll go back to the mainland smelling sweet.'

'I've shrivelled away, I'm impotent. And look at you, all blue goose-pimples!'

But we swam together, noisily, shouting and gasping with the cold, and, as I warmed up with the exercise, I relaxed. I swam, face down, eyes open, and said, 'Thank you, sea,' underwater, laughing and choking as my words bubbled out.

'I've dreamed of this, swimming in the sea with you.'

I swam up to where he stood, wiping the water from his face, and we hugged each other tightly for warmth. I was shivering and his teeth were chattering, but we locked our bodies together, straining to stay upright against the nudging of the sea. The water crept between us and encircled us, so that we were, all three, united, and I dipped my fingers in the water and wiped Jos's forehead.

Twenty-six

I saved his letter until I reached home. It's been ten days since he left, and I was certain that he would be on the boat today. I waited on the high ground behind the village, and watched as the boat came in. Today, there were two passengers and, even from such a distance, I could tell that neither was Jos. Nobody wore his clothes or was bent beneath his rucksack. Nobody was young and male and single. The two passengers were a couple, in long raincoats; I saw them later, outside the shop. They were old, and together, cast ashore on this bleak island in early autumn, and wondering what they would do. I watched as the boat went out. It became small and dark, trailing a pencilled line of black smoke, before I walked down to the shop, to buy something, anything. And to collect my mail.

There was a letter, soft and fat, for the pages were too large and had been folded several times. Jos's handwriting was on the envelope. Jos had addressed it. He himself had not returned, but he had sent a letter.

I sat on the mausoleum steps and pulled out the wad of folded sheets. He had only written on one side of each page, because the paper was thin, with finely perforated edges.

'My dearest, darling Harriet,'

Perhaps one is less inhibited on paper. 'Darling' was not a word that Jos had used before.

'My dearest, darling Harriet, This letter will have arrived in my place. I wish there were some way of contacting you. I wish you were holding *me* and not these scribbled pages. Even as I write this, I *ache* to be there with you. I wonder where you are reading this? I can see you so clearly sitting on the mausoleum steps, or on the stones outside the crypt (because I'm sure you won't be reading this letter until you get home!) I wish I'd never left you, I miss the island and I miss you terribly. It's hard to believe that *this* (the university, the city) can exist at the same time as *that*, where you are. I keep remembering our evening out in the boat with the jellyfish, and our expedition to Red Sand, etc., and it's hard to believe, from here, that it really happened! I've just been to Safeways and to the launderette – but two weeks ago I was washing socks in the burn and wondering if I had enough powdered milk to last until I left! Two weeks ago I was with you – it seems months. I'm not sure that I can take it, actually – I'll probably end up a schizo. What have you done to me, love, I feel so *old*! Saw my ex-girlfriend the other day (not to speak to!) and she seemed like a schoolkid! So do most of my friends. One of the lecturers is your sort of age, quite good-looking, too – think I'll have to chat her up, just to keep in practice (only joking!). Seriously though, it's been quite a shock getting back here. I was a bit pissed off, too, to find that a girlfriend of one of the girls in my flat had been using my room for the past month – she'd split up with her boyfriend, and Liz (the girl in my flat) had let her stay here. She hadn't made any mess or anything (and she's moved out into the sitting room now I'm back, it's okay!) but I think it was a bloody cheek, even so. I suggested she could pay my share of the rent – but that pissed *her* off, too, so things are a bit tense. As for work, now that I've analysed some of the data, some interesting trends are becoming apparent. Peter's given me some useful ideas on how these might be followed up. You remember that I was telling you about the possibility of a link between tidal cycle and haul-out times, and how it didn't look as though there was any pattern? I broke it down with reference to season and sex, and there's evidence for some correlation. I haven't examined the faecal samples yet (they're in formalin), but have decided to wait until I have a bigger batch, as it will require a considerable amount of lab work. By the way, do you remember the seal that was porpoising above the jellyfish? (I'll never forget that amazing, wonderful evening. I'm drawn towards the west coast all the time, not just in July!) As I was saying it turns out that porpoising is a characteristic of common seals, reason unknown; please keep your eyes open for any recurrence. Now that I've analysed and written up as much of the data/information as possible, I've got quite a good behavioural dossier on many of the seals in the group – not bad for one year. It's a start, anyway, and I'm pleased with the report, so I felt reasonably confident about the oral presentation. I think I did the talk fairly well – people certainly liked the slides (thanks again for your help in getting the close-ups), but I got absolutely hammered during the questions afterwards. I suppose, in all fairness, some of the points were useful (at the time it was Hell!), but there were one or two really aggressive people, one of them a mol. biol. hot-shot (who doesn't know a mouse's arse from its ear-hole) who really laid into me about "what was the point of it all?", and so on. I churned out the usual garbage about "helping our understanding of factors affecting the seal population, implications for the salmon-farming industry" etc. I also said "because it's fun. And because it teaches one to appreciate the relationship between other species and our environment – perhaps we could learn a thing or two." At least, I think that's what I said – it didn't go down too well, anyway. I wish you'd been there to whisper in my ear, I'm sure you'd have thought of a convincing reply. *Can* you? What *is* the point of it all? Somebody was muttering afterwards, in the corridor, about self-indulgence. I suppose it is, really – to get away from all this, the stink of traffic, squatters in my room, and the hassle of justifying my existence. I can see why you did it, getting right away. If only I had some way of making money so I could do it all the time, too. (All these double-meanings. Let's do it, my darling, let's *do* it. I want to be with you, right now!) So, that wasn't a very good experience. (I'm talking about my talk, of course!) I'm feeling pretty depressed about all this nonsense. To make matters worse, Peter had a go at me after the talk. (I guess he felt a bit threatened, being the project supervisor, so I suppose he just took some of it out on me.) Not only about the work, and what we (i.e. I!) should be doing, but about you, too. How had I got so close to the seals? That I seemed to be spending a lot of time sunbathing and sightseeing (I'd put in a few slides of views, esp. Red Sand, and made some stupid crack about perfect 'beach weather' and good swimming. That last is a joke! I still can't believe how cold it was) – and so on. More or less told me to stop messing around and get on with the work. I was angry at first, and we had a bit of a row, but I can see his point of view. (I've apologised, don't worry!) If it weren't for him, I wouldn't have gone to the island at all – we can't put everything down to that nosy sod, Ferguson, you see. I'm sorry, I'm blethering on – it's late at night, and I'm sitting on on my bed. I do love you, Harriet, I think of you all the time, and can't believe my luck.

'I've managed to get most of the odds and ends you asked for (my bank accepted your cheque!) plus a few other things that I think might come in handy. There'll be quite a big load, so I hope I'll be able to manage it on the boat. By the way, could you bear to go over and check that the tent is okay? I put most of the valuables inside poly bags, so they shouldn't have got wet anyway. It's been raining here for several days, but I hope the clouds passed you by before dumping their load. I'm intending to get the boat on Tuesday. My favourite fantasy is of walking back to the tent and finding you there, in my sleeping bag, waiting for me. Will you try it? Sometimes I can hardly bear to think about you, I want you so much. I

> *hate* being here – I see now that my *real* life is on the island, with you and the seals. Harriet darling, I love you so much. I can feel your fingers on the page – I kiss you, over and over again. Jos'

I leant back against the pillar, closed my eyes and listened to the sea. Letters are such an unpredictable method of communication; I thought about Jos's first letter to me, the careful composition, the unwritten anguish that had, nevertheless, cried out from the page. At that time, I could not have imagined that, a year later, he would write to me again, as my lover and companion, freely expressing his bewilderment, and his love. A long letter, less careful, and yet, for all that, written about a matter of long-lasting importance, his life. The pressures of love escalate, in letter-writing; the temperature rises, as letters fly backwards and forwards, until the reader shakes with excitement as he or she rips open the envelope, yearning for further assurances and protestations of desire, glancing through quickly for references to love.

How should I have replied? What would he have wanted of me? Maternal comfort and reassurance, commiseration with his misfortunes? But he might have awakened, the morning after he wrote this letter, burgeoning with optimism and a positive approach to his difficulties; in which case, would he have preferred to read of birds and beasts and flow'ring things, of rowing trips and wanderings? Or should I have ignored reality, and written a love-letter, full of delicate descriptions and passionate poetry, with couplets and odd phrases gleaned from the poetry anthology and Shakespeare?

I sat there by the mausoleum and I knew I would not write. The bracken was yellow-amber and the heather flowers crisp and brown. I saw myself, sitting poetically alone and love-struck on the moor, and the picture made me smile, and yawn and stretch with amusement. At the crypt, I tucked Jos's letter among my papers in a cardboard box, then I drank some tea, and left to check on the tent.

The tent was neat and characterless, his belongings tidied

carefully into polythene bags; tins and pots were piled inside the flysheet, and the tent pegs were weighed down by boulders. I took out the sleeping bag and unzipped it, spreading it out across the ridge to air. I was embarrassed to remember how I had lain here, naked, in Jos's absence, almost in another life. And in order to conform to his written fantasy, I would be required to unpack his belongings and reorganise the tent, then calculate, to within half an hour, the time of his return! Fantasy so rarely resembles reality, it requires too great an effort in timing and stage management. Meanwhile, I needed to stack peats, and lift the late potatoes, and bring up kelp to the garden for burning and composting; there were clothes to wash, and water to be fetched, and kindling to drag home from the copse. That was reality! Organisation, foresight and hard labour! I rolled up the sleeping bag and stowed it away, and went back to Camus Beag.

Twenty-seven

Jos wasn't on the next boat, either. Once again, I had walked over towards the village and waited on the hill and, once again, he had not disembarked. I went home and continued to be busy at the crypt and on the croft, but on the day of the next boat's arrival, I found that I no longer wanted to go to meet him. Certain that he would return today, I was now slightly peevish at his delays and changes of plan. The day was grey and heavy, with the dampness of rain in the air, and the sea wallowed in the bay, its grumbling muffled as though half asleep. I didn't expect Jos to reach this side of the island until mid-afternoon, and I spent the morning clearing brambles, nettles and straggling couch grass from the edges of the garden. Therefore, I was hot and dirty when I heard the low drone of an engine. At first, I thought it must be a trawler, but the seascape was empty apart from a white yacht sailing in the distance. The noise of the engine stopped, and I realised then that I had heard the Land Rover, and that it must have stopped on the track, at the end of the footpath to Death Bay.

It must be Jos! And he must have been able to persuade John MacGregor to bring him across with his purchases. I was surprised, for Mr MacGregor didn't like to leave the shop on the day the boat arrived, because there were goods to receive and sort, and the occasional visitor to be advised and entertained. And I was such a mess! I had planned to wash and change before Jos arrived (my feigned indifference didn't extend to sluttishness! I might be intending to be busy when Jos arrived, but I also intended to look good at the same time), and now I became flustered and uncertain. I washed my hands and threw water on my face, wiping it dry on my sleeve, and then, despite my intentions, I could no longer bear to be ignorant of what was happening on the other side of the ridge. Keeping low, I crossed the moor to where I could observe the track. As I reached an observation point, the Land Rover door slammed, and I saw that Jos stood on the track, alone, next to a large pile of goods. Jos stooped to put on his rucksack but, as he straightened up, he must have seen me move, for he put down his pack and waved, and shouted. He came striding up towards me, leaping on to rocks and tussocks, and his smile lit up his face.

'Harriet! I'm back!' he cried, unnecessarily, when he came within earshot.

I couldn't help smiling, my irrational petulance was instantly forgotten, and I went down to meet him. The Land Rover was making a jerky three-point turn, bumping and revving on the rocky track.

'Harriet!' Jos squeezed me tightly, and rocked me backwards and forwards.

'I'm so glad you're back.' I meant it.

There was a long blast of the Land Rover's horn, making us jump and pull apart. Jos grinned, and shook his head.

'Cheeky bugger!'

'John MacGregor?' I couldn't believe it.

'Ferguson. That'll give him something to talk about, won't it?'

He was still grinning, pleased that we had been seen. Robbie's elbow was resting on the open window and I could see him watching us; he didn't wave.

'Ferguson offered to drive me over. I had all that stuff—' he gestured to the pile on the track '—at the quay, but MacGregor was there with the Land Rover collecting his stores and I persuaded him to take everything over to the shop for me.'

'That was good of him.'

'Yes, he's okay. And I asked if he'd be able to bring the things over here when he was next free – expecting it to be next week, you know what he's like. Ferguson was loafing about, chatting and having a good poke around, and he told MacGregor that he'd drive me over today, if that was all right. So there we are!'

'And I'll bet he interrogated you on the way over.'

'He kept trying to. He asked me how you were, which surprised me – something about how well you looked. You *do* look well, actually. But I got him talking about the fishing, instead. He still needs a crew, did you know? His dad's not at all keen to keep going, apparently. He said he'd asked you.'

'Yes. As you say, a cheeky devil.'

'Worth keeping in mind, though.'

'But I don't want a job, Jos!'

'No, not you. Me! If I ever decided to, you know, give up this job. Pack it in.'

'Jos!' I was stunned. 'You can't mean this.'

'Well, you read my letter. You did get it, didn't you? Explaining why I'd be late back, and everything.'

'It was a wonderful letter. There's obviously a lot to talk about. You know, I was so disappointed when you weren't on the boat – but then I got your letter! I checked the tent, as you asked – everything is fine. Or was, when I looked. It hasn't rained, either, surprisingly.'

The ground beneath our feet was only soft, not squelching.

'I suppose I'll have to move over to the bothy soon.'

There was an unspoken alternative behind his statement, but I decided to ignore it.

'You look well, too, despite all your trials.'

'*You've* got mud on your face.' He laughed, and brushed it away. 'Were you gardening?'

'Mmm. The brambles got me!' I showed him my hands.

'Well, if you're not too battered we could take some of these things over to the crypt. We can use the new sledge.'

Down on the track, Jos proudly showed me the plastic sledge that he'd bought at my request. I didn't tell him that, although beautiful, a blue sledge would get lost amongst the heather more easily than fluorescent orange! There were also two boxes, a six-foot roll of heavy-duty polythene and a taped bundle of six-foot laths, as well as his rucksack, so we had to make two journeys.

While I stoked up the fire to boil the kettle, Jos opened one of the boxes and pulled out a bottle of whisky.

'A present for both of us, to celebrate my return home.'

He stressed the last word, and we looked at each other for a while.

'Very prodigal. But I'm afraid I've only got tinned tuna and potatoes – not much of a feast.'

'Oh, there are all kinds of goodies in here. Some of which you asked for, and some of which you didn't.'

He pulled out a dozen paperback novels, science fiction and thrillers, which, he explained, were his and had been sitting, unread, at his flat. There were new batteries for the radio, and more nails and staples (my requests).

'Ah yes! I always said you should have one of these – it's getting muddy outside the entrance.'

He handed me a rolled-up doormat, bearing the message, 'Welcome'.

'Unfortunately, they didn't make one that said "Welcome, Jos", but I'm sure it's understood that the greeting is entirely exclusive.'

'I shall turn it upside-down if anyone else comes calling.'

In the other box was a miscellany of tins and bottles of food, some Cox's apples, ballpoint pens and several pads of file paper, several well-thumbed *National Geographic* magazines and a pile of photocopied articles.

'Some of these things are mine, obviously. I got the mags in Oxfam, I thought you could look at the pictures. Nearly bought you some cartoon books, too, but I was running out of money!'

He grinned at me, and I was overwhelmed. I stood up and caught his head between my hands, tangling my fingers in the roughness of his beard.

'You're so – good,' I whispered.

'There are some joss-sticks in the bag, too, by the way!'

'Rose and jasmine! It'll be like a harlot's boudoir! You've thought of everything, you must have spent ages hunting for all these wonderful things.'

'The polythene took a bit of finding. And everyone wanted to know why I had bought a sledge! I had fun thinking up wild explanations.'

Our reunion was curiously lacking in passion, as though, for both of us, the expectation had used up all our energy. Jos was clearly tired; he became restless towards early evening, keen to return to his own base, and I did not dissuade him.

Twenty-eight

The questioning of Jos by his supervisor about our relationship had apparently elicited the information that Jos might be able to gain future access to my boat. A few days after his return, Jos asked me if I would be willing to take him round to the haul-out rocks on several occasions, so that he could catch and mark as many seals as possible. Now that he had found suggestions of sexual and tidal variations in haul-out frequency, he needed to be much more certain about the identity and sex of the seals that he was observing. His own system of recognition was not infallible, he admitted, and at present he could only be certain of the sex of unrecognised seals if they were lying with their genitals in view. If each seal were individually marked, there could be no ambiguity; and now was the time to do it, when they had already moulted, and when there were pups old enough to mark. It wouldn't be difficult, we could catch them in a long-handled net, that was what the pole inside the roll of polythene had been for.

I was annoyed, for now it seemed that the success of the project depended upon my cooperation. Like it or not, I was being drawn in; Jos could not row well enough to take the boat out on his own.

'And Peter was insistent that the department would pay – naturally, for wear and tear on the boat. And also for your time . . .'

He must have seen the expression on my face; his voice trailed away.

'*Peter* says. It seems to me he hadn't thought this project through very carefully. What would you have done if I wasn't here to help? Or if I say no?'

There was a bitterness at the back of my mouth, a burning, as my anger began to boil up from my stomach.

'Well, Peter thought I might get Ferguson to help, if you weren't willing.' Jos sounded miserable. 'He talked to him that day we went up to the old haul-out site. Ferguson wasn't very keen, actually. It wouldn't be very convenient, of course – he'd have to motor right round the island, and it would be difficult getting his boat alongside.'

'So I'm more *convenient*, am I? I'm here for your convenience, so Ferguson won't have to hang around! Well, that has truly made this invasion worthwhile. It's so nice to know that you have been fucking me with an eye to the future.'

I knew I was being unjust, but the fury filled my mouth with foulness. Jos's face was stiff and white, but I didn't care how much I hurt him. I wanted to! All the tensions and uncertainties of the past few months ached in my throat.

'For all I know, you and Robbie Ferguson set this up right at the beginning. Including the business with Finnghail!'

'Harriet, what are you talking about? You're going crazy.'

'Oh, go *away*! I knew it was a mistake having anything to do with you. You only wanted me because I'm useful. Listen to you! Count my seals, look after my tent, I'm feeling frustrated so give me some sexual relief! Take me out in the boat, please, act like a whore, please. Mummy, I'm hurt, look after me!'

Oh, it was wonderful, unstoppable, incidents and associations crowding in, a cathartic stream of consciousness. Harriet, all things to one boy-man!

'I'm nothing better than your – your *coxswain*!'

As soon as I shrieked that, there was a sparkle of laughter in my mind. I turned away, wanting the anger to continue, relishing it, and dreading the inevitable return to reality and apologies. Jos made a strange, choking noise, and I turned back, to see that he was no longer white, but red, and even as I looked, laughter bellowed and shook out of him. Then I was crying, crying and laughing, and we held each other, speechless, while my tears trickled on to his beard.

'Coxswain! What made you think of that! "Come on, baby, cox my boat". Don't shout at me like that, you terrify me!'

Despite his laughter, he was still tense, wiping my face.

'I'm so sorry, love – I don't mean to take you for granted. I really am sorry, I keep forgetting what it's like for you. All these people! I keep forgetting that you're not used to all this. I suppose I just thought that you might like to help. Typical selfish male! I didn't really even *think*, did I? I shouldn't even have discussed it with Peter. I'm so stupid.'

'Oh. I suppose you had to. But there've been so many changes in the last six months – I'll have to get used to it.'

'You know, several of our arguments have been about seals, haven't they? I'm not surprised you don't want anything more to do with them.'

'No, it's all right. Of course I'll take you round in the boat.'

I looked up at him, and rubbed my cheek against his, smearing my tears. 'I'm not sure how easy it will be to catch the seals, though. Won't they bite?'

'We'll just have to be careful. If only we had some thick leather gloves . . .'

'Of course! Sure! I've got drawersful of them, come and choose a pair!'

He smiled quietly, and held me against him; we stood like that for a while, and I could feel him relaxing against me. Then, gradually, the silence built up between us with an extraordinary, tingling intensity.

'You don't really think that, do you? Any of those things you said. That I just wanted to use you. Or that Ferguson and I discuss you?'

Jos's voice had become soft, and strangely distant. I shook my head against him. His hands were round my waist, under my pullover.

'Harriet, I love you so much. You must believe me.'

He was whispering, his eyes closed and his head tilted back.

'*How* I love you.'

His hands moved up slowly, I was holding my breath and my legs were weak. The wind was rough and loud around us, and the sea was smacking against the shore. Spray blew in the air, and when I opened my eyes I saw, unseeing, that the gannets were there again, silently questing. There was no place for us to go except the cottage. I took Jos's hand and led him there, and the sea clapped and roared. We went in through the gaping room, through the dust and leaves and trailing ivy. We went into the fusty gloom of the bedroom, where the frame of the empty bed loomed like a skeleton, and I pulled out old clothes and laid them on the floor. The sea echoed in the shell of the roof above our heads, and cradled us in a thick cocoon of sound. We knelt, our fingers tracing mandala on each other's skin, until the sea-spell made us one, and we dived, gasping, into the dark waters of the soul. And afterwards I understood that, whatever had happened to me in the cottage, I had been blessed by the sea. With Jos beside me, the pattern would unfold and there was nothing more to fear.

There was, in the weeks thereafter, a deep peace and stillness between us, as though we moved in slow motion and dreamed the same dreams. A balance had, somehow, been achieved, an understanding; we both sensed it, I think, and tacitly accepted the alteration, because it brought with it an intuitive awareness of each other's needs, and the gift of compromise and consent.

We were now in a hurry to mark the seals because the weather was becoming more variable, building up towards the unpleasantness of winter. Rowing was strenuous work, and wet, and we beached the boat temporarily at Death Bay, both of us lifting it high above the strand-line. The seals were not keen to lie and wait, and the landing at the rocks was made hazardous by the swirling waves, but we made four trips and marked sixteen seals, more than half the maximum number that Jos had ever observed. In late October, there was a lull; the rowan shone with gold and rubies, and the birch trees by the gorge were shimmering yellow. We went out again, from Camus Beag, switchbacking on a deep, smooth swell. Jos's rowing had improved and his pull was now directed as well as strong, so that we soon reached the haul-out rocks. We bagged and marked five more seals, females that Jos thought he had not seen for several weeks; the red numbers stood out brightly against their fur. It was my turn to row home, but before we were even halfway there, I began to feel cold and sweaty, and slightly sick. I continued rowing, trying to ignore the shaking of my legs, but suddenly I had to thrust the oars into Jos's hands, and I learnt over the side to vomit. I scooped sea water over my lips and forehead, and wiped my face on my handkerchief. Now that I had been sick, I felt much better.

'It must be this swell! I can't believe that I'm sea-sick.'

'You look terrible. Swap places and I'll row. What have you eaten that I haven't?'

I sat in the stern and tried to remember what I had eaten in the past twenty-four hours, but there was nothing that was obviously strange – although the powdered milk had been past its 'sell-by' date for some weeks. Perhaps the fault lay there? By the time we returned to Camus Beag, I thought I had quite recovered, and I was thirsting to replace lost fluid, but my legs were still weak and I was relieved to reach the crypt. Jos was anxious, and would have stayed, but I assured him that I was improving and could manage on my own. I wanted to be alone, to go to bed. He made me a warm drink, without the powdered milk (at which he sniffed and grimaced), and he finally, protesting, left me to sleep, closing the new polythene and lath door behind him.

November brought gales, and the last remaining leaves were ripped brutally from the trees. The glens and hollows became bare and bleak, but the moor remained timeless and unchanging. The crypt was cold, and Jos helped me to make a chimney, so that the fire could be brought inside. I needed oildrums and large rectangular tins, so I went down to the sea, privately, and asked that it would provide. It grumbled, and shook spray in my face, but I climbed out on the rocks and stretched out my hands into the water, accepting the wetness creeping into my clothes, and asked for help. So the sea provided, as I knew it would. We found old fence wire by the copse, and we hammered out the metal cans. Our first attempt was weak and leaky, but with modifications and much swearing we made a hood and curving flue, that conducted the greater proportion of the smoke to the exterior.

Jos had already moved to the bothy, and was now walking the coast each day, spotting seals. We saw each other less frequently, because he was so busy, pushing himself to collect information before his return to the university; but perhaps it was also because I felt weary, and was content to stay inside as long as possible. The warmth and foetid comfort of the crypt were preferable to shouldering through the wind and squally showers, visibility reduced to a small circle seen from inside the hood of my oilskin coat.

I stayed only once at the bothy; there were two chairs and there was no smoke, because it spiralled warmly up the chimney. The wind had buffeted me on the way across and I was tired and didn't want to eat, but I accepted what Jos gave me and forced it down. Later I went for a short walk and was sick behind a boulder. I covered the mess with stones and dead grass, and washed my mouth in the cold, fierce water of the burn.

We sat by the fire, listening to the driftwood crackle and watching the salty green flicker in the flames. Rain clattered on the roof and window, and although the fire sucked in draughts so that my back was cold, I remembered the warmth and security of winter evenings in my cottage. Jos showed me the bothy's log-book, and we talked about the few visitors who had stayed: occasional walkers, who had recorded their successes or failures, and exclaimed about the weather; others whose address was given as *Melissa* or *Sea Sparrow,* yachts that had anchored briefly in the small bay, allowing their crew a few hours ashore to stretch their sea-legs and investigate this remote western outpost. Jos had only once seen someone here, and in the last year I had twice seen figures on the skyline of Sgurr Mor. It was a lonely place and no one intruded upon us.

We were profligate with the wood, and had a large, hot fire as a grand finale. When the contents of the log-book had been dissected, conversation became awkward, desultory, peppered with 'don't forget', our anxieties and uncertainties moving us forward in time. I thought of similar evenings with my mother, each time I left for another term at university; how she would prepare my favourite meal, and slip some chocolates or perfumed soap into my suitcase, and how we would spend the evening together but already mentally apart, conversation reduced to much-repeated trivialities. Why hadn't I appreciated, then, her loneliness? Why hadn't I asked for her help more often? She had loved Tom, and I realised, much too late, that if he had lived, she would have devoted the rest of her life to caring for him. But instead, she had been allowed neither her grandson nor her freedom; she had had to care for me, her grown-up daughter who had temporarily again become a child. If she were alive, would she be happy for me? There was no place for her here, and she would be unlikely to recognise me, but I could imagine her concern. I longed to lay my head on her bosom, and for her to hug me and promise me it would be all right. My throat constricted, and Jos must have seen my misery, for he took my hand, and we stared at the fire together.

'You know I don't want to go back,' he said, eventually. 'But I'll come back again in a month, maybe less.'

'And then you'll go away again.'

It had been planned that he would make monthly visits throughout the winter, for a few days at a time.

'I'm not sure I can cope very well with this – all these partings. This is terribly unsatisfactory, isn't it?'

He turned sideways on his chair, looking at me, his knees touching my thigh. I remained silent, because I was unable to make decisions, the future was becoming unclear, there was no discernible pattern.

'I don't want to be based over there, and coming to you as a visitor. There's too much instability in that, and, in any case, that would feel like a lie. This is where my life is – not just because of you, but everything else, too. I have everything here that I want.'

'I know. I've watched it happen to you in these past two months. I wasn't sure at first – nor were you. But if that trip of yours, back in September, had been happier – if you hadn't had so many disappointments – you might have been less convinced. I don't know – you'll have to see what happens when you go back this time. You'll be there longer, you'll have more time to become used to treating it as your proper base.'

'If, even as you say, that last trip had been better, I'm sure I would still have come to think this way. It would have taken longer, that's all. Anyway, this is all hypothetical. It's *you* I want to be with, Harriet. For Christ's sake, Harriet – I want to live with you, to live *with* you. I don't want to be always parting from you, and not knowing whether you'll have determined to be a permanent recluse again, in my absence.'

'No.'

'I don't even want to leave you at night, let alone for days or weeks. What? What does "no" mean?'

'No. I don't want to be a recluse again.'

I was too frightened by the uncertainty of the future to be alone, but I couldn't tell him that. I am supposed to be his invincible Harriet, self-reliant, capable, unafraid; not this pathetic middle-aged wretch, longing to lean weakly on the arm of her decisive young man. Courage, Harriet! Be strong! Be patient, for the path forward will soon be visible through these thickets.

'That's a major barricade withdrawn, anyway. Perhaps there's hope for me yet.' He was smiling, faintly, hopefully. 'Harriet?'

'Yes.' I smiled back, though my head was full of tears. 'Progress is being made. There may yet be more concessions. But don't advance too quickly. Change the subject, quick!'

'No, I can't. There is no other subject. Can't you see that I'm desperate, I hate all this uncertainty. I need to know that you want me, and, if I can find some way to arrange it, you will let me come back here – to you, not just to the bloody seals. And that you will let me stay here with you. Always. Me and you. Permanently.' I could see that Jos was near to tears. 'Think of this as a proposal – except that I'm completely helpless, I can do nothing but *beg*. You hold all the answers. Do you realise that? That I'm totally powerless – other than going away and forgetting about you entirely. And how can I possibly do that?'

His agony and helplessness were inside me, too. Of course I knew that I had to make decisions. And both of us knew that the rehabilitation of the cottage was the only solution. But I could not yet be certain!

'I can't. I can't decide now, I'm too confused. Jos, my love, another month. Wait another month, and we'll both be certain.'

'And then another. And another . . .'

'No. When you come back in December, we'll each be sure.'

'Is that a promise?'

'Almost.'

The opened sleeping bag was slippery on top of us and the makeshift mattress of clothes was lumpy. I spent a cold and wakeful night, and Jos was restless beside me. I helped him tidy the bothy, and he stowed his cooking equipment and tent in the loft; he had already carried some of his belongings to the track, where John MacGregor had arranged to meet him, and everything else was hidden above the ceiling. I knew that he would have preferred to store things at the cottage, despite the damp, but I had not offered and he had not asked. (Another month. Only another month.)

We parted miserably, early in the morning, with few words other than a wish for the time to pass speedily.

Twenty-nine

How could I be pregnant at my age? I'd assumed that I was infertile, my womb incapable of conceiving and holding another child. All those unprotected years with Graham, after Tom's birth, when I eschewed contraception as the work of the devil, waited to be blessed again by God's will, and remained a stubbornly empty receptacle. It had been my punishment, my just reward for earlier sins, and I had, finally, accepted the failure meekly. In my solitude, conception would have been miraculous; but I was almost amenorrhoeic, perhaps as a result of my strenuous lifestyle and irregular eating habits (for I had become accustomed, through boredom and necessity, to eat lightly). The relative absence of menstruation was a convenience and, because it was so irregular, I was rarely reminded of its meaning, and so the possibility of conception was disregarded. And Jos? On that first day, there hadn't been time to question the result. We'd been unprepared; and afterwards, perhaps an understandable dread of the consequences had prevented him from asking. I was 'the older woman', I must know what I was doing. He perhaps assumed, with the ignorance of youth, that I was post-menopausal, but was too embarrassed to ask. Because I never referred to contraception, he must have assumed that we were safe.

Pregnant: a minute embryo, curled up and cushioned in fluid, growing inside me. Surely I must be imagining the symptoms? In the lonely darkness, and on the empty hills, I had dwelled too long on my body's changes, magnified them, imagining myself also magnified. I must have misunderstood the significance of the changes: my body, that had for so long existed merely to keep my mind and senses alive, was now blossoming in response to attention; my breasts merely ached to be caressed; my skin was swelling into a pretence of voluptuousness. This wasn't pregnancy! Meanwhile, the vomiting and backache were no more than psychosomatic symptoms, triggered by Jos's absence.

As I sat on my bed and listened to the wind and rain, and thought of the cold and vicious weather yet to come, I was nauseous with fear.

'I don't understand! Why? Why must this happen? Tell me the answer, dragon, you're supposed to know!'

Neither the sheep nor the dragon answered. They had abandoned me, had withdrawn into stony silence. What had I done wrong?

Slowly, through the suffocating panic, threads of logic began to form. I would need to go ashore, and have my pregnancy confirmed; not with a doctor, nor a family planning unit, however far away, for then I would be marked down and under surveillance. There were kits, weren't there, at the chemist's? I should buy several, in case one lied, and test myself. If the results were positive, I would then start to plan for our futures. Only then, if the pregnancy was confirmed, would I start to plan, to think about Jos, and the cottage – and the child. Only then. The fogs of panic closed in again and, exhausted, I fell into a troubled sleep.

I set off early to catch the boat, walking slowly through the winter darkness. I arrived with half an hour to spare, but weak and shaking, and I bought some chocolate and a large carton of orange juice at the shop, to help my body recover. John MacGregor was surprised when I told him that I might be away for a week, for I hadn't left the island for many months. I told him that I had business with my bank and elsewhere, and he nodded wisely, then smiled and asked me to give his good wishes to Jos, if I should see him. The thought of visiting Jos had not occurred to me, and I responded quickly, surprised.

'Oh, I'm not going there! I'm going over to Edinburgh.'

'Aye well, I daresay he'll be back soon enough – the middle of the month, I think he said.'

'It's possible.' I nodded, knowing it was true. I had a week, at best ten days.

So began a week of intense activity and concentration. I was sick on the boat and huddled by the rail, the taste of orange juice acid in my mouth. The sea held no charm, the dumpy guillemots that buzzed across its surface were scarcely a distraction. I caught a bus, and then a train, and it was late evening by the time I arrived in the city, so that I took a taxi with the last of my cash, to a small guesthouse in the suburbs. I had stayed there before, and the woman seemed to recognise me, although there was a slight hesitancy in her manner, but perhaps that was due to my late arrival, or it may have been that I smelt like a smoked and briny haddock. I lay, like a bloated white fish, in a hot bath, deep, hot water, in which to wallow like a seal, enjoying the luxury of sinking into warm wetness. I sat in the guest lounge, read magazines and watched the television news, the names and events a mystery, dislocated fragments, unconnected with me. At ten o'clock, the woman brought me tea and raisin scones, and, with some embarrassment, I asked her to lend me some money for the bus fare to the city centre. The bed was soft and warm, and, now that I was actively seeking solutions, I was able to sleep.

The bank was in the city centre, a monument to Victorian wealth, and, like the mausoleum, it held itself erect with polished granite pillars. Footsteps echoed and discreet voices reverberated in that marbled, church-like interior, where supplicants queued between thick, red ropes, waiting to be summoned to the mahogany counter, where they might be permitted to make their petitions on coloured slips of paper. I rang a bell, beneath a glass banner that announced 'Inquiries'. I waited on a buttoned leather bench, and was eventually ushered into a small room where I discussed the details of my account with a young man, Jos's age, who explained to me about tax relief and interest, and who tried to conceal his astonishment at my negligible annual expenditure. Despite his city suit and smooth, soft countenance, he was bemused, apparently unaware of a wild island race that lived at the extreme margins of his country, subsisting, perhaps, on seaweed and potatoes. I had a sudden urge to uproot him, abduct him for a day, and show him that far-off kingdom, and the image made me smile, so that he perhaps thought that I was simple. It wasn't entirely necessary for him to speak so slowly and loudly, because his explanation was clear and faultless, but I thanked him. Then I signed several forms, writing my name against his pencilled crosses, and was assured that my capital could not fail to grow under the terms of the new high-interest scheme.

With real money in my purse, I walked through the main shopping area until I found a large, impersonal chemist's shop. The shoulder-high displays were piled with goods, and I searched slowly, moving through bands of different odours, perfumes, soaps and household bleach. Near 'Personal Hygiene' was a shelf of pregnancy-testing kits. I read the instructions on several different packets, and chose three. In the queue at the checkout desk I held them against my chest, but when I placed them by the till, the girl spread them out, on public display, to check the prices. What stupid impulse made me say: 'They're for my daughter?'

Her face was blank, uncaring, but I was sure that my bare left hand shouted the lie. Blushing, I thrust the packets into a carrier bag and waited for my change. I hid amongst the hustling Christmas shoppers and searched for a store that sold picnic equipment, where I would be able to buy disposable, clear plastic cups.

By now, I was finding that the crush of people was exhausting, and the shops were stifling and enclosed. A board advertised a coffee shop on the first floor of the store, and I stood still, thankfully, as the escalator bore me upwards. Fluorescent lights made the tables two-dimensional, lacking shadow, and a voice interrupted the piped carols to announce special bargains in the china department. The sugar on my doughnut coated my lips, and I licked them and washed the sugar away with frothy, sweet hot chocolate. The warmth was soporific, and I rested my head against the wall and dozed briefly, surrounded by my shopping, a bag-lady seeking refuge from the streets.

I had been so self-engrossed, so caught up in my own concerns, that I'd forgotten about Christmas. Last night, when I arrived at the station, I was astonished by the coloured lights and gaudy baubles that festooned the shops and lamp-posts. Although it was seven o'clock, shoppers pressed in and out of plate-glass doors, entering and leaving shops that were brightly-lit, windows glowing with gifts and rich clothing. Even the taxi had been decorated, small fairy lights fastened around the edges of the glass partition. Last night, the hectic bustle had distressed me, and I hadn't wanted to acknowledge the possibility of Christmas, but now, refreshed by my snack, listening to people discussing their purchases, I became caught up in their infectious present-hunting. I would buy Jos a present; and I would buy a good pudding, brandy butter and a Christmas cake. We'd have an early Christmas dinner, a feast! Red candles? Why not! And indoor fireworks! I would take John MacGregor a bottle of port for his kindness. Everywhere I looked, potential gifts enticed, and I shopped enthusiastically, but it was not until the sharp edge of a shopping basket nudged viciously against my stomach that I remembered why I was here.

Would Jos think that the gift of a child was in bad taste? I had tried to ignore the displays of baby clutter in the chemist's, the teething rings and bottles, the potties, plastic bibs and tiny socks, but the enormity of what had been made (what we might have made; surely it can't be true?) punched me in the midriff, and I held on to a counter for support.

'Are you all right, hen?'

A small, square woman took my arm, and summoned a crisply-lacquered girl from behind the counter. I couldn't breathe, but I tried to shake their help away. They guided me past interested stares to a chair by the door, and my small protectress stayed proprietorially beside me, while an assistant fetched me tea. I was sure that the kits were visible in their bag, clues to my embarrassing behaviour, but my helper was too busy talking, commenting on the heat of the shops and the crush around us. She asked me where I came from (doubtless, there is something in my manner that suggests I'm not a city person!) and when I told her, she was amazed. A thought struck her, and she leaned forward and patted my arm.

'You'll not be used to these crowds then, will you, hen? It'd be a good thing if we forgot about Christmas altogether, wouldn't it, the amount of fuss. It's enough to make anybody feel queer.'

Her sympathy was warming, and I smiled up at her, already feeling better.

'Must be a bit quiet, in the winter. Have you got family over there?'

She nodded towards the door, presumably indicating the island.

'No. Just me!'

Family! Oh, yes, I think I may have one. Inside me. Family. A year ago, wee woman, I would not have let you touch me. And now I have a lover and, perhaps, a child. Does it disgust you? And my dead son is all around us, and part of me. The woman was saying something else, but someone knocked my chair and the empty cup clattered on to the floor. I stood up, and thanked her for her kindness, and said that I was quite recovered. We wished each other 'Happy Christmas', and she hoped I'd have a safe journey home.

I wanted to go back to the guesthouse, to go to bed and sleep so that morning would arrive more quickly. I couldn't do the tests until morning, and this near-certainty was too exhausting. I needed to be certain, to be able to plan positively for the future. There was a bookshop nearby, and the piles of glossy titles were comforting. I spent two hours surrounded by the luxury of words, and bought myself two Christmas paperbacks. Then it was late enough to return to my room, a meal, and an evening by the fire.

There was only one bathroom, so I had to be discreet. A 'midstream sample' was collected in a plastic cup, and I took it back to my room, hidden by my sponge-bag, and laid out the instructions, the vials and the indicator strips.

All three tests were positive, there was no longer any doubt. Inside me a curved and pulsing foetus grew, partly its father and partly me, and partly with its own identity, pulsing in its own warm, salty sea. How long had it been there? When would it be born? My body seemed suddenly so big it seemed impossible that neither I nor Jos had noticed, and I knew that I should go to a doctor. But I wouldn't, I couldn't; I would manage on my own, as generations of women had done, before me. And Jos would help! Surely Jos would help? I tried to imagine his face as I told him the news, and the laughter-creases around his eyes, the way his beard curled forward when he threw back his head in laughter, were so bright in my mind that I wanted to hug him. A child! We would be a family. We would be together, and our needs would be small.

Jos could carry on his work from our home. I had promised him an answer, and I had slowly come to accept that the cottage must be rebuilt. That would be the right thing to do, because that I knew was where the child had been conceived and must grow up, lulled by the sound of the sea. Even until last night I'd been unwilling to take the final step and admit to myself that that was what I was going to do. But now there was no longer any alternative, and I imagined our child toddling in and out of the front door, playing in the peat-cuts, and collecting pebbles on the shore. Jos would be typing his notes at a table in the bedroom, occasionally glancing out towards the sea. And I? What would I be doing? I would be fifty when the child was five. But I would be strong and happy – and complete. I saw the three of us, climbing up above the gorge, our boy asking again for the story of Finn. We sat amongst the moraines up by the lochan, watching the red-throated diver on her nest as we ate our picnic lunch. I imagined the boy's face as he caught his first trout, and his frightened fascination with a crab's snapping claws. In the evening, he would help to carry in the peats, and I'd heat water to wash his face and hands at the kitchen sink. He would learn to love the sea and the earth, he would grow up knowing of his links, in total awareness and acceptance.

For *he* was the meaning, wasn't he? A child was conceived of the sea and sky. For him, both Tom and Finn had died; I had waited for him all these years, and Jos had been brought to me to help.

Now there was so much to do. I wished it were not Sunday, for I wanted to sort out my affairs. I cleared up the mess and hid the evidence, wrapping the test kits in a carrier bag, to be disposed of in a dustbin. After breakfast, when I complained about a day of forced inactivity, my landlady told me that the shops would be open, happy to work longer hours for the prospect of greater income. I caught a bus into town, and now there was an added delight to shopping. I was careful and did not hurry, and stopped to drink and eat. I had worried about Jos's present, because I realised that I knew very little about his likes and dislikes, but finally, on impulse, I bought him a large, chunky woollen pullover. It was expensive, but he would need the extra warmth in his winter watching. My dearest seal-watcher, the intended father of the foetus in my belly. I felt as though my shape had changed visibly in the last few hours, and I bought new, comfortably elasticated clothes. I found a public toilet and changed into a new blouse and jumper, and smart trousers, then I spent the afternoon in the art gallery, enjoying the hushed atmosphere, the soft seats, and the click of heels on polished wooden floors.

The next morning, after breakfast, I telephoned my solicitor and made an appointment for that afternoon. I found a hairdressing salon that looked half-empty, and had my hair washed and cut. The girl made disapproving noises at the previously untidy cut, but was quietened when I told her, shamelessly, that I had cut it myself.

A brighter, tidier woman looked back at me from the mirror, and I thought that my pale puffiness had disappeared, to be replaced by the smug glow of motherhood.

My solicitor was surprised to see me; he was kind, avuncular, near retiring age, and he knew the story of my past. He must have been reassured to see me in good spirits for, although I was nervous at what I had to do, I was also feeling cheerful and positive. I explained to him, not expecting comment and receiving none, that I had come to make my will, as I now had someone whom I wished to benefit. I explained also that my cottage had been damaged in a storm, and that some of my capital would be needed to repair it; I had not been insured. I told him that I had reverted fully to my maiden name, and together, impassively, we drew up a short document in which the croft and cottage, and all my money and possessions, would be left to my child. After my signature had been witnessed, we chatted for several minutes, and he told me how pleased he was to see me looking so well and taking such a positive approach. Incidentally, he said, *à propos* of nothing whatsoever, my ex-husband's firm was doing well. I asked if Graham had remarried, and was pleased to hear that he had, six or seven years ago. Yes, there were children, teenagers apparently, his wife's, of course. Of course, I said.

There were two days left, because I would need a day to travel. I spent one day at the guesthouse, reading and relaxing, temporarily drained of energy. I wandered through the suburban streets, hunched up against the biting east wind, and found a steamy café with formica tables, where I ate haddock, peas and chips. The greasiness regurgitated as acid heartburn, for several hours. The next day, I bought a cheap, two-handled sports-bag, convenient to carry although it looked incongruous, and I finished the last of my Christmas shopping. I also bought a modern book on pregnancy, and this time did not say for whom. That night, I sorted and packed my purchases.

By the time I reached the harbour on the following day, it was early afternoon. There were no taxis in such a small place but there were, surprisingly, left-luggage lockers in the small building that housed the ferry office. I left some of my bags there, and then took my rucksack and went to the builder's yard. When I had first moved to the croft, this builder had carried out the minimal repairs that had been necessary; he knew the cottage, he had friends on the island, and I needed his help again. He was at home, this being a poor time of year for outdoor work, and I explained what I wanted done. I wanted some temporary repairs to be carried out as soon as possible, to make the building water-tight and habitable, and I wanted him to return in the spring to replace any rotten timbers and rebuild the chimney. He knew, of course, what had happened, and was cautious at the amount of work involved. There was the transport, he said, what about that? I reminded him that, last time, the Land Rover had come over the moor to bring the corrugated sheeting; it had been difficult, I knew, but it would be possible again, and perhaps Ferguson's boat could help . . .? Then we talked a while about the fishing, and the salmon farms, the difficulties these days, and the Russians that had come ashore, but finally he agreed that, if I could perhaps pay his fare (I had already offered), he would come across next month and take a quick look to see what could be done, by way of a temporary patching to the roof. Meanwhile, there was Christmas and, of course, New Year. Yes, I could see the difficulty, and I looked forward to seeing him next month. Was his daughter visiting him for Christmas? Ah, that would be good. Aye, well. He would do his best. What with the bad weather coming on . . . I thanked him, and decided to telephone at the start of the year. With luck, the cottage might be habitable by March.

I stayed the night at my usual bed-and-breakfast, aware that this was my final night of comfort, and that a week away had made me soft. In the morning, I wandered down towards the quay. Once, I thought I caught sight of Father Peters, and I stepped into an alleyway; I felt so different that I was almost sure that he could not recognise me as Harriet Falmer, Catholic, but I could not be sure.

The wind was strong down by the harbour and I had to put my hood up to protect my ears. The water was oily and flecked with scum and rubbish, polythene bottles, plastic cartons and half-submerged newspaper, but out beyond the harbour wall the sea was grey-green and turbulent, the crests of waves jostling in all directions against the confines of the bay. I sheltered in the lee of the fish-packing shed, and watched as a bus came in. Several passengers climbed down, mostly locals, but one of them was Jos. The driver got out and opened the flap of the luggage store, and Jos collected a large cardboard box. He chatted with the driver, and they both laughed; another passenger was drawn into the joke, and I marvelled at the relaxed manner in which Jos related to the others. I was jealous, too, unreasonably. I wanted him to show that he disliked the outside world, and longed to escape, to find his refuge in me – and the child. I remained where I was and watched him. He looked around, but didn't recognise me. Why should he? My face was hidden by my hood, and I was out of context. He picked up the box by its strings and began to come towards me, towards the office. I pushed back my hood.

'Jos!'

He stared, disbelieving.

'Harriet? *Harriet*. What are you doing here?'

He was astonished, almost peevish, but then he must have heard the echoes of his voice because he put down his box and came towards me.

'Harriet. I can't believe it. I'm sorry, you gave me such a shock! Did you come to meet me?' Then he frowned. 'But of course you didn't. Stupid question.'

I wanted to blurt it all out, about the baby, to tell him that I wanted him for ever, that I would repair the cottage, and I wanted to hold him and be held. But we were both in public view, and I could see that he knew it, too, and held back.

'We'll have the whole boat trip together.'

'And the next few days. Stay with me, Jos, at the crypt. I want you to!'

'Some of the time, yes. This is so amazing. I've never seen you here, it makes you look different, somehow. Look at the box – it's full of Christmas goodies!'

'I've got a box, too – Christmas pudding, the lot! We'll be able to have our own Christmas, just the – two of us.'

We continued to stand and look at each other, saying silly things and smiling. I yearned for privacy but, conscious of interested glances, we moved over towards the office to buy our tickets.

There were few passengers on the boat, it was the wrong time of year, but the cabin smelt of diesel and old vomit, so we found a corner out of the wind and huddled, heads down and close together. Hoods up, zips closed, hands in pockets, close contact was scarcely possible. Jos's moustache was damp against my face when we kissed, and I licked the salt off his lips with the tip of my tongue, trying to force down the lust that was building up inside me. I longed to take his hand and press it against my belly. I was bursting with pride, I was the mistress of love, superior, accomplished in the art of child-bearing. See how my body changes! While you were away, involved in childish things, I have been doing all this – I am making a child. But my waterproof was stiff with cold, and the time wasn't right.

'So why were you on the mainland? You haven't told me, yet!'

'Christmas shopping! And I had some business to attend to in the city.'

'Business! I've never thought of you as needing to do business, you seem so remote from all that sort of thing.'

'I have to check on my investments, you know. How else do you think I've managed to live here, unemployed, for so long? No, I'm joking – there's not much money, but there's enough. Enough to rebuild the cottage, anyway.'

'To rebuild? Harriet! You're going to *rebuild*?'

'Yes. Are you pleased? I talked to the builder yesterday, and he's going to come across and see what needs doing.'

Jos seemed stunned: he just sat and stared at me.

'Aren't you pleased? It's for us, Jos.' I grabbed his arm. 'I promised you that I'd give you an answer – and this is it. Come and live with me. As soon as the cottage is repaired, it'll be ours.'

He was so pale that I was afraid that he was going to cry.

'Oh God! You've been over there, organising all this. For me! I couldn't believe you would, it was far too much to ask.'

'I'm doing it for *us*.' (I couldn't tell him, yet, who 'us' included.) 'I know now that I want us to live together. You were right, it's the only way that it will work. We can re-arrange the cottage so that you have a place to work. There'll be chairs and a table, and we'll get a double bed. The more I think about it, the more excited I am. Imagine! We'll be together all the time, no more walking over the cliffs or sitting on the ground!'

I really was excited, now that I had begun to think of the implications. Jos still seemed shocked.

'I don't know what to say. It's too much to take in.'

'Had you really thought that I would say I didn't want you?'

'Yes. No! I don't know what I'd thought you would say.'

'You seem so unprepared, it's strange. I suppose the question has been so much on my mind since you left, last month, that I thought you would have produced a stream of arguments and suggestions.'

'I've been so busy. It's been a Hellish month, actually. I don't know what I've been doing, half the time.'

'You do look a bit worn out. I wish you could stay, I'd look after you.'

He smiled, rather wanly.

'You'd like to mother me, would you? You look good, though. It looked as though you had a new hairstyle, when I saw you on the quay. I really am so glad to see you, it's been very difficult without you.'

He leant forward, pushing back his hood so that he could kiss me, and his lips were so stiff that I longed to warm him.

I didn't look so good, half an hour later, when the boat hit the open water in the sound, but I managed to reach the rail in time.

It was a relief when we finally reached the lee of the island, and it was very good to step ashore.

John MacGregor's face was a picture of benevolent surprise when Jos and I disembarked together. I almost expected him to start humming 'Here comes the bride' and to ask to see the ring. Our boxes and baggage were unloaded on to the quay, and the wind and rain were making life unpleasant.

'Are all those boxes yours? To go across?'

We both nodded.

'Well, seeing as it's the season of goodwill, I'll let you take the boxes and Miss Falmer across on the Land Rover, once I've unloaded here. But you're to turn round and bring it right back, mind. I can't be doing without it. You'll have to walk back over in the dark, you know that.' He looked at Jos. 'Will that suit you?'

'You're fantastic! Santa Claus will be really good to you this year!'

'You see that he is!' MacGregor laughed. 'And mind how you drive! I don't want you getting the wagon stuck anywhere. Not like young Ferguson!'

'Did he? When?'

'It would have been last summer, did you not hear? When the shearers were over. They'd had a wee dram too many, which is nothing unusual, and got bogged down across the way,' he indicated the west, 'on the moor. So they said.'

'What happened?' I asked.

'Too far gone to move, they were. Slept in their seats. More like passed out. Then had to walk across in the morning and get a shovel, when they'd sobered up.'

John MacGregor's eyes creased and glimmered, and Jos and I exchanged grins.

We carried as much as we could across to the crypt, because it was the nearest point to the track. It was cold and miserable work against the rain, and when we reached the crypt I was dismayed. The paths to the entrance were slimy with mud, and water had run down inside the door. I hadn't been away from this home before, but now, as I opened up the entrance, the smell of dank, enclosed air was overpowering. It was so dark! I went inside, dripping water, and found the lamp, but its light only accentuated the gloom. Jos didn't say anything as he lifted the bags inside, but I was ashamed. The sky was already darkening towards night, although it was only mid-afternoon, so Jos took the sledge and we went back to the track. I felt weak, but I had another load to pull and this was not the time to break the news.

At the last moment, Jos decided to keep his rucksack, for the weather was deteriorating further, and he thought he might stay at the village. I could see the sense in that, but it was not quite the manner in which I had expected us to spend the first evening of his return, and I said so.

'I know. Not mine, either. But I feel knackered, Harriet. I'm not sure I can face a three-hour walk back here, in this. I'm really sorry. But it'll give you time to get sorted out, yourself, and I'll come over tomorrow night, and stay. I promise.'

There was such a deep weariness in him that I was concerned; it was as though the life had drained out of him and he had given in to a sort of helplessness. I couldn't understand it, inexplicably it frightened me, and I wondered if he was ill. I could only hope that he would have recovered by tomorrow.

As the Land Rover ground away in low gear, I began to haul the sledge, slowly, carefully, towards the crypt.

The weather continued foul the next morning and I stayed at home. I let the wind blow into the crypt to clear out the fusty corners, and I aired the bedclothes in front of the fire. My animals had not greeted me, and I supposed they had been sulking in my absence.

Tonight would be special. I didn't know what was in Jos's box, but I unpacked my food and presents. I had the ingredients for chicken stewed in wine, into which I would stir cream. I raked out the fire so that the heavy pan would simmer slowly, and I went down to the croft and picked out some big, old potatoes for baking, from the store. The pudding would also need to simmer for a long time, but it would wait until later. I dressed in my new clothes, and brushed my hair, and tried to read.

The crypt was warm and scented by the time Jos arrived. His clothes were wet and his hair was plastered to his head, but he had brought dry clothes in his pack. A day of exposure seemed to have suited his temperament, for he was bright and talkative, the lassitude of the previous day blown away by the wind.

'What a transformation from yesterday.'

'Me, or the crypt?'

'Both!' He peered down at the saucepan, and sniffed appreciatively. 'That smells good!'

'Christmas dinner – no roast turkey and stuffing, I'm afraid, but poultry, anyway. And pudding.'

'We'd better eat the pudding I bought tomorrow, then. We'll need to run up Sgurr Mor to make room. You've put on weight, it suits you.'

I laughed, and poured wine, watching as he changed his clothes. I sat on the floor, and he lay on the bed and told me about his day. He had left the village early in the morning, walking most of the way in the dark before the dawn. Everything at the bothy was safe and undisturbed, and he had spent the day wiping rain off his binoculars and trying not to tear the sodden paper in his notebook. His book was drying by the fire, and he showed me two scribbled pages of sightings; despite the poor visibility, he had spotted several marked seals, and he was pleased at the prospect of a few days in the field.

I think we were both avoiding the topic of our futures; it was a subject that would provoke too much emotional tension, and Jos seemed to feel, as I did, that we should enjoy ourselves. I got up, grunting, to check the saucepans, and then went back to sit on the bed.

'This is perfect.' I stroked his face. 'It's perfect having you here.'

'Mmm.' He sighed, and stretched, smiling back fondly. 'All we need is music. Why don't you play something? I haven't heard you play in ages.'

I had forgotten about the penny whistle, and now it suited my mood perfectly. I played the three tunes that I knew best, and Jos hummed 'The Skye boat song' as I played, because he didn't know the words. We drank more wine, and then we ate, in no haste, enjoying each other and the food. The wind snapped at the polythene door and the red candles guttered in the draught, but we were safe and together.

Jos unpacked his box and produced brandy. I was worried that he had overspent his grant, but he was still delving in his box. His cheeks were flushed with the warmth and alcohol, and his eyes glistened.

'Would you like your present now, or shall I leave it here for you to open on Christmas Day? No, on second thoughts, it might be better if you open it now.'

The rattling packet contained seeds: flower seeds, sweet peas and forget-me-nots and blue nemesia; vegetables, sugar peas, courgettes, land cress and capsicums.

'I thought you might be able to use some of that polythene to make a lean-to greenhouse, against one wall of the garden,' he explained. 'It wouldn't need to be large. I don't know if the green peppers will be any good, but it might be fun to try.'

I stood up and hugged him.

'You're so inventive. My present to you is very dull.'

'Well, I thought you might need something to keep you busy, in the spring. I didn't know, then, about the cottage.'

'I'll make sure there's time, don't worry. It's a wonderful present.'

In the growing season, my time would be devoted to my family. Jos was pleased with the pullover, and its rough woollen pattern suited him well. The crypt was hot, and my face was burning, my breasts were taut with life. I made Jos close his eyes; the buttons on the blouse were troublesome, but I cupped my breast and lifted it to Jos's lips. Soon, soon, he too could drink! The endless circle would be fulfilled. He murmured and opened his eyes, perhaps he hesitated a little, but then at last, the barrier between us was broken and we were caught up in our own rapture, the alcohol within us slowing our encounters to exquisite sweetness.

Later, as we lay on our sides, hollowed against each other, Jos' hand against my stomach, I wanted to tell him what he held; but the effort was too great. Just before I fell asleep, he put his beard against my ear and said,

'I'm so happy about the cottage.'

I think he had a hangover the next day. I certainly did, and it took two aspirin and several cups of tea to improve the view. I apologised silently to the child inside me, and was happy to let Jos set off on his own.

On inspection, the damage to the cottage seemed less extensive than I'd thought. I supposed, now, that I had exaggerated it in my mind because I had wanted the cottage to decay and become part of the natural landscape. The main roof-timbers, as far as I could see from the safety of the ground, were intact, although they might eventually need to be replaced. All the corrugated iron needed replacing, and the plasterboard ceilings, but that was not a difficult job. A new back door and a new front window would keep out the weather, but I wasn't sure what could be done about the chimney. We would have to manage, somehow, but we couldn't do without a fire. The repairs would have to be basic, but as long as the roofing was securely fastened, we would be safe enough in a storm. I patted the wall, and fetched a broom from the outhouse, in order to sweep out some of the accumulated rubbish.

Jos found me there later in the day, and I showed him what I thought could be done. There were dark rings under his eyes, where the skin looked creased, and he was thoughtful.

'This is the best decision you could have made. It's such a relief to know that you'll be living here again, in a place that's warm and comfortable. I just wish it could happen now, this minute.'

'It won't be too long, I hope. We should be in by the end of the winter. I can't imagine what it will be like. It's so strange, to think of sharing it with you.'

'Do you mean that you're changing your mind, about wanting me to live with you?'

'I'm longing to share it with you. I want to share everything – for ever!' I couldn't help laughing, the idea was so novel!

'Even the sugar peas and the courgettes?'

'That depends how much you help with the garden! But there'll be too many for one person, if they all produce, so I suppose I'll let you have a few. But I have changed my mind about the cottage – I'm convinced, now, that it's lucky for us.'

Why couldn't I bring myself to tell him? 'By the way, I'm carrying a child'; 'By the way, I'm pregnant'; 'Oh, by the way, we'll soon be having a little addition to the family.' I tried; several times during the next twenty-four hours, I planned how I would say it, how I would lead up to the topic so that its introduction was not too sudden. Was I frightened to send Jos away with this knowledge? I wanted him to be with me, all the time, to understand about the baby, I didn't want to tell him and then let him leave, so that he would be alone in his paternity. He needed to be here for longer, to feel the baby growing, so that he would develop with us in our sense of belonging. By the afternoon of the final day, I knew I wasn't going to tell him. I rationalised my cowardice by telling myself that he would stay longer next time he came, and the signs would be more obvious, the idea less abstract. I had already given him one major surprise when I'd agreed with his wish for us to rebuild the cottage and to live together. It was his future that we had thus decided. (Had we? Perhaps we hadn't, after all, discussed the details, but it was too early to make firm plans.) I couldn't overburden him at this time, when he was required to deal with the mental and physical upheavals of moving here; and I could manage on my own, there was no necessity to tell him yet. He would be so proud!

We had so little time together, for Jos was to spend his last night at the MacGregors', in order to avoid an early start to catch the boat. The days were short, the visibility poor, as the grey sky loured down towards the sea. On the final day, I joined him, and together we strode along the wind-blasted paths, stopping, with streaming eyes and buffeted arms, to peer through our binoculars. It was a happy time and, in sheltered corners, where the reduction in wind permitted conversation, we told each other about some of the events and encounters that had happened in the previous month. He was able to unravel the background to some of the stories I'd seen on the news when I was in the city, and he attempted to bring me up-to-date. I knew better, now, than to be surprised at his sharp eye and perspicacity, and his descriptions made me laugh. I gave him my impressions of the Christmas streets, and of the builder's (expected) procrastination, but there was so much that I couldn't tell him now, because it related to our child. It would be *our* child, he had a right to know, but I, too, procrastinated; my reasons were much sounder than the builder's.

Gulls spun upwards from the cliffs, catching the updraughts, screeching over our head, and cormorants stood rigidly to attention on a rock, ignoring the spray that each wave threw towards them. We said goodbye in the afternoon. We had run out of things to say, and there was the stiffness between us that precedes departure. Once or twice, I thought Jos was about to say something, but when I looked at him, inquiringly, his face was blank and his eyes sought the low horizon. Finally, the time had come, and we held each other tightly.

'A whole month.'

My throat was tight. Jos's lips were against my hair, and he rocked me gently.

'Don't, my love.'

We were quiet a few moments, then he said, 'I want to thank you for asking me to live here with you, in your cottage. I never imagined that anyone would ever do anything like that for me. No, listen! If I've seemed a bit subdued, it's because I've felt – oh, it's hard to describe – overwhelmed, really. Harriet, you are the most extraordinary and generous person I've ever known.'

No matter that what he said sounded stilted, rehearsed, I knew he meant it. There was such a depth of love and of misery in our parting, that I couldn't bear to let him go. But finally he left.

'Take care, my love. Be strong. And keep harassing that builder. Get it done as soon as possible.'

I stood and watched as he walked away, and the greyness closed in around me and my beloved child.

Thirty

Only a few days remained until Christmas, and I had walked across to the village to deliver the bottle of port. I needed to get outside, for the crypt had become oppressive, and the animals still remained stubbornly silent. The dragon no longer seemed to glow with fire, and when I held the lamp towards him, I saw that his scales were coated with a thin film of mould. I apologised, and rubbed him with a cloth, hoping he would be invigorated, but I was shocked when the friction dislodged a tile. It fell to the ground, and a small, black leprous hole appeared on the dragon's flank. I was able to push the tile back in, but I could feel that others might be loose. I realised, then, that the humid warmth was affecting the cement, and I hoped that I would have left before irreparable damage was done.

Outside, the weather had lifted slightly, and I could see the lower third of the hills. The burns were full and white, and the moorland darkly wet, but I was plump with life and feeling well.

John MacGregor was delighted with the port, and invited me in for a cup of tea and cake. It was the first time that I had been inside his house, and he and his wife ushered me into the warmth of their living room and made me feel welcome. Did they notice? Did they guess? His wife was plainly curious, and longing to ask me questions, but I explained that I couldn't stay long, as I wanted to be home by nightfall. Before I left, John gave me a box of chocolates, and three letters.

'There's one of these addressed to Harriet Longmore, but I don't know if that's for you.'

I looked at its postmark; it would be a card from my solicitor.

'Yes, that's me. There's been some confusion, but I've reverted to my maiden name.'

Let him sort that one out! I avoided his astonished stare. The other letter was probably from the bank, as usual, but the third had the printed label that I had always associated with St Thomas' parish. So Father Peters had seen me, after all, and this would be his way of indicating that he had seen through the lie. I pushed the letters into my pocket, sighing, and wished the MacGregors well for Christmas and Hogmanay.

The wind was against me as I came over the pass, but, before I pulled my hood up and put my head down, I saw a group of stags and hinds sheltering in a dip on the hillside. I looked back, once, and their long necks were tall and straight as they watched my progress. I carried the picture of them with me, all the way, my mind otherwise blank apart from repeated snatches of Christmas songs, lodged there during my shopping expedition. Plod, plod, plod, plod; in her master's steps she trod. Or, where the track was smooth and downhill, 'I *saw* three ships come *sail*ing in, *sail*ing in, come *sail*ing in, I *saw* three ships come *sail*ing in, on *Christ*mas day in the *morn*ing.'

The sea was framed in the broad U of the slopes that swept up on each side of Death Bay, and the mausoleum stood at its base, unyielding, protecting the spirits who lovingly touched the countryside then flew home to roost in its stern shelter.

I was tired, but wanted to fly with them, and I went down to sit beneath the sonorous roof. The envelopes crackled in the pocket of my waterproof, and I took them out and opened them. I didn't care about Father Peters, or what he had to say, but I tore open the envelope, nevertheless. It contained a printed letter. 'My dear Harriet.' It was from Jos! I snorted with amusement, half-shocked to think that I might have thrown the envelope away, unopened. The letter was dated 19th December, several days after he had left.

'My dear Harriet, I came back to the island prepared to tell you that I had changed my mind. I've come to realise that I can't possibly live permanently on the island, however much I care for you. I wanted to tell you, but I couldn't, because you beat me to it, and showed me what you were prepared to do for me. I hadn't known that you cared for me so much – if only you had told me earlier. But it was too late, Harriet. I don't know what to do, or where this leaves us. I don't think I'll ever stop loving you, I think of you all the time. It's killing me. You said once that our affair would be like a holiday romance, and I realise now that it's doomed to stay that way. I haven't the courage to make the break. I'm so sorry. Believe me when I say that I really do love you. I still look forward to seeing you next month, although I can understand that this arrangement will hurt you, and that you may not want to see me again. I don't know what I'll do if you won't let me see you. Please look after yourself, Harriet – you really do need to be back in the cottage. With all my dearest love, Jos. PS. Happy Christmas. (I hope it will be and that you won't be too sad.)

I rested my head against the end of the tomb and closed my eyes. The music of the sea swelled around me, like a chorus, and the voices spiralled and rose up to the sky, enfolding me in their hymn of praise.

It was dark when I finally stirred, and I was cold and stiff. The hymn had gone: a dull murmur remained. Joseph, most prudent; Joseph, unjust; Pillar of families; Terror of devils . . . Jos's letter was still in my hand, and I symbolically tore it into small pieces and threw it up into the wind. Brandy gives me heartburn, but I poured out a glassful and ate some chocolates and a tangerine. Just before I fell asleep, I remembered the visions I had had, in the summer, when Jos's supervisor was on the island: how I had seen myself, as from outside, solitary, walking alone through the seasons and their scents. Yet not alone, because I knew, and was greeted by, every plant and animal, rock and lichen, as a friend. I had not seen my child, but he must have been there, somewhere, unseen but tangible, and the feeling of warm companionship was so very strong.

Thirty-one

Something tore inside me. I felt it ripping, like a cord attached to my navel, tugging sharply at my womb. I was pulling the empty gas cylinder on the sledge, it was the empty one, it wasn't heavy. John MacGregor had promised to bring me a new one, but this was the empty one. The sledge jammed against a boulder and, unthinking, I tugged sharply. And something snapped, but it was inside me, not the rope.

The pain was sharp, and my baby screamed. But then the hurt lessened, and I left the cylinder at the track, and came down to Camus Beag. Now the pain is there again, but dull, heavy, and there is a warm wetness between my legs. My body is big and unseemly, the wetness is warm, and faintly pink, but I am cold and faint. I have to get down to the sea, it will heal me and tell me what to do. I can't lie here any more, the cottage creaks around me and, inside it, I'm all alone.

I am coming. Help me, give me strength to reach you. The whiteness of foam, cleansing in its purity. Help me wash away the blood. Tell me what I should do. I'm not close enough, I cannot hear you speak. I must bring the boat. So far to push, and I can feel the warmth again. Pull the boat for me, I beg you – you once helped me push it free. You are leaving, sea, your tide is going out, see how the beach is wet from your tears. Help me. Pull with the seventh wave, lucky seven, tall and strong.

There are waves of fear inside me, eroding, scouring; waves of pain, one wave after another. I want to lie down, so that you will rock me and comfort me, but you're too rough with me near the shore. Give me strength, and I'll come out to you, where I can hear you speak. Fear gives me strength to pull the oars. I am coming. Pull me out, moon, with the tide, to where the waves swell and fall. Push me, wind, out on to the sea.

The tide of pain recedes, leaving damp footmarks. There is warmth in the bottom of the boat, I try to curl up beneath the seat, but I'm too large and cold. I can hear the sea, it gurgles and mutters beneath the boards. It whispers in my ear, and lulls me to sleep, soothing my pain. There is a deep, distant throbbing, coming closer.

Droplets of water leap over the bow and trickle down to find me, but the cold has dulled my senses and I can't feel their tender touch. Nothing hurts. The wind smells of northern snow, pure white snow that will fall down on to the purity of foam. I will be healed and cauterised, with cold caresses. The loving murmur in my ear, how the sea loves and wants me. I have slept on its bosom, we have become intimate. I've been intimate with so many, but it is only you that matters. It whispers its thoughts to me, and tells me of vast treasures that will be mine. It has been waiting. Waiting for the two of us, my child and me. We shall be One.

I want to come to you, to submerge myself in adoration, to sink beneath the pain. I hear you trying to climb the side to reach me, but I have no strength left to rock the boat. Yet I can let you in, my body is a microcosm, the boat a shell. Do you see my fingers? I have pulled out this bung. Enter, and take me quickly, don't let me be afraid. We are yours. I feel your soft caress, creeping up my body. Embrace me in your ecstasy, and make me yours.

Renew in me the ecstasy of belonging, swamp me with your floods of everlasting joy. The deep pulsing is coming closer, closer. My child and I surrender ourselves unto the world.

Thirty-two

I've been burning garden rubbish. The heat of the flames was on my face and the warmth of the summer sun on my back – everything is warm and whole: the soil is rich and dark, the peas and courgettes are burgeoning but, although I decided to try some green peppers in the greenhouse, I don't think they're going to come to much – despite the warmth, the growing season is too short.

Alastair is sitting on the path putting little stones into a pot and burbling to himself saying I know not what, a little boy's conversation with himself; I want to look at him all the time, everything he does just makes me smile!

Before the fire dies down I'll burn the contents of the cardboard box that I once kept in the crypt. The crypt's closed up again now, of course, and the dragon and the sheep mosaics have been left to rest in peace. I'm mildly curious to see what the box holds: an assortment of letters, that I don't want to read; some legal-looking papers and odds and ends, all of which probably have copies in some office; a photograph of me, not very flattering, I'm too thin and my head's tipped back, eyes screwed up against the sun, mouth slightly open as though I'm talking to someone; and; strangely, a packet of mackerel hooks. I don't remember putting them in the box.

I burn them all, except the red packet of mackerel hooks – I'm not sure what to do about them, whether to burn them with my past; but we might need them, the mackerel will be running soon – and although the hooks are old, they've not gone rusty. I put the red paper bag in my pocket.

I thought I heard a curlew call up on the moor, but I think it was only Alastair making his funny little sounds.

'Mum-mum-mum!'

'I'm coming, love. Mummy's coming!'

He totters along the path towards me, giggling, sure that I'll catch him. And I love him so much, and I'm so happy, that I start to giggle too.

Because all the other Harriets have fled: they were all mad and incomplete, their minds full of unexplained blank holes and refusals to recognise the truth. They were lost in a weird wilderness and they disappeared finally with the birth of our son. And my garden fire got rid of even their shadows, so I'm never going to think about them again. *This* Harriet is complete, and lives in a warm, complete cottage, where her warm and complete son was conceived, with her surprisingly warm, and complete husband! We are *all* complete, we're a completely Happy Family!

I nuzzle my nose into Allie's hair and he giggles even more loudly – but then I hear the noise for which I've been waiting.

'Listen!' I say. 'Sssh! The boat!'

We both stop giggling and listen – and can hear the unmistakable deep throb of its engine, coming ever closer.

'Dad-dee, Dad-dad-dad, Daddee!'

'Yes, Daddy's back. Let's run!'

Allie wants to get down to run on his own, but he's still too precarious on his feet, so I stand him on the wall and piggy-back him down towards the shore. And his father, bringing in the boat, sees us, and waves and calls. We all smile at each other across the water, and Alastair shouts,

'Dad-dee, Dad-dee!'

Thirty-three

The rowan tree by the front door reaches out its leafy twigs towards the cottage's dormer windows. A neat drystone wall draws a line between the tidy, well-ordered garden, where rows of vegetables flourish, and the disordered wildness of the moor.

A woman with short grey hair is stoking a garden fire and she pauses, briefly, as a curlew's call bubbles across the moor, but then turns and holds out her arms as a small boy, perhaps eighteen months old, toddles down the path towards her. Both mother and son are laughing, and she picks him up and buries her face in his short, dark-red curls.

At that moment a boat putters around the northern point of the bay, its trailing wash slapping on the shore beneath a mausoleum, an airy thing of polished pillars; the boat's deck is piled with bright plastic boxes and coloured floats, and the deep throb of the engine echoes back from the cliffs. On the moor above, several hinds stretch up their long necks to catch the sound in their furry ear-trumpets, but the attention of the boat's skipper is concentrated on the figures at the cottage, the waving, smiling figures of his wife and son.

A practical man, used to working in this landscape, he picks up the mooring buoy and secures the boat, and unloads the boxes into the waiting black inflatable dinghy. The family call to each other across the water and his wife helps him to pull the boat ashore. There are big red crabs in the boxes and when the little boy shrieks in frightened delight as they wave their claws, the man laughs, and the sun glints on his red curly hair.

He puts the crab-boxes into the back of an old van that is parked on the newly-bulldozed track, and looking towards the smoke that curls up from the garden, says something to his wife. The woman answers quietly, with a smile, and then pulls a small red paper bag from her pocket, and looks at him, unspeaking. He has been bouncing his son but now he pauses, and his face is still; he looks at her – and she reaches up and strokes his face, shakes her head and smiles.

He asks a question, and she nods and, when he takes her gently, almost shyly, by the arm, she puts her arm round his waist and they go, all three of them, round to the back garden, where he throws the red packet on the fire.

Then, as though in wonder at their late-found happiness, the middle-aged couple link fingers, and smile down at their son.